THE
FIELD
EQUATION

A.A. TRENT

For my husband,
When all else feels like a bad dream,
you are the reality I can count on.

1

A faceless being visits me every night. Its depthless face watches without eyes, a blank canvas of judgment, and I stare back, forgetting all else. Then I wake up, and it's another day to get through. The visitations drive me crazy, but they don't *make* me crazy.

Dr. Sternan, a psychotherapist assigned to me through military court, has become a broken record, repeating every week a variation of the assurance she voiced in our first session: work and life will distract me until what I remember becomes nothing more than a bad dream.

But will the disturbing dream ever go away?

The real world is still worse, though. Anything can happen at any moment out here, and there's no waking up from it. I can't confide in Dr. Sternan about this, because I fear she will send me to a psychiatric ward. According to her and every other interested party, there is nothing more I can do except move on. But how do I move on when I'm being told nothing was in that laboratory—that I suffered from a stress-induced episode?

I didn't, though.

I didn't hallucinate or fabricate what I witnessed.

I remember everything about that night.

I remember the distinct squeak of my black loafers on the waxed beige linoleum in the hallway. The elevator didn't open when I punched the down button, so I used the emergency stairs; my rubber soles prevented any slipping as they connected with each smooth gray cement step.

I remember the metallic tang of the stair handrails, and the *absence* of other smells. A sign of how clean the lab building was, as protocol dictated.

I remember poking my head into each level's entrance corridor, but could tell the sound was rising from further below by its muffled quality. Red squares flashed on malfunctioning security screens attached to retinal scanners installed at various checkpoints along the corridors, each leading to higher security clearance labs.

I remember the incessant buzzing that drove me on, getting louder at three-minute intervals, goading my insatiable curiosity after the initial worry of what was happening wore off.

Yes, I timed it. I'm a scientist.

Within fifteen minutes, I felt like my eyeballs were vibrating in my skull.

I remember not having encountered another scientist or guard. Did they flee when the noise became too much to bear? It was nine o'clock on Thursday evening. But scientists were always working late, needing to meet the deadlines set each week by their superiors. I never came across another living soul—or otherwise—until I opened the door to that subterranean laboratory.

I remember that there wasn't the usual big yellow sign hanging on the outside door handle, warning of the type of experiment being performed. And why were all scanners and elevators not working, but the security alarms not blaring? The handbook on emergency protocols and safety measures presented to me on my first day was thorough; I took a test to verify my comprehension.

Something had gone wrong, and I felt an obligation to figure it out. I was more qualified to handle a malfunctioning piece of equipment than the lazy, pot-bellied security staff who watched movies in their little box by the front doors instead of walking their patrols. Employees are supposed to call the Air Force security office if an emergency were to happen below the ground floor. But there hadn't been time to follow protocol. The sound and vibrations accompanying it were escalating too fast. And I was still an enlisted soldier, with a duty to protect my fellow man.

Steven and I used to get a kick out of listening to scientists and Air Force cadets whisper to the children of colleagues at holiday parties of lizard people and extra-terrestrials being experimented on down in the vast maze of rooms and corridors at Rosebud Research Facility. Everyone loves a good conspiracy theory. Not me, though. I knew better as a physicist with a doctorate and as a soldier. I'm grounded in reality. Science-based reality. I was going to switch off whatever machine was making the noise, chastise the scientists causing the problem, and *then* call security.

But now that I've been down there, I'm not sure of anything anymore.

And that uncertainty makes me an excellent scientist, not a nutcase.

"All right back there, miss?"

I blink, released from my trance by watching the windshield wipers' rhythmic back and forth, whispering their secrets across the glass. The heavy steel and charcoal-stained sky rolls and twists beyond. I glance up at the same instant the cab driver does; his striking blue irises meet my brown ones in the taxi's rear-view mirror.

"Yeah, I'm okay," I mumble, and glance away and then back to find him still peering at me. Preferring to keep my demons to myself, I ask, "I heard it rains here nine months out of the year. Is that true?" It rained a lot in Montana, so this won't be a tremendous shock if it does.

The driver shrugs, making the raindrops still clinging to his jacket wink in the dim illumination from the dashboard, and turns his eyes back to the road. "I don't think so. I've lived here all my life. There are plenty of dry months. You should come back in July. It's gorgeous then. Green as far as the eye can see, clear running rivers, and blue skies. How long are you staying?"

Such a straightforward question shouldn't require a lot of thought, so why did it make my throat constrict and my mind go blank? "I-I don't know yet. Um, I'm curious about the town you are driving me to. Deadwood is such an ominous name."

"Deadwood goes back a long way to when loggers and miners came up the river. The logs clogged the waterways and messed with the ecosystem. An old legend says that because of a curse on the white man from the indigenous peoples, wherever the white man staked, crops never grew, so they had to rely on logging for income. The town remained unincorporated until a reclusive billionaire fell in love with the area, bought up the land, and built the college. These billionaires are obsessed with legacies. I think I read somewhere that it was the Umpqua Indians who were here. Same name as the river. OPB airs the documentary occasionally."

I pull out my phone and search Wikipedia, thankful for the two bars of cell service. For once, I'm fine with small talk. It will take an hour more in this cab from the airport to our house along winding, lush, forested roads. Steven was smart enough to upgrade our phone plan to get guaranteed service wherever we were, no matter how far from a major city. He thinks that will be enough to get me out hiking someday. What Steven doesn't understand is that it's the act of hiking, not the inherent dangers of the outdoors, that keeps me from adventuring. "The Confederate Tribes of Coos include the Lower Umpqua and Siuslaw Indians. You were close." I read on for a bit in silence. "Well, that's a sad history."

The driver harrumphs. "Most history is."

With a hum of agreement, I drop my phone back into my purse and lean my head back, closing my eyes. The cloying remnant of upholstery shampoo rising from the back seat draws up a fading memory of opening a fresh pack of alcohol wipes to clean my workstation. Cleanliness was just as important to our bosses as the research we conducted; taxpayer money paid for our multi-million-dollar equipment, after all. I exhale low and slow. Going from working in a prestigious building to traveling a thousand miles to work for pennies at a brand-new, middle-of-nowhere community college still feels like a punch to the gut. A once six-figure salary down to a paltry five. Riches to rags with no savings, no security.

The headache behind my eyes travels further into my skull, and in this momentary lull in conversation, the ache dances anew in my temples to the beat of my heart. I recall the first twinge of pain after the plane took off in Louisiana, and the throbbing didn't let go upon landing in Portland, Oregon. Then the loud propeller plane ride to Eugene thrummed the headache deeper into my skull before receding for a time once I had disembarked and collected my bags.

The driver remains quiet; he turns down his radio.

My eyelids flutter. It's four in the afternoon, but I've been up since four this morning. Saying goodbye to my parents as they dropped me off at the airport wasn't easy. I felt like a kid leaving for the first time for camp or a birthday sleepover, and a primitive part of my brain screamed not to leave the safety of my parents' arms. Not that I'd ever admit that to them. I'm an adult. A married adult. A soldier. No, I *was* a soldier. I must keep reminding myself of that. Another gut punch.

My parents agree with both Dr. Sternan and Steven that it's time for me to dip my toes back into society after a month-long sabbatical convalescing in my childhood bedroom, sleeping on the single bed with the bookshelf still displaying all my scholastic achievements. Momma and Poppa assure me everything will work out. I'm not as confident. Even the lawyer we paid gobs of money to hadn't salvaged my career. I had lost everything. Okay, not *everything*. I still have Steven.

There had been so much excitement in his voice as he talked about the house he'd found for us that I couldn't say no. He had done all the work—all the paperwork, walk-through, inspection, and check-writing. I just had to sign under his name and hit send on the fax machine in my mom's office.

"This is your time for some much-needed rest, honey," Steven had articulated over the phone after telling me about the house for the fifth time. "Let me do this for us. I've got an interview tomorrow with a construction company, and will hone my skills with this fixer-upper. I'll be the main breadwinner while you lie low with your teaching position for a year or two. Just as Dr. Sternan suggested."

As the sound of tires splashing through puddles and indistinct murmurs from the radio fill my ears,

I ponder what kind of experience slow living will be. But the paramount question remains: will it quiet the monster living in my head?

I am not crazy.

2

I jolt awake. When did I fall asleep? My chest tightens as I rise and claw at the cab door's window ledge, squinting out the fogged-up glass, ignoring the patient ache in my skull, waiting for my eyes to adjust to the bleak, wet world beyond. Homes bathed in shadow crouch far behind dark lawns around each bend in the road. Does no one use lights here? Where are the street lamps? What time is it? Has everyone gone to bed already? The cab tires crunch on gravel. Weighted, bruised clouds blanket the world in premature darkness. The stabbing needles of rain have ceased, as has the caress of windshield wipers.

"Where are we?" I don't mean to sound panicky, but my voice comes out several octaves higher than normal. Every possible horrific scenario and horror movie scene plays through my head.

The driver's head tilts toward me. "We are on Deadwood Creek Road. The address you provided is a few more turns up this canyon, according to my navigation."

"Oh, okay." What happened to the confident soldier? The flop sweat soaking through my blouse contradicted the fact that I had gone through basic training and traveled the world. I lean back and press two fingers against the right carotid artery in my neck, my pulse racing, and start counting backward. One hundred, ninety-nine, ninety-eight…

*

My index finger taps on the worn spine of *Physics for Scientists and Engineers* in time to "Waterfalls" playing through my phone's speaker as I ponder my organizing strategy. The dark hardwood floor isn't entirely uncomfortable to sit on. More books wait their turn stacked on my right.

I'm still wearing the thigh-length black wool coat I traveled in. Steven warned me it would be cold tonight, a wet cold just like back home. He had set the thermostat to sixty-five degrees before flying back to Montana yesterday. The heater kicked on when I got home, but I'm not any warmer.

Remnants of airport disinfectants, stuffy planes and the cab waft off my sleeves when I move my arms. But I don't care. I'm too comfortable right now to change clothes while surrounded by my books. Like old friends, these tomes comfort me in this empty-walled room, the same way my favorite ducky blanket as a child kept me safe from the boogeyman under my bed. Two painkillers have eased my headache, putting me in a better mood already.

A pale-yellow flame bounces on its wick inside the rosemary-scented candle gifted to us by Momma. Remnants of pizza crust on a paper plate grow cold and stale next to the candle where they sit atop the bookcase.

Momma says the woody scent and smoke will cleanse any stagnant energy. I thought she had meant the house, but now, as I inhale the perfumed air, I wonder if she had meant it for *my* stagnant energy, my reluctance to work again; to show my face anywhere least the billboard on my forehead announcing my failure as a soldier and as a career woman.

My momma and poppa had exchanged a worried glance when Steven announced over speakerphone that he'd found an abandoned house for sale. Steven had been apartment and job hunting here in the county for a week after I got hired as a teaching assistant in the Physics department. I almost cried when I heard the pitiful wage offered; it will be half of what I was making last year. But I couldn't turn it down; not when it was a chance to stay in my field. Hiring sites and Momma's college board connections had come up dry for leadership roles.

This house was a bargain that Steven didn't want to pass up, had pleaded over the phone with me, and we discussed the pros and cons. After getting married, we bought a new condo, and I didn't want to downgrade. My parents took Steven's side in that they were more concerned with my mental health than the quality of the house. I'm not crazy, I had to remind them. My final stipulation was that Steven check the inside for leaks, critters, and creepy crawlies. Fresh paint could fix the rest.

The candle flame dances wildly on its wick. I glance out the curtain-less window facing the driveway and street. The starless night and lack of streetlamps make it seem as if our house is in the middle of nowhere; the darkest part of the middle of nowhere. A cold, wet void. I frown at the realization of how alone I am. Steven's dark blue work truck is a reassuring presence in the driveway. It'll do for transportation tomorrow, but my apprehension about exploring this town built up a mountainside will ease once I'm behind my all-wheel-drive Subaru when Steven returns with it.

Raising my hand, I wait to sense the breeze that's affecting the flame. Then I sniff the air. Besides the scented candle and pizza, staleness fills my nostrils with a hint of the pines from outside. No tiny insect wings flutter nearby. Nothing tickles the tiny hairs on my knuckles.

There must be a tiny gap in the wall paneling around the window, or disintegrated weather-stripping somewhere in this old house. After walking around the place while I was munching pizza, I saw what Steven meant by proclaiming the house has sturdy construction, but needs a facelift. The faux wood wall paneling will go, and so will the shag carpet.

My phone chimes, and I scramble to grab it, hoping it's Steven checking in again. It was Dr. Sternan.

"You missed your 7:30 appointment call. I can squeeze you in right now or reschedule."

I swipe back to the home screen for the time. Nine forty-five. "I've been here for four hours already?!" Time flies when you're organizing books, I guess. Well, better now than rescheduling. Dr. Sternan is the first psychologist who might help me. She's a straight shooter and doesn't use big words to unbalance me. I know big words, and even bigger theories. I'm a physicist, for crying out loud. I pause the music and dial her number.

"Mrs. Simmons, I'm glad you got my message," Dr. Sternan answers. She has a pleasant voice; one I imagine would be great for audiobooks. Clear and not too deep, but also not too high-pitched. Calm. Focused. Images of a middle-aged woman wearing a pantsuit and spectacles spring to mind whenever we talk, since I've never met her in person.

I stand up to stretch my legs and stare at the blank wall above the bookcase, a separate part of my brain mapping where to hang family portraits. "Hi, Dr. Sternan. Sorry about that. I didn't arrive home until after five and have been unpacking since. And for the umpteenth time, please call me Claire."

"Alright, Claire. I understand. But court orders are court orders."

I roll my eyes at the mention of the board of Air Force officers that reviewed my case after I filed a complaint about the breach in security and the resulting horrors I witnessed that night. The officers and I had argued for an entire afternoon. First, they claimed what I saw was none of my business, since I didn't have security clearance in the bowels of the building. Then they claimed there were no scheduled experiments that night on Level Five. Therefore, I must have fabricated everything. I questioned how all the scanners and locks could have malfunctioned. It was my business if it put civilian workers in danger. There was a lot of glancing among themselves and pursing of lips after that.

The blame had to be placed somewhere, though. When the review board couldn't find a satisfactory answer, they threatened dishonorable discharge from the Air Force and a permanent note on my record because of my false statement, ensuring I'd never find work in a government-run facility again. I found an excellent lawyer and threatened a lawsuit for defamation of my character and the threat of unsubstantiated discharge from the Air Force. A new panel of ever higher-ranking Air Force officers claimed I couldn't substantiate my account of events with any evidence and that I was sue-happy. I had taunted them using their own words and walked out.

But I should've known better.

What little evidence I had scrounged together, for what my lawyer explained as whistle-blowing, disappeared. The copy of video evidence showing me running out of the building to find security? Gone from my locker at work before I could mail it to my lawyer. The corrupted tape showing footage of me inside the building—all the cameras appeared to glitch that night—disappeared from the security room, along with the recording of me being interviewed by lab campus security after returning from checking out the now silent, evacuated building. Lucky for me, campus security testified that all the elevators and security pads were still malfunctioning, or else I would have believed the whole evening had been a hallucination.

Still armed with my lawyer, I took a psych evaluation to prove I was sound of mind. It held up in court.

As a last resort, the Air Force, in coordination with Rosebud Research Facility, offered a plea deal. I sign a non-disclosure agreement that outlines I won't talk about the details of what I claimed to have seen with anyone from this point forward, including any medical professionals and family members, and they would medically discharge me from the Air Force with half retirement benefits and bankroll a psychiatrist for the first year provided I never miss a session. According to the panel, I was displaying anger management issues.

I have every right to be angry. I'm not crazy.

After some research and cross-examination, my lawyer told me to accept the deal. It would be the best we could hope for. Furious, I had yelled, "What's this 'we' business? This is my life and career you're talking about."

It had taken me a further week of talking everything over with Steven and my parents before I relented and accepted the plea deal. More than once, they had to talk me down from shouting.

I'm angry, remember? Not crazy.

The laboratory then laid me off indefinitely, granting me, in their words, "graciously", a severance package for twice the amount calculated based on my employment length.

So, now, here I am, talking with Dr. Sternan long distance since she is based in Montana, about a psychotic break that didn't happen, and I can't tell her what I saw because she came after signing the non-disclosure agreement and three other psychologists that I believed weren't taking me seriously.

"At the end of our last session, you were telling me how you felt through the trial process before agreeing to sign the non-disclosure agreement," Dr. Sternan prompts me.

I tap my foot and force my jaw to unclench. "Right. I was angry as all-hell for being called a liar after they admitted to something going on in the facility that night."

"Ah, but Claire, the court records show they never admitted to knowledge of an experiment in progress. They acknowledged that there might have been a malfunction of all things electronic in the building that night. A power surge of some sort." Papers rustle through the connection. I can only assume she is rifling through my extensive file. I'd seen the two-inch-thick folder sitting on a previous therapist's desk. The government is good at keeping notes when it wants to.

Static crackles through our connection before her voice comes through. "The first doctor and psychologist concluded they believed this power surge may have caused your hallucination." I imagine her taking off her spectacles and rubbing her eyes. Perhaps she regrets allowing me to call back so late.

"Right. I mean, no," I say in quick succession, clenching my free fist. "Read between the lines, Dr. Sternan. Military buildings don't have malfunctions. Not with the gobs of money they pour into construction and maintenance, not to mention security electronics and firewalls. There are buffers in place to prevent unauthorized use of electricity. Do you know how much energy a physics experiment uses? Tons. Each lab has its own allotted amount of power. Each is separate from the building's own power supply, so that wouldn't happen." My burning lungs remind me to inhale. Dr. Sternan remains quiet. I inhale once more and proclaim, "I had to pass a test on lab and building security and safety measures when hired because it's a government-managed lab with civilian scientists on staff along with military personnel overseeing them, like me. I know what I'm talking about. Besides, if a power surge affected me that way, don't you suppose they would classify it as a terrorist attack on the facility?"

"It is possible. I'm sure there is a reason they handled the situation the way they did, but that is not why we are having these sessions. Let's get back on track. What conclusion did you draw versus what they told you happened?"

I roll my eyes again, imagining her reading the non-redacted bits, skimming ahead, noting if I deviate. But I don't need to. "I told them that, from what I saw, someone must have tapped into the building's power to boost their experiment. It compromised everything. They must've also disabled the alarms to the security system. The whole thing stank of incompetence and abuse of lab protocols. I can't believe they denied my clearance to work on that level a month prior." I pause in my rant and scrunch my eyes, counting backwards from one hundred. A lump lodges in my throat. I deserved to get that position. I was confident throughout the whole interview, having more hands-on experience than other PhD holders. A team leader badge was there for the taking with level five clearance and tons more lab toys. I didn't care what they wanted me to do, so long as I got to use the big computers and whatever else they hid down there. I still don't know who got the team leader position, but whoever did must be the one who botched their experiment. Incompetence and favoritism could have destroyed the building. And I'm who got the shaft. I make a noise not dissimilar to a whine.

"Inhale a couple of deep breaths, Claire," Dr. Sternan tells me. "In fact, I'd like you to practice box-breathing. You inhale for four counts, hold for four counts, exhale for four counts, and then hold again for four more. I am here to help you work through your emotions. But first, you need to acknowledge that you can't change the past." She pauses. I chomp on my tongue so I don't blurt out something that'll lose me another therapist. She continues. "I know you crave vindication, Claire. You're frustrated because you want the world to see you as a scientist—a very intelligent, logical individual. You live by facts, and when your testimony got dismissed as delusion, it made you question your own intelligence. But I am here to tell you that you don't need to question your intelligence. It didn't go anywhere. My goal, as I have stated before, is to get you to accept the fact that vindication may never come and move on."

My forehead thumps with the drum of yet another approaching headache. "They took everything from me, though. Everything I've worked for. My job, career, friends, you name it. It's all back in Montana. Along with my sanity, too."

A sigh comes through the receiver. Gentle,

measured. "They haven't taken everything, Claire. You are still a physicist. You still have your husband, your family, a roof over your head, and a new job starting tomorrow. You can't control what others control. The United States government, not you, controls that lab. I implore you to accept your limitations and love the person you already are. You claim this incident is the root of all your anxiety and loss of success, but I wonder if it goes deeper—further back than that. The root of your need to climb the proverbial corporate ladder faster than anyone else may have been what rationalized your actions that night."

Acid fouls the lingering meaty tang of pepperoni in my mouth. I swallow twice and purse my lips while I pick my words. "No, absolutely not. I was just trying to do my job. No one else sensed that something was wrong and investigated. I alone did that. I have conquered every fear and obstacle that's ever been in my way. I was rising in my career. I was managing an entire team of scientists. Just because I'm career-minded doesn't make me a bad person." The blank white wall of the living room looms in front of me, solid and cold. I felt like I was talking to a brick wall with each of the first appointed therapists. I'm overdue for questioning Dr. Sternan's motives as my court-appointed therapist. Is it her job to get me to admit wrongdoing on the record?

"I never said that, Claire. But there remains the fact that you sensed something wrong, knew that you'd have to go where you didn't have clearance to go, and still went without getting help first. As you have just reminded me, you felt you deserved higher clearance. Did your teammates share your disappointment when you didn't receive that promotion?"

I scrunch my face and exhale through my nose. "I don't recall. But why does that matter? You can't imagine what it felt like when my coworkers wouldn't even look me in the eye after the investigation. Who spread the rumors? I didn't. People who I thought were my friends and younger recruits who had admired my work acted like I didn't exist anymore, like I had become—" I suck in my next words. *Like I had become one of the things I saw down there.* Then I had signed a non-disclosure agreement that owns a part of me now, a part I can't share with anyone else. A part that still scares me. Those figures found a way into my dreams, stalking me for some unknown reason. Taking that sabbatical at my parents' house helped a bit. The figures didn't visit as often. But now I'm in a new state, a new home. I hope to God the memory and the visitations cease with time. Where are the Men in Black with a neuralizer when you need one?

"Claire? Like you had become a what?"

Is she hoping I will slip up so she can sell my story to the newspapers? I can see it now: **Former Military Physicist Spills Beans On What's In Our Government Laboratory Basements**. Does Dr. Sternan fixate on getting a breakthrough like the shrinks on television get excited about?

"Nothing. Look. I know who I am. I know I'm angry. There's nothing to accept. Like you said, I live for facts and logic. The review board didn't take any of that into consideration. They acted as if I were a simpleton who had wandered into the lab. The week before this happened, I was becoming something my..." My train of thought drifts as a humming drones in my ears. I close my eyes and count backwards. Ninety-nine, ninety-eight. I'm not stressed, just frustrated. The hum increases in volume, as if fifty bees sharing the room with me are multiplying. The hum becomes a buzz. Is it my phone? Maybe the refrigerator? "Dr. Sternan, do you hear a buzzing sound on your end?"

A momentary pause, then, "No, I hear nothing. Try taking some deep breaths. Try box breathing. This may be your anxiety speaking." Her last two words crackle and fade away through the receiver. This three-year-old cellphone is dying already. Great, another expense.

I clench and unclench my fist. "I'm not anxious,

doc, I'm frustrated. And extreme anxiety causes my ears to ring, not buzz. This is different. I think it is my cellphone. Ah, it's getting louder again." I freeze. The sound is all around me now and has taken on a certain pitch that is familiar. Like what I heard coming through my lab's open door right before I went to investigate the source that night. "Dr. Sternan, are you sure you don't hear a buzzing sound? It is very important to me that you listen. I'm going to hold my phone away from my ear and walk around the room."

Dr. Sternan acknowledges. I raise the cellphone above my head and shout, "I can hear it in both ears. Its pitch has just risen."

As I rotate, the room darkens. I blink, then whip around, sensing movement. There's a dark mass where the floor lamp was. The top of the mass is flat and continues down with a body-like shape. But it's fuzzy on the edges, like an artist had raced their paintbrush back and forth to blend it into the background. Suddenly, I'm entering that door to the underground laboratory, with the stuff of nightmares waiting. My throat constricts as a gasp dies on my lips, and my vision tunnels.

I drag my cellphone back to my ear, not daring to blink. The figure isn't moving, and neither am I. But I could swear its edges are expanding. "He's here," I choke out.

"Who?" Dr. Sternan asks. Her voice sounds so far

away, crackling in and out. The buzzing drills into my skull, filling my ears, hurting my eyes. My bones are vibrating now. I can just discern Dr. Sternan's words. "Claire? Who?"

"Gheee," I squeak out, hurling myself through the adjoining dining room and out the back door. I have to get out, get away from that *thing*.

I scramble down the patio steps, swing around the left side of the house and slide in mud, slamming into the plastic trash cans. My hands claw for grip on a trashcan lid until my feet stop slipping and try to listen to my surroundings above the frantic beating of my heart. A small voice calls my name. The figure knows who I am. They found me. Steven will discover my body tomorrow. I'll be face down in the mud, one hand clutching my chest. He will grill the coroner about what happened, who will peer at him with a grave expression, perhaps even pull off his glasses, and announce, "Your wife died of fright. She got scared to death."

My name is called again, screamed. The voice is familiar. I'm clutching my cellphone in my right hand. Dr. Sternan must still be on the line. "Oh, thank God," I breathe out in relief. The faceless figure can't speak. Yet.

I lean against the house, gulping air, and bring the phone up. The shaking of my hand makes it rub against my ear. My eyes dart back and forth, just in case the monster followed me.

Why is it here? What does it want?

"I'm here," I whisper. Cold beads of sweat run down my spine, but I'm still in one piece, at least in the physical sense. Moisture on the wall soaks through my hair, chilling my scalp.

"Jesus, Claire. You scared the shit out of me. I'm sorry for my language, but what the heck happened? Where are you? Are you safe? Where is Steven?" Dr. Sternan's voice comes across steady, harsh, mad. Excuse me for almost dying.

I lick my lips and press my free hand against the house to stand straighter. *You were a soldier, Claire! Pull yourself together,* I chide myself.

"I'm okay." I shake my head, trying to dispel the image burned into my brain. "Just scared myself, I think. I thought I saw something. Steven is driving back from Montana. He'll be home tomorrow." I had just seen what I hadn't seen outside of my dreams since I walked into that subterranean lab. I inhale once more. The damp, chilled night air is too heavy for my lungs, suffocating me with the essence of wet bark and pine needles. My eyes ache as they try to discern all the dark shapes nearby. I focus on steadying my shaking voice. "I don't hear any sounds outside. I'm standing along the side of the house. It's silent."

"You uttered something before you ran. It

sounded like you were going to say the word ghost. Do you reckon you saw a ghost in the lab? I won't tell anyone, Claire. This moment could be a steppingstone for you. Psyches can manifest preconceived demons we need to face in order to move on. Or is there an actual intruder in your house? Do you want to call the police just to make sure?" Dr. Sternan's voice transitioned from sounding excited to concerned.

"No, no. I—I just made a sound because I—it was just a reaction." I won't break the non-disclosure agreement. Those uniformed thugs took enough from me. As the seconds tick by, I'm able to convince myself it's just my anxiety showing its ugly head. It has been a long day. Moreso, I don't want to earn a reputation with the locals as the girl who cried wolf on her first night. "My stress got the better of me, I think. I'm going to walk through the house to make sure it's all secure, regardless." I inch my way towards the backyard along the house, my sneakers squelching in the mud. Dr. Sternan can proclaim it was a breakthrough all she wants; I just want to live to see another day.

"Claire, keep me on the phone. I won't be able to sleep tonight if I don't know you are safe."

"You've got it." What a fool I acted! What if I hadn't had shoes on? It will be gross enough washing all this muck off my Converse.

A dark shape contorts by the back fence. The porch spotlight that came on as I ran from the house doesn't illuminate the back half of the yard. I freeze with one foot on the porch step and watch. The crunching and rustling become fainter. But on which side of the fence? The darkness is affecting my depth perception. I wonder if I still have my night-vision binoculars, or did the military confiscate those, too? The military police had rummaged through my belongings in our apartment as if they were expecting to find drugs or stolen government secrets. Steven hovered around them as they searched his belongings too, until an officer made us wait outside.

Just to reassure myself, I ask in a shaky voice, "Raccoons live in Oregon, too, right? And they can get big?"

"Yes, I reckon so. Why? Do you see something?" Dr. Sternan whispers, as if she is standing right next to me.

My grip tightens on the soggy porch railing. I squint, but the shape has melted into the night. "Or it could be a stray dog. Something was by the back fence." In this moment, I'm more afraid of what's out here than what might be inside and make it to the screen door in two giant leaps. The house within is silent. "Okay. I'm going in. I'm—"

"Claire? Do you have something you can grab for protection? Just in case?" Dr. Sternan's voice breaks above a whisper, sounding more scared than me, though my heart is pounding in my chest.

"Steven might have some tools in the kitchen." I slip inside. The house is silent except for the hum of the refrigerator. A few moving boxes wait to be unpacked on the counter. The closest box is open; I peek in. Mixing bowls, a spatula, whisks, and, ah, yes, Steven's wooden rolling pin his grandmother gave him. The weight in my hand boosts my confidence. I squint at the corners of the room and the dim living room beyond. My candle is still lit but burning much lower. Did the demon suck the flame like a lollipop, relishing the heat that reminded it of home?

"Okay," I whisper into the phone. "I've got a heavy rolling pin and will go room by room." Not that a physical object will affect a paranormal being, or whatever that figure is. I try to ignore the fact that both my hands are still shaking.

"Okay," Dr. Sternan exhales. "Remember your military training and trust your instincts. That will help keep any hallucinations at bay."

I flinch. I hate the word hallucination. How dare my brain, with all its knowledge of the hard sciences, make up such nonsense? But here I am, states away, and I witness the same thing in my dreams and in our living room as in the lab? Is it because I was reliving the moments before I opened that lab door and saw what was inside? My fear dissolves into anger. How dare something or someone invade my home?

I creep up to living room and lunge toward the floor lamp, holding the rolling pin above my head.

I'm greeted with an empty room. No noise except the squelch of mud on my sneakers and the creak of the floorboards underfoot where I land. No black shapes. No ghost. The floor lamp with its antiquated wrought iron stand and beige lampshade is standing in the corner as it has been all afternoon.

"The living room is clear," I tell Dr. Sternan, and hear her sigh. I'm not so ready to let my tense muscles unravel.

At the hallway entrance, I remember my muddy shoes and slip them off. Then I tiptoe onto the brown shag carpet that is throughout the rest of the house. Each creak of a floorboard makes me flinch, and an owl's screech outside makes me shriek, which causes Dr. Sternan to shout in response, but I'm alone. We both release nervous giggles after I explain what startled me. There's nothing here, save for me, moving boxes, and furniture worth hauling.

Back in the living room, I rotate once more, checking every shadowed corner. Nothing twitches. Nothing buzzes. The candle burns lower still, but the flame is true. "Okay, Dr. Sternan. I am alone, and every lock is secure. Perhaps you are right about my anxiety ramping up," I admit, my eyelids heavy and shoulders aching.

Dr. Sternan makes a noise of agreement. "Call me if you need to. Let's schedule our next session for Monday of the following week at five in the evening. And remember to focus on living in the present, not the past."

3

Steven's rolling pin goes to bed with me for a feigned sense of security. I sleep in my underwear, too tired to dig out my thermal sleeping shirt. With the thick comforter and heater, I won't be cold.

Too soon, my alarm clock blares its maddening beeping, set to the highest volume so I wouldn't sleep through it. Something cool and hard is in my left hand. I recoil and throw back the sheets. It's just the rolling pin. I slap off the alarm and collapse back onto my pillow for a moment, waiting for my heart to stop thumping. Then I trudge, still warm from bed, half-naked into the kitchen and turn on the coffeemaker.

Gooseflesh sprout along my arms and legs. *Stand*

at attention, soldiers; we must conserve our heat! I shiver, wondering if I should turn up the thermostat. Movement catches my eye, and I glance upwards from observing the sentries on my arm. Beyond the curtain-less window, someone is passing by on the street walking a dog, and here I am, sporting my leopard print underwear and nothing else.

I bolt to the bedroom, hands shielding my breasts. The memory of my first month in a freshman college dorm floods back. My roommate was another female, but the dorm itself was co-ed. Our room had an en-suite half-bath. I had thrown back the covers, clad in just boxer briefs because I have always been a hot sleeper, and through the fuzzy haze of morning eyesight, made my way to the sink to freshen up and dress. My hand had just reached the doorknob of the bathroom when the laughter and whistles erupted; my roommate had left the door to the hallway wide open for all to witness instead of confronting me with how uncomfortable it made her to see my half naked body for all of fifteen seconds. I had screamed and locked myself in the bathroom for hours, wedged in a tight ball on the floor between the toilet and sink, bemoaning what had happened until the resident hall director and a counselor coaxed me out with a promise of a room to myself.

When my parents questioned why I was moving out of my original quarters, they had flown up to Montana for moral support and negotiated a single room for the entirety of my school career. But my reputation never recovered, and the college guys who asked me out always brought it up on the first date. So you can imagine my happiness upon a chance encounter with a sweet construction worker who didn't know of this humiliating incident. And if he did, Steven has yet to bring it up.

The dog walker hadn't looked over, but what if they had? I would have had another death. This time, out of embarrassment. The local coroner has their work cut out.

After dressing, having enough sense to ready my outfit last night, and swiping mascara on without taking out my eyes, I go back to the kitchen to gulp down a cup of lukewarm coffee before hopping into Steven's truck to make it to my first day of work on time.

*

The morning commute is a breeze. A car or two at each intersection, all wet with morning dew, headed in the same winding direction down the valley towards the college. I have donned my favorite orange blouse and black slacks for my first day. Not just because it's October, of course, but because orange is my favorite color. I love eating orange foods, wearing orange clothes, and sleeping in orange sheets. If it weren't for Steven and his equal love for the color blue, I would live in an orange world, surrounded by different shades for every mood and season. Want to be cozy? Throw on a spice or ginger-shaded sweater, or heat a bowl of pumpkin or carrot soup. Need a mood boost? A bright glass of orange juice or don a blouse in the shade of orange peel, like the one I am wearing. Orange is a flavor for the senses. Taste orange foods. Look and listen to the drifting and crunching underfoot of orange leaves in fall. Experience rust-colored sand slipping through your fingers in a desert. It all feeds my soul. I had even requested my parents and grandparents to call me Orange when I was five. They declined and instead offered the nickname Pumpkin, which I agreed to.

No holiday or school picture was safe from my obsession with the color. I had insisted on dressing up as something orange every year for Halloween. Pumpkin, princess, goblin—it didn't matter, the dominant color scheme had to be orange. Christmas and Valentine's Day were a challenge for my parents to dress me. In exchange for wearing pink or green to school functions, my parents would include orange treats in my lunch.

One day when I am wealthy, my car will be a Corvette in the shade of persimmon.

I was wearing my proclaimed lucky orange blouse when I met Steven. With that happy memory quirking up my lips, I arrive at campus and find a parking spot in the third row of the faculty parking lot. After three calming breaths, I exit the truck with my briefcase and look around. The science building is in the northwest corner of campus, if I remember the map on the website correctly, and this parking lot is in the southwest corner. What the online map didn't tell me is that the county's ancient forest still thrived in this part of town. Towering pines, oaks, and maples hide the buildings from view. Moss and vines dangle from limbs like streamers. And the pathways are semi-hidden by overgrown ferns. Am I working at a community college or *Jurassic Park*?

Two women in business casual pants and blazers in shades of green stroll past, deep in conversation, so I follow behind at a distance, hoping they will lead me to a teachers' lounge or the main office.

After a minute, the women wave to one another, with one going down a few stairs eastward and the other veering north towards a building with a timber frame jutting out at odd angles and an art installation that moved with the wind out front. I pause. The building across the way has a plain brick facade, except for a silver plaque above the door announcing the science subjects taught within. Physics is third on the list. I breathe a sigh of relief and head that way.

After stepping around some students chatting inside the front door, I pick the hallway carpeted with what I discern to be a tree pattern on the right to start down. I wasn't told where to meet the professor, just the classroom number. Up ahead, there's a map of this building's layout on the wall, as if the universe is throwing me a bone.

"Claire? Claire Simmons?"

I twist around and take in the sight of a woman so unlike the plaid and jean-clad students. She's what I stereotype as a "corporate woman": blonde hair pulled back in a severe bun, light gray eyes framed by tortoise shell, horn-rimmed glasses, a subtle mauve lip, a tailored dark gray pantsuit, and black kitten heels so shiny, you could check your teeth in them, standing three feet from me.

Wearing kitten heels all day like this woman makes me sore just thinking about it. And on such a campus as this, with all its winding paths and steps! I don't know whether it's my feet or my stamina giving out at the thought. Perhaps both. Today I'm wearing my Steve Madden loafers. One day, I hope to own a beautiful leather pair from Coach, but for now, these synthetic uppers will do.

At least they're comfortable.

"I believe you are my new assistant. I'm Professor Bayer," she says. The corners of her lips stretch down as her eyes inspect me from top to bottom. It doesn't intimidate me too much; the officers in boot camp used to scowl at me so hard, my knees would tremble. My spine straightens regardless.

"Oh, thank God! Hi!" I rush forward with my hand extended, plastering a smile on my face. Her fingertips graze mine before she retracts them. *Is my hand sweaty?* I rub my palm on my hip. "I don't know where I should go before class. This is my first time in a teaching position of any kind." I tug at the cuff of my blouse and roll my shoulders back.

Then I notice her briefcase. A supple, shiny leather in honey brown with gleaming gold hardware. That exact bag has been on my wish list for two years. I was going to buy it when I got a pay raise with the level five clearance position. This woman's outfit was supposed to be what I wear now. I swallow the lump in my throat and look up.

Professor Bayer raises an eyebrow. "Just to be clear, you won't be teaching unless I'm absent, which I never am. You are to assist me in my teaching duties. Grading papers, running errands, and meeting with students for tutoring."

My cheeks heat. Wow. How far I've fallen from

managing a research team in a government-owned lab. Even in college, my advanced physics professor had me and a few other students working alongside him on his current research computing project. At least in this position, it sounds like I'll be able to help the students if they need it. Learning physics was like a gateway drug for me, and I'll be happy to get more people hooked. My chest spasms. I pat my sternum, wishing I had had the sense to pack some antacids.

"That second door behind you is the teacher's lounge for this building. There's a small keypad just inside the door that you will use to punch in and out every day since you are not salary. The front office should have provided you with a digital badge and pin number," Professor Bayer explains, waits for my acknowledgment, then leans over me and points to a spot on the map. "And there you will find my office. It's a small faculty building right next door to the one we are in. You can find me there before and after class. I'd like you to arrive earlier, beginning tomorrow, so I can go over every lesson plan. The term started weeks ago, so I need you to be punctual and focused. I teach three classes a day, from entry-level to advanced. There are two different entry-level class sets, two intermediate, and one advanced, as the classes alternate days, giving the opportunity to teach more students."

I nod. How much did the hiring board tell her about me? Why the over-explaining of how college works? My PhD should hold clout, which I completed two years ago. I remember scheduling college courses. As we get to know each other, I'll slip my credentials into the conversation and ask her to recall research stories, and inquire if any of her previous colleagues are at prestigious labs around the world. I will use my intellect, build up contacts, and climb towards the top again.

"… and we have just enough time before class to show you my office."

Professor Bayer is halfway down the hall before I realize she walked away, so I jog to catch up. She stops long enough for me to use the time clock, which is identical to the one used at the lab, and then continues on until we are in front of a door in said small outbuilding. Her nameplate reads Dr. Danielle Bayer, PhD, Professor of Physics. I hope one day to have my name on a gold plate like that. Even though I oversaw a team of civilian scientists, I didn't have an office for personal use, much less a nameplate.

"What is your PhD in? Mine is in quantum computing. I love everything to do with math. Should I address you as a doctor?"

"Professor or Doctor Bayer is fine." Danielle's

keys jangle when she turns one in the lock and pushes the door open. I spy a large mahogany desk, shining from a layer of polish. She gestures inside, but her body still blocks me from entering. "I am the only physics professor on campus, and they had to bribe me with these accommodations for me to agree to come teach. My PhD is in theoretical physics."

I gawk at her. No wonder I got the job so fast; how does one teacher teach all these students? She scrutinizes me, and I snap my mouth shut.

"This is a natural science community college, so students don't fill the seats. Don't expect a raise in pay next quarter unless the school can get more funding. I can't imagine any actual teaching positions becoming available soon, either."

I fight the urge to roll my eyes. "Noted." I'll be taking the first lab manager job that becomes available, wherever it may be in the world, and kissing this job goodbye. What's the point of being a scientist and not working in a lab? Then I could buy us a sleek apartment with superb views. I'd rather have a view than a white picket fence.

Dr. Bayer has us arrive at each class five minutes early and goes over the syllabus with me in the time between. She introduces me to the students after they file in. The first class, Intro to Physics, has twenty-two students, and each class after has fewer. The advanced class at two in the afternoon has seven students. Most of these advanced young adults transferred from more prestigious colleges for various reasons, Danielle explains, like changing their major or having a change in their financial situation. She explains all students must live on campus the first year as if it were a university. A ploy by the college founder to feed the budding town's economy.

She is more attentive to the advanced students; knows each by first and last name and asks after their other classes. I notice a few of the advanced students ogling me during the lecture. Male and female alike. Are they sizing me up? Wondering what credentials I have since Danielle didn't think to mention them? Or is it out of sheer boredom? The screen that Danielle lectures in front of becomes the subject of my warm-cheeked focus for the latter half of this class.

After observing Danielle's attentiveness to the advanced students, I intend to cast my energy behind the students in the intro classes. They had the decency not to stare and didn't whisper amongst themselves as much as in the other classes. Also, if the first years don't understand the fundamentals and have someone rooting for them, then they'll never have the confidence to join the field. And it is such an exciting field! My degree and time in the Air Force allowed me to travel, build computer parts, and code programs. Until that fateful night lured me astray…

*

By three in the afternoon, our classes are done, and so begin office hours. Danielle announces she will take the advanced student's questions while I "practice" with the first and intermediate level pupils that request tutoring.

"Would you like some coffee from the teachers' lounge, Professor?" I need a caffeine hit. The multiple flights yesterday and the hour-long taxi ride were draining to begin with. Coupled with my scare last night, my eyelids are heavy and I'm yawning uncontrollably. Professor Bayer also drones on in her lessons. I spotted one or two heads nodding throughout the day. It's not the professor's fault, though. She, like me, wants to be anywhere else in the world than here.

"We'll stay in. I don't fancy interacting with other professors today. They are nosy, and their conversation topics are mundane, trust me. Dealer's choice for coffee flavor from the bowl behind you." Professor Bayer falls into her desk chair. "So, tell me about yourself."

A waist-high walnut bookshelf abutting the left

wall houses coffee-making paraphernalia on the top shelf. It's empty of any textbooks or reference books. Strange. I had assumed books would crowd every surface in academic offices, like in the movies. Maybe it's because we are living in the digital age. Or the professor may have hyperthymesia, so she doesn't need reference books because she remembers everything.

I suck on my lower lip, running through what I like about myself that I might share with her, and rummage through the bowl of coffee pods. Powdered creamer, a box of sugar cubes, and a paper cup full of wooden stir sticks live on the next shelf down. An empty box of strawberry Pop-Tarts lay on its side next to four coffee mugs that sport flying pigs with different colored backgrounds. Red, orange, blue, and purple. Funny choice of mugs for such an intellectual, but what do I know? I've heard it said that brilliant minds are unfussy about things such as decor. All the mugs at the lab were plain white, so we had adhesive name stickers to use on them, and only drank from them in the designated eating and drinking areas. I pick a French Roast for us and plop the first pod into the machine, then turn around.

"Which mug do you prefer?" I hope this will teach me more about her personality before I reveal any of my own. I want to show her that I am at her level, or near her level, or *aspiring* to be near her level of mental acuity. Theoretical physicists are pioneers of the unknown in our field. They can explain possibilities that the average person reads about in science fiction books. These scientists take the fiction out of it. I must hold back all my burning questions so I don't annoy her, and pepper them in throughout the semester instead. The non-disclosure agreement burns like a brand in my mind; she would have some theories about what I saw on level five, I'm sure.

"I'll tell you when you tell me about yourself. Fact for fact," she states flatly. I want her to glance up and wink, to put me at ease, but her face remains straight and focused on her task at hand.

I lean against the bookcase to feign nonchalance, even though my insides clench. "Okay. I joined the Air Force right out of high school, which paved the way for my degrees in physics before landing a position at Rosebud Research Facility. But then I got, uh, hurt, and am here now."

She peers up at me over the rim of her glasses. "Hurt? A lab accident or military accident?"

"No... I can't talk about it because of security protocols and all that. The Air Force gave me a medical discharge of sorts. But you don't need to fret about my abilities." Does it sound like I'm a badass from the scientific front lines yet? I consider that what I used to do was cool. Like in the movies, I had access to places that required a retinal scan and an ID badge.

The professor shrugs. "Ah, well, that's admirable. I'm glad you are in one piece. My turn. I always drink out of the blue mug. Where were you stationed?" she asks, steepling her fingers and resting her chin on them. Her picking the blue mug makes sense to me. Stability, calmness, and intelligence are the key attributes of that color. Just like my Steven.

I grab the orange mug with a pig flying upside down. "Never had to leave Montana after receiving my doctorate. Before that, I deployed to a few places, my favorite being Greenland. They have a state-of-the-art science and computing building that I basically lived in. Then I hopped between South Africa and Germany in subsequent years." I point to the condiments and try to match her casual tone. "Cream? Sugar?"

Her lips purse while the corners stretch upwards. It comes across as cartoonish and scary, like the Grinch. I'm staring. I know I'm staring. But I can't blink, can't fathom what she is trying to convey, or fighting to hide. She leans back in her chair; her face relaxes. "How fortunate for you. Two teaspoons of cream and one sugar." There is an undercurrent of "who cares" in her tone. A little on the icy side. Is this a meet-and-greet or an interrogation? Is she judging my time in the military? Or is it the small talk? I've come across quite a few intelligent minds who hate small talk.

I shake off my trepidation and switch gears to ask about tutoring protocol. The professor's shoulders loosen. There's a tightness around her eyes that softens as well, making her appear younger.

"Ah, yes. That's why there's the small desk behind you, or you may meet with the students out on the benches on the east side of this building. Don't go too far in case you need me to help with a question."

A knock sounds at the door. Timid. Maybe one or two knuckles used; two raps. Professor Bayer glances at her wristwatch and nods once. "Right on time. I appreciate punctuality. Let the first student to tutor in, Claire. Sit at the small table here so that I may observe your interaction with a few students. I would like to make sure you are a good fit for this position."

I gulp. Was getting hired not a promise of at least one term's employment? The woman who congratulated me over the phone for being hired mentioned a probationary period, but I thought it was more of a formality than something I needed to stress about.

My head bobs while I try to find my voice and

scurry over to the door, as if I'm a maid rather than an assistant. The young lady waiting at the door is wringing her hands and avoiding eye contact. I recognize her from the entry-level physics class and give her a reassuring smile as I reintroduce myself and motion for her to sit. She shows me the lesson on waves that's stumping her. I dive right in, feeling as happy as a cat in sunshine talking about physics.

I am not crazy.

4

Steven is unloading my Subaru when I pull into the driveway after work. I throw the truck's clutch into park and vault into his arms. Lord above, I hadn't realized how much I missed his warm embrace, his kind eyes, his reassuring presence after a month apart. His brown hair hangs untrimmed after a month's neglect around his ears, and whatever cologne he may have splashed on this morning has long since faded when I bury my face in his shoulder. The stubble on his chin scratches my forehead as he rests his face on my head. Then he leans me back and kisses me like *V-J Day in Times Square* by Alfred Eisenstaedt.

That's our thing. Whenever we spend any length of time apart, he sweeps me off my feet. He got the inspiration from said picture that hung on my wall in my dorm room when we first started dating. "Hey, look. It's us!" he'd announced, pointing to it. I had shaken my head, explaining that though it was a sweet picture, the girl was furious he had kissed her. They were total strangers and went their separate ways afterward. But Steven had grinned and shaken his head in response, declaring, "Then we'll have a better story." That night, he surprised me with that exact sweep at my door when saying goodnight. It was a perfect moment, and my heart was his.

That memory pops up every time he does it; an instant dopamine hit, and I'm giddy when he rights me.

"You're wearing your lucky orange blouse. Did you have a good first day at work?" There's a sparkle in his brown eyes, but tension in the corners of his mouth.

I've always been able to read Steven like a book. He wants me to have a good day every day. Good days mean I am healing. So he doesn't fret, I wiggle my shoulders and smile. "I don't call this my lucky shirt for nothing."

Steven grins like a youngster who had just hit a home run, and then implores, "What do you think of the house? She's old but still got life in her. I imagine we can make a home here." He glances from the house to me, doe-eyed. "For now, at least," he adds. We had agreed when I said yes to his marriage proposal that my career, since I made more money, would come first. If that meant moving because of a work opportunity at a prestigious lab, he would follow me, no questions asked.

But now he's the breadwinner. Does he not want to move anymore because I failed once? I swallow hard at the reminder. If Steven gives up on my aspirations as a physicist, I don't know what I'll do.

I make a show of contemplating the house and give a slow nod. The jury will remain out on calling this small town a home for a couple of years, as he suggested. I don't know how long I should wait before I apply for leadership jobs at laboratories again. Does Dr. Sternan tell me? Or do I have to wait until Steven says we can sell the house for a profit? My thoughts flit to the town of Deadwood's internet page Steven had sent me when he was selling me on the idea of purchasing this home. There's a five-shop strip mall, one farmer's market, one corner market, one gas station, a couple of hotels, three bars, and that's about it. I had asked two students I had tutored today what they did for fun. All of them proclaimed they hike and play video games. Thrilling.

Also, my eventful phone call from last night with Dr. Sternan has been weighing on my mind all day. Should I tell Steven and die a little inside when that worry creeps back into the corners of his eyes? I'll make the poor guy age prematurely from the stress I cause him. Maybe it was just nerves. Who could blame me for getting spooked? I was alone in an old house in a state I'd never been to. My brain was tired. My nervous system is still recovering. That's all.

"Yeah," I say, crossing my arms. "She's got character, that's for sure. And a bit of a draft. My candle kept flickering last night."

Steven had grabbed a box labeled 'Claire-clothes' from the trunk and handed it to me. "You know what your mom would say about that," he proclaims with a wink.

Yeah, I know. I suppress a shudder. Ghosts.

"This is the last of your stuff if you want to focus on unpacking or resting. How was it, by the way? Your first day?"

I had pecked him on the cheek and skipped away before he changed his mind about needing my help; unpacking was just the distraction I needed. "First day was simple," I holler over my shoulder. "I sat through classes listening to the lessons and then tutored students. Nothing I can't handle."

CAW! CAW! I freeze and glance up at the nearest tree. Six crows bob their heads, examining us with onyx eyes. "Don't poop on my car!" I shout at them and hurry inside.

*

"Stev— Oh!" My shout reverses back into my lungs as I slip on the mossy front step. I pump my legs, using the momentum to keep from faceplanting into the wet, leaf-strewn front yard overgrown with ankle-twisting weeds and waist-high brown grass. Steven appears at my side and grabs my arm to stop me, his fingers biting into my skin.

"Honey, be careful! I told you to slow down on that step until I can pressure-wash the walkway."

I'm happy that he's home to scold me. I don't want him to let go. And I never want to be alone in that house again. "We've got bigger problems, Steven." I inhale and try to keep the last slice of pizza I just ate from coming back up. This can't be happening. I was happy when I came home. Steven was home. I was singing along to "Hit the Road Jack" by Ray Charles blaring through our Bluetooth speaker. I *never* sing. But now I'm out here on the lawn, holding my stomach, trying to explain what I had just seen as I peer into Steven's face.

"Why—" He freezes, watching me glance wide-eyed back at the house as my heart slams against my ribcage. It wouldn't amaze me if he can hear my heartbeat because it's quiet except for the sound of New Orleans soul blaring through the speaker. No buzzing. No birds chirping. I peer into the trees by the driveway. The crows are gone. No bug is humming. No car sounds are traveling from the main road down the hill. As if the outside world were being smothered by some unknown force.

"Why has it gone so quiet?" I whisper. This anomaly is unnerving me more than what I just experienced. For now.

Steven's eyes dart around and then back at me with concern etched from the crease on his forehead to the tight line of his lips. This intense gaze was born the night he picked me up at the security office after the incident. He never used to examine me like that, as if he were weighing what to say next, so as not to say or do anything to make the situation worse. I don't blame him; what I had recounted sounded like something you'd watch on *The Twilight Zone*. Something absurd in its believability.

"Unhinged" was the word I had heard whispered in the halls behind my back as I passed scientists and military personnel alike in the weeks of going back and forth to court and hearings.

People I used to call my friends found excuses not to eat lunch or grab coffee with me. My assigned doctor on base had written *stress-induced psychotic episodes* in my file and had passed me onto a psychiatrist who was more eager to hand over a prescription for anxiety than he was to listen to my side of what I witnessed at the lab. I never took those pills. They sat in the medicine cabinet collecting dust at our condo. I told Steven to toss them out, but he insisted we take them to the new house in case the move caused a panic attack. I don't even know what box they live in now.

The higher-ups must've already got to the doctor, I remember thinking. Something had gone wrong during that experiment, and someone with a lot of pull was covering it all up. But I hadn't backed down. What that experiment had brought forth was terrifying. Things not from this side of reality. I saw what I saw. It wasn't a dream. Just like I hadn't been dreaming last night. Or a few minutes ago.

Steven rubs my arm. "What do you mean, quiet? It hasn't been quiet since I arrived. Birds have been chirping, a dog barked for a while, and three cars passed by. The music is still on. Are you okay?"

I crave to reassure Steven that I scared myself when a cobweb touched my face, but I won't deceive him. I point back at the house. "From inside our bedroom, I heard the speaker skip. I thought it was weird because it's not a CD. So I raised my head to listen, and then a buzzing sound began, like what I had heard that prompted me to investigate that night in the physics building. Remember?" He nods, so I continue. "I twisted around and... and..." My body shudders. It was much closer today than last night.

"And what, love?" Steven prompts. His hand comes up and cups my cheek, warm and scratchy with calluses earned from working without gloves because he likes the reassurance of his own grip on the boards, knowing the structures he builds will stand for longer than a human lifespan. Steven doesn't even glance back at the house as I stare up at him; all of his attention is on me, concerned that the monster—a term coined by one psychologist—living in my brain was at it again. A monster named anxiety that causes hallucinations and paranoia.

Another therapist had offered to refer me for an MRI. Maybe I had a tumor. I had sneered at such a ridiculous theory, but then saw the fear in Steven's eyes when I told him, and had agreed to the test. Nothing scares Steven. But the therapist scared him enough to believe that his wife was sick. Scared that he didn't know how to protect me from this invisible monster.

The scan came back clean. So did every other test

they performed. Nothing was medically wrong with me, and yet, the military still gave me the proverbial boot because I wouldn't, and still won't, revise my story. I will go to the grave swearing that I saw what I saw. I was awake and lucid. I was there. And so were others. But the question remains: Where did they escape to when I got security for help? Why didn't anyone come forward? Who stole the video footage? Who were the scientists who created or brought in, or conjured those *things* into the lab?

I inhale until my lungs are full, returning to the present moment. "And I turned around, looked at my reflection in the mirror that's glued to the wall, and my reflection reshaped—shifted. Like static lines on an old box television set. Steven," I grab his arm and hiss, "It was no longer me reflected. It was something taller and, and, like, bigger." So big that I hadn't noticed a head. Then I remembered what I saw last night, which I am going to keep to myself for now, and added to the description. "And the top of its head was flat."

"Flat?"

An image of a beheaded person pops into my head. "Or lopped off." I gag and place a clammy hand on my throat.

Steven's mouth drops open. Then his head tilts to one side, much like a confused dog trying to pinpoint a sound. "Wait. You said you heard a buzzing sound right before you turned around?" The concern on his face dissolves, and he straightens, looks at the house with a cynical eyebrow raised. The silent nineteen-seventies built single-level two-bedroom house we signed papers on, that we are still moving into, stares back. Its white siding and light gray edging and door look a little too clean in the mangled, overgrown lawn that betrays how long it has been empty. The bank did the bare minimum necessary to sell it. *How did the figure follow me? I didn't encounter any at my parents' house. Am I never going to be safe from these monsters?*

Then I remember my mom has a lot of protective charms around the house, burns incense, and keeps wind chimes by every door. They live in Louisiana after all, the ghost capital of the United States, according to some. Their home might as well be called a safe house. I need to locate a new-age shop for some quartz and wind chimes. Perhaps found in the coastal towns nearby.

He lets go of me and stalks towards the front door, trampling down the weeds beneath his thick brown leather work boots. "I heard it, too."

"Really?" Hope flares in my chest. Vindication is nearer than ever; I'll be free of this monster that I know lives outside of me, and not in my head, that these medical kooks claim to be controlling me. I shake my hands to dispel my nerves and follow him inside. If it's still in there, I don't want Steven to face it alone.

Steven shouts over his shoulder, "Could be a power surge causing something to make the sound. Maybe the vibration affected your inner ear or something. It is an old house. One guy on my job site doesn't seem half bad at electrical stuff. Maybe I can get him over here in exchange for some odd jobs around his house or a few square meals. All he eats for lunch is gas station food."

My husband lived with his grandmother the second half of his childhood, who cooked everything from scratch. Fast food was an abomination to him when we met. My balanced love of healthy and convenience helped to broaden his menu if we are ever too tired after work to cook.

He clicks the speaker off and disappears down the hallway. I pause in the hall and watch him peek into our bedroom. He looks back at me. "All clear. The mirror looks fine." He steps inside the room, out of my sight.

I tiptoe the rest of the way, my footsteps creaking the wooden floorboards under decades-old matted brown carpet, and poke my head around the door. If only he knew all the laws of physics I do, he'd know that a house-level amount of electricity wouldn't cause someone to hallucinate. Unlike at the lab, where the power was being used for the experiment itself, which caused the incessant buzzing and generated or opened a portal to whatever I saw. But right now, I don't have the energy to correct him. No pun intended. I'm just plain scared.

Steven is standing in front of the mirror. He places his palm on the glass and shoves. Did he think he was going to fall through it like in the horror movies?

"Just me in this reflection. I thought if it were loose and the pitch strong enough, that it could vibrate the glass, distorting the image," he says, scratching at his five o'clock shadow. "Maybe it was a minor earthquake? I was too focused on organizing my tools in the truck to notice."

"I might have felt vibrations. But the mirror isn't loose, is it?" My whole body felt as if it vibrated. But as I reevaluate, it may have been that I was shaking from fright. It was over so fast. Both times, last night and just now, I had sprinted from the house before I could collect any data. Maybe next time I'll have the courage to stay and take notes. At this frequency, it seems inevitable. My chest and shoulders deflate. I look up, expecting that concerned look again. But he's just gazing at me, considering something in that sweet, overdue for a trim, head of his.

"No, it isn't loose. But I'll tear it off the wall tomorrow. Tonight, we'll cover it with a towel." He scratches his brown stubble again. "I seem to remember we watched a show that said it's bad luck to hang a mirror in the bedroom."

I hug myself and mumble, "Feng Shui."

Steven snaps his fingers. "That's it." He gestures for me to come into his outstretched arms.

I oblige him, kissing his chin before he has time to react. When I pull away, he smiles down at me and smooths back strands of my chestnut curls that have come loose from my messy bun.

"If you say you saw a ghost in the mirror, I believe you."

I hug him tight, squeezing his midsection. All I ever want is to be believed. I've felt so alone these past few months, almost believing the lie that it's all in my head. But Steven had heard the buzzing.

I'm not crazy.

He strokes my back. "And if Buzz shows himself again, he'll have me to contend with."

"Buzz?" I peer up at him.

"Yeah, you said the figure had a flat top, like a buzz cut. And if it's a bigger spirit, I'll assume it is a male. What if he used to live here and died in Vietnam or something?" He chuckles as I arch my eyebrow higher. "Because of his haircut. Get it?" I roll my eyes, and he waves one hand toward the mirror. "Anyway, I'd tear it off right now, but I want to get ready for work tomorrow, and I'm dog-tired. Remember, love, this is a big change for you—for us. Be gentle with yourself. Every house has its quirks, even the new ones, and we will soon get used to the little noises and shadows it makes." He kisses the top of my head and walks away as I gnaw my lower lip, unconvinced. "Everything will be okay, you'll see. What happened to you in Montana won't happen—"

DING DONG. The loud noise echoes through the empty house, its wood-paneled walls amplifying the acoustics tenfold.

"Jesus!" I hiss after my initial flinch, and mentally apologize heavenward. Raised by a fair-weather Catholic father and a mother who dabbles in her native voodoo beliefs, the constant struggle of good versus evil instilled in me makes me cautious of the power of words. And I need all the help I can get from the good side right now.

Steven spins around. "Expecting anyone?"

I shake my head. I don't know anyone in town yet, except Professor Bayer. Everyone else is just a face on the street.

"Stay here," he says, and hurries down the hall.

The front door is still open, I remember, thanks to my wanting a fast escape route if the house offered another apparition, and the screen door doesn't have a lock on it. So whoever is standing outside has a clear view of the interior and could barge in if so inclined. There aren't any curtains up either. I pause, then decide to creep after him since I know some self-defense learned in boot camp, and hover at the end of the hall, out of sight.

"Can I help you?" Steven calls out, his voice an octave deeper than usual.

5

"Howdy," a hoarse voice replies. "I'm your neighbor to the left in that white barn-shaped house through the cluster of trees. I just wanted to come by and introduce myself. Name's Gary. Gary Tubman."

Our rusty screen door complains on its hinges.

"Hi Gary. Steven Simmons. Hang on, my wife is here too." A pause. "Honey? Can you come here for a moment? Our neighbor is saying hello."

I smooth down the front of my blouse and roll back my shoulders, then attempt to slip around the corner as if I hadn't been eavesdropping. Steven smiles at me as I approach, stretching out his left hand to me as his right shoulder blocks the screen door from closing on this Gary person.

"This is Gary Tubman, from next door. Mr. Tubman, this is my wife, Claire." Steven snakes his hand around my waist as I extend my hand and paste on a tight-lipped grin for this weathered man who's my height, wearing jean overalls, a red unbuttoned plaid jacket, and rain boots.

"Nice to meet you, Mr. Tubman." I have to restrain a grimace as I watch his pale brown eyes travel up and down under bushy white eyebrows as both of his dry, leathery hands grasp mine a little too eagerly. He doesn't let go when I relax my fingers. Then Gary clears his throat; it sounds wet, and I yank my hand from his. Germs are gross by themselves. But when they travel in a stranger's spit? I'm out. Steven's grip on my hip tightens, pulling at my hip bone. I step back.

Gary mumbles something as he pulls a red handkerchief from his jacket pocket, with large white embroidered initials, MT, on the corner surrounded by multiple embroidered white daisies, and coughs into it. Something dislodges deep in his lungs. I turn my face away to hide a grimace. Gary recovers and stuffs the cloth down into a pocket of his overalls. "Sorry about that. I thought I was over that cold, but it seems to still have me in its grip. Call me Gary, please. I said you are an exotic beauty, Claire, but you must not have heard me. Where did you find her, Steven?" He winks at my husband and smiles, revealing crooked, yellow teeth. Combined with his voice, it makes me assume he is a smoker, or was one.

My "nice girl" act for strangers has reached its limit. "Being called an exotic beauty is not the compliment you imagine it is," I deadpan.

Steven nods. I appraise his schooled expression and catch a hint of steel in his eyes.

Gary gapes and puts his hands up in a defensive posture, as if he had heard my thoughts. "Oh my, no. Sorry, I... I." His face crumples as his arms fall limp to his side. "Well, now look what you've done, Gary. You old, sad fool. I'll go." He steps away.

"Wait," Steven says. I glare at him, trying to convey my distaste for this man. I want Mr. McSmokey-Voice gone. Steven gives me a reassuring pat on the bottom. "Gary, wait. Come back. Let's not start off our relationship like that." Steven always gives people grace; it's something I don't have the patience for.

Gary gazes at us; his bottom lip wobbles, and a pool of tears gathers along the bottom rim of his eyes.

I grit my teeth for a moment and then relent. "Who's MT?" I ask as a steppingstone. I will never beg or demand an apology from someone I've just met, but the door is open if Gary wants to give one.

A tear spills over onto Gary's weathered cheek. He takes out his used handkerchief and dabs his eyes. "My wife, Mary, was the best thing in my life. God rest her soul. I'm sorry, Mrs. Claire, if I offended you. An old man and his outdated mind, I'd say, but that's no excuse. Mary had big white hair and a bigger personality. She was always the life of the party—turned heads wherever she went." He gestured toward the street with one hand and met my gaze. "I—I think I meant to say you are a natural beauty. Your looks are your own. All these young women today wear makeup as if they are plastering a house. Mary could carry off bright eyeshadow, but it suited her somehow. Nothing like the amount of makeup these young people wear nowadays." He peers at Steven. "Mary would have given me a right good hiding for saying something like that. And goodness knows what I would give to have one more day with her, hidings and all. You cherish your wife, young man. God takes the ones you love in His time, not yours."

Steven nods and pulls me close. "Thank you for coming by and introducing yourself." His tone is kind but final. I nod in agreement.

"Ah, yes. You're welcome." Gary's eyes brighten for a second and then dim, and his shoulders droop. "You have unpacking to do. Old Gary will talk your ear off if you don't shoo me away." He waves both hands and turns around. Then spins back to face us. "Uh, I'm sure you won't need any, but I am available if you need anything, as in help. I'm not too old yet, and all alone rambling about my house and garden." He brings his hand up and scratches at the white stubble sprouting along his jaw. "Good weather for unpacking today."

"Yes, sir," Steven agrees. "This Oregon weather is unpredictable. We got lucky."

Gary takes a step back and points to the sky. "I think you did, too. The Nor'easter should pick up soon. I advise you to keep your cars parked in the garage or away from the trees. These on your property line are pretty brittle. And, being no one has lived in this house for a good long while, they could do with a trimming. The birds sure love 'em though." He takes another step back. "Well, I'll leave you to get settled in. Come over anytime." Gary puts his hands into the pockets of his overalls, turns around, and leaves.

I watch as the old man walks between our cars and continues on between the pine and oak trees. "I want a fence between him and us."

"Ah, he seems harmless," Steven says with a shrug and walks out into the front yard. "I'm more worried about these trees. I wonder why the birds like them. There were a bunch of crows here earlier. I assumed there'd be more blue jays and other forest-dwelling birds. Maybe the buzzing and town construction scared them off."

I follow him out, not wanting to be in the house alone. "Who cares about trees and birds when we might have a haunted house and a creepy neighbor?"

I am not crazy.

6

Professor Bayer sips from her shiny black thermos Tuesday morning as I finish pouring coffee into my orange thermos before heading off to class. I've noticed a small smirk playing on her face since she arrived to unlock her office.

"Having a good morning, Professor?" I hope to build a rapport with her within the week. Throughout the tutoring sessions, I wanted to squirm in my seat so much. Once both the advanced student *and* the professor were staring at me, then whipped their heads together and began whispering when I looked up. The students' ears I had been tutoring at the time went bright red when I turned my attention back, and it hit me. Maybe they weren't gawking at me, but were peering at the student. A crush, or a spat. Disrespectful and immature of a professor to be encouraging such behavior, regardless.

Professor Bayer glances over and drops her smile, causing me to drop mine as well. We stare at one another for a moment before she offers a saccharine grin. It says, "Not invited. Now I have to make something up." My stomach drops, and I avert my gaze.

"No better than usual." Then the professor proffers me a textbook and three file folders while still wearing the sticky-sweet facial expression, complete with a bat of her lashes. "Listening to you tutor yesterday showed me you have a firm grasp on the material, so please work on grading these papers while class is in session. That book is my copy of the answers. Just pop your head up every so often to note where I'm at in the lesson."

I nod and step into the hallway, eager to distance myself from the awkward moment I had created. Something about her tone hit me all wrong, grating with the rough side of dismissal. Those words should have felt pleasant with their hint of approval, but they didn't. My haunches bristle. My last boss had a superiority complex and wore the same disingenuous smile. I will not feel less-than. I've worked too hard.

"Does that include the students' opinions of me in this evaluation also? I noticed a lot of staring going on yesterday during the last class and tutoring," I ask in a waspish tone.

That elicits a momentary eyebrow raise and pursing of lips. "My advanced students are perceptive, Claire. Most are too intelligent for this school, and I treat them as full-fledged adults. Their opinion of you matters to me because they deserve the best education I can provide them, and you are a part of that educational influence now."

"That's not fair to your other classes," I bite back, clutching my free fist and widening my stance. "Or me. You know my credentials. Just because the Air Force discharged me doesn't mean I'm any less of a person or scientist. I care about psychics and the students. All the students."

An amused grin spreads across the professor's face, and she nods to a few people as they pass us in the hallway. I assume they are other professors, since we are still in the faculty building. I swallow hard and attempt to compose myself; my feet pull back together, and I unclench my hand. It won't do to have other teachers side with Professor Bayer about my insolent behavior, no matter how justified. The grin on her face doesn't falter when she turns her attention back to me. "My, my, you have some whip in your tongue. You can handle your own, I'll give you that."

I raise my chin and step past her, biting back smugness that could have been tears had my low-key insubordination ticked her off.

"You know, word has spread about you," Professor Bayer croons.

My eyebrows shoot up, and I spin around, clutching the textbook and folders to my chest. "What word?"

Dr. Bayer winks at me, any hint of scorn gone from her face as she locks her office door. "Oh relax. It's a good thing. Though by your expression, you'd reckon I know one of your innermost secrets."

She chuckles. I choke. There are too many secrets that I don't want to keep. Dr. Sternan has mentioned that my quick-to-react disposition stems from everything I keep bottled up inside. But what can I do when a non-disclosure agreement has my tongue? I catch her rolling her eyes.

"Come along, Claire. I meant that word has spread about your enthusiastic tutoring. I had so many emails requesting tutoring time that I had to draw up a sign-up sheet. My beginner students might pass the class this semester." She shakes her head and marches forward at a brisk pace. "I may need you to stay an extra hour for a little while. If you can manage."

I whistle and say I will make the time. I need to keep this job to rebuild my resume and get good references. Plus, the extra pay is an incentive. The students like me so far. And Professor Bayer, though through unprofessional means, has confirmed my abilities as an assistant. As long as our resident "Buzz" doesn't keep interrupting my life, I may get through the first year here in one piece.

I am not crazy.

*

"Why don't you stay in here to eat your lunch with me and chat?" Professor Bayer offers as I collect my briefcase.

Yesterday I had walked around campus to get better acquainted while I ate a ham sandwich purchased from the cafeteria, since the professor hadn't invited me to stay inside. After washing up, I poked my head into the teacher's lounge of our building and introduced myself to the five professors in there. Two male chemistry teachers, Harry and Carl, both sporting gray hair and deep laugh lines, sat at one table with two biology professors, Don and Amy. They introduced the fifth adult, Baxter, as the resident environmental biologist, who didn't raise their head from deep in an upheld book to acknowledge my hello, at a table sitting by themselves.

Harry leaned back in his chair and pointed at me. "You come and eat in here if that Doctor Bayer ever gets too up on her high horse, Claire. You are always welcome here. Not everyone here has a steel rod up their a—"

"Harry!" Carl shouts and hits the other man's arm. Then he turns and gazes up at me with soft hazel eyes. "What he means to say is that we don't look down on our fellow faculty because of the amount of education or experience that they've had. We are here for the students. That's what matters."

I had let go of my held breath as a nervous laugh escaped and thanked them, then excused myself. In the hallway, I had taken a moment to reflect. Though she may be intelligent, Professor Bayer sure isn't making any friends. If I want her help to get back into a lab, I'll have to bring my physics A-game to class.

Now, I glance around Professor Bayer's office and wonder if I shouldn't head down to the lunchroom. It will be awkward after our tense interaction this morning. I cringe at the thought of eating in silence for an entire hour.

As if she read my thoughts, Professor Bayer says, "Just pull up a chair to my desk. I'm not too fussy about crumbs. A janitor comes along in the evening and vacuums, anyway. Come, come, it's not every day I want to chat."

I drag the chair over. One small step for Claire, one giant leap for humankind. We settle into a comfortable silence among the rustling of her lunch box unzipping and my sandwich bag opening. The professor has brought a salad with grilled chicken. Such an adult lunch compared to my white bread with peanut butter and strawberry jam. But a classic is a classic for a reason.

After a few minutes, Dr. Bayer pulls back the sleeve of her right hand and scratches her wrist. I spy a flash of color on her wrist and lean forward. A small blue-inked tattoo is on her pulse point. One solid dot nestled into a dip in an otherwise straight line beneath the dot. I choke on my mouthful. My tongue pries the peanut butter glob from the roof of my mouth, and I take a long swig from my thermos. Her eyes flash my way, and she pulls her blouse cuff down again.

"Are you alright?"

I nod and wipe my mouth. After a few throat-clearing coughs into my elbow, I point to her right hand. "I have the same representation of a field equation tattooed on my ankle! Though I imagine you lean more towards quantum field theory than classical field theory."

Professor Bayer's eyebrows rise and her eyes widen. She glances at her wrist and then back at me. "Wow, it's rare someone knows what my tattoo means, much less has one of their own. Call me impressed, Claire." She smiles at me, sincere this time, which I return, and we regard each other for a moment. Professor Bayer straightens. I peer behind me, expecting someone to enter, but the door remains shut. I face back to see the professor eyeballing me. She leans forward. "Claire, can we start over?"

Start over what? The conversation? The day? "What do you mean?"

"You and I. I meant for us to be coworkers and leave it at that, you know, professional. But your enthusiasm for physics mirrors mine. Perhaps we can be friends outside of work?" She clasps her hands together. I would say she is pleading with that gesture, but what little I know of her makes me think she wouldn't be caught dead pleading. Danielle is a doctorate recipient, like me. We know how hard we had to work to get where we are, and can imagine all the sacrifices needed for where we want to go. My face might split open from my Cheshire grin.

I force my facial muscles to relax and sit up straighter. Momma lectured to act out how you desire the world to respond. I need a friend who might help me get back on track with my career. And here, an opportunity has presented itself for being myself. "I would like that very much, Professor Bayer."

"Please call me Danielle from now on when we are alone. I worked hard for my doctorate and need my colleagues to acknowledge that by still calling me Dr. Bayer. We are here to leave a mark on this earth, aren't we? Especially as women in the sciences."

My head is going to pop off if I keep nodding anymore. "You are right, Prof—Danielle. I'm honored."

Professor Bayer waves her hand at me. "Don't go all schmulzy on me. I don't do huggy-feely."

I clasp my hands in my lap like a scolded student. "Understood. Thank you, regardless."

Danielle gets up and gathers her trash and lunch containers. I check my watch; we need to be in class soon. *One day at a time, Claire,* I tell myself. *Rome wasn't built in a day, and neither are friendships. She just needs someone to break through that hard exterior.*

As we stroll together toward the classroom, I make a mental note to compose all my questions for her. There are so many. Like, where she's worked, what research papers she's written, and can she help with my ghost problem once I prove it's not just my anxiety causing a hallucination? I may be getting ahead of myself, but I don't care. I made my first friend in this town.

*

Between tutoring students, Danielle locks the door from the inside so we might snag a break. I get the coffee pods picked out and ready. Hazelnut latte for me and plain for her.

"The dean mentioned you relocated here from out of state. Have you found housing yet? I've heard they are building more apartments north of town," Danielle questions when I hand over her filled blue flying pig mug.

I pull a chair to her desk and cup my hands around my mug. The temperature outside is reaching the low fifties, and the air conditioning is still blasting. I'm glad that I came from a cold climate, so all the clothes I already own are warm. "My husband, Steven, found us a house. We snatched it up using my VA loan and discharge stipend for the down payment." I take two swigs, enjoying the hot liquid flowing down my throat and hitting my stomach. "I can confirm the building projects are apartments. Steven works in construction and is on the site. How about you?"

Danielle leans back and takes another sip from her mug; she had buttoned up her long black cardigan like I had my dark orange wool sweater. She had mentioned earlier that someone else, like the janitor, has control over the thermostat. "I am hoping to secure a position at one of the national laboratories once funding comes through again. The request could arrive any day, even though the government is handing out fewer grants these days. I remain optimistic since my current research isn't mainstream, so a small apartment suits me just fine."

I lean forward, soaking up her words, seeing an opening. "You'll have to tell me about your research someday. I worked at Rosebud National Laboratory, where my, er, accident happened. It was nice…" I trail off, worried about how much the non-disclosure agreement allows me to say. My lawyer dumbed it down for me, but since I don't retain him anymore, I don't suppose he'd appreciate me begging for a refresher. I decide to change the subject, just in case. "But I'm stuck here for a while since I am a homeowner now. Steven wants to fix it up and flip it, but it needs a lot of work, and we're not exactly rolling in the money. The yard itself is a nightmare. I've never seen such a weed-choked jumble. At some point, I've got to get out and start weeding before the neighbors gossip. Though I'm sure they've found something to talk about already." I was thinking about Gary.

If he could come talk to us new neighbors, I'm sure he had no trouble making his way around the neighborhood, even with the houses further apart than most cities I've been in, informing everyone what we dress and sound like. Are the neighbors as grossed out by him as I am?

"Yardwork, you say?" asks Danielle, sitting up straighter in her chair.

I snap out of my thoughts and nod.

She places her cup down. "I dabble in landscape architecture if you'd me to have a look? For free, of course, since my level of expertise is akin to that of a hobbyist. Living in an apartment doesn't give me much opportunity to practice. I have a soft spot for landscaping. My father did landscaping in his retirement years. He helped pay for my college that way, and I would help him on the weekends."

"That would be amazing. You can come over after work today, if you'd like, since it's supposed to storm beginning tomorrow. Your input would be invaluable." I plaster on my biggest, genuine smile. All teeth. I make my dentist work hard so I can flash my polished chompers when I so desire. Momma never let me forget three things: sit up straight, brush your teeth, and keep your curls tamed.

"That works," Danielle says, picking up her coffee once again and checking her watch. "I'll follow you home right after work."

7

Danielle, in her shiny black BMW that stands out amid the few older trucks and sedans like mine, follows me home. I warned her about the abundance of birds in our yard, so she parks on the street and walks back to meet me in the driveway.

I watch as Danielle approaches the trees that border our property line with Gary's. She taps the bark of several trunks, and her lips move, but I can't catch what she's saying. I fidget with the handle of my faux-leather briefcase while I wait. I'm glad I could tell her it had been an abandoned property the bank repossessed; otherwise, I'd be red-faced and stammering my apologies for the state of the yard.

"Um, would you like a drink? I can bring it out to you if you still want to look around some more before coming inside," I offer. It wouldn't surprise me if she said we should bulldoze the lot and start fresh. That might be what I suggest to Steven as an option either way. "We have little in the way of food yet. I haven't gone grocery shopping."

Danielle shakes her head as she walks past me in her heels with the ease of one strolling across a marble floor and not a loose gravel driveway to the other side, concentration etched in her brow, a distant look in her gray eyes. Waist-high yellowed grass and giant hogweed dominate the space, while a large patch of thistle grows in the northwest corner. I spot where I had stumbled into the yard yesterday afternoon after seeing the mirror apparition, aka "Buzz", and a small path that was trodden where Steven had dashed to intercept me. I'm glad there aren't any thistles where I had stopped; their barbs would have ruined my trousers and favorite blouse.

"I'll have a cup of tea with you, but not until I examine the backyard, too." Danielle clucks her tongue. "I see what you mean about being overgrown. The trees might have a bug infestation, which would explain the birds. An arborist may save them, or you could chop them down and start with fresh saplings. I'm out of my depth there. But this lawn," she sweeps her hand over the yard, "will take days."

I roll my lips. Both sound like jobs that Steven would need to do. I've never done yardwork on any scale other than pulling weeds with Momma in her vegetable and herb gardens. Steven had hired high school kids to do the yard work at our condo. "We don't own any yard tools yet. There is a shed out back, though. Steven hasn't mentioned whether the bank cleared it out. Ivy is covering most of the building." It might not even be ivy. I know the names of mathematical equations and theories, not plants.

Danielle places her hands on her hips and motions toward the house with her head. "Let's look. Lead the way."

We go through the house because both our shoes are clean. I'll have to guide her around the side of the house or offer to wash her shoes after we're done. I had glanced out the patio door this morning, and it was nothing but mud and small tree branches and twigs littering the yard. The vining plant, with its leaves going through the color change of fall with splotches of orange and brown, is dominating every board of the side fence and the few trees along the back.

Both of us pause on the back porch steps and survey the giant mess in front of us.

"Oh my," Danielle whispers. "Did the previous owners have a dog? Grass is missing in a lot of spots. Or that could be a sign that the soil is too heavy in clay. The ground appears to be dipping there in the middle of the yard. Water will pool, and nothing will grow." Another cluck of her tongue. "I hope you got this place for a steal because just fixing up the two yards will be expensive."

My heart drops to my stomach. Steven already works so hard at his job; I can't expect him to fix the house and the yard as well. "I'll find time," I say, wincing. What I mean is that I'll be staying up late learning how to do yard work from YouTubers. I'll have to buy a pair of garden gloves and galoshes and a big floppy hat and a knee pad and... Momma will help me type up a list. I point to the back-left corner of the yard. "There's the shed. I can't tell if it's leaning because of the ivy or because it's rotten and needs to be demolished."

Danielle surveys the rectangular, swampy yard. In Steven's measuring terms, we could fit the equivalent of three pickup trucks back here. Steven liked the idea of a larger backyard for a potential dog or garden opportunity in the future. Danielle turns to me. "You don't have a spare pair of work boots or rain boots around here? My shoes are leather and definitely not mud-proof."

And probably cost you five hundred dollars. "I have a pair of sneakers. Hang on." I skip back into the house and grab my running shoes and a pair of socks. Bright orange Nikes I bought five years ago, still in new condition. I don't run often.

"Here you go. I wear size eight, so let me know if you need to borrow an extra pair of socks," I offer.

She smiles and shakes her head. "No, this is great, thanks. I'll step carefully so they don't get too muddy." Then she crouches on the porch steps and begins changing into my shoes. "I wouldn't worry about doing much until spring. That will give you the winter to plan what you need to do. An overhaul will be time-consuming, but worth it. I can picture stone steps to a fire pit in the middle. A rubble foundation beneath it will help the excess water to drain throughout the year."

I half-listen and shrug, swapping body weight from my left foot to my right. The whole yard might be quicksand for all we know, waiting for one false step to suck one of us into its muddy depths. I shudder and search for a path to the shed area that has sturdier ground. We could go along the right side where dense ferns grow, using the frond arms as mats and holding onto the chain-link fence to mitigate a slip and fall. A faceplant into a mud puddle would be beyond humiliating. My cheeks burn just thinking about it.

Danielle stands and walks a few steps, testing the shoes. "Very comfortable. Thanks." She glances at me, and I offer a tight smile; she turns to face the yard. "Hmm, I'd like to inspect those vines. They might be poison ivy, but I want to be sure for your sake."

I gasp. "Poison ivy in a residential area? Who would allow such a thing to grow in their own backyard?"

"Maybe not on purpose, since it is an abandoned lot. Poison oak and ivy are common in this climate. Same with nettles. Some gardeners grow nettles for their culinary and medicinal properties. The poison ivy might have helped keep intruders or kids out of the yard if cultivated on purpose. Do you know how to identify such plants?"

I don't. I'm not outdoorsy, and never cared to learn. I just want it to go away. My limbs itch, and I scratch my forearms at a phantom rash. "Something about leaf shape?" Suddenly, I need very much for this consultation to be over and go inside where nature won't get me. "There's thicker grass and less debris along the right fence."

Danielle nods twice. "It'll be fine as long as we go slow. Would you like to stay on the porch? I'd hate for you to dirty your work shoes. And no offense, but you don't seem very keen. I understand and don't judge you for a second."

Is she a mind reader or my guardian angel? An impulse to hug her comes over me, but I don't give in. I don't need to be fired on my second day for inappropriate behavior. Instead, I shake my head and scowl at the yard. "I couldn't let you go alone. It's treacherous. Maybe neither of us should attempt it."

"No, no. You stay here. I've dealt with worse with my father. Trust me," she says. "I'll just peek at the vines and trees along the back fence. You should know what is growing in case you or your husband ever need to venture back there."

The guardrail for the porch, tinged with green moss, gets a strength test as I hold on tighter and tighter while Danielle picks her way around the yard. She discovers a long stick leaning against the fence and uses it to nudge aside grass, fallen tree debris, and untamed weeds before taking another step. It's like watching a movie. Our brave heroine became lost in the wilds of the Pacific Northwest. Will she make it back to civilization before the brambles devour her, bones and all?

Once Danielle makes it to the back fence, I cheer and clap. She humors me by giving two thumbs up; she's too classy to cheer or shout. I compose myself and watch her peer at the trees. Vines are choking the trunks. Danielle continues weaving her way along the back fence toward the shed, using the stick to pull or push vines.

She reaches the shed and tries the door. The wooden boards creak in protest. From here, I can just make out a telltale metallic jiggling to deduce there's a lock on the handle, but can't tell if it's a combination or key lock. She doesn't get it open and turns her focus to the flora around the edges instead. A moist breeze picks up, and the sky darkens by degrees. I bounce on the balls of my feet and chew on the tip of my tongue. The forecast must be right about a storm on its way. Danielle straightens and scrutinizes the sky; I gesture and shout for her to come back, lest I have to send Steven out to rescue her when he comes home.

She makes it back, and I insist she changes back into her shoes in the kitchen since the linoleum is easy to clean and the wooden bench on the porch is sodden. The sky has darkened further, and the smell of rain is thick. I flick on the water kettle and get two mugs down from the cupboard while Danielle explains what she observed.

"Most of those vines are a type of oak, invasive but harmless. There are some thorny blackberries, too. But there is also poison ivy all around the shed. I'd advise you not to handle anything until someone can help you next year. You'll need to wear protective gear and rent a dumpster. I used to wear painters' jumpsuits when I worked for my dad. The hardware store might even sell those paper hazmat suits. A box of those is worth it if you'll be working for days on end in the yard and don't fancy laundering clothes every night to get the plant oils off." Then she gestures back outside. "There's a strong key lock on that shed. I suspect the bank did that since it's not rusty and you didn't mention Steven putting one on. You should ask Steven if they gave you a key. I peeked into the shed through a gap between the wood siding and spied a couple of shovels leaning against the far wall." She stands up and goes to the small window next to the back door, her mouth morphing from a frown into thinned lips before one corner pulls back, then relaxes. Her eyes squint.

My heart skips a beat. "What's wrong?" Something else I should stress about? The world darkens, and I release a small gasp, grasping the edge of the counter and eyeballing the living room, expecting Buzz in his large, TV-snow form. The house lightens, and I exhale. It was just a dark cloud passing overhead. I dash around and flip on every light switch in the kitchen, dining room, and living room.

Back in the kitchen, I set milk and sugar, along with the mugs of tea, on the table. "Danielle? The tea is ready," I call over to her; she is still staring out the window with her arms folded. "Professor?"

She takes a hesitant step back and then turns to me. "Oh, yes, thank you. Sorry, I thought I saw something."

8

My hand pauses in lifting my orange Garfield mug. Hot steam rising from the butterscotch-colored tea within hazes my vision as I stare at Danielle. She saw something. Was it the animal from two nights ago? Is Buzz going to pop in for a visit? My ears strain to hear the telltale drone. How would I explain my experience without sounding crazy? I'll have to run from the house with her and ruin both our shoes. "Like what?" I croak.

Her left eyebrow raises high on her forehead. "You look like I just said I saw a ghost. Is everything all right?"

I lick my lips. "You proclaimed to see something. What was it?" I'm not disclosing anything about

Buzz until I'm certain he's not a hallucination. I need this job. I need her friendship.

She tilts her head, then shrugs. "I'm sure it was just a raccoon or something. This untamed yard is attractive to wildlife." A smirk plays on her lips. Is she making fun of my reaction?

"Oh yeah, of course," I say, and fake a chuckle. "I saw that raccoon a couple of nights ago, as well. I can understand why it made you pause. He scared me half to death when I was…" What do I say instead of admitting I was running from the house, scared senseless from a hallucination in my living room?

Danielle sips her tea. The small upturn at the corner of her lips expands to a full grin. "You are a city girl, huh? But you trailed off there. What were you going to say?"

Now my cheeks are on fire. I thank my dark skin for hiding the flame as it travels down my neck, swallowing me whole. "Uh, I guess I am. I was taking out the trash at night—my first night. What I mean is, Sunday was my first night here, and I was alone and…" *Shut up, Claire!* "I'm rambling. Sorry. You get the picture."

Her grin softens, and she nods. "A large raccoon would make anyone startle, I'm sure." Danielle's gaze wanders around the room, and she drains her cup. "This is a cozy little house. Does it have more than one bedroom?"

"Yeah, two, in fact," I chirp, happy to be on a different subject. "Would you like a tour? I've turned the second bedroom into an office." I spring up, ready to insist on giving a tour if she declines. I want to show her that I have my life together; that I may be poor now but am a reliable employee and friend, and a capable scientist.

Danielle stands and straightens her cardigan. "Okay. I can't wait for more grant money to come my way. The last one allowed me to afford to rent a furnished two-bedroom townhouse with a pool."

"That sounds nice. I can't wait to get on with another lab somewhere in the world, too. Like you, it's been hard to find work. I guess people aren't as interested in the workings of the world as they used to be." A white lie is harmless, right? I hadn't even searched for job openings anywhere since I came here, and my wallowing took up time when I was on sabbatical at my parents' house. It's a miracle that I found this teaching assistant position… with my momma's help.

Danielle nods and smiles as I show her around. She understands it's our first week in the house and that we are still unpacking. Perhaps the professors in the teacher's lounge misjudged her.

"You'll have a pleasant view of the backyard once it's all fixed up," Danielle offers when we enter the second bedroom, which is occupied by my desk and a few of Steven's more expensive tools that I don't know the names of. They're big, bulky, ugly metal things. One is a wrench-like contraption the size of my arm. Another has a saw blade at the end. It reminds me of a robot arm.

"I don't need a view to stay focused," I say and shrug, needing to make it known that I'm a hard worker without outright saying it. The girl with stress-induced hallucinations will get back on track. Someday, Rosebud Research Facility will offer me a job again, and I'll be able to refuse, throwing in my old boss's face that I've advanced to bigger and better things. "Once I get into a good routine with you at work, I may begin drafting grant requests. I could start my own coding referral business. Maybe we can collaborate or help each other with what we hear for opportunities, you know, since we are both physicists." Help-me-help-you-help-me, and all that. At some point, I may have to admit I've never applied for a grant. I'm sure there is a how-to manual online.

The corner of Danielle's lip quirks up, and she leaves the room, throwing a "Mmm, quite," over her shoulder. I am left alone in the room for a moment, wondering if my intentions were too on the nose. No one ever said I was good at tact, but no one ever said I was bad at it either.

The front door opening snaps me out of my overthinking sandpit, and I charge out of the room. "Please don't leave, Danielle."

I skid to a halt, short of running into Danielle, in the living room. Steven is closing the door behind him, white plastic bags with red Chinese characters hanging from one arm, keys and his tool belt dangling from the other hand. Based on the condition of his work shirt beneath his unzipped jacket, it was a muddy day on the job site. It's not uncommon for his neon-green and orange work shirts to come home smeared with dirt and sweat stains, and sometimes jagged rips and tears from being caught on a rogue nail or jagged end of a two by four. When the stains don't wash out anymore, the shirts become cleaning rags. He says we need to buy stock in construction worker clothing, with how fast he wears them out.

"Oh, hi, honey! Sorry Danielle. This is my husband, Steven. Steven, this is Dr. Danielle Bayer, the professor I assist," I rush out.

Steven smiles through his dusty face. This man's smile has dispelled many an awkward situation I've created. It's sweet and honest; I don't picture him ever using a fake smile like I do. Danielle smiles back and nods her head. Steven hoists the bags higher and says, "If you'd like to stay for dinner, I've brought home enough food to feed an army. They just opened the restaurant last week."

"Or enough for you for one meal," I say, nudging his arm and winking before taking two bags from him. "Yes, please stay, Danielle. You can tell Steven all your observations about the yard."

"I accept your offer. Thank you," Danielle says. She steps back to let us pass.

Steven sets down the bags next to the kitchen sink and turns to Danielle. "What's this about the yard?"

"Danielle has experience in landscaping as well as a doctorate in theoretical physics," I explain, shooting her an appraising smile. "She offered to lend her professional eye."

Steven whistles. "That's some resume, Professor. I would appreciate any notes you can give. But if you ladies will excuse me, I'd first like to get cleaned up for dinner."

We nod in agreement, and I pretend to smell him, then wave my hand in front of my nose. He hooks me around the waist with one arm and kisses me on the forehead. I screech and smack his chest until he releases me and heads toward the bathroom, chuckling to himself.

I catch Danielle's eye, and she smirks, shakes her head. My cheeks combust. "Sorry about that. It's like being married to a Labrador, I swear."

With her help, we have the table set and various

entrees poured into serving bowls we can pass around our small, round four-seater dining table by the time Steven comes back with a clean upper body and fresh clothes. Danielle requests water since she needs to drive home, while I pour Steven and me each a Heineken.

The bowls get passed while Danielle brings Steven up to speed on what she's told me so far about the state of the trees and to be wary of the poison ivy in the back. "It's quite rural around here, so I can't imagine the neighbors will report the state of your yard if you leave it until spring," she says between nibbles of Kung Pao chicken.

"Is that legal?" Steven wonders aloud after draining his glass of beer. I hop up to grab him a fresh one. "People call the cops if someone doesn't mow their lawn?"

Danielle shrugs. "It's more common with H.O.A. properties, but yes, my father got hired sometimes because of derelict yards. Some places can't have bushes or trees within five hundred feet of the house because of wildfires. Have you met any of your neighbors? I'm sure they'd understand if you explained." She slices a veggie dumpling in half and eats it with the grace of a queen. I wonder if it is her few years more in age or her upbringing that imbues her with elegance. Then there's her nice car, clothes, and briefcase. My thoughts travel back to

Dr. Sternan and how she told me that I need to love myself where I am right now. Could I love being here in Deadwood, eating mediocre, greasy, MSG-laden takeout Chinese food with Steven and a new friend? Perhaps at this very moment, sitting here in this small dining room, yes, yes, I could.

"We've met the old man who lives to the left of us," Steven says. His face disappears when he tips his bowl of egg-flower soup up to his lips.

I roll my eyes. Danielle notices and tilts her head, so I lean forward and hiss, "He called me an 'exotic beauty' when Steven introduced me."

Danielle has the decency to express shock. As a fellow career woman, I knew she'd understand. Steven leans over and pats my arm. Danielle tuts.

"He apologized, Claire. And he warned us about the condition of the trees, too. We should have him over for dinner sometime. I bet he could tell us about the previous owners and this house," Steven says.

I grimace, remembering his wet cough, grasping hands, and yellow teeth. "Just him? What if you leave the room? He's gross. What if he tries to hold my hand again?" I wail.

"What about a housewarming party? Or you could say it's a meet-and-greet if you're not comfortable requesting gifts, as is customary with a housewarming party," Danielle suggests. Then she straightens up, her eyes bright. "Oh, you could use Halloween as an occasion! It falls on a Friday this year. This Friday, if fact."

"This Friday is Halloween?!" I squawk. How did it sneak up on me? I've never missed carving a pumpkin or hanging a paper skeleton in the window. Didn't I notice the extra orange-colored decorations around campus and in the few shop windows? This move has thrown me out of sync.

Steven stands up and collects our plates. "Oh, yeah! That's a great idea. There's a pharmacy-type place next to the hardware store on my way home, honey. We can get some lights and decorations and have the immediate neighbors over for drinks. We might even get some trick-or-treaters this year since we're in a house."

Bless him, Steven needs to be a homeowner, I muse, swiveling my head between him and Danielle, who is nodding with a grin. He gets excited about everything I don't: handing out candy on Halloween, yard work, talking to neighbors—

"Oh, and you're invited, of course, Professor," Steven adds.

I nod and pick up a couple of bowls from the table. "Yes, I insist. Please." At least there would be one person there I could count on for intellectual conversation. I set the dishes in the sink and switch on the hot water, intending to let them soak overnight. I'll load the dishwasher that came with the house and find out if it can handle me not scrubbing the dishes beforehand. I face Danielle. Steven comes over and wraps an arm around my shoulders, tugging me to him. I flash him a smile.

Danielle holds onto her smile. "Alright, but then I insist on helping you with the invitations, since it was my idea. I detest store-bought ones, don't you? We can use my laptop." She stands and collects the last of the dishes from the table before I can. "Now, I hate to dine and dash, but it's getting late and my houseplants still need to be watered. But it was kind of you both to have me stay for dinner, and like I said, don't agonize about doing anything with the yard until spring. I can mention it to your neighbors on Friday night as well." She squeezes my left biceps with her left hand and offers her right hand to Steven. "It's been a long time since I've had such a cordial evening. Claire, we'll make those invitations tomorrow. I'll see myself out."

9

I wake up to Steven's gentle snoring next to me on Wednesday morning and check my phone. Five thirty. I've woken up half an hour before my alarm. The shadowy figures visited my dreams as usual, but my heart isn't thumping. And it's getting harder to hold on to their image when I wake up. I rise, peering through the darkened room at the area where the wall mirror used to hang. I always check that corner, just in case Buzz shows up again, and am relieved as usual that there is an empty wall. This could count as tangible evidence of my healing that I can present to Dr. Sternan.

As my eyes adjust, so do my ears. Nothing buzzes or whistles or hums besides Stevens' breathing. *Slow down, heart; everything is okay.* Four-second inhales, then four-second holds, and then four-second exhales. There, now I should be able to sleep for a few more minutes. I ease back onto my pillow and close my eyes.

Somewhere in the distance, a car honks. My eyes pop open. I'm not tired. Did I finally get a good night's sleep? I slide out of bed, pull on a sweatshirt, sweatpants, my orange fuzzy slippers and tiptoe out to the living room to do some yoga, which I haven't done since I was staying at my parent's house. I can't wait to report to Dr. Sternan.

By the time Steven's alarm goes off and he walks into the kitchen, yawning, I have started the coffeemaker and plop two pieces of bread into the toaster. He scratches his stomach and smiles at me. I sidle over and wrap my arms around him.

He makes an "Mmm" sound deep in his chest, and I pull my arms tighter. It's going to be a good day.

*

I arrive at work light on my feet, swinging my briefcase and orange thermos. A peanut butter and jelly sandwich with apple slices bounces around in the otherwise empty case. The contents of our pantry and refrigerator are down to these ingredients, along with a bit of milk and a lone carrot in the crisper drawer. I told Steven that I'll shop for some groceries and pick out a couple of large pumpkins to carve tonight. Since I'm buying the food for the party and some other pantry staples, Steven agreed to shop for discounted decorations on his way home before Friday night.

"Good morning, Professor Bayer!" I sing as I enter her office.

She straightens up by the printer set up on her desk as her hand flies to her chest. "Good Lord, Claire, you scared me! But at least you can hold a note. Good morning."

The ruffled collar of my dark blue long-sleeved blouse lifts with the sound of crackling static as I strip off my overcoat. "I woke up after having the best sleep I've had in a long time. I even had time to practice my favorite yoga poses, make Steven his breakfast and both our lunches, and get a decent parking spot." I place my briefcase on a shelf in the bookcase and lift my thermos for a drink, the other hand holding down my dancing collar edges. There's enough product in my brown curls that the static doesn't stand a chance of wreaking havoc.

Both of Danielle's eyebrows raise. "That good, huh? Well, I hope the rest of your day continues the same way. I'm refilling the ink cartridges since I wasn't sure how many invitations you'd like to print off. The office supply police were reluctant to give me color ink, claiming it's more expensive. But that's rubbish. They get it from a warehouse for cheap, like any other business."

I gulp the still too hot coffee so I won't spit it, and wince as it burns my esophagus. "Office police?" I choke out.

She chuckles and closes the printer's front cover. It makes a series of whirs and clicks as it realigns itself. "That's what I call office secretaries. Didn't you ever request supplies at the lab you worked at? Aren't they the stingiest? It's easier begging for a raise than staples and paper clips."

"Oh, I never did, I guess. I would send one of my civilian team members to get anything I needed. Whoever oversaw supplies at Rosebud Research Laboratory never complained. None of my team ever came back empty-handed or with a reprimand to pass along." Except after I filed a complaint about the unregulated use of power the night of the incident, and rumors spread. Then, my team members started transferring to other labs, showing up late, misinterpreting instructions, returning with the wrong supplies, and whispering amongst themselves more than working. It was exhausting and aggravating. The board that reviewed my case added this to my file: "Claire cannot keep her team on task, and it is putting all other projects behind schedule." The facility couldn't have that. It was another excuse to get rid of me. A shudder wracks my body.

Danielle clicks her briefcase shut and leans over her desk. Her mouth contorts into a frown. "It doesn't sound like a happy memory, though. You just shivered. Or are you that cold?"

I try to fake a smile, manage a strained grimace, give up, and relax my facial muscles, shaking my head. "No, I'm fine. Working at the research facility was wonderful at first. But then my incident happened, and my life fell apart for a little while." I blink and straighten. "But I'm better now, I promise. A change of scenery has done a world of good." Another misrepresentation of the truth. I would pack up tomorrow and drive to, well, not Montana—I need some space from there, but perhaps New Mexico for a warmer climate and bigger research facilities, or the east coast so Steven could be nearer to his family for a while. This town seems so sleepy! Even the students don't jostle one another or shout or sing in the walkways like when I was in college.

A light pat on my arm startles me back to the present, and Danielle is walking out of the room. She waits for me to leave before locking up and says, "I can attest to a change of scenery doing a body good. But it's also okay to acknowledge one's own demons that may have hitched a ride with you."

"That's one way to look at it," I murmur, thinking of the buzzing and the figure that has scared me twice so far. Has Buzz given up and left? I hope Buzz is a demon of my imagination and my psyche is righting itself.

*

Since I didn't bring my laptop, I doodle several sketches on a notepad while Danielle plods on in her classes about particle characteristics and oscillating waves and light theory. Do I want neighborhood kids running amok at our place? No, just adults this year. How many neighbors do we want over? Not that many, and make a notation of five copies, circling it in the page's corner. So far on the page I have:

Come by and say hello on Halloween!
The Simmons would love to meet you and
share a drink!
6PM-8PM
21+

Rudimentary pumpkins and leaves float around the words. At lunch, I should have time to race home to get my laptop that has Adobe installed or use a computer in the library here if Danielle needs to use hers for work.

*

"Don't waste time going home for your laptop, Claire. I can just as easily draw this up on my laptop while you eat your lunch. Then we can tweak it to your liking after classes and have it printed off before the first student arrives for tutoring," Danielle says when I show her my sketches as we head to her office for our lunch hour.

I want to hug her. But I don't. So instead, I say, "That's very kind of you. Let me know how I may pay you back in kind." She nods, sits at her desk, and pulls her laptop closer.

When I set my briefcase away a half hour later and make her a fresh hazelnut latte upon her request, she spins her laptop around and shows me her work. It's perfect. I can't help but clap and lean over the desk.

She found the same fun font as I had sketched and placed an orange shadow behind the letters. Then, as I had sketched as well, she had scattered little graphic jack-o'-lanterns and fall leaves and candies all over the background.

"Oh, you got it perfect on the first try, Danielle! Is there anything you can't do?" I gush. I would have worried about fonts and graphics for another half hour or more. "I wish we were inviting more people than the five households just to show these invitations off. But five couples plus Steven and me are all I imagine we can fit into our little house. Plus you, of course."

Danielle rotates her laptop back around, beaming. "I'm glad you approve. We will print them off when I print off some coursework later. Perhaps you can cover me for tutoring this afternoon, so I may pop out on an errand? Then we can say we are even for this project?" She glances at me, and I nod in agreement, then she paws the scroll pad. "It will be fun. You never know what interesting people live right next door."

*

I spent an hour in the local supermarket picking out two pumpkins for us to carve, as well as some snacks, drinks, and meal ingredients. Identifying perfect carving pumpkins is an art. They can't be too big or too small, too round or too oblong, or have skin ridges that are too deep. Then there are stencils and carving tools to consider, as well as LED tea lights or the usual wax ones.

In our first year together, Steven had suggested using his power tools in his bachelor apartment to carve pumpkins. He had handed me his power drill, which I had never used before. I got the brilliant idea to tape a big spoon to the drill bit, and within seconds pumpkin innards were spattering us and the walls of his kitchen. He had laughed until he cried while I sat there gaping at the juice running down the walls and pulp in his hair.

"Good thing you're majoring in science and not medicine," he'd wheedled, then howled with laughter again while I pelted him with more pumpkin guts.

That became one of our favorite memories together. I've gotten much better at using the tools since then.

My phone pings with an incoming text while I scan the beer choices. It's Steven reminding me to get extra paper towels and newspaper for pumpkin carving tonight. Then a second text pops up from him, saying to pick up painter's drop cloths and tape to protect the kitchen. Every year I get that text. He'll never let me live that one night down. I roll my eyes and shoot back the middle finger and wink face emoji, and head to the checkout. My stomach is growling, and the frost on our frozen lasagna dinner has already melted.

Steven pulls into the driveway just as I do. He helps me bring the pumpkins in, holding one in each hand. "You picked out some excellent candidates for lobotomy practice."

I giggle and smack him, admiring his bulging

biceps stretching his sawdust and sweat-grimed neon green work shirt sleeves.

"Did you have any luck with your invitations?" he shouts over his shoulder, oblivious to my ogling.

I snap out of my gaze and turn back to the car. "Yeah! They turned out great with Danielle's help! I'll drop them into the mailboxes right now." Using envelopes had felt like a waste, so I had just folded the invites into thirds with our address written on the outside. A cute pack of pumpkin stickers at checkout rounded out the look to seal the edge down. I grab the invitations from my briefcase and hasten to the neighbors' mailboxes, one to each house on either side and then one to each of the three houses across from us.

I jog back to help Steven bring in the rest of the groceries and prepare the kitchen floor for our poor pumpkins' demise.

10

Thursday at work is the usual lounge in class as I listen to Danielle teach. It's getting easier to ignore the stares of the advanced students. After almost a week here, they still go to Danielle for tutoring, opting to reschedule instead of giving me a chance when Danielle is busy with another student. Though there is one male who stares more than most, who strikes me as familiar. The line of his jaw and his heavy brow are hard to miss. Did I work with a sibling or parent of his at Rosebud? Or drill with a family member in the Air Force? I shake the irrational fears of silent judgment and ostracizing from my head and decide to wait for him to break the ice if he chooses. There are worksheets to grade from the previous class to fill in the free time, anyway. Danielle had printed these class assignments after printing my invites, commenting on how these students were struggling to retain any course material and that repetition was the key for it to stick.

"Well, stick until their final exam, anyway," Danielle reiterates over her cob salad at lunch. "After that, I don't care what they do with their brains."

This makes me sad. I hold my tongue against the questions that crave to hurdle out. Does she figure she won't be teaching for long? Does she just not like kids? But this is a college with young adults who need all the encouragement they can get to succeed. My goal is to have the students leave my tutoring session with a smile. Physics is fun when you understand it. I want the students to have fun, too.

*

My brain is tired; my eyes are heavy. Danielle's lessons are progressing too fast for these students, and the sign-up sheet for tutoring reflects that. Today, I had three students drift away after my tutoring sessions, looking more perplexed than when we started. Danielle had to leave at three for an appointment, so I had a fourth cup of coffee to stay upbeat and tutor two students at once in the last hour. Yet another advanced student peeked their head into Danielle's office, saw it was just me, and left before I could ask what they needed help with. I even photocopied Danielle's lesson plan for next week that she left on her desk so I can gear up for more confused students and research fun teaching methods for class, and try to make it appear like something I ran across on the Internet over the weekend.

Now I'm sagging in my car seat, driving home, worrying my lower lip as I try to come up with a tactful way to approach Danielle about her lesson speed and teaching style. "Danielle," I want to say, "You are too monotone and skip to new lessons too fast. These kids became lost three classes ago, if you hadn't noticed." Yeah, that's going to go over great.

The weather doesn't help; mist and fog test my car's headlight beam strength on these winding dark roads that blend with dense undergrowth. Bloated gray skies every day get interrupted by the odd cloudburst, soaking everything in minutes, no matter what kind of jacket or raincoat you're wearing. As I pull into our driveway, I'm thankful that not only is there some dark blue sky peeking through the cloud cover as the sun sets ever earlier, but there isn't the usual flock of crows and small birds in the trees on our property. One of these days, bird poop is going to drop into my hair, and it will be so gross.

I step out of the car with my briefcase in hand and inhale. Wet earth and wet pavement odors fill my nose. That smell reminds me of morning walks to school with Poppa and long walks around campus in college when Steven and I were getting to know each other.

Honk, Honk.

A classic V-shaped flock of five Canadian geese heads south, almost over our house. Their long necks stretch out in front as their wings flap at the same pace.

Bzzzz.

Every muscle in my body tenses. I'm scared to take my eyes off the geese. I fear what is watching me is in the house or right next to me.

The buzzing speeds up. And then rotates away, as if it's in a car driving around a corner. That's new. The vibrations leave my body. That's new too. But in what direction is the phenomenon moving? I glance at the house's front window; no shadows lurk.

HONK, HONK, HOOAK!

My eyes veer up at the odd sound. Two geese collide and fall fast towards the house as they hit each other with their frantic wings flapping. I gasp and drop my briefcase, taking a few steps back. The rest of the geese honk louder, heads swerving side to side like they're crazed, and swoop down, headed straight towards me.

I scream, cover my head with my arms, pivot, and run.

"Claire! Over here! This way!" someone hollers. I sprint towards the voice, eyes on the ground, my right elbow scraping across the bark of a tree trunk.

"Come inside! Hurry!"

I've reached a neighbor's house and peek between my arms. Someone has just darted back inside and is holding the front door open for me. I bolt up their porch steps and leap into their entryway.

"What in the Sam Hill made that noise?" a man hollers. "Was it the birds or you?"

I double over, wheezing. It's been a couple of years since I did any sort of sprinting. And in cheap loafers, nonetheless. I don't know what I just witnessed, but I'm glad I didn't experience it alone.

I'm not crazy. I'm not crazy. I'm not crazy.

"Mrs. Claire? You okay? Can I get you some water? You can sit in my recliner to catch your breath."

I pause my inhale count. I recognize the voice. Old and weathered. I recognize the smell. Old cigars, unwashed clothes, and dust. I stifle a groan and stand up straight. I've just charged into Gary Tubman's house. He continues to peer through thick lace curtains at his living room window while my eyes adjust to the dim interior. Then he glances back at me; he's still wearing the same outfit from Monday afternoon. Does he still have the same handkerchief in his pocket? I shudder.

"I've never heard a noise like that in all my life," Gary says. "You sit down if you'd like." He motions behind him to an orange and yellow fabric three-seater with sagging cushions and two deflated brown decorative pillows by the armrests. A dark wood coffee table with cup ring marks and a small box television on a rolling stand occupies the middle of the room. Moss-green shag carpet stretches into the hallway beyond. Black and white and sepia photographs in frames clutter the top of the television. His recliner is brown, with darker brown areas that look more like stains than any sort of pattern on the seat and armrests. I clamp my jaw shut and try not to think of those spots too hard. It's like I've stepped back in time to the nineteen seventies.

"No, thank you. I'm better now," I mutter, afraid of breathing in too much air from this decrepit room. My elbow stings where I scraped it. I try to ignore the pain and instead stare at the old man. My feet, which ran in fear moments ago, can't seem to move. Gary is holding back the curtain. There are various brown smudges on the fabric's trim. Those curtains haven't seen soap and water since his wife died, I bet. Part of me pities him, while the rest of me desires to get the hell out of here. But what about the birds? It's like they blamed me for the anomaly and told each other to attack.

I roll my lips, and my eyes connect with his. He's staring at me, motionless. I sidle to the door. "Um, I—did you hear the buzzing, too?"

Gary puts his hands on his hips. "Buzzing? Is that what made you go all wonky?"

"No, Gary. The noise before my scream was a flock of geese's abnormal honking and diving at me. There was a buzzing sound before that. When I got out of my car." I gesture toward the window.

He peers outside once more. "I hear buzzing sometimes, but just assume it's my hearing aid. So, you heard a buzzing right before the birds? Was it your car or phone? Birds are sensitive to electricity. They use the Earth's magnetic field to migrate. Did you know that?" Gary looks back at me.

"What? Wait." There were too many questions in that rambling, and my brain can't tell which question to answer first. Ringing starts up in my left ear. I scrub my face with my hands, more exhausted than before. The fabric of my blouse is sticking, tugging on the area of dried blood around my elbow. I eyeball the decrepit sofa and deliberate my options for a moment. Should I wait for Steven? Should I call animal control? In my peripherals, Gary stuffs his hands down his overall pockets and keeps them there.

"No," I say, straightening up. "We've heard the sound before, too. It starts off as a hum and then gets louder. I was in the house the last two times, and Steven was outside when we heard it on Monday. It's not our phones or cars. I'm sure of it."

Gary presses his face to the window. "Well, I don't see or hear the geese or any buzzing either. Maybe it was a plane."

I shake my head. Why is it the human condition to write everything off as something that sounds logical, just so they can go on with their lives? There was no way a plane could have caused the birds to react like that. Planes have been flying for decades. I can't let this go; Gary is the first person other than Steven to have witnessed what's been happening to me. "No, it wasn't. I had just got out of my car and was watching the geese fly over. Then I heard the buzzing, and that's when two of the geese collided with each other and fell out of the sky, and the rest of them veered down towards me. I screamed and started running. Then I heard you calling me."

Garry nods, pointing to himself. "I had just opened the door to go get the mail. When I stepped out, I heard the peculiar honking and your scream and saw you run between the trees with your hands over your head. That's when I called you. I didn't see the geese fall. The trees block my view."

"But you said you'd heard buzzing before, or thought you did?" I grill him, hopeful for another witness of the phenomenon at our house. Then I hug myself. If only it were as easy as a plane overhead. Then I could plan for it by deciding what kind of plane and calling the airport or writing a letter to the mayor, or attending a town hall meeting. But if it was a plane, wouldn't it follow the same flying patterns as all the rest day in and day out? It's been days since any buzzing sound tormented us, unless it's sporadic and happens when we're not home. Thank goodness we don't have pets! The crows must've flown away on Monday before I ran from the house. The wheels spin in my mind. I know very little biology, but have had PBS animal shows on enough times in the background for a few facts to stick. Maybe that's why the crows and other birds stick around. They are intelligent and have learned to wait for their next meal to get weakened by the buzzing, like those poor geese. Or the bugs to wiggle free from the infested bark. How long has this phenomenon been going on at our property? Could it be just a coincidence that I witnessed a similar thing at the lab building? Is this why the previous owners abandoned the house? What if there is a curse on the land? I need Steven. He'll know what to do.

Gary approaches me. I raise my hands, blocking him from coming any closer. "Stop. What are you doing?" I was going to pull my phone out but realized it's still in my briefcase. It's just me and this old man in his house. No one knows I'm here. He may be old, but he could hide lean muscles and sinister motives.

He stops and gesticulates to the door behind me. "I need to check that the coast is clear. I don't want you to leave in case they attack again, like you say they did. What if they're disoriented or diseased? It would be mighty un-neighborly of me to make you go first, Mrs. Claire."

I step back and allow him to pass, moved by his courage. But then I get a whiff of unwashed clothes, old man, and dirt. Nope. I'll risk the birds. "I'll come out with you. I need to see for myself, too, Gary." And to get some fresh air. Had it been summer here, I would have fainted by now from his odor.

We inch out into the middle of his manicured front yard. It's muddy, but has enough grass coverage that neither of us slips much. He holds his weather hand out for me to hold, but I pretend to be preoccupied scanning the darkening blue sky seen between big gray clouds rolling past and condensing.

The late afternoon is quiet again. No one else appears to have come out of their house to investigate my scream or the birds' commotion. Or they had poked their heads out and had either seen Gary helping me or I was already in his house. Others had to be home from work by now.

Steven won't be home from work for another half hour, plus the time to shop at the party supply store. Oh, yeah. The party.

I search the sky, then face Gary when I'm satisfied no geese are going to attack. He stares back and shrugs.

"I gather we are safe, Gary. Thanks for the help. But before I go, I was wondering what you thought of our invitation?" I stuff my hands into my coat pockets, trying to stave off the cold creeping down my collar.

His head tilts. "You mean that slip of paper in my mailbox with your address written on the outside was an invitation?"

"Yes, Gary. Didn't you open it?" I'm beyond exhausted; there is a vice-like pressure around my skull now. Any more stupid questions, and I'm going to walk away. "What did you think it was?"

He blinks at me and scratches his chin. "Well, I ain't ever received an invitation like that. Do you need a special light to read it?"

I grind my teeth and one heel down. My loafer squelches. I groan and hop to a thicker patch of grass to wipe mud off the sides of my shoes. The pressure in my head increases. "I am in no mood for these games, Gary. I've had a long day, and then those kamikaze birds were the icing. I used thirty-point font. I placed the folded invitation into your mailbox within an hour of printing it. You shouldn't need a special light, not to mention glasses, to read it. If you don't want to come to the party, then just say so."

"What party?" Gary sounds as exasperated as I feel. I glare at him; I can't tell if he's fibbing or serious. He raises his palms up. "Mrs. Claire, the paper you deposited in my mailbox is blank."

I stare at him. My brain has told me what he said, but it doesn't tell me how to react. So I wait. And wait. He drops his hands and makes his way back to the porch, gesturing to me twice to follow. I need him to repeat himself; I heard wrong. But every time my mouth flops open, nothing comes out. This is a prank, or a ruse to get me back into his house. I'm not going back in there. Not for all the tea in China, or grant money for a quantum computing job in Sweden. Okay, maybe for grant money to be used in Sweden.

"I'll show you, Mrs. Claire," he says from the

porch, gesturing to me once more to follow.

I place my hands on my hips and say, "I'll wait out here."

He disappears inside, not taking off his shoes, which are covered in mud. I grimace. All that mud on his green shag carpet. At least it goes with the color scheme. I wipe my shoes on the clump of crabgrass I'm standing on again. Not that it'll do any good since I still must cross the rest of his yard to my house.

Gary's screen door squeaks, and he steps out with a folded white paper in hand. He hesitates on the porch steps until he sees that I'm not moving and makes his way over. "See, Mrs. Claire. I'm no liar. I may be old with poor eyesight and hearing, but I am not a liar." He hands me the slip of paper.

On the back of the folded part, my address is visible, scribbled by hand. I purse my lips and unfold it, noting that the little pumpkin sticker I used to seal each one has some paper on it from when Gary had ripped it open last night or this morning.

It's blank. As if I just pulled it out of a fresh ream of paper. I gape, unbelieving. I hold it up to the sky, hoping to find remnants of ink somewhere on the page. Nothing is there. It appears just as he described. A blank sheet of printer paper folded into thirds with my address on the outside. How has one side—the more important side— disappeared?

I want to scream and stomp my feet. I had two good days in a row. Now I'm starting back at square one. Why did I bother coming home? Why did I bother moving and starting a new job? What's the point of anything if I can't make one thing go right in my life? I sniff and let my shoulders sag, whispering, "I don't understand."

Gary gestures across the street. "Mr. Davis is home now. Did you give him an invitation? We could ask to see it. Your printer skipped a page, I bet. It'll be alright."

"I slipped invitations into those three boxes," I point to each house, "and into the mailbox for the house on the other side of my home." I suck my lower lip and scan the sky once more for geese. Why is it always so quiet after something happens to me here? Gary's house and body odor may gross me out, but his presence is reassuring out here. And his patience soothes my frayed nerves. "Would you come along and introduce me? Then I can explain and re-invite the neighbors if all the pages got messed up somehow, starting with him." I hope it's just Gary's invitation that was misprinted. This has been embarrassing enough as it is. I could swear I glanced at each of the five pages before folding them, because I'm used to double-checking my work before turning it in.

Gary's eyes widen, and his bowed spine straightens. Yellowed teeth expose themselves as a wide grin stretches the lines on his face. "I'd be happy to!"

This time, when he offers his hand to me, I place the very tips of my fingers in his hand to placate him. Under all that wrinkled skin and dirty clothes, maybe, just maybe, there's a harmless old man like Steven claims.

But you never know until it's too late. I plan to live, unlike all the unlucky bimbos in those horror movies I watched growing up. How naïve I was back then, thinking monsters lived just on the big screen.

I pull my hand back when we reach the street and allow Gary to lead. I don't know which house Mr. Davis lives in, or what he looks like. Gary will be a welcome middleman in this awkward introduction. I wish Steven were here with his disarming smile.

My ambassador marches to the front door of the house across from mine. The front yard of this robin's egg blue painted ranch-style home is just as muddy as everyone else's, with a gunpowder gray F-150 truck parked in the gravel driveway. A porch light turns on just as we step up to the door. The rusty white screen door covers a dark blue storm door.

Gary uses his thumb to ring the doorbell.

Woof. Woof. Deep baritone barks emanate from just behind the door, and I backpedal.

Gary pats my arm. "Don't worry, Hamlet is a big softy. I've seen the kiddies play all over him in the front yard."

"Back, Hamlet. Back," a booming voice shouts from within. "Go, you damn dog! Get out of my way."

Who names their dog Hamlet? Then I wonder if there's a breed of dog that a name like Hamlet suits. It doesn't roll off the tongue. An image of a small chihuahua in Shakespeare outfit pops into my mind, and I crunch down on my tongue to stymie the giggle bubbling; I don't presume Mr. Davis will appreciate my humor when I already have to explain a blank invitation. I can't explain it, though, if it is. Not the hows or whys. All I can say is sorry, and here's the missing details.

A head pokes through a crack as the storm door opens. "Who's there? What do you want? Make it quick," the head demands.

I blink. Words don't come. It happens when I'm scared. Why am I scared? I've seen scarier things in my home and in dark alleys around the world. He's just a man who's had a long day at work. I can smell garlic and some kind of cooked meat wafting from within.

"Good evening, Mr. Davis," Gary says. "This is Mrs. Claire Simmons. She lives with her husband, Steven. They moved in across the street." He gestures with the blank invitation toward me.

I swallow and attempt to smile. It wavers and dies as I manage a small "Hello."

"Claire Simmons?" The annoyance is clear in his Southern drawl. Not a great sign of the conversation to come. It also makes me wonder how many other Southerners like me have moved to this corner of the state. Opportunity or necessity? Another question for another time. He steps forward and pulls the storm door shut behind him. The screen door squeals for oil just like mine and Gary's and swings outward, missing my face by an inch. I step back, and my heels sink. I'm off the porch and into the muddy yard. My poor shoes.

Mr. Davis gazes at us, pale lips in a thin line, and thick eyebrows furrowed. As he takes us in, I size him up. About five foot ten inches of white man with a balding round head, and wearing an undershirt that's two sizes too small if the enormous gut exposed near his waistband is anything to go by. The lines around his eyes place him at around fifty. Or he's younger and never wears sunscreen.

"Are you a relative of the Galloways?" Mr. Davis

asks.

"Who are the Galloways?" I shoot back, the question if he is from Tennessee or Louisiana burning in my throat.

Mr. Davis juts his chin out, gesturing. "Tim and Laura owned that house before you did. Up and disappeared one night. No one knows what happened to them." He cocks an eyebrow at me. If I try to step anywhere, I'm sure my foot will come out of my loafers stuck in the mud, so I stand still and meet his gaze.

"I wasn't aware. Look, I wanted to explain my invitation—"

"You call that an invitation? George from next door and I thought it was a Halloween prank. Young lady, it isn't funny, whatever it is. We don't need you city-types disturbing our peaceful community."

"Now wait a minute, Mr. Davis," Gary says. He appears even older and frailer next to the fat man. God bless his confidence. "Claire is just trying to explain—"

A sausage finger flies up and pokes Gary in the chest. "I bet you're in on it too, you old kook."

Gary backpedals. His face crumples, and one hand rubs where the fat man poked him.

"Hey!" I shout. Shoes be damned; I pull my feet free of the mud with a gross *slurp* and step back up onto the cement walkway next to Gary. "Don't push him, and shut up for one minute so I can explain what happened to the invitation I put in your mailbox."

Mr. Davis leers at me. I give him my best glare back. He snorts. "No one tells me to shut up. Get off my property or I'll call the cops on you for trespassing."

I suck in a breath through gritted teeth. "Mr. Davis, I am a scientist and upstanding citizen. Just let me explain."

A sharp bark of laughter escapes his lips, and he steps back into his house, the screen door slamming shut. Then, his form looms up on the other side. "And stop feeding the damn birds. They're pooping all over our cars and harassing my dog. I'll report you for damages."

I try again. "Mr. Dav—"

"Go away," Mr. Davis shouts over me and slams his storm door shut. The windows of his house rattle.

My chest deflates. Ever since the inquest at Rosebud Research Facility, I have been getting nowhere with anything or anyone in my life. Have those figures I saw cursed me? A figure conjured from that lab to haunt me, hunt me, or drive me into madness? Perhaps it's already succeeded.

Gary grimaces and gestures for me to follow. "I'll

walk you home, check for any poor birds that fell on your property, and call animal control tomorrow."

After we cross the street to my yard, I ask him, "Why was he so mean to us? To you? How did that go so wrong?"

He shakes his head and shoves his hands into his pockets. "I was nice to the Galloways when they lived here. That made the other neighbors dislike me, I guess."

We trudge to the driveway, and I pick up my dropped briefcase. Gary slips past me, looking around, then spins about and spreads his arms wide as I straighten up.

"What are you doing?" He may have extended a kindness to me, but I'm not hugging him.

"Go on inside, Mrs. Claire. Don't look past me. A couple of geese on the side of your house didn't make it." He gestures with his head towards the house. "Go in and I'll take care of the poor things. Try to have a better evening."

I blink and hug my briefcase to my chest. "Oh. Oh, okay. Thank you, Gary. You too." Then I scurry past him and into the house.

11

Once inside, I lock the front door behind me and fall into a dining chair. What just happened? Geese falling from the sky, senile Gary coming to my rescue, and cranky neighbors yelling at me is not how I imagined my first Thursday night in Oregon to go!

It could be electrical.

That's what Gary suggested, and Steven before him. Is that why the previous owners acted weird? And what's been affecting the birds?

It could be electrical.

Is that why the buzzing and the vibrations that accompany it and the terrifying specters?

If the Galloways couldn't handle the haunting

experiences anymore and felt alienated by their neighbors, I don't blame them for up and leaving in the night. If it becomes too much for me, I may do the same thing.

But it hasn't come to that yet. I am a scientist. I live by scientific methods. Steven and I will figure this out. Old wiring won't bully me out of the roof over my head.

It could be electrical.

I huff and place my briefcase on the table in front of me. It's taken a beating. There are long scratches along one side and a bashed-in corner where I suspect it met the driveway.

The front door bursts open. My heart leaps into my throat. Footsteps clomp towards me, and several things hit the hardwood floor.

"Claire! Claire, where are you?" Steven's voice calls out.

I scramble up, tripping over the dining chair leg. He collides with me as I enter the living room.

"There you are. Gary hobbled over as I pulled in and told me what had happened. Are you alright?" He squeezes me tight once, then his calloused hands cup my cheeks, his eyes searching my face.

I pull his hands down. "I'm fine. Very confused, but fine."

Steven grasps my hands in his, and his eyebrows furrow. "He said geese attacked you, and then you two talked to the neighbor, Mr. Davis, who yelled at you. Gary said he felt terrible about what happened to your invitations. What happened to your invitations? What happened with the neighbor? I left Gary mid-sentence and ran in. Are you okay?"

"Yes, honey. Go excuse Gary to go home because he seems the type to stand outside until you do. I'll explain everything over dinner. I just came inside for the first time myself."

He stands there gazing at me with that new concerned expression reserved for me. "Did you see Buzz?"

I shake my head and wander to the refrigerator. "No, thank goodness. But I heard what sounded like buzzing right as geese were flying overhead when I got out of the car." I glance back at him. "A couple of geese collided and fell to the ground. Gary took them away for me. He said he'll call animal control tomorrow. Gary also suggested it's an electrical problem since birds are sensitive to electromagnetic fields."

Steven rubs his forehead. "Yeah, this is something we need to figure out soon. I'll go thank Gary." He turns and walks out of the room.

I sigh and twist back to the fridge, opening it and scanning the contents. I don't have the energy to cook, and the leftover lasagna was our lunch today.

All I crave is a glass of wine and an early bedtime. But Steven deserves to have a meal, so I scoot over to the cupboard and open it, searching for inspiration.

The screen door squeaks open and shut once again, and plastic bags rustle. He enters the kitchen, waving a piece of paper in his free hand.

My tired, unfocused eyes fixate on the bright logo of the bags in his grip, comprehension of the company not hitting me yet. "Are sandwiches okay for dinner? I'm too exhausted to make much else."

"Mr. Davis was mean to you because something happened to the ink on your invitations?" Steven frowns, waving the paper in his hand again. I gaze up at him and nod with a grim smile. He looks at the invitation, front and back. "I'll go speak with the neighbors on Saturday." Then he sets the bags on the counter. An orange streamer rolls out. That's right, the Halloween decorations. Steven folds the paper in thirds along its creases, sets it down, and hunches over the sink. "Yeah, sandwiches are fine. I'm too upset to obsess about food right now. No one yells at my wife and gets away with it."

I sigh and walk over to him. "Oh, Steven. It'll be alright. The invitations were just the cherry on top for that man after a long day at work. I'm sure he'll quiet down and come to apologize. It sounds like the previous owners here were outcasts, and I get the impression Mr. Davis isn't keen to make friends." I toss a loaf of bread on the counter along with two tins of chicken and then go to the fridge for lettuce and condiments. "But I would like to sort this buzzing noise out. I don't want it to drive us away like it may have done with Tim and Laura Galloway, who the neighbors say owned the house before us. And I'll talk to Danielle tomorrow about the ink disappearing. She printed out some worksheets at the same time, too. I graded some of them during class yesterday, so I know the ink was still there in the morning. It's an unfortunate occurrence. Danielle witnessed that there was ink on the pages since she herself typed them up and printed them in her office. Otherwise, I would believe I've lost my mind. There must have been a chemical reaction when I put them in the mailbox. Too much moisture? I knew I should've used envelopes."

"Do you still want to decorate?" Steven asks, motioning to the bags. "I don't want neighbors here anymore if they are going to treat us like that. We are decent people. I can try to return everything since I have the receipt."

"Don't bother. We can save the nonperishables for next year. Go wash up. I'll fling a few decorations on the front window tomorrow and have a bowl of candy ready in case we get any trick-

or-treaters."

12

Rain lashes at the bedroom window when I wake up to my alarm on Friday morning.

Steven rolls over and throws the sheets off his body, stretching. "I don't reckon we're going to get any trick-or-treaters tonight if this weather keeps up. I'll get sent home early if the site is too wet. They warned me that it might happen. My paycheck may not amount to much this month."

I pull the covers off me and step into my sweats and fuzzy orange slippers. The temperatures have been falling. Bed socks will soon be required if we don't want to crank the thermostat. "If you do, you could beg your electrician friend to examine the house. Since we're not having a Halloween party,

I'll have the energy to make red beans and rice for dinner. Perhaps he'll accept a free meal as payment."

"Ah, you spoil me, love," Steven says and kisses me as I pass him. It's his favorite dish. He deserves it if his friend can squash this buzzing. I'll make him red beans and rice every day of the week if he solves this problem. Then, we can speak to the neighbors again and start anew. Mr. Davis will be sure to have a different tone when Steven arrives on his stoop with his magic smile.

I get to Danielle's office at the usual time. Upon opening the door, I find Danielle absent. My eyes travel to the piles of papers on her desk. Before I know what I'm doing, I have crossed the room and am rifling through papers, searching for the worksheets that we printed right after the invites. We are supposed to hand them back today, and if the ink is missing, we'll have to reprint them and have the students do the assignment again.

"Claire!" Danielle's voice shrieks. "What are you doing?"

I flinch, lose my balance when I straighten up too fast, and fall back into her leather desk chair. My free hand grasps the soft material of the armrest to right myself. "I found the worksheets," I gasp, holding them up. "You wouldn't believe it if I told you, but my invitations—"

"I don't like people rifling through my property, Claire," Danielle interrupts. Both her fists clench. If she could breathe fire, I'm sure I'd be a pile of ashes right now. "Get out of my seat."

My cheeks flame, and I scramble out of her chair and around to the other side. Danielle marches around her desk and puts her hands on her hips, surveying the clutter.

"Look at the wreckage. I had this all organized."

Wreckage? I didn't make that mess. Your desk is always in this state. I suppress these words and instead hand her back the worksheets. When her mouth opens, I raise one finger to stall whatever harsh rhetoric is about to come out. Her eyebrows furrow as I spin back around to snatch Gary's crumpled invitation from my briefcase.

"Look, Danielle, please. Just look at this invitation. I needed to see if the ink on the worksheets disappeared, too," I shout and shove the blank invitation into her face.

She grabs it and unfolds the paper. Her furrowed forehead softens, and one eyebrow raises. She turns the page around again. Then she raises it to the light. "Where did the printer ink go?"

"That's what I want to know. Can the problem be that there was a chemical reaction on the paper from the air or moisture in the mailboxes? I didn't use envelopes," I explain.

Danielle flips the paper over to the side with my address. "But the pen ink didn't disappear on this side," she says with a mystified air. "And the worksheets are still in the same shape as when we printed them. How peculiar."

"Should we ask the chemistry professor? I know Harry eats in the teachers' lounge every day."

Danielle purses her lips. "I'll hold on to this and show it to one of them today. I'll mention the ink isn't printing properly to the administration office as well. They're probably buying cheap ink. We can't be the only people that this has happened to. But right now, we need to get to class."

*

After classes, I agreed to tutor two students at once, like yesterday, so that Danielle could track down one of the chemistry professors and ask them to test the paper and talk with the administration office. I had offered to go since it was my invitation, but she said she was going to make up something else up since they frowned upon the use of school resources for personal use, even cutting off the portion of the paper with my address penned so it won't raise questions.

Danielle returns and goes straight to her laptop without acknowledging me as I twist my thermos in my hands, staring at her. She glances up. "The last student has canceled their tutoring session. I suspect they'll be getting ready for all the Halloween parties tonight. You can leave now if you'd like," she offers. Was this her olive branch for how she had reacted this morning?

"No, I'll help you grade the second batch of worksheets so we both can leave a little early." Points all around. Plus, I want a hand in grading because Danielle circles wrong answers, whereas I find where they went wrong in their formula or calculations and write out the correction so they understand why their answer was wrong.

Danielle smiles. It's the first time today. The pinched expression is gone. I had told her about the geese at lunchtime, and she had nodded in agreement about the possibility of an electrical issue.

"You or Steven should check the attic for an old antenna. I've heard of people building their own to get free cable. If it's still connected but malfunctioning, that could explain it," she had offered in response.

I now remember to check my messages; Steven has confirmed his electrician acquaintance will come home with him. My back slouches against the chair, and I place my thermos on the desk. *Another small step for Claire.*

"What did Harry or Carl say about the paper?" I

ask.

"He said he'll perform some tests when he has time. What would you like me to bring tonight for the party?"

I wonder which of the two teachers she means, open my mouth to ask, but then pause. It would be too tempting to harass those nice men for an answer, and then they might refuse to do it. So, I will wait for Danielle to tell me the results. "There's no party. Sorry, I forgot to mention it. After the geese incident, I went to a neighbor's house to explain that something had happened to the ink, and he was rude. So Steven and I gave up on the idea. Instead, Steven is bringing over his electrician friend tonight to check out the house, since the problem is getting worse. Maybe I'll try again next year."

*

When I finally get home, Steven is alone in his sweats, watching college football highlights.

"What do you mean he didn't come over? You told me that he was," I ask, and stir in spices to the red beans and rice in our soup pot he had started. The dish doesn't deserve quite the gusto I am giving with my aggressive stirring, but I need some way to vent my frustration. This dish is a labor of love and was supposed to be payment for a quick walk-through with his electrician acquaintance.

Steven pops the lid off his beer and sits down at the dining room table. "He was, but then got a better offer. Cash in hand. You know how much I love your red beans and rice, but even you have to admit, it's not worth the two hundred dollars he's earning under the table at the truck stop that called him."

"Two hundred dollars?" I cry out and spin around. I'm still holding the ladle, and sauce splatters onto the linoleum floor. "What is he doing? That seems excessive." I set the ladle down and rip two sheets of paper towels off the roll, bending down to clean up the spill.

In the process of my wiping the floor, Steven plunks his bottle down, and the chair legs scrape. Much nearer now, he says, "Certified electricians make bank. I'll investigate the attic while I still have the energy. Danielle's theory makes sense." Then his footsteps recede. The attic trapdoor squeaks open, and the extendable ladder hits the carpeted hallway with a soft thud. A shiver runs down my spine. Better him than me. Attics and basements are places I avoid. I don't even know what my parents keep in theirs. And now that I seem to be a magnet for paranormal moments in the house, all the more reason to stay in the kitchen.

The amazing aroma of Cajun spices fills the house. I always go heavy on the cayenne pepper, and Steven always requests that I use extra smoked paprika. Any time I make this recipe, we both have a pile of napkins saturated with sweat and snot, and two glasses of iced tea or water downed by the end of the meal. And I always end up craving more of the dish. So does he.

Out the back door, sheets of rain pour down. Halloween decorations and a bag of candy lay discarded in the corner of the dining room. There's no way kids will be out in this weather. I shuffle to the front door and flip off the porch light. Steven's footsteps continue their thumps from one end of the attic to the other. The creaking ladder rungs mark Steven's descent.

"I take it from the lack of screams there's nothing scary up there?"

He chuckles and hoists the ladder back up, then shoves the door until the latch clicks. "No. The place is empty. Everything is dusty, but is up to code. I got the place inspected before signing." He brushes stray clumps of cobwebs clinging to his broad shoulders and sniffs the air. "Smells like I'm just in time."

"Yup, come plop down and I'll fill you a bowl. I turned off the porch light, too. No kids should be out in that storm."

Steven falls into a dining chair and scratches his scalp, making his shaggy brown hair stick up at different angles. "I heard it hitting the roof. Thank goodness we have a good roof. The air may buzz, but at least we're dry."

We eat and talk about different colors we might paint the rooms (I want the office to be a shade of orange), ripping up the carpet, and when we can set aside time for hanging pictures. Over the last couple of days, I've been taking pictures out of boxes and leaning them against the various walls.

I stack the dishwasher after dinner and call first dibs on a shower. Then I'll catch up on shows or call my mom while Steven takes his shower before bed. My parents and I have been texting since I left, but there is nothing more comforting that hearing a loved one's voice. I will tell my mom and dad about our electrical problem. They might have some theories we can test, too.

The telltale ding confirms a Bluetooth connection with my phone when I click the shower speaker on. Justin Timberlake blasts as I turn on the hot water. It's been a long first week of work and living in this new place. Someone said it's always the first week in a new place that is hardest. I theorize they're referring to homesickness, but it's been such an eventful first week that I haven't had time to miss our condo in Montana any more than I miss sleeping in my old room at my parent's house. The endless hot water from the large water heater is a small consolation prize for the tight muscles in my shoulders.

I scrunch my eyes and rinse the shampoo from my hair. Something scurries over my foot, a few tiny, tickling movements. Rivulets of water mixed with shampoo suds run into my eyes. "Ah!" I shout, competing with Justin Timberlake's high tenor. I shake my foot, hoping it's just a clump of hair, but then the same sensation travels over the grounded foot.

"Please be hair. Please be hair," I pray while scrubbing the soap from my hair, face, and eyes, standing like a flamingo.

When I'm confident that I won't go blind if I open my eyes, I wipe the water away, peer down, and scream.

Bugs.

Brown bugs. Green bugs. Red bugs. So many bugs.

They're climbing out of the drain that's clogging with their bodies and the draining water. More beetles and long, multi-legged crawlers are dropping from the tub faucet. The bathroom ceiling light flickers. On, off, on.

I scream again, forget about my left foot still aloft, and step back down. The sickening crunch of bugs underfoot makes my stomach lurch.

"Steee-ven!" I howl and vault from the tub, snatch a towel on my way and dash from the room.

"I'm dealing with something!" he bellows from the kitchen.

I sprint that way, trying to wrap the towel around me and not trip. "Bugs are—"

Bugs are crawling over the sink's edge. Steven is batting them back into the sink with his bare hands and has the faucet turned on full blast. More are crawling up his arms, onto his back. I wretch, hot bile and dinner spilling onto the kitchen floor.

"Hand me something to stuff down the drain! They keep coming!" Steven cries out, grabbing bugs off his shirt and throwing them into the sink.

I hurl myself across the kitchen against my better judgment and almost hit Steven in the head with the paper towel roll when I toss it his way. I'm not coming any closer. My skin tingles as if they're on me again, crawling in my hair, along my back, a thousand spiny, tickling legs marching over my body. My stomach roils from its impromptu purge, and I double over, one hand on my stomach and the other wiping my mouth as saliva collects, trying to ease the acid burn in my throat.

I brush off my legs to get rid of the phantom sensation while Steven turns off the taps and corrals the bugs back into the sink and down the drain. Then he rips a fistful of paper towels off the roll and stuffs them down the drain.

"Get my duct tape from my toolbox by the front door," he instructs.

I hasten to retrieve it, holding my towel up with one hand, giving my vomit a wide berth. He layers tape over the paper towels in the drain and then takes the paper towel roll and tape, turns around, and freezes, looking down.

"Go, I'll clean it up," I croak, my cheeks burning. Steven frowns, edges around my mess on the floor, then runs to the bathroom. I shudder. How many got out of the tub and are marching to other areas of the house, or straight for our bedroom? I dry heave once more and hold my free hand against my stomach. "Get it together," I chide myself, then grab a fresh roll of paper towels and start laying them over the bulk of my vomit before grabbing the kitchen gloves. It came out of me, but that doesn't mean I want to touch it.

"Honey? Can you bring me the trash can?" Steven calls from the bathroom.

I reach for it, keeping my eyes diverted from the kitchen sink inches away while holding up my towel that's slipping.

Something tickles down my back. I shake my head like a dog, and my wet hair slaps me in the face. Nothing falls to the ground. I pray it's just the water dripping from my hair, and wrap my towel tighter around my torso. After tossing the gloves on the floor near the paper towels, I pick up the trash can.

Something flashes by in the dark beyond the patio.

I gasp and drop the trash can. The rain is still pelting down, distorting the back porch light. Was it a tree branch falling? Or is it that big raccoon again? Is it living under the house? I strain my ears to listen for any animal sounds, but the television is still on, distracting my focus. It sounds like the Weather Channel based on words reaching my ears like "low pressure" and "wet weekend".

"Honey! Trash can!" Steven shouts.

I jolt out of my frozen watchfulness and sprint to the bathroom.

Steven is on his knees near the tub, wiping the floor near the rug. I hand over the trash can. "Is it bad?" My voice is husky, my tongue sour, my throat burning.

He throws the wet paper towel into the trash and then picks more up from inside the tub. There are small, dark shadows within the folds of the crumpled, damp towels. "I stoppered the drain and duct-taped the faucet for now. I've seen bugs on building sites, but nothing like this. That was really gross. Straight out of a horror movie." He looks up at me and offers a weak smile. "You squashed some when they joined in for a shower. That's one point for us. Are you okay?"

My hand flies up to my mouth as bile rises once more. "Stop," I gag. "I've already lost my dinner. What in God's good name was that?! I can't live here, Steven. I'm not staying here tonight." The more I talk, the more hysterical my voice becomes. This situation is abnormal. Some might even say paranormal.

Steven stands up and turns the speaker off. I spin on my heel and go back to the kitchen to clean up my mess while holding my breath, then stomp to the bedroom to dress and pack an overnight bag. Who knows what other crevices those bugs will find to crawl through? Or if the creature outside finds a way in. The coroner's report will read: *Couple dies of asphyxiation from bugs in their orifices. Raccoons ate their toes.*

Steven enters the bedroom as I am pulling on my orange blouse from the hamper. Dirty or not, my favorite shirt won't perish at the hands of bugs or animals until I'm buried in it.

"Honey, calm down. A few bugs can't hurt us. It was the storm. The extra water scared them into finding higher ground."

I shudder and pull my Calvin Klein slacks on. "A few bugs, Steven? A few? That was like, like the,

the, well, I don't know. But I had my eyes full of soap when they were crawling over my feet!" Another shiver wracks my shoulders. Which shoes should I wear? My work loafers are clean. But my Converse are my favorite. Classic blue with white soles. But I'm not wearing them out in that mud and rain. I snatch my Converse and running sneakers, placing the former in my backpack, stuffing my feet in the runners. The bright orange shoes remind me of how brave Danielle was to traverse the muddy backyard in them. If she could do that, I could leave the house in them. "Will this happen during the next storm? How about the one after that?"

Steven walks around the bed and pulls me into a hug. My spine stiffens. He hugs tighter. Tears press against my closed eyelids. One tear escapes, then another. I bury my face in his shoulder. "I couldn't see them until I washed the soap out of my eyes. But I could *feel* them!" I cry. I've never had such an adverse reaction to animals or bugs before, but they've never been where they shouldn't. "And this storm is making things move around in the backyard." I gulp. "And the buzzing on top of it all. I've reached my limit, Steven, and we've only been here a week. Are you sure nothing felt amiss before leaving for Montana and my arrival?"

He pulls me away and wipes tears from my

cheeks. I look him in the eye and watch his brow crease. He sucks in a breath, lips quirking and stretching. "I'm sorry, honey. I forgot your threshold is lower now. Those bugs terrified you, didn't they? I didn't mean to be insensitive. Is your stomach better? Do you want a chewable Pepto?" I nod. He nods. "Okay, if you can wait one minute, I'll get the bottle and pack a bag with you and we'll stay at a hotel tonight, okay? I don't want you going off alone in the night."

"Okay," I agree between sniffles.

I am not crazy.

13

Steven white-knuckles my Subaru's steering wheel through a torrential downpour along a particularly dark and steep street as I hunt for the two hotel locations around town on my phone. The connection is shotty, and I keep getting the little blue progress bar that pauses more times than not when a page loads. He advises me to pick the hotel away from the college campus in case of drunk and unruly students, so I zoom out on the map. There's a Motel 6 at the end of W Fork Road for just seventy-nine dollars a night.

I'm still a bundle of nerves, slapping at phantom, or real, bugs crawling on my legs under my pants. I peer down at the car floor a fifth time. Steven had checked the car over with a flashlight before I agreed to get in. Walking in the rain had seemed safer than going into an unchecked vehicle in the dark; another lesson I learned from horror movies.

Not today, bugs. Not today.

"I had the television on too loud to notice if there was any buzzing. Did you hear it?" He leans over the steering wheel further as rain lashes the windshield.

"Turn left at the next intersection," I instruct, then say, "No. I had the shower speaker on. Like I said, I was trying to rinse shampoo out of my eyes when they started surging out of the drains. There were so many." I stick my tongue out.

"They must've got washed back down the drain then, because when I went in and turned the shower off, I counted five tiny beetles attempting to climb up the sides. You terrified them by stepping on their friends."

I sneer. "Don't humanize them, Steven. Have you ever stepped on bugs barefoot? I didn't do it intentionally. That will haunt me forever." It was like stepping onto a raw egg, hard shell giving way to a wet, viscous center. At least an unfertilized egg doesn't have a soul, a nervous system, or a brain. My hand flies up to cover another dry-heave.

Steven reaches over and squeezes my knee. "Okay, okay. No more bug jokes, I promise. But my point is, there was no buzzing."

"That's no comfort to me," I say through my teeth. "No buzzing means it's a separate problem. Another problem we don't know the root cause of. I'm not crazy, Steven, but I am under attack in my home. Since day one, in fact."

"Since Sunday? You didn't tell me anything happened Sunday night."

I freeze. Oh, yeah. I had chalked it up to nerves. But this isn't nerves anymore. It's deteriorating what's left of my nerves. There's something going on at that house. "I'm pretty sure I heard buzzing Sunday evening. I forgot to tell you," I say as a half-truth. The fuzzy specter was there, too. But Steven has never seen it, so I can't say it as scientific evidence like the buzzing phenomenon. "What if an animal is chewing wires under the house? I swear I saw a dog or raccoon out back twice. Do you know whether security cameras are expensive?"

"Yeah, they are. Most people have them installed through a security company. We can't afford that yet. But don't assume it hasn't crossed my mind. I want you safe. I'll get an electrician to the house, I promise. They'll know where to check for bad wiring."

I chew on my lip and glance at my phone to make sure we are still going the right way. "Turn left in two blocks, and the motel will be on the left." I envision the swift movement of something I saw when Steven asked me for the trash can. I saw something Sunday night, too. Was someone or something lurking, playing pranks on us? I face Steven again. "Do you suppose our phones can record all night? We can set up yours in the kitchen and mine in the bedroom."

He pulls into the motel and parks, cutting the engine. "Why those locations? Our phones might record all night if we leave them plugged into their chargers. I'll do whatever you want to get you to come home tomorrow. We can't afford to live in a hotel while I sort the problems out."

I rub my hands together as the cogs in my mind rotate. *Stay logical,* I tell myself. "Um, well, we could catch an animal going under the house. Or the camera could catch someone like a neighbor playing a sadistic prank on us to make us leave. That Mr. Davis is on my radar just based on how antagonistic he acted. And I know you like Gary, but he still gives me the creeps. He smells of unwashed clothes, and his house is stuck in the past. Real creepy."

"Retired people rarely have money to redecorate, Claire. You can't hold that against him," Steven snipes and gets out of the car, slamming the door. I should've known he would side with Gary. His own grandmother is about the same age. But there is an enormous difference. Grandma Simmons keeps an immaculate house and smells wonderful no matter the time of day, and she's been a widow for twenty years.

14

Saturday morning brings a break in the weather. Patches of baby blue peek through white puffy clouds as morning fog burns off when we check out of the hotel at ten o'clock.

Last night, as we lay in the lumpy queen-sized bed covered by a multicolored pastel comforter, staring at the popcorn ceiling and waiting for sleep to snatch us, Steven proclaimed he'd spend all weekend getting the house sealed up and bug killer sprayed around the foundations. "With an overgrown yard, I bet it's invited an extraordinary quantity of bugs and small creatures to burrow in the lawn and trees. It's just nature trying to reclaim its space. You'll see, sweetie, once we have the yard cleaned up and the electrical problem fixed, living there will be nice." He kissed me and turned over, snoring within minutes.

I'm glad he's so content with that answer, but I'm not so sure. If it turns out none of these issues existed when the Galloways owned the house, what happened to it between when they left and now? And why and how did the bank not catch it?

I stared at the back of Steven's head on the pillow next to me. He wouldn't lie to save face so I wouldn't get mad, right? What if he knows something is missing or something happened to the house that he's not telling me, putting his own selfish desire of home ownership above my sanity? I rolled onto my back, pulling the sheets up to my chin, and closed my eyes. No, I can't believe that. It's not who he is. It's just my stress talking, the monster in my mind whispering its devilish, contradictory ideas, scheming against me.

*

After stopping at a coffee shop for some breakfast, Steven drives us to Jim's Hardware, a weathered, timber-framed store on the outskirts of town.

We grab a bucket of wall stucco and a large roll of weather stripping first. Then we wander the creaking wooden aisles and stare at the selection of bug sprays, rat traps, and mosquito nets dangling from pegs.

An employee hobbles over in his large denim apron. His liver-spotted head doesn't have a single hair left on it, but the man has clear eyes and, from Steven's wide-eyed expression, an impressive grip when they shake hands. He introduces himself as Jim, the owner, as the sign states. Steven explains our pest problem and then mentions the buzzing issue as well. We both wait while the old man stands with his hands on his hips, one index finger tapping.

He reaches forward and grabs a box of large poison traps for cockroaches. "Well, the buzzing sounds like an electrical issue since it's not constant like that of a hive of bees. And it is possible that the bugs got affected by that if the excess water from these storms is short-circuiting something under the house. They have a will to live, just like we do. And if it is an older house... We don't have cockroaches in these parts, but the traps work well for a few types of forest beetle."

A memory of Mama explaining to me about the balance of creation and karma while we checked for pests in the garden makes me reconsider. "No, I would rather not resort to poison yet. It's not like the bugs did it on purpose. Don't you have anything that will just deter them from the house?"

"But we can't go without showering or using the sink for more than a day, honey," Steven says.

Jim nods. "You might check out the military surplus shop that's about five miles east. They might have a bug zapper of some sort that just stuns the buggers. If they don't, I'm open until five o'clock tonight, and you could try these traps in the meantime."

We buy a few nails along with the stucco and stripping and thank Jim for his help. Then, when we reach the car, I hop into the driver's seat.

"Call your electrician friend to come on Monday. Danielle will understand if I miss half or whole day because of a bug infestation. We need your wages more than mine to pay your friend, anyway," I say, and Steven doesn't argue.

He makes a few calls while I drive and then reiterates the conversations after hanging up. Steven's friend is due to be on the construction site with him all week, so he referred Steven to a self-employed electrician new in town. This electrician has agreed to show up at our house at eight in the morning on Monday.

The surplus store turns out to be a metal hangar big enough for a small plane, surrounded by a barbed-wire fence. A gigantic, faded American flag hangs limply above flags representing each branch of our military below.

"That's a bit on the nose," I mutter.

A man wearing hunting, rather than military, fatigues and sporting a buzz cut walks out of the hangar and watches us park along the edge of an adjacent gravel road. He reminds me of a G.I. Joe, if Joe had stopped working out and let all his former chiseled edges grow soft, plump, and saggy. We get out and nod to him. The man gestures to my car. "You have military plates. We give discounts to active and retired service members if it's one of you. I'll just need to verify your ID."

Steven puts an arm around my shoulders and smiles at me. "That would be my Claire. Air Force."

I nod, and the man snaps me a proper salute. Call me impressed.

"How can I help you two today? You will find something new on every visit. Got friends around the states and can make more if you're in the market for something harder to get." He winks at me.

What the hell does that mean? My mind goes to the black market. Shady deals with shadier people. How far would I go to rid our house of the anomaly? Time will tell.

"We're scouting for some pest control options. Something to keep bugs, rodents, and fowl at bay," Steven says, taking the lead.

The man's face brightens. "I'm sure we will find just what you need. Right this way, folks." He turns on his heel and starts marching to the hangar. Then he spins back around and walks backwards, peering at me. "What base do you report to?"

Of course he would ask something like that. If it hadn't been for Steven holding my hand, my shame and embarrassment of the truth would have had me turning on my heel and waiting in the car. "I'm retired now." A white lie is easier to live with.

He tilts his head. "You look young to be retired."

Stevens' hand tightens. It's his signal for me to tap him in. He would pounce with just one tap of a fingertip on his hand. I just shrug. "Retired. Honorable discharge. Same thing."

The man's thick brown eyebrow raises. "Not really."

"She's got ID *if* we decide to spend our money here," Steven says, and throws him a smile. Threat and disarm. It's the one-two punch Steven has in his arsenal. He would have succeeded in big business.

I nip my tongue to cut short the giggle bubbling up as the man chokes and gesticulates, spinning back around.

Steven winks when he notices me beaming at him.

We make our way through the various piles of

camping gear and paintball equipment. Mr. Buzz Cut shows us some battery-powered and solar-powered bug zappers. There are lanterns with long tubes that electrocute bugs when they land.

"And over there I have a roll of electric fence if rodents or deer are tearing up your yard. It might work for the birds if the trees aren't too tall. All prices marked are firm. I've got bills to pay, too."

Steven nods, telling him we'll browse for a while. I can tell Steven doesn't like Mr. Buzz Cut any more than I do from the way he glares at the man each time his eyes wander over to me.

"Was there something else?" Steven's tone drips with annoyance. The shop owner is still hovering at the same table we are perusing, gawking at me.

Mr. Fake Fatigues McBuzz-Cut steps nearer and shrugs. "It's a curious thing, is all. Been here a long time and had no Air Force members stop by. Then, within a few months, bam, there's two." He surveys his bunker as if expecting another person to pop up.

"We're not segregated to just one part of the country," I snort.

The owner steps closer still, lowers his voice, and gives us a conspiratorial look. "I know. I'm not ignorant. It's just an interesting coincidence. This other person is very different from you, though, so far as I can tell. They drove an old Nissan without military stickers and asked about a military discount, but then were hesitant to show us proof. They've bought some odds things."

Steven makes a nondescript noise in his throat, but I'm curious, bordering on the nosy. "Did you get a name?"

Mr. Buzz Cut's shoulders drop. "No. It was my daughter who worked in the shop both times while I was out at auctions. She prattled on about how she assumed this person was a doomsayer type. They wanted to keep their identity a secret. We have quite a few of those here who try to live off-grid in the woods."

I nod, acting as if I understand. But I don't. I love running water and electricity and every other modern convenience way too much to give it up. I spot a security camera on the hangar's roof and point up at it. "Did you get video of them? I'm curious if I know them and our paths just haven't crossed yet."

What I wasn't saying is that I want to compare their size with the hunched figures I've seen twice now in the backyard. What if it wasn't a large wild creature, but a person who traveled here to harass me from my former base or the Rosebud Research Facility? And then there's what I saw down in the depths of that physics building…

"Nah, they're fake. Wait. Why do you want to

know?" Mr. Buzz-Cut's eyes narrow at me.

I roll my eyes. "Just curious. Like I said, it would be nice to reconnect if we are already acquaintances, or that we just have a similar background. This is a small town, after all." I paste on my best fake smile. "I'm sure you understand the camaraderie one makes in the military."

His mouth guppies and Steven turns his laugh into a coughing fit. *Gotcha.* My smiling facade becomes genuine. This buzz-cut tomfool has never been in the military. There is a gut feeling with these types. Maybe his dad was in the military, or some other family member piqued this man's fascination at a young age. But between the haircut, non-official fatigues, and all too perfect salute without offering what branch he was in, real or otherwise, I would place what little money I have on the fact that he has never done one hundred pushups in the mud during a rainstorm at one in the morning while a drill sergeant screams in your ear.

Mr. Buzz-Cut kicks at the ground. "The cameras are a deterrent, and I don't sell actual weapons. I recall my daughter yammering on about the person wearing dark glasses and what she thought was a cheap-looking wig. Cross-dresser was her first thought. I reckon it's just a case of a doomsday prepper trying to hide who they are, so no one tries to get access to their bunker of canned beans." He snorts and then waves us over. "Come over to my desk. I'll show you some bug deterrents for camping tents that emit a frequency we can't hear. A city-looking bloke sold them to me last week. I doubt they're even used and will give you a good price."

His "good price" was a dollar less than something similar at Jim's Hardware, so we bought one that's supposed to deter all bugs within a radius of fifteen feet. After showing him my veteran ID card, he gave us a ten percent discount.

"That's five percent more than I usually give," he says with an all too broad smile, as if he were offering more like a fifty percent discount. On goes the fake smile of mine.

Back in the car, I announce we should place the new contraption, that's about the size of a box of cereal, on the floor between our bedroom door and bed. "I don't want to wake up with bugs crawling on me."

When we get home, I hold the vacuum at the ready with my face turned away while Steven pulls the duct tape and paper towels off and out of the drains and faucets. Besides the unfortunate few that died from being squashed in the paper towels or stuck to the tape, the rest of the hoard has retreated down the drain.

We then go around the house and apply weather stripping and fill in any cracks or holes in the walls and along the baseboards. Even the tiniest nail holes.

"A bug can't fit through that," Steven complains when I point out three more nail holes in the hallway at nine in the morning on Sunday. It's my third pass through the house this weekend.

"Ants can get in anywhere. It's them or me." He sighs and covers the holes. I peck him on the cheek. "Now I'll make you pancakes."

"And bacon!" he yells after me.

My nerves are fraying beneath my careful facade, and I am very aware of it. Every half hour, no matter what I am doing, I freeze and listen for the buzzing sound. Then I scramble to the back door and peer out into the soggy yard. I strain my eyes to stare along the back fence through the window, willing myself to spot the creature or human that lurks there. Like a harbinger, or the perpetrator themselves. The vines and moss swinging from the lower tree branches keep tripping me up. I keep expecting to see a marsupial doing acrobatics. Regardless, if it is a living being that is tripping a mechanism causing the buzzing, the apparitions, and now the bugs, I need to know what I'm dealing with.

Because I still don't know what I witnessed in

that laboratory.

What's worse, everything and everyone was gone when I came back with campus security. Scrubbed. Not a computer on. There were no fingerprints in sight. It was like they pulled the old stage trick of rooms on a coaster. One minute is one scene, the next another.

I won't let that happen to me again.

I am not crazy.

15

I called into work at six forty-five Monday morning to let the administration office know I won't be in. After I hang up, I realize I don't have Danielle's phone number, so I call the office again and ask for her cellphone number. I've never noticed an office phone in her room or classroom.

"We don't divulge that information, Mrs. Simmons," the office personnel states. "We will let her know."

"Okay," I say. "Please include the reason for my absence."

There is the shuffling of papers on the other end before the voice on the other side says, "You don't need to include that, but I can if you'd like. What is the reason?"

"A bug infestation."

"Gross."

"Yeah."

They assure me that Danielle will get the message and hang up.

*

I've followed our hired electrician, Corey, around for half an hour, making sure every fixture gets tested, every outlet secured. He explains he is searching for loose wires, overloaded wires, or an improperly grounded wire that is causing the sound anomalies. I didn't follow him into the crawl space or attic. Dark, dirty, and possibly haunted places are no-go areas for me.

He'd never heard of an electrical problem from a house affecting bugs and birds, and ends his examination where he started in the kitchen, washing his hands that are covered in grime from under the house. "The buzzing doesn't happen all the time, does it? I couldn't hear anything out of the ordinary."

I stare at the dusty cobweb in his blond ponytail. "No. But I swear when it does, it's terrifying," I explain. "I'm not the only one who hears it, either. Can you check the refrigerator?"

Corey puts his hands on his hips. He did his best to dust himself off with a towel from his car, which I appreciate, but still has large brown spots on his knees and the aforementioned cobweb in his hair. "I don't doubt that it is unnerving, Mrs. Simmons. But I don't check appliances. You'll have to hire an appliance specialist for that."

I cross my arms. "Okay. But there is something going on. There's something *causing* this noise and disturbing us and the wildlife here. Were you getting any weird readings at all? Anything in the attic?"

"None," he says, shaking his head. The cobweb doesn't budge. "Wiring is in good shape. Got another ten years of wear, I'd say. Same with the breakers. A lot of dead bugs and bug poop behind sockets and under the house and in the attic, though, so I believe you when you say you have a bug problem. It's an older house, though. Just make sure none of the bugs are destructive, like termites. That'll ruin the value of your house." The electrician sticks the sensor end of his testing device into a light socket by the stove. It beeps and the screen flashes. "Same reading as before. Monitor your electricity bill for any spikes in usage at odd times, like when you are not home. And call me again if you notice anything out of the ordinary." He turns to me. "Abandoned houses often become bug hotels. They can wreak havoc when no one's around."

"We just moved in here, so it might take a couple of months to figure out the pattern of usage on our bill. Wait, aren't termites warm-climate bugs?"

"Can't hurt to check. Before summer is ideal. The bug company rates are cheaper this time of year."

My hands drop limp at my sides, and I stare at the sink. "Do you know of any that work weekends?" I never want to experience the sight of bugs crawling out of our drains again.

"No. We small-towners love our weekends." He pulls out his wallet, flips through a stack of business cards, and hands me one. "This guy is legit and not too expensive. I used him myself for hornets one year. Call sooner than later. He's popular."

I examine the plain white card with the words, THE BUG GUY, on one side and a phone number on the other.

Corey takes his leave, saying he'll mail the bill.

I watch his truck pull away from the driveway and call the exterminator.

"The bug guy speaking. What can you pester me with today?"

"That's the cleverest tagline I've heard in a while," I announce. It makes me grin; I needed that.

"Thanks. Those who call me usually need a

laugh. How may I help you?"

I drift from the living room to the dining room. My ritual of checking the backyard for critters is still going strong. This time, I focus my attention on the lower trunks of the trees and gaps in the bushes. "Well, I just had Corey, the electrician, over, and he recommends you since he couldn't help us find the source of our problem." There's nothing moving around the yard. I head for the bathroom to check the tub and sink for bugs. It's misting again, harder than yesterday, so if the water is causing the bugs to surge upwards, it might be today.

"And what seems to be the problem?"

No bugs yet. I stopper the sink and tub and return to the kitchen to do the same.

"Bugs swarmed up our drains Friday night. Corey also explained that we have a ton of dead bugs in the walls and under the house. He advised us to check for termites."

"My goodness, that's unfortunate," the bug guy sympathizes. "This isn't termite country, but I'll be happy to diagnose the abundant bug issue for you. Is it one type of bug that is overwhelming your house?"

I scrunch my nose and try to remember while keeping bile down. So. Many. Legs. I swallow. "Well, the ones that came through our drains appeared to be beetles and many-legged creepy-crawly things. I don't know the scientific names."

The bug guy chuckles. "That's alright. Creepy crawlies is the usual description I get. You mentioned there are some dead ones in the walls and crawl spaces. I'd be happy to appraise the situation and set traps or place poison around if necessary." The line goes quiet for a moment. "I can come by tomorrow at one in the afternoon. Would that work?"

I tap my free hand on my hip. That would mean another day off work. Should I wait until Steven has a day off because of the weather? But how would we coordinate that?

"Uh, miss… I didn't catch your name?" the bug guy asks.

I blink back into the present from my scheduling conundrum spiral. "Oh, uh, Mrs. Simmons. Claire and Steven Simmons. I was just thinking it over since I haven't discussed it with my husband yet."

"Mmm. I understand. But I must warn you, I only have tomorrow available because of a cancellation. That is rare for me. I have a conference in Orlando next Friday and then obligations the following week. Every opening booked."

My shoulders sag, and I lean against the wall. More lost wages and another bill. We might have to eat rice and beans for a while. "Fine. Come over tomorrow. I don't want a repeat."

The bug guy clucks his tongue. "I'll try to help prevent that, Mrs. Simmons. See you tomorrow."

He hangs up, and I text Steven that Corey didn't find any faulty wires, so the exterminator is coming over tomorrow. Then I mosey to the refrigerator and hunt for lunch.

My phone dings on the counter. It's an unknown number texting me, but the preview box announces it is Danielle. So she can have my number from the office, but I can't have hers? That doesn't seem fair.

"You have a bug problem? Understandable to miss work. Call me using this number. At lunch."

"Claire? Is everything alright?"

I fall into a dining chair. "Yes, everything is alright for the moment. It was awful, Danielle. Bugs were coming out of every faucet and drain. I bought a bug contraption to keep them at bay in our bedroom in case they come back. We had the electrician here today to check for faulty wires, and an exterminator is coming over tomorrow."

"That's awful!" Danielle exclaims, then groans. "Does that mean you will miss work tomorrow, too?"

"Um," I start, roll my lips, and jump up, beginning my pacing of the house once more. "Can I do a half-day? The guy won't be here until the afternoon, and Steven's paycheck is bigger than mine, so it has to be me to miss work. I'm so sorry,

Danielle. I can make it up to you. You can email me worksheets to grade, or lessons to type up, or anything else. I'll even work on the weekend. We need to figure this problem out. Please. We already spent a night at a motel and can't afford it," I blurt out, and halt. I've made it to the second bedroom. "I have my laptop all set up right now."

There is silence for a long moment, and then, "We don't do half days here, Claire. I'm sorry. Call in again."

I peer out of the bedroom window, scanning the backyard once more for creatures or figures up to no good that might assume I'm at work or not paying attention. The rain has paused, and the yard is a treacherous muddy lake. I half expect a tentacle or two to rise from the middle, hunting unsuspecting prey. "Okay, I understand. I'm sorry again. I have to sort this out. I can't live like this and function."

"I sympathize. I know you are doing your best. Just try to come to work on Wednesday, okay? We are falling behind. I accept your offer of help from home. Not for today, but perhaps tomorrow. I'll contact you."

I head back to the kitchen with a growling stomach and eat leftover beans and rice from the freezer. Then I collapse down on the couch and flip through the television channels, settling on a soap opera. As long as the TV or music is on, my mind won't wander to its dark corners where fuzzy figures and multi-legged creatures dwell.

My phone chimes.

"Hi Momma!"

"Hi pumpkin! Did you get the house fixed?"

I hit mute on the controller and lean back onto the couch. "The electrician says there's nothing wrong with the house's wiring, and we have an exterminator coming out tomorrow to evaluate the bugs we have in the walls. They're dead, though, so I'm not as creeped out as if they were alive."

"That's good to hear. Electricians aren't cheap." Then there is a pause. "And have your nightmares stayed away? Is your new therapist helping you?"

Ah, the worries of a parent. It never ends. I squeeze my eyes shut. "Yeah, Momma. Dr. Sternan is helping me work through my anxiety a lot." Though, in truth, I can't tell if she has helped me. The figures in my dreams are further in the background when I remember I dreamed, but they seem to have manifested in the real world now. "We have a phone appointment in a couple of hours."

"And your job?" The tightness in Momma's voice hasn't left. "Are you at work right now?" I crave to tell her that I am living in a utopia with unicorns and sleep in the clouds. I don't want her to worry.

My parents have done so much for me as it is.

"Work is fine. The professor I assist is nice, and she and I may collaborate on writing grant proposals to work in a lab again. I missed work today. We need Steven's paycheck more." I inhale and hold it. Steven and I have been trying to come up with a payment plan for the portion of my lawyer fees my parents covered. I won't know just how little we have to contribute until the end of the month. "Momma, it may take longer to pay you back for the lawyer fees than expected."

Momma tuts. "Oh, you silly child, I've told you both you don't need to pay us back. What happened to you was an injustice. The justice system is flawed, and it's not your fault."

I sigh. "You know Steven and I won't accept that. We will pay you back. It'll just take time. You guys have done so much for us that it's time I stop taking advantage—"

"Advantage? Child, it's mine and your poppa's right to help and support you when needed. If you have to pay us back, then pay us what you can, when you can. We are not concerned. Do you understand? We just want you to have the best life."

The last sentence was strained. I can picture tears springing into her eyes, and squint my own, swallowing the lump in my throat. "Thank you,

Momma," I whisper.

"You're welcome, pumpkin. Don't forget to send us pictures once you have the place decorated. We love you both."

It is all I can do to choke a "We love you too" before hanging up.

I then fill the time before my appointment with Dr. Sternan by cleaning the house and doing a load of laundry. Steven had gotten new hose attachments for the washer and dryer that came with the house. Same with the dishwasher. After I run any machine, I stand vigil for a few minutes, training my ears to find the familiar buzzing noise.

Not a single machine makes more racket today than any I have used in the past. It's both a good and bad thing. Good, that we don't have to spend money on new appliances, and bad that we still haven't figured out the source of the buzzing. Thinking back to my conversation with the electrician, it adds to my frustration that the phenomenon isn't at regular intervals to date. There's no rhyme or reason behind it. Unless you count the appearance of Buzz those two times. But even his figure just stood there like in my dreams, not saying anything or moving. Useless.

I sniff twice and trudge to the back door, scanning for movement. Then I check my phone. Steven hasn't texted me back all day. I hope his phone battery hasn't died. Buying a new phone would be another expense we can't afford.

When it's time to call Dr. Sternan, I decide to set up in my bedroom with my phone and a cup of coffee for comfort and privacy, even though I'm home alone. At least in here, I can close the curtains against the darkening world outside.

"We ended last session with me wondering if your deep-seated need to rise in your career at lightning speed is based upon a need for control and perfectionism stemming from your childhood," Dr. Sternan prompts after the usual pleasantries.

"That's what the last shrink lectured," I complain. "Why can't you entertain the idea that I was just doing my job and trying to prevent a disaster in the building?"

"Because you had motivations other than that, Claire. We shrinks, as you call us when you are upset, are listeners. We hear much more than what you say. You admitted to being upset that you got passed over for a promotion to have higher clearance at your lab a month before the incident. That is proof of something else going on in your mind. Whether it is conscious or subconscious."

"I had every right to be upset," I shoot back. Pain pricks my knee. I glance down; I've drawn blood where my long, untrimmed nails are digging into my kneecap as I perch on the bed and try to hold my composure. Two nails broke while cleaning today, leaving the ends jagged. I swipe the welling red dots away and continue my rant. "And so what, then? Okay, let's say hypothetically that I was curious to find out who had clearance down there, and have them witness I am competent in an emergency and offering my expertise. That doesn't scream control and perfectionism to me. My career choice is to be a world-renowned physicist. Successful people often apply for higher positions. So what if I'm ambitious? I'm a woman in a male-dominated field. I'm not afraid of shattering a glass ceiling or two."

"And I applaud you for your efforts. What I am trying to have you acknowledge is that your blind ambition may have contributed to not following protocol. You chose not to alert the authorities before trespassing into a security level for which you had no clearance," Dr. Sternan counters, unfazed by my argument.

Air whistles through my clenched teeth as my lungs expand. I'm overheating in this sweater. "Why do I need to acknowledge that?" Blind ambition? Where did she come up with that? Everything I've ever done, I've known the why and how.

"If it is something that stems from long ago,

you're doomed to repeat yourself whenever not handed every promotion you assume you deserve." Dr. Sternan's voice remains even and low. It reminds me of myself when I tutor the students, so I remain silent. Dr. Sternan might have something to teach me.

But what if it's not me dooming my career? What if it's someone or something else that followed me here? What if this has been going on longer than the incident? I rack my brain. Who would gain from my failure? A past coworker? A friend? A family member? A family curse? A curse on this land? I lick my lips. "What do you mean, doomed?" The fuzzy figure of Buzz pops into my mind. Was he sent to finish the job? Is he working on a different plane, puppeteering everything?

"Most of us are our own worst enemies. We can't alter our past, but we can learn from it. Please, Claire, just humor me and let me do what I do best."

"Delve into my psyche to find what's broken and all that?" Or haunted. I swear to God, if she says Buzz is my brain reflecting who I am, I'm going to fire her. I hate symbolism, especially in the world of psychology. One of these days, I'll ask Dr. Sternan what school of psychology she follows. If she's a Jungian, I'm in trouble.

"Not broken. Shaped or formed by our

environment and the people in it," she explains. "Many renowned psychologists agree that one's upbringing molds personality."

I sip my tepid coffee and ease back onto my propped-up pillow. If I'm not mistaken, the doc is referring to developmental psychology. This could be interesting to hear what she has to say, seeing as my momma was an educator and I'm sure she and poppa used a bit of psychology on me. "Okay, doctor. Let's see what you can find."

"Thank you, Claire. Get into a comfortable position in a quiet room and close your eyes."

"All set," I mumble.

"Let's go back to your childhood to find the root of your drive to succeed. Tell me about your parents," Dr. Sternan prompts me. Her voice is soft and melodious. It reminds me of the hypnotists I've watched on the internet.

My back and shoulders relax on the pillow as I visualize my parents. The truth is easy, and I am proud to tell her about the amazing couple that raised me. Everyone deserves parents like them. "They are the best. Everything a child could desire. Loving, helpful, 'give the shirt off their backs' type.'"

"Do you feel indebted to them for that?"

A yes pops into my conscious mind. I suspect the yes is to the money I owe them, but something deeper says that's not what Dr. Sternan is asking, so I say, "I guess I want to make them proud of me."

Dr. Sternan makes a faint humming noise. "From what you've already admitted in previous sessions, I can deduce that they are proud of you. It's clear that they love you very much. And since they already love and support you in all the ways a parent might, why is there such a need to show them that you are the best at everything before anyone else?"

"They came from nothing and built their careers from that," I say, sitting up, my pulse racing. "They have endured so much as poor emigrants from very different parts of the world. It may be the twenty-first century, Dr. Sternan, but prejudice is still very much alive. My father started as a janitor and now runs a successful shoe store. My mother has climbed from being a grade school teacher to being on school boards and committees." I gulp the last of my coffee. "They have opened so many doors for me. I conceive it's fair to want to prove to them that all their hard work was not in vain and to prove to myself that if they could do it, so can I." I will never disappoint my momma and poppa if I can help it. I'm their only child. But maybe I already have by getting let go from the research facility and discharged from the military. They are better than

I am at putting on a happy, brave face during tough times. I deflate back onto my pillow.

"Okay, that's very good, Claire. Thank you. Hold on for one moment while I jot down some notes." A minute goes by with me listening to her gentle breathing as I stare at the ceiling before she continues. "Now let me postulate this to you. They love you unconditionally. They chose careers based on what they wanted to do, not just for—"

"But doesn't every parent work hard for their kids? Or most parents? They hope for their offspring to be better off than they were, right?" I interrupt, scrunching my eyebrows to focus on a brown spot on the ceiling. Is that a stain or a bug? It's not moving, but I keep my eyes trained on it.

"Yes, but we are going wide. Let me refocus our discussion," Dr. Sternan directs, her voice still subdued. "Wouldn't you agree you've proved to your parents that you can succeed in life already? You are a scientist with three university degrees and are in a healthy marriage. You were a soldier and worked in a national laboratory."

I let out a cynical chuckle. "Was a scientist. I *had* a career. Past tense. And now I owe my parents half the lawyer's fees they kept on my behalf. I lost. All that achievement is dust in the wind." I exhale forcefully. Is my hour up yet?

"But the important takeaway is that their love

and support for you have not wavered. Same with your husband. I want you to reflect on this until our next session. This is your life, not your parents'. I can tell that they understand it. Now it is time you did."

I allow myself a second of mind-wandering before her second message digests in my brain. "My life is my own... Yeah, I'll consider it." My eyes wander around the room and freeze where Steven pulled the mirror off the wall. The plaster is a different shade from the paint where he patched the holes. If my life is my own, then why can't I find and control what's happening to me here?

"Dr. Sternan, can I ask you a question?"

"Of course, Claire."

I scratch the forearm holding the phone, formulating my question so I don't sound like a lunatic. "Remember my experience last week? Well, since then, I've heard the droning sound twice more," I rush to say, hoping to block her from jumping to her previous conclusion of an anxiety attack. "Steven and a neighbor have experienced the buzzing, too. Can you explain that? The electrician couldn't find the source of the sound and heard nothing during his visit. I didn't either. The anomaly is sporadic."

There is a long silence. Just when I'm about to ask if she is still there, Dr. Sternan answers. "That is interesting. It could be a case of tinnitus, which is a ringing in the ears. Your brain could understand it as a buzzing sound instead, since it seems to cause a panicked reaction."

"But all three of us at the same time?" I will ask every expert in every profession until I get an answer that fits. I can't live and grow and heal in a house that scares me.

Dr. Sternan hums a note. It seems she does this to let me know she is thinking and that her mind isn't just wandering during our phone calls. "There is much we don't know about the human brain, Claire. There are cases called mass hysteria, where several individuals experience the same mental or physical sensations or sounds, even though only one of them is the true experiencer. The modern medical term for it is Mass Psychogenic Illness, or MPI. A shared delusion could be the culprit. Have you explained the noise to the others before they announced they heard it, too?"

"Yes," I draw out. It sounds like she is pinning the blame on me again. Why is everything my fault? My heart thumps in my chest. "Are you saying they lied? Am I wasting my money trying to find the source of a sound that exists in my head alone?" I roll onto my stomach and grasp the edge of the bed. How would I explain this to Danielle? Or my parents? Or Steven?

"Don't panic, Claire. They didn't lie. It just means the others may imagine they're experiencing the same thing because of their compassionate nature. They may fantasize that the buzzing is as real as you hear it. Regardless, I'm saying it is a possibility, not a definite fact. The idea came to me because you said the sound is at random times. You could get a physical done at a veterans' hospital. I wouldn't rule out migraines or an inner ear condition."

I rub my forehead and huff. The psychiatrist's reasoning makes sense. Steven didn't hear any buzzing at the house before I arrived, and Gary assumed it was his hearing aid. "Okay, yeah. That is an idea. You're right. It sounds plausible. Thank you."

We agree to keep Monday evenings as my appointment time and say goodbye.

When Steven comes home, he mumbles about something his boss did, that he's hungry, but wants to get cleaned up first. I fry fish and rice for dinner while he showers.

While he wolfs down his food, I tell Steven what the electrician announced about nothing being wrong and how nice the bug guy sounded. He wipes his mouth and focuses on me.

"You didn't believe me when I said I had the house inspected? I told you that the inspector found nothing except these outdated appliances."

I stand and snatch his plate, stacking it onto mine, then let them clatter into the sink. Steven's eyebrows rise when I spin around. I point at him. "You agreed that the buzzing could be electrical. You and everyone else. It's a hundred dollars well spent. And I never said I didn't believe you. That inspector cashed our check the day you gave it to him. But he could have overlooked something. We need a different professional to find the source, Steven. We need a science-based, in-reality, hard fact of proof." I drop my fist onto the counter and return his gaze. "I need this for me, for my mental health. Please."

What I don't admit is that the anomaly could be all in my head. But I don't want it to be. I don't want to go crazy. I don't want to be shoved into a padded room, drugged up.

Steven raises his hands and stands. "Alright, honey. Just do what you need to do and keep me informed. I'll be watching television before I fall asleep. I'm exhausted."

He falls asleep on the couch within half an hour. I set the dishes to soak and tiptoe to the bedroom, making a mental note to search for a local veterans' hospital to make an appointment.

16

I wake twice to a humming noise. It lasts for a few seconds and then stops. A while later, Steven stumbles into the bathroom, knocking over something on the counter, and then makes his way into bed. Before I let him drift off to sleep, I ask if he hears anything. We lay there for a while, in complete darkness and silence, until his gentle snores begin. I smack him awake, harder than I should have, I'll admit. He shoots up, shouting. I pretend the noise is going strong for posterity's sake.

He scrubs his face, listens for a moment, and then turns to me. "It's just the bug machine on the floor. Please let me sleep. My boss is prodding us to finish twice as much a day because of the sudden housing demand. I'm so tired." He falls back down and covers his head with his pillow.

I sit up for a half hour more, straining my ears, and almost get up and unplug the bug deterrent, but upon sneaking a peek at the floor from the bed and not being able to guarantee a safe path through the inky darkness around discarded shoes and clothes, I think better of it. I never, *ever* want to step on another bug again. And if the contraption is shooing away insects like it should, I shouldn't turn it off.

*

Steven is jostling my shoulders, telling me to shut my alarm off that my tired mind and ears have chosen to be oblivious to. I swipe it off, groan, and roll out of bed, yelp, and leap back onto the bed.

"What now?" Steven grumbles, throwing his own sheets off and standing up, stretching.

I crawl over to his side and peer at the floor, remembering the reason behind my interrupted sleep. "Are there bugs? It's been raining so much. The bugs are bound to come back." *Please don't let the sounds be all in my head.*

Steven crouches down and inspects the carpet. "Not a single bug. Either the machine works, or you dreamed the noises." He studies me, and his eyebrows scrunch together. "Honey, you look exhausted. Why don't you go back to bed since the exterminator won't be here until this afternoon? You don't need to make me lunch everyday like I'm a kid."

I slide off the bed and step past him. His remarks bite. Did I dream all those sounds last night? "I'll nap later. I'm not tired right now." That's a boldfaced lie. I could stress-cry myself back to sleep. I'm so tired of the mysterious buzzing. It's splintering my brain, allowing slivers of doubt and worry to grow in the depths of my sanity. But first, I need to check the drains, the faucets, and the floors for bugs. Then I'll check the backyard. I had heard something. The noise woke me up multiple times, nagging at my consciousness until I acknowledged it. So, is it my inner ear, like Dr. Sternan suggested, or something else?

I don my slippers and slip a hand into the dark bathroom to flip on the light. No foot of mine is stepping blindly again.

The floor is clear. So are the tub and sink. Then I make the mistake of glancing in the mirror.

Nasty dark circles frame my under-eyes. Frazzled curls stick out at all angles. My lips are pale. A day at boot camp left me looking in better shape.

I wash my face and try to comb my hair into a sort of tamed nest until I can fix it after Steven leaves.

"Are you almost done in there? I need a hot shower before I leave," Steven shouts from another room.

I swipe on some tinted lip gloss and traipse to the kitchen, passing him in the hall. "All yours," I announce sweetly. He doesn't reply or pat me on the butt like he does when we pass each other in close quarters. I pause and glance back at him, but he's already closing the bathroom door behind him.

"He's tired, and it's cold," I say to console myself. And there's a good possibility he's annoyed that I woke him up last night.

Not seeing anything lurking in the backyard through the paned glass, I force myself to open the back door and step onto the porch. A dark, soupy yard waits patiently for its next victim as the cool hand of morning air wraps around me. The stench of leaf decay and soggy wood overpowers another, more animalistic scent on the edge of my senses. Is it wet dog? Wet raccoon? Bird? I look up at the dark limbs looming against a black sky. Assured no glint of eye or feather betrays what may sit in wait to attack, I peek over the railing.

It's too dark. Everything is in a void of shadow. What shapes I can make out through the poor illumination of the porch light casts shimmers from being drenched in constant rain. It doesn't smell right, like fresh rain in Montana. All I can smell this morning is smoke from chimneys and mud when I raise my nose in the air. The wet animal smell is still there, stronger on the breeze. My rational mind wakes up, telling me the neighbor on the other side must have a dog.

I've been here for a week. One week stuck in a dark and rainy purgatory. No lights from the neighbor's houses are on. Our porch light and the light from our bathroom window are the dim signs of human habitation.

After a violent shiver wracks my torso, I head back inside, locking the door behind me. We need curtains. Soon. I don't like that what lurks outside can see inside. Can see me. Watch me. Hunt me.

Steven manages a half-hearted peck on my cheek before leaving for work. I curl up on the couch and pick a cartoon channel to have on while I call into work with the same bug issue excuse and then shut my eyes.

I jolt awake. Buzzing. There's buzzing, angry buzzing right next to me. I roll off the couch and pull the blanket with me. A rectangular object slides off the cushion and clatters onto the wooden floor.

It's my phone vibrating with an incoming call.

Maybe I am losing it. "Oh, geez," I say aloud as I grab it.

Ten o'clock flashes on my home screen. Then a voicemail pops up from the exterminator. He is requesting to come over sooner since another client switched appointment times. Am I available in fifteen minutes? He will give me a discount on the eighty-dollar consultation fee if I do this.

If I don't shower or fix my hair, I can. The discount is an additional incentive. Who cares what I look like, right? He's here for the bugs. I call him back and confirm that I am home. Then, I hustle to the bathroom to wrap my hair up in a bun, moisturize, and dress in jeans, an old gray long-sleeve shirt, college sweater, and my orange running shoes in case I need to follow him around outside.

He rings the doorbell just as I am pouring myself a cup of coffee.

I answer the door to be greeted by a six-foot tall barrel-chested man with a full auburn beard and head of hair, wearing a magnifying eyeglass set that reminds me of a character from a cyberpunk comic. His button-down dark blue utility shirt has The Bug Guy embroidered on the left breast pocket. A medical stethoscope hangs around his neck. He's holding a clipboard in one hand and a laminated badge in the other. Bob Hassleman, the identification reads. The Bug Guy. Certified since 1999.

"Nice to meet you, Bob," I say, opening the screen door wider so he can pass through. "I understand the glasses help you find tiny bugs, but why the stethoscope?"

Irish Spring infuses the surrounding air, and the lines around his eyes crinkle as a smile graces his face. A Santa Claus-like belly laugh rumbles from his lips. "To listen for the critters in the walls, of course. Sometimes they like to hide from me. But I always find them."

I grin and gesture to the kitchen. "That's great to hear because they are not welcome in this house. Can I offer you a coffee before we start the tour?"

Bob shakes his head. "No, thank you, ma'am. I'd rather just dive right in. Sounds like you've had a bad time of it. This place is not big enough to run a motel." He tugs on his ear and winks.

I tilt my head to one side. Oh, he's referring to a roach motel. It's too early for jokes. I offer a fake laugh, stuff my hands into my pants pockets, and say, "Yeah, the fire marshal would shut it down pretty quick."

Santa Bob nods, his smile faltering, then glances around the room. "I dare say they would."

I never said I was funny.

I fill the awkward silence that follows by texting

Steven. It should put him in a better mood knowing we're getting a discount. "Alright, lead on, Bob. If you don't mind, I'd like to shadow you to learn what I can."

Bob assesses me for a moment, then nods. "Sure, why not?"

I follow him around, answering questions he has about where we've seen bugs and how many. Every few feet, he sets the stethoscope to the walls or floor and listens, then scoots forward.

He finishes inspecting the inside and steps onto the back porch. I've been nothing but useless and in his way. There was also a curious look from him when I refused to go up into the attic. "I'm sorry I can't provide any definitive answers for you. I've been living in this house for a week, and Steven has stayed for a little longer than that. The previous owners abandoned it, and the bank took it back. Steven says it passed inspection and the electrician couldn't find any faulty wires to explain the issues we've experienced."

Bob remains silent, steps into the muddy yard, and squats down, poking at the ground with a stick. His head disappears under the deck for a moment. He stands back up. "Well, ma'am, there are a lot of common beetle bodies all dried out in the walls and attic, and there're a lot of drowned worms and beetle bodies here and out front in the yard where I poked around before ringing your doorbell. For these critters to force their way into the sewer system and up to your sinks and tubs is very odd. It doesn't seem to be an infestation because nothing I found is alive, like the house was tented years ago and never vacuumed. There's nothing to exterminate." He then frowns.

Another dead end? Really? But they were alive, crawling over my feet and up Steven's arms. I shudder, crossing my arms. "Is there anything you can do to prevent it from happening again? I'm getting desperate. The neighbors are mad at me, saying that I'm feeding all the birds that are pooping on their cars and maddening their dogs. I've been here a week and might actually go crazy from this nonsense." I sweep a hand around. I can't let this guy leave until he understands what a nightmare these seven days have been for me. "Something is buzzing. The same something or the rain is causing a copious number of bugs to rise from the ground and attract wildlife. Geese dive-bombed me the other day right after I heard the noise." I rest a hand on my chest. I'm hyperventilating. Bob bounds up the stairs, panic in his eyes; I hold up a hand to halt him, calm him. I am calming him. Hilarious.

"Should I call an ambulance?"

"No," I wheeze. "Just hold on."

Then I begin the box breathing technique Dr. Sternan taught me, and force my body to inhale for four seconds and hold for as long. By the time I've done it twice, I'm able to speak again.

"It's all right, Bob. I'm alright. Just a panic attack," I assure him.

Bob peels his hand off the railing and puts his phone away. "I don't know CPR, ma'am, I'm ashamed to say." He then fusses with the pen attached to his clipboard. "I'm sorry to have upset you. I was telling the truth. There isn't anything for me to do for you. There are no signs of common buzzing insects like bees or wasps, and, as I explained, the bugs coming up from your drain are something I've never heard of. That's not in their nature. They rarely live in sewers. It sounds like something out of *The Twilight Zone*, if I'm being honest."

I smooth wisps of hair off my forehead. "You can say that again. So you're sure you haven't heard of anything like this happening to anyone else in this town or abroad? I'm running out of time and ideas."

Bob surveys the yard once more while stroking his beard and then shrugs. "Nothing. I suggest that when the weather clears up, get rid of any dead brush around the property. That will take away their natural habitat. I'm truly sorry. In fact, I'm so sorry that I will not charge you for this consultation. I'm perplexed. I will do some research and question some colleagues on message boards. If I find out anything, I'll call you." He steps back into the swampy yard. "I'll walk back using the side here so I don't muddy up your house. Good day, ma'am." Then Bob, the best bug guy in town, walks away.

*

Steven arrives home covered in sawdust with dirt streaks on his forehead around five thirty, eager to hear what the exterminator had to say. He sighs when I explain that there is no infestation.

"My parents also say hi from yesterday, and they aren't expecting payment for my lawyer's fees, so we can take our time on that front," I offer with a lopsided grin. "The eighty bucks saved can go towards what we need to work on the house next."

Steven beelines it for the kitchen, retrieves a beer from the fridge, and takes a swig. "That's a literal weight off my shoulders, honey. I didn't realize how stressed I was about the condition of this house and the money we owe. I am responsible for anything that happens since I pushed so hard for us to purchase this place." He takes another drink and holds the cold bottle to his forehead. "It may be cold and rainy outside, but I worked my ass off today. If they demand any more of us, the other workers say they'll walk. I don't have the balls to tell them I won't. We need the money."

I wrap my arms around him even when he tries to evade me, saying he needs to change out of his sweaty work clothes first. "I don't care, Steven," I say, squeezing him tight. "I'm back to work tomorrow, I promise, and we will clean up the yard when it warms up, which will evict the bugs and therefore the bird problem. Heck, maybe those geese hit a power line or tree branch, and it gave the illusion that they were attacking me. It's been a week for the books, and can only get better from here."

I am not crazy.

17

While Steven is showering, Danielle texts me that she has emailed me documents with instructions to work on ASAP. I message her back that I will begin right away and that I will be at work tomorrow. Then I walk to the kitchen. I'll need extra free time, and the time I can rob is what I would spend making dinner. Thank God for frozen pizza.

Steven doesn't complain and offers to make the salad so I can print off the file Danielle emailed over.

*

"These proposed class lessons are all jumbled.

It's like she didn't even try to go in order with the textbook. This is going to take forever to fix," I bemoan to the empty room. The coffee on my desk went cold an hour ago, and even the crickets and croaking frogs have gone to bed. I've spread Danielle's lesson calendar for the next semester in front of me on the floor. A legal pad scrawled with notes balances on my knee as I sit cross-legged. I twirl my pen like a baton in my right hand, the speed increasing with my frustration.

Steven taps on the room door I had left ajar. "Honey, drop the pen and go to bed. Remember, Danielle doesn't need this done tonight."

I cast him a grateful smile. He always has my well-being in mind. "I'll be quiet and work for half an hour more. Then I'll come to bed."

He nods and retreats, shutting the door. I stand up, stretching my arms above my head, and look out into the backyard. All is still. The drumming of rain on the roof and the whoosh of wind have petered out as well. I rub my eyes and yawn. Even caffeine can't keep me up for much longer.

I squat down to collect the pages; I'd rather use that half hour to sleep. A low buzzing wiggles into my right ear, and then my left ear. "Oh no. Not now. I'm going to bed, I swear," I hiss, hoping my consciousness is listening.

The pitch rises. I snatch up the last pages and

stand, placing the stack on my desk, and shutter my eyes, willing the sound to subside. This stress response has to stop. "I am in charge of my body. I am in charge of my brain," I chant, willing my psyche to control my body's response. A vibration snakes up the arm of my hand that's still resting on the stack of papers. "What the hell? Is it an earthquake?" I step back, and my whole body vibrates.

"Steven!" I shout and lunge for the door. The handle turns, but it won't open. The world sways around me. The buzzing increases to that of a power drill. I'm shaking. Tears spring up. My hands try to turn the handle, grasping and rotating, but now the round handle doesn't rotate with them. "Steven, I can't open the door!"

"Claire?" Steven calls out. "Claire, unlock the door." He rattles the doorknob. "It's an earthquake, I think. Unlock the door."

"There's no lock on this door!" I shriek. The vibration is making my head hurt. Don't earthquakes roll or rattle things, not vibrate? I let go of the doorknob and splay my hands against the door itself, trying to steady my body and my vision. I can't think straight. How does a door lock that doesn't have a physical lock?

Steven slams against the door, cursing the house and its settled foundations. I survey the room for something to anchor between the door and the frame to rip it open. Steven stores his more expensive saws and tools in the closet. A crowbar or hammer would work.

The dark window draws my attention. There's something outside. Someone. A fuzzy humanoid shape. Buzz. I freeze, ogling as the black and white grainy figure shifts. It's at the window, holding its hands above its head. Why? Why is he doing this? Is he trying to get in? But he has already been in the house.

My legs remember how to move, and I slam myself into the door. "Steven, get me out of here!" I scream. Tears stream down my face. I pound on the door with both fists.

"I have to go get my crowbar," Steven yells. "Don't panic. I'll be right back." His voice recedes with each word.

"Don't leave me! He's coming for me!" I sob.

"Who's there?" Steven shouts much closer. The door rattles violently. "Stand back. I'm going to kick it in."

I step to the side, hug myself and sink down to the floor.

Then, I do something I know I will regret.

I peek over my shoulder.

Buzz is growing, filling up the window. His television snow form is vibrating side to side. How is he doing this? Is he trying to communicate? If I go to him, will he stop?

Then there's two. Two figures separating and expanding from the one. Two Buzzes. Double the nightmare, double the fun.

I shrink back, fighting the sound, the vibrations, and the figures, and curl into myself. "Please, no," I groan.

The door bursts open with a splintering of wood. I shriek, covering my head with one hand and pointing to the window with the other. "There!"

But when I look up, Buzz and his companion are gone. I gasp, and a choked squawking sound escapes my throat. Steven walks to the glass and peers out. The sound is still vibrating in my brain. I cradle my head and shout, "Stop it, Buzz!"

Steven picks me up and walks into the bedroom, kicking the door shut behind him. He sets me down on the bed and grasps my face in his hands. "Don't move. I'm going out there."

Then he's gone. Cold air replaces his body heat. "Don't take him," I sob, still hearing the buzzing, vibrations running through my body. My hands shake as they clamp over my ears. Steven is gone, and I'm all alone. Buzz is going to attack Steven, then kill me, freeze my heart, and report back to his masters in the physics building at the Rosebud Research Facility. *"See?"* he'll somehow communicate. *"I didn't need help after all. I finished the job. The only witness is dead. Our world domination can recommence."*

"Claire? What are you saying? Who's coming? Honey, there's no one out there. Honey, look at me."

Was I talking out loud? Was Buzz talking through me? Where did Steven go?

Strong, calloused fingers are prying my hands away from my face. A weight shifts next to me on the bed, and Steven's arm encircles me. I climb onto his lap and sob into his chest.

"I thought they took you, Steven." Screw the non-disclosure agreement. Screw Rosebud Research Facility and the military for lying to me. The rumors are true. Monsters are being created in the bowels of the buildings there. "They've sent the beings to kill me because I saw them," I moan. "It's Rosebud facility, or the military, or both. They won't stop until I'm dead."

"No one is after you. It's stopped. It's over. It's okay now," he soothes. "It was just an earthquake, sweetie. I bet there have been tremors all week, and those brought on the hallucination caused by your anxiety, like the doctors told us."

I peer into his face through hot, blurry eyes. "Are you sure?" There's no fight in me. I'm as weak as a baby, clinging onto his t-shirt. "The monster is still in me?" Is that why I can see Buzz? Is he haunting me from the inside out?

Steven's soft brown eyes gaze down at me while his fingers smooth hair from my face, soaked from sweat and tears. "There is no monster. I'll confirm the earthquake tomorrow. I bet it's going to be headline news. There are many volcanoes in this state. I promise it's okay. Let's get you tucked in. Do you need something to help you sleep? Your anxiety pills? A Benadryl? Or chamomile tea?" As he offers suggestions, he pulls me to my side of the bed and tucks me in. If I weren't in my pajamas, I wouldn't have had the energy to undress. Then he offers me a tissue box. I'm a snotty mess. I can't remember where I put my anti-anxiety medicine.

"Why are they doing this to me?" I whimper, curling into a ball, pressing my eyes shut.

Steven doesn't have an answer for me; he leaves and comes back with a pill and a glass of water. "This will help calm your nervous system, honey."

I blow my nose once more and swallow the pink tablet, not caring what he gave me, and pray that the television snow figures will be too tired to attack me again tonight.

I am not crazy.

18

There is no earthquake discussion on the morning news as Steven and I skirt around each other getting ready for work, still in the haze of sleep. The newscasters speak about college football statistics and the countdown to Christmas. The meteorologist talks of a slight reprieve from rain and a reminder to weatherproof our homes for the coming winter snow.

"Maybe we missed that bit of news, honey," Steven assures me, kissing my forehead before leaving.

I race to work through rising fog, running yellow lights dimmed by the heavy air, finding that I'm already more confident with the turns and steep grade of the roads here.

"Good morning, Claire," Danielle says, walking towards me. For the first time since I started, I have beaten her to the office, not wanting to be home alone. She takes her time rummaging for the key, looking and smelling fresh, and eyes me with curiosity. "Eager to get to work, are we?"

"Um, yeah. I want to do some research on," my mind races for excuses to be on my laptop during class, "current articles related to today's lessons. Complex subjects always stuck better in my memory when the professor paralleled them to real-world scenarios." I pat down my hair and touch my cheek, hoping I blended my cream blush and concealer so I don't look like death frozen over.

Danielle opens her door and walks in first. "I don't recall requesting you to do that in the instructions," she says over her shoulder. "Did you glance over the lesson plans I sent you? I just need you to make sure I didn't overlook any major lessons highlighted in the book."

I lick my lips. The earthquake research will have to wait. Her teaching method needs to be addressed, and this is a perfect segue. I set my laptop and battered briefcase on the tutoring table and face her. "Um, about that, Professor." I decide on a professional approach since that seems to be the tone she is taking this morning. "Would it be possible to slow down on the lessons for a week so that the students can catch up? They struggled during our tutoring sessions last week." I stand taller under her hard gaze, clasping my clammy hands behind my back.

Danielle's hands go to her hips. "I have fifteen weeks to cram twenty weeks of lessons into these students' brains in time for exams. So, no, I cannot slow down for their benefit. All their other professors are doing the same. It is the students' responsibility to learn the lessons. And that is precisely why you are here. To help me. That's why I can't stress enough how important it is that you make it to class."

Air rushes from my lungs as if she has punched me in my gut. I didn't *want* to miss work. I want to have a house that doesn't buzz and a brain that doesn't hallucinate. It then occurs to me that the phenomenon only occurs at the house. Why would my broken brain pick this home to break down? Is it because it's a new environment? But then so is everywhere else I go day to day. I also get stressed at work sometimes, or if I get stuck at a red light for too long. So why don't I sense anything ominous during those times?

"Claire? Are you listening to me? Your eyes are distant. Do you understand my predicament?"

I blink and refocus on Danielle. She raises her

hands in the air.

"Yes, Professor. I will do my best to improve my attendance and be here for the students. I have looked over the lessons to get acquainted with your teaching patterns, but have not cross-referenced them with the lesson book yet. I'll continue to work on the lesson plan after work," I say in my most professional, monotone way. I am here to work. Danielle may not consider me a friend anymore. My house, and or brain, has issues that's affecting my life and relationships. These are the facts. I need this job for the money to keep my head above water. Career first, then survival. I inhale and meet Danielle's gaze.

Her shoulders relax. That wasn't a fun exchange for either of us. I need to remember that Danielle is under more stress than I am at work. But she's not being attacked. She hasn't seen what I've seen, lost what I've lost.

"Okay. Thank you for understanding my point of view." Danielle walks around her desk and picks up her lesson binder and a stack of papers. "Let's get to class."

*

When the last students trudge away from tutoring, with one young man side-eyeing me with a smirk on his face as he passes by, I lean over to collect my briefcase and laptop. The nonverbal judgment from advanced students will have to be addressed some other time. My mind dissected Steven's earthquake theory all day, so I didn't notice any students staring during class. Nowhere on the internet was anything announced about tremors in the area. So if it's not tremors or the rain causing the buzzing, or an electrical issue, or insects surging, then what?

"Can earthquakes cause visual hallucinations?"

Danielle's head snaps up. "What's this about hallucinations?"

"Like, say there was an earthquake of some magnitude and then a bunch of people said they saw a ghost during the event. I—I saw a ghost hunter show once." Not once. More like binge-watched a series once I settled into my parents' home for my sabbatical. I became obsessive, trying to rationalize what I saw. It took way too long for me to realize that the shows were making me neurotic, scared to go out after dark, scared of cemeteries—which I used to be so at peace in—and scared of death.

She tilts her head and scrunches her eyebrows. "There's no such thing as ghosts, Claire. You're a physicist; you should know better. Besides, earthquakes are rolling waves of energy. It's not the correct frequency to affect the inner ear."

I should know that, having advanced degrees in physics; I'll make time to beat myself up later. She hasn't seen or experienced what I have. I roll my lips. I need a different approach. "Did you feel the earthquake last night?"

"What? No, Claire. There was no earthquake. What connection are you trying to make? Are you well?"

"I—I don't know. Steven felt it, too. It lasted for minutes. Or maybe it was just seconds, and it felt like minutes. Vibrations. Or some sort of tremor. It's hard to explain. I thought I saw something. My office door locked, and Steven had to break down the door."

Danielle's hand flies to her lips. "How awful! What about a burst water line? I've heard those can make a terrible racket. Do you have water pressure today?"

I incline my head, trying to remember. Whatever Steven had given me to help sleep had worked a little too well. I drank two cups of coffee, one after another, before the medicinal hangover abated. Two more cups after that, thanks to Danielle's bottomless supply of coffee pods, and I'm still not jittery. "I—yeah, maybe. Neither of us showered this morning."

"I'm sure there's a logical explanation for this.

Perhaps the bugs were getting wet feet from the pipe before it burst, and that's why they came up. The water-main break could have been far enough away that it didn't affect you, but close enough to feel it."

"Wow. That makes sense. Thank you, Danielle." A rational mind. It's just what I needed. "Logic and science make the world go round."

"Indeed," Danielle says, smiling back at me.

I am not crazy.

19

I drive up the canyon past our house, testing the Subaru's second-gear durability on winding streets that become steeper the further I go, snooping around for utility trucks or blocked-off streets, anything that could signal road or utility damage. All appears normal and quiet as cloud cover rolls in to obscure the darkening blue of the sky. I turn back when the paved road turns to dirt.

Steven pulls into the driveway just as I do.

"Hello, honey," he greets me and returns my kiss. "Having a better day?"

"Kind of," I admit. "There was no news of an earthquake, but Danielle deduced that there may have been a water-main break or burst pipe of some sort. It would explain the bugs, at least."

He drops his work belt on the floor once we are inside and sits on the couch to untie his shoes. "That would make sense. None of the other workers heard or felt anything. But none of them live near us. Do we have water pressure?"

Through our front window, I watch someone walk by with their dog. I don't recognize them, but it gives me an idea. "How about if we interrogate our neighbor on the other side? It will give us an excuse to introduce ourselves and gauge whether they are experiencing anything similar to us. Gary is not that helpful since he has a hearing aid. He says it buzzes sometimes. Would you be up for that?"

Steven glances down at the boots he just pried off his feet, then gazes up at me. "I will go with you if I can shower first. I'm not introducing myself like this. And again, do we have water pressure? Because I will not shower under just a trickle of water."

"I just got home, like you. Go take a shower if you can before we interrupt their dinnertime."

Half an hour later, having confirmed our water pressure is fine, I've pulled on my wool coat and Steven zips up his blue windbreaker, his hair still dripping wet.

Something shrieks from the thicket to our left as

we traipse down the driveway. Steven and I freeze and scan the visible branches amid the evergreens. Another creature answers above us. And another. The shrill calls grate on my ears.

Steven points to a tree. "Birds. Right there. Must be fighting for dominance."

"Or food. Probably told their friends about the bug feast," I whisper, peering up at the countless dark shapes with beady eyes reflecting our porch light. I shiver. "They can have them and leave."

Steven throws an arm around my shoulders and pulls me close. "Nature finds a way."

A floodlight blinds us as we make our way up the two stone steps to the black front door decorated with an autumnal wreath. Steven raises his hand to knock, but the door swings inward. I try to step back, but Steven still has his arm locked around my shoulders.

A man of Poppa's age emerges. More light pours out from behind him. Smells of a pot roast wafts out. I steel myself for an onslaught of verbal abuse about feeding the birds and interrupting their dinner.

"Howdy, folks. You are the new owners next door, right? We got your newfangled calling card in the mail. It made me chuckle with the blank interior. So modern and edgy. Names Charlie, Charlie Devon." He thrusts his hand out towards

Steven.

I watch as Steven displays his award-winning smile and shakes the man's hand, introducing himself and me in kind as I drown in a pool of embarrassment over the disappearing ink Halloween invitation.

Charlie nods and smiles at me but doesn't offer me his hand. Why not? Do I have bird poop on me? Did he think that the invitation was a prank like the other neighbor, and just trying to save face since both of us are here? Then I realize I have both hands in my pockets. The man is just going off my social cues. I bob my head. My hands are warm and safe. They can stay where they are.

"We won't keep you long, Mr. Devon," Steven begins. "We were wondering if you felt or heard anything like an earthquake last night? We had a strange buzzing noise in our house and then one of our doors jammed shut. It was the weirdest thing."

I'm glad Steven took the lead. He has a better way with words and people than I do.

Mr. Devon purses his lips for a moment and then glances behind him. "No, I didn't experience anything. I don't reckon my wife, Barb, did either. She would have said something. We were in bed by nine." He takes a step to the left and gazes over our shoulders.

"What about your water pressure? We were

worried it might be a burst pipe." My voice comes out small, timid. Have these recent trials made me afraid of conversing with strangers now?

Shadows hide Charlie's facial expression. "Our water has been fine. Maybe it's down the canyon?"

Steven and I nod in unison, thanking him for his time.

I halt. "Mr. Devon? May I ask something that's going to sound strange?"

Our neighbor tilts his head. "Sure. What is it?"

Steven squeezes my shoulder and shakes his head as if he reads my mind, but I ignore him. "Are there any ghost sightings around here? Does any paranormal stuff happen? Are there disturbed gravesites?"

"Ghosts? Maybe at the old fuel station or something. Haven't heard of anywhere in this area. But that house of yours," he trails off and clucks his tongue.

"Yes?" Steven's voice is rife with curiosity. "What about our house?" He takes a step toward our neighbor.

Charlie takes a wider stance, grabs both his elbows, and motions toward our house with his chin. "Well, it sounds made up, but I swear it's true. The couple who lived there before you were quite odd. They disappeared not long after we moved in, so we didn't get to know them. But the other neighbors said they were doomsayers—worried the world was going to end any second. I remember they always kept their blinds shut. They never had visitors, and many of us spotted them buying extra canned goods, candles, and the like at the corner shop. They left the house at night." He pauses and glances from Steven to me. We remain quiet and still. He continues. "Local gossip was that they were Satanists using the cover of being preppers to hide their weird mannerisms. Then they got up and left in the night one day. House was still full of their belongings."

"Is that all?" I ask, rolling my eyes, then whistle a nonsensical tune. Steven squeezes my shoulder a little harder than necessary to vocalize his disapproval of my attitude.

Seriously, though. Satanists?! Who knows what they invited into our home? I've heard of weird rituals that invite demons into our world. What if that's what they were doing in the underground lab? My brain spirals down the what-if trail. Momma always says there is evil in the world we need to fight. After seeing Buzz, I am a believer.

Charlie waves his hands as if shooing a fly. I snap back to the present. He eyeballs me. "Ah, but it was all gossip. I wouldn't stress. We didn't really know them. I shouldn't have said anything. Gary is the person to talk to. He did yard work for them, and my wife used to witness his wife leaving loaves of her wonderful bread on their porch. She used to give us all bread. We miss that. Mary passed away around the time that couple disappeared. Poor Gary was never the same."

"What happened to her?" Steven and I ask in unison.

"Not sure," Mr. Devon admits, recrossing his arms. "Gary and I never talk, to be honest. He's always out there when the weather is nice, working in his yard. Sometimes my wife waves to him, driving by, but we do little else. We saw an obituary in the paper, and my wife dropped a sympathy card in his mailbox. I don't mean to make us sound unfriendly. We travel a lot."

"We won't keep you any longer, Charlie. Thanks for indulging us," Steven says. "It was nice meeting you." He takes my hand and pulls me back down the stairs.

"You're welcome. Have a good night," Charlie says, and waves.

Once we are almost to our driveway, I rage at Steven. "Why did you pull us away? He could have told us so much more. Satanists, Steven. We may need to get a priest in to bless our house."

Steven shakes his head. "Utter nonsense. It's all rumors. I excused us because I knew we could put all this to rest with a quick word with Gary. Your pulse raced when he started talking about that rubbish. I need sleep, and so do you."

He pulls me along to Gary Tubman's house and raps on the door twice.

It takes a solid minute before the door cracks open. The same whiff of unwashed clothes and old cologne greets us. I groan.

Then Gary flings the door wide open. "Ah! Claire and Steven Simmons! Come in, come in out of the cold."

At least he isn't wearing the same clothes as last time. Tonight he's donned dark gray sweatpants, a beige thermal undershirt with a waffle-weave pattern, and a brown cardigan in good repair. He ushers us inside before I can protest, my limbs stiff with resistance. Then Gary waves us toward the sagging brown and yellow couch and says he'll be right back with tea and cookies.

We don't sit. Instead, I hold my sleeve to my nose when a sharp smell, sour with decay, enters my nostrils, and watch Steven appraise Gary's house for himself. Has Gary not taken out his trash in weeks? Steven swipes at his own nose twice, disguising his desire to pinch it shut.

The room looks the same as last time I was here, but beneath this new malodorous scent, the air smells musty, smoky. Cigar butts rest in an ashtray atop a stack of newspapers on the coffee table.

Gary shuffles into the room and splays his hands. "I can't seem to find my serving tray. Would you join me in the dining room?"

I want to make an excuse and grab Steven's biceps as a signal. I want to fill my lungs with cold, fresh night air. But Steven prods me across the room, telling Gary we'd be happy to join him.

Steven and I plop down in high-backed dining chairs with worn blue paisley cushions. A yellow Tiffany-style glass shade, dulled with a layer of dust, casts the room in an amber glow. Gary rambles on about the weather from the adjoining kitchen. Did we know that we have already gotten a quarter inch more rain than last year? A jigsaw puzzle in progress of a cottage scene covers the back half of the table. I lean forward, find an edge piece in the box, and click it into place.

"Don't do his puzzle," Steven scolds in a hoarse whisper.

I recline back and shrug. Gary sets down three faded floral mugs filled to the brim with murky tea, a small pink ceramic cream pot, and a crystal bowl of sugar with various beige lumps here and there. It reminds me of a cat box. I cover my gag reflex with my hand.

"It's alright, Mr. Simmons, your wife can help herself. That was my wife's favorite puzzle. I bring it out once a year to finish it in her honor." Gary offers me a sad, yellow-toothed smile and proffers me a box of tan wafer cookies. I accept one and dunk it into the cup in front of me, preparing my taste buds for disappointment.

Steven accepts a cookie, too, and avoids the condiments like me. "Have you felt any earthquakes or heard anymore buzzing, Gary?"

The tea is bitter without cream and sugar, but I'm not sure I could avoid the mystery lumps in the sugar or sniff the cream to make sure it's not rancid without appearing rude. The entire house smells as if the kitchen needs to be gutted. And the cookie is stale, breaking in half with much effort. Gary might as well have offered us croutons. I place the other half on a napkin. If Gary insists on taking it with me to finish, I'll feed it to the birds, if they'll even eat it.

Gary sticks a finger in his ear. "You hear that too? Gosh, I thought it was just a sign of getting old. It's been faint when I've heard it. Oh, there it is again. Is that what you hear?"

Steven and I angle our heads. I clasp my hands tightly in my lap, forcing myself to sit still and not bolt. There is buzzing, but not of the right pitch that makes my blood run cold. It's more of a hum.

"No, that's just your fridge," Steven says after a moment. "It sounds like it could use some maintenance. Remember to vacuum the coils at least once a year. Did you hear anything louder last night around eleven?"

"I couldn't have; I'm asleep by then. Usually on the couch with the television turned all the way up," Gary says, and shrugs.

"How about bugs?" I implore. We need to get through this interview before the smells of the house embed themselves in our clothes and hair.

Gary takes a sip from his mug and shakes his head. He had added three heaping teaspoons of sugar to his tea, lumps and all. "No, can't say any more than usual. But those birds love your yard. They are coming to my yard now, too. Must be yummy bugs."

I swipe a hand across my forehead. "Alright, well, we'd better get—"

"Hold on, I need to ask him one more thing," Steven interrupts. I gape at him. He wants to stay *longer?* Steven turns his full attention to Gary. "Can you tell us anything about the past owners of our house? We are curious about its history and how they maintained the yard so we can bring it back to its former glory."

I bob my head in agreement to Gary. My husband is learning to tell white lies for our benefit. Good for him. Or he is excited about doing yard work. I sag back into my chair as Gary clears his throat and takes another sip of his tea.

"More tea?" When we both shake our heads no, Gary begins. "Hmm, let me think. They were curious folk, the Galloways, but nice. Tim and Laura paid me to upkeep their yard—just the front yard, mind you. I hate to imagine what you two have to deal with in that backyard. They never invited me back there. And then when my wife died…" His eyes moisten. "A part of me died as well. The Galloways disappeared not long afterwards. I lost my best friend and then the other friends I had."

"Just the front yard?" I wonder aloud. Steven's foot taps mine under the table. I glance at him, and he motions to Gary with his head. I peer back and watch silent tears falling down Gary's face. Oh, I'm focusing on the wrong thing again.

Steven slides a hand closer to Gary on the table. "Our condolences, Gary. Mr. Devon on the other side of us said the same thing. There isn't a correlation, is there?"

"A corro-what?" Gary asks, then pulls out a handkerchief with his wife's initials embroidered on it, like last time, and snots it up. I purse my lips. It grosses me out even when I have to blow my nose.

"Did your wife's death have anything to do with Tim and Laura leaving, Gary?" Steven reiterates louder.

"No, I don't reckon so. Those two didn't tell me anything about their troubles or family. My Mary died of cancer." Gary's head falls to his chest, and he mumbles, "I—I don't want to talk about it."

"We're sorry," I rush out. "We didn't mean to upset you, but we've been having strange things happen at the house and are trying to find out why." I peer at Steven for support. He nods his approval and glances back at Gary. I try once more. "Can you tell us where they might have gone? We might track them down. Maybe something spooked them away?"

"Spooked?" Gary lifts his head and strokes his stubbled chin. Then he chuckles low and blows his nose again. "Oh, you've been listening to the local gossip too much. There ain't no such thing as ghosts, Mrs. Claire. Tim and Laura left for their own private reasons, I think. A few men came snooping around one afternoon, searching for them. The sharks—that's what I call them because of the shiny gray suits they wore—wouldn't say much except that Tim wasn't paying his bills." Gary stuffs the snot-filled handkerchief into his cardigan pocket. "You two have not seen a picture of my beautiful Mary yet. Come with me to the hallway. I've got an entire wall of her."

We are slow to stand. Me because I'm reluctant, Gary because he's old, and Steven because he worked all day doing a physically demanding job. Steven raises two fingers in my direction behind Gary's back and mouths, *"Two more minutes."* I nod once and follow him through the living room.

Gary beckons us to where he stands in the hallway, lit by a lone bulb in the ceiling, and points to each picture frame, telling us when and where Mary was that day. There is no oohing and awing from me, though; I'm beyond distracted, nearing the point of gagging. That same sour funk is much stronger here. It smells moldy and foul, making the primal part of my brain scream for me to run and not look back. Something is emitting this smell from nearby.

I examine the floor and notice a square outline in the matted shag carpet. "Do you have a cellar?" I interrupt.

"Claire!" Steven admonishes. "Don't be rude."

"Oh, there's nothing down there," Gary rushes out. "I don't go down there. My knees don't like stairs anymore."

I ignore both of them and continue to survey the brown square as Gary prattles on about his deceased wife. The smell is rising from something down there, perhaps caught in a long-ago flood. My eyes freeze on a point of white in the corner. Is it the tip of a white feather? I squat down and pull at it. The tip turns into a full-length downy feather.

"Honey, what are you doing? What is that?"

"Mrs. Claire, really," Gary pleads. "Nothing is down there."

I detect panic in his voice. He should be panicking. I comprehend the decaying smell now. A suppressed memory from childhood surfaces. Poppa took me trick-or-treating one year before I was old enough to go alone or with friends. We turned a corner, choosing a shortcut through an alley, and there was a heap of something in the shadows. The smell had hit me before I saw the tail and realized what I was looking at in the same moment Poppa grabbed my hand, backpedaling. I screamed. Poppa had picked me up and taken the long way home that night. He had the "death talk" with me the next day after I woke screaming from a night terror. So, yeah, I recognize the smell of a dead animal. In this case, two dead animals. I'd bet money on it. I stand up and hold the feather up to Gary's weathered face. His eyes widen with new tears brimming on the red lower lids.

"Did you slaughter those geese?" I shout. "That's illegal! Were they even dead? Or were they just dazed, and you dispatched them for food?"

"Jesus, Claire," Steven shouts at me. "Knock it off with these insane theories."

Gary takes a step back, shaking his head. "No, Mrs. Claire, they had bad wing injuries. The animal people would have just euthanized them. I didn't want their bodies to be wasted. I gave them a quick death, I promise." He clasps his hands. "I'm poor. Their meat will last me for weeks. I was going to cook one of them for Christmas and invite you two."

I dry heave. "You're sick," I declare, then turn and dash out of this stinking den of death and dust.

"Jesus, Gary," Steven exclaims. "Claire, wait."

I don't slow down until I'm inside our house. My vision sways. I collapse onto our couch and put my head between my legs, gulping air. Clean air. Those poor geese.

Steven walks in and locks the front door. He steps closer, pauses, then plops down next to me. His hand rests on my back. "Well, that explains the smell. I'm not sure if it is illegal for him to eat them, but it is concerning." His palm travels in circles on my shoulder blade. "I'm sorry I didn't believe you. We won't go over there anymore. That… that was the line for me. But we will still be cordial to him."

I sit up and study his face, raising an eyebrow. He can't be serious. His expression remains passive. "You can stay friends with him, but I don't know if I can even talk to him ever again. You can't make me. That was gross. He's senile, Steven. He should be in an old folks' home. He smells as if he hasn't washed himself for weeks."

Steven nods once. "He needs to be checked out. Maybe we can get hold of a family member for him, or call in a non-profit service to evaluate his condition."

I stare at the empty wall across from us. Framed pictures are still leaning against it on the floor. Maybe this is a sign I should start repacking. We still have boxes in the garage to be recycled. Then my eyes wander to our carpeted hallway. The layout of Gary's house is like ours. Kitchen to the right and hallway to the left. "Did these houses get built around the same time? Do we have a cellar?"

He shrugs. "Our realtor didn't mention it, and I've yet to see a trapdoor like his. She said that Gary's house is the oldest and that the original landowner who built that house had sold off acres to developers."

I hug myself and lean back. "The electrician and bug guy didn't even ask to check the cellar or ask if we had one." Then I bolt upright. "Unless the Galloways disguised it as something? Maybe there's a separate electrical system in there that's gone off." Anything to foil this madness, to clean up this house, and to sell it as fast as possible. I don't want to live here anymore. I miss Montana, I miss Louisiana, I miss my parents, I miss familiar surroundings, and more importantly, I miss being unconcerned by my surroundings.

Steven taps his boot on the floor. "Interesting idea. Maybe it's under the house or near the porch, and the trapdoor got covered in mud. If the Galloways were as eccentric as they sound, perhaps they had one installed and the bank overlooked it in their haste to sell it."

"How do we find out if we have one?" Hope flares up in my chest. I hold tight to this sensation, knowing from the past two weeks that such moments are fleeting. Something else is bound to snuff out this glimmer of light.

Steven stretches and yawns. "Besides crawling around and tapping the ground with a hammer to find a hollow-sounding spot, which I don't want to do, we could go to the Deadwood planning office to get a blueprint of the property."

"I'll do that after work tomorrow," I volunteer. "But right now, I need to shower Gary's house off me."

I am not crazy.

20

I drive to work through milky wisps of morning fog on Thursday with the radio blasting a local station's morning talk show. Each DJ is trying to make the other laugh with jokes and farting sound effects. I prefer music, but this is effective in distracting my mind from thinking about butchered geese in Gary's basement. I'll make Steven ask Gary for a relative's phone number soon. We could use the excuse of wanting an emergency contact in case something happened to him and give him Steven's cellphone number. He sure as hell isn't getting mine.

A cold ball of orange light rises in the east above the frosted campus streets. Bodies scurry through the fog in front of me as I make my way to class.

"Mrs. Simmons? Mrs. Simmons?"

I freeze, glancing around, clutching my briefcase tighter with numb fingers, wishing I had worn gloves today. I don't recognize the voice.

A student runs up from behind an enormous evergreen further up the path. It's a young woman from the advanced physics class in the afternoon who sits in the front row. I relax my grip and stand straighter, pretending I wasn't just about to run away.

"Mrs. Simmons." She bends over, catching her breath. Then she straightens. "Can you talk to Professor Bayer on our behalf? We are all so far behind. Two of the students are talking about dropping the class since they expect to fail the final exam. I'm an excellent student, and I barely passed the midterm. We can't keep up."

I chew on my inner cheek and regard the woman. I remember she had tutoring with Danielle last week. I had overheard Danielle explain some rudimentary laws again, that if not memorized and understood, the rest of the semester would be like listening to a foreign language. I also remember being annoyed at how Danielle had flown through those crucial laws as if they weren't of any importance. "I've already mentioned something similar to her, but I will bring it up again."

The student grins. "Thank you, Mrs. Simmons. I knew you would understand. Just so you know, a few of us wish you were the teacher. We like how you explain things to students from other classes when we are tutoring with Professor Bayer."

My heart swells, but I maintain a stoic expression. A part of me has been worrying about my qualifications to even tutor since I have never taught before. I guess I can let that part go, but not how I've felt ostracized by the students of said classes. "That's very kind of you. But if you all feel that way, why do they always stare at me in class and never seek me out for tutoring?"

"Oh, well," she draws out, the tips of her ears red from embarrassment or cold. "Dr. Bayer instructed us to sign up with her to tutor us since you cover the lower classes and aren't as knowledgeable about the material. The hierarchy made sense, so we never questioned it. Sometimes we look at you, hoping that you will interject and advocate for us when she talks too fast, and Kerry and Tyler think you're hot." She shrugs when I blink at her, trying to digest her rapid firing. "Dr. Bayer said not to ask questions during class at the beginning of the year. I guess each of us had assumed the other had talked to you about the signal, and then assumed you didn't care or didn't think speaking up was necessary." Another shrug. Her gaze lowers.

"Hmm. In my defense, that rule was never told to me, nor have any of your classmates spoken up about any such signal. Also, it's hard to believe she said that knowing I have a doctorate of my own. I just chose not to go by the name Doctor Simmons. I'm worried it's too late. Like I said, I have noticed her teaching shortcomings and am trying to address them with tact. Don't give up yet, though." An idea occurs to me, and I pull out my cellphone. Perhaps the other professors were right all along about Danielle and her superiority complex. I believe I can still help these kids, though. "If you tell me your email address, I'll send you mine so you and others can shoot me questions you have. I'll check my email throughout the day and in class to help more."

The young lady beams and relays her email, then shifts her books around to check the time on her wristwatch. "Thank you so much, Mrs. Simmons. I need to get to my first class. What should I tell Kerry and Tyler? Can I give them your email for help also?"

I roll my eyes. "You tell them they may use my email for physics-related questions. I am happily married and don't appreciate being ogled. Go on, I'll see you in class."

*

Professor Danielle Bayer is not speaking to me. She's upset that I rearranged all the lessons for next semester so that they are in order with the book. I held my tongue while she lectured me about how I am wasting time we don't have. Then she stormed out of her office to class, not bothering to lock the door once I had followed behind.

I ate lunch in my car and stayed out of her office all day. When she still hadn't said a word to me after students left the last class, I strode up to her. "The students are becoming lost, Professor. I have highlighted the topics that are most asked about in tutoring." I point at the page I handed her, then gulp when she throws a glance full of daggers my way. "Please, Danielle."

She drops the page onto her desk. "If you hadn't noticed, I'm very busy with three classes a day, five days a week. Your job is just to do as I say, not to improve the way I teach. There is a reason I'm the teacher and you are the assistant."

Her venom doesn't have the desired effect. I was a student once and still remember the fear and anxiety of hard classes and believing that the professor didn't care about us. That small conversation with the student this morning solidified my confidence in my conviction. "Why don't you just copy this quarter's coursework?

Your new version is out of order based on the textbook's layout. You didn't miss any, but there are lessons that are too advanced early on."

Danielle runs a hand through her loose blond locks and sighs. "Because I'll become bored stiff if I don't customize what and when I teach, Claire. I'll teach all the laws and equations necessary for each lesson beforehand." She taps one of her gel nails to her temple, painted orange with brown leaves, a full set. Those can cost sixty dollars or more. I called the salon in town for a quote because I would love to have a fresh set of nail gels every two weeks, like I used to. But sixty dollars twice a month is too dear on my meager salary now. It makes me wonder what a professor's salary is. She waits until my eyes meet hers once more to continue. "Teaching is a test of patience and creativity. And attendance."

I bite my tongue. That was a dig at me. Though my gut tells me she'd lie, say she meant the students, if pressed. Annoyance engulfs me, and I seek a quick exit. "Message received. It's about four now. Mind if I take the rest of this stack of worksheets home to grade? I need to go to the planning office before it closes."

Danielle's fierce gaze melts. "Why? I mean, yes, you can leave. Have you started remodeling?"

Ah, nosiness. Juicy gossip for an afternoon snack. Danielle loves personal details; I've observed this multiple times while overhearing her conversations with others. Some people prefer to live vicariously.

Great, I'm delving into other psyches. I've been in therapy for too long. *This is just her switching to friend mode. But are we still friends?* I rub my palms on my hips. How can I condense everything without sounding like a lunatic? "Well, we talked to our neighbors about the, er, goings-on at our house. We found out that one of our neighbors has a cellar. That reminds me, I need to ask Mr. Devon, too." I shake my head to refocus. "Anyway, I got the idea that there is a hidden cellar at our place, and that's where the disturbances are emanating from."

"Who's Mr. Devon? Wouldn't the realtor have told you? Or the house inspector? Oh, Claire, tell me you and Steven didn't skip getting the house inspected before buying it?"

I pick up one foot to stand like a flamingo. "I— well, yes. Steven did everything. I wasn't here. Mr. Devon is our other neighbor."

"You didn't house hunt with Steven?" Her eyebrows rise. "That explains a lot."

"I was indisposed," I huff. The planning office will have to wait until tomorrow with all these questions.

Danielle nods. "Oh, because of the incident you

mentioned?"

"Yes." I twist a curl around my finger and mutter, "Not hurt physically—more mentally, err, emotionally, or well, my therapist and I are still trying to work it out…"

Danielle steeples her fingers. "Oh? You didn't mention the mental aspect before. You're not prone to rage or anything? You shouldn't ignore it. Especially if it is PTSD."

I watch the clock on the wall strike the hour. So much for going home early. But what she just touched upon has me curious. "You know about post traumatic stress disorder?"

Danielle nods like a bobblehead. "Oh, yes. My father developed it after coming home from Desert Storm."

"How does he cope?" I had read that symptoms vary from person to person, ranging from bad dreams to constant tremors and becoming nonverbal. No therapist ever mentioned that they suspected I suffered from it. What I'm experiencing is, well, to be determined, I suppose.

"It destroyed him. Destroyed us," Danielle whispers, her eyes glazing. Then she leans forward, and a strangled expression takes hold of her features, gray eyes boring into mine. "Don't let it destroy you too, Claire. Seek help before it's too late."

I gulp. "I, um, okay. I'll mention it to my therapist."

"You'd better go now before you miss the office," Danielle declares, one hand waving me away while the other dabs at her lower eyelids.

21

Steven arrives home with the usual clunking of his work belt onto the floor and groans as he pulls his work boots off. I take the wild rice off the stove and leave the fragrant lemon-pepper chicken to brown in the oven.

He walks over, pecks me on the cheek, and opens the fridge. "How was work?"

"Up and down," I admit. "An advanced student requested I tell Danielle to slow down during lectures, and I did. It didn't go over very well." I switch off the oven and open a drawer to get the oven mitts. "At least I found out why most students are staring at me. Some sort of code that is useless because no one informed me of it. I was getting worried those kids were siblings or kids of people from Rosebud Lab."

Steven gulps half of a blue Gatorade, then wipes his mouth. "It wouldn't matter anyway, even if they were. I can't imagine their opinions hold any sway in your employment. But let me guess, Danielle told you she knows better since she's the teacher?"

"How did you know?" The glass casserole dish containing the chicken slips through my grasp and clatters onto the counter. I flinch and then inspect the dish to make sure it didn't break.

"Even though Danielle seems nice, it's just a sense I get about her. Maybe it was the way she held her head or that nice car she drove when she came by," he says, placing two stacked plates near the still sizzling chicken. I toss the oven mitts aside and stare at him as he turns and pulls cutlery out of a nearby drawer. Steven always goes on about how we shouldn't judge others without getting to know them first, and here he is admitting that he did just that! He looks at me and shrugs. "It doesn't surprise me that's how she reacted. But it makes me worry about you."

I grab the cutlery from him and set it down on our napkins. "Why would her personality make you stress about me? So what if she wants to keep up with the life she has left behind? I would if we could afford it." All I want for Christmas is a pair of patent leather loafers, an alligator-skin briefcase, and a shiny new BMW. Who cares if I live in a small college town? I would cherish them, clean them, and wear them every day. Steven doesn't understand.

"Someday we will, honey. But my point is that I can envision her taking advantage of you. You idolize her, I can tell." He dishes chicken and then rice onto a plate. "Don't let her walk all over you. This is supposed to be a chill job until you get back on your feet."

I cackle at the absurdity, grab a plate and splat a piece of chicken onto it. The residual brown grease makes it slide across to the opposite edge. "What are you talking about? I am back on my feet with this job and building a temporary life here with you. I don't idolize her. I don't know if we are even friends still—if we ever were. It's becoming too hard to separate our friendship and work relationship. I just want to do a good job so I can get a good reference for a team leader position at a lab somewhere." I add a heaping spoonful of steaming rice to my plate and join him at the table. "I miss the lab environment. I miss the excitement, the unknown. These textbooks are all filled with everything I've already learned. It's like I'm stuck in college all over again."

Steven sets his Gatorade down. "Well, if you don't idolize her, then you admire her. You have the same level of education but act as if she is so much more intelligent. I worry. It's my right as your husband. I love you and don't want to see you get hurt."

We gaze at each other across the table. He thinks he understands, but he doesn't. Steven never rebuilds on the same job site or has to teach a class about how to do construction. Every day is a new challenge for him, just like it was at the lab for me. But seeing me miserable is what he is focusing on. I take a deep breath and slump back in my chair. "I know you worry about me. You wear it on your face all the time," I relent. "I am in awe of her, I'll admit. But her teaching style leaves a lot to be desired, and I don't know what else I can do as a teacher's assistant. I'm used to being in charge. I want to be on top again." I forgot to get a drink, but I don't know what I want. Water should be a priority, but it's so boring.

"Maybe there's nothing to do this year, honey. Wait until next semester. If the complaints become a pattern, then bring them up again." He shoves another mouthful of chicken and rice into his mouth. His plate is already half empty, and I haven't even taken my first bite. "Who knows? Maybe a teaching position will become available.

Math or more physics classes."

I nod, mentally rolling my eyes, and stand back up, resigning myself to drinking a glass of plain water like a mature adult. "Yeah, you're right. I'll do that." Steven loves me even though he doesn't understand my point of view. He cares about my health.

I am not crazy.

"Grab me a glass-uh water, if you don't mind?" Steven asks and scoots his chair back while I fill the glasses. "Oh, I wanted to ask you. Did you call an animal control company out here?"

I return to the table with our drinks. "No, there doesn't seem to be any point since the last two guys found nothing. Why?"

He gestures with his thumb behind his back. "There's an animal control van parked in front of Mr. Devon's place. The truck is facing us, and I saw two guys sitting in the front seat when I drove up. Maybe the neighbors are having some kind of issue now?"

"Are they still out there?" I set down my fork. Maybe the animal control people will have some answers for us. What if Mr. Devon deceived us? What if there is something wrong in the entire neighborhood, but the neighbors are keeping it under wraps so their property values don't fall? I've heard my friends and parents talk about things like that. I stand up. We need answers. Or a lead. Something. Steven covers his mouth, full of food, and mutters something.

I ignore him and hurry to the front door, fling it open, and run outside. The pavement is cold and wet. Sharp pebbles poke into my feet the entire length of the driveway.

The van is gone.

I stand in the middle of the road, my shoulders drooping.

Every time I get my hopes up, they evaporate.

"Honey, please come inside," Steven yells from the porch.

I hop back to him, my feet protesting at all the foreign objects digging into my soft soles.

Steven frowns when he opens the screen door for me. "If you had waited for me to swallow my bite, you wouldn't have needed to run out barefoot. I was trying to say that they had probably left by now, but I saw the name on the side of the van when I glanced over on my way inside. Deadwood Animal Control."

I sit on the couch, listening, swiping embedded pebbles and a few thorns from my cold, wet feet. "Ah. I'll find a phone number. They wouldn't have a reason to hide anything from us."

"Hide anything? Who's hiding information from you?" His eyebrows furrow, and he points to the kitchen. "Go eat your dinner first. You haven't eaten a single forkful yet."

"I'm not hungry anymore," I argue and stand.

Steven spreads his arms, blocking my way to the hallway. "No. Please eat something first. It's excellent. You seasoned the chicken perfectly."

Why did he tell me the name if he didn't want me to keep searching for answers? He's acting like I'm starving myself, which I've never done. I run my tongue over my upper teeth and give him a hard stare. "Fine. I'll eat first. But we have to be proactive about this before it gets on top of us. I don't want to miss any more work." Then I stomp back to the kitchen.

I expect Steven to follow me, to argue his case, whatever it may be, but he doesn't. Instead, his footsteps retreat down the hallway. I swallow a mouthful and gulp down some water while I run through scenarios. The neighbors might all be conspiring together against us. Maybe they ran the Galloways off, too. Is there something valuable on our land? Does our house sit on an oil field?

Steven walks into the dining room, holding my laptop. His face remains neutral as he sets it on the counter and clears his side of the table. I watch through my lowered lashes and nibble on another piece of chicken, pretending I'm less interested than I am. After all, he is welcome to use my laptop anytime.

As if he can sense me near bursting with curiosity, the side of his mouth ticks up and his eyes twinkle when they meet mine. "I'm looking them up while you eat."

My eyes widen, and I nod, understanding. My handsome, sweet, caring husband. Bless his big heart. He understands, at least, my anxiety surrounding the house. I eat faster while he types and clicks. Every once in a while, he leans forward and squints, then leans back, but says nothing.

Why isn't he saying what he's found? Is there a damning article or page about critters in our area? Are the animal control people reporting something more sinister? A mutant lab-grown raccoon programmed to destroy our property? After what I've seen, I don't discount the possibility.

I finish eating, then rip plastic wrap off in large squares, covering the leftovers in their cooking vessels, and chuck them into the fridge. When I twist back around, Steven is closing the laptop. Post-it Notes within his reach have nothing written on them. "Didn't you find a phone number or email?" I step toward him. "An address?"

He slumps back and rubs his eyes. "Nope. I can't find the page or an address. Nothing," he reiterates. "I can't find the company. I must have gotten it wrong. The parked van was at an angle." Steven jostles his chair back and stands, yawning. "I'll try to keep an eye out tomorrow. Maybe I'll ask my coworkers if they've seen them. I'm assuming you'll be doing the same?" He closes one eye and peers at me.

I giggle. "Yes, One-Eyed Simmons." Then I drop my smile. "I'm not crazy. And neither are you. We must find the cause of all this nonsense if we are to clean this place and sell it."

Steven opens his other eye, his lips slack, and gives a reluctant nod. "Yeah, I guess I was just envisioning us here longer, you know, since I plan to put some blood, sweat, and tears into remodeling it. It's got good bones. Perhaps just a haircut will allow us to put it back on the market for more and go back to living in an apartment for a while. The ones we are building are nice. I know we are not crazy, just dog-tired." He grabs the laptop and trudges past me. "I know I am."

Later in bed, I stay sitting up against my pillow, rewinding our conversation. Steven had sounded so sad, so dejected, talking about selling this place. But it's just a house. Not a home. At least not for me. I pull the sheets up to my chest and glance toward the wall where Buzz showed himself. There is no way for me to know where he will pop up next. While I'm on the toilet? Or scrubbing the kitchen floor? Or while Steven and I are making love? Where is the line for Steven? How long can I go on living like this, being the only one to see Buzz? Glancing over, Steven has his eyes closed, his breaths slowing, measured like they always do before he falls asleep. I wiggle down so that my face is next to his and whisper an olive branch. "Maybe they are new in town and a neighbor has a number, but it's not yet listed. Maybe they'll take care of all the crows. There were tons of them in one tree when I got home."

Steven grunts and turns over, his back to me. "You're probably right," he mutters.

I need to be right. Because I am not crazy.

22

Someone has unzipped my scalp and replaced my brain with a twenty-pound bowling ball. It's leaden on the pillow, and my body is warm and cocooned under the blankets. I remember someone in my dream calling my name, but I can't remember who. Steven? Buzz?

Steven's voice rises, short sentences spurting. The sound of glass cracking. Steven cursing. I stick my nose above the sheets and glance around. What's he mad about? What broke? Rain lashes the windows. I roll into a seated position and rub my eyes. Steven curses louder. What is his problem? It's cold, so maybe the heater stopped working. I reach for my phone, but it's not on my nightstand.

That's weird. I remember placing it there before turning off the lamp.

I scoot out of bed and shiver. Did Steven forget to check the pilot light before bed? I fumble through the dark toward the dresser. Steven flips on the hallway light, and it blinds me for a moment. As my eyes adjust, I can make out that the little hand is on the three on my watch. Why the hell is Steven up in the middle of the night?

My stomach drops. Something else has gone wrong with the house. There are no bugs surging around my feet, so I perk my ears to listen for the telltale buzzing. But there's nothing audible besides Stevens' grumbling. I sniff the air, but there is no smoke or rotten-egg odor of a gas leak.

I shuffle out of the room, trying to suppress a yawn. "Why are you up? It's three o'clock. Come back to bed."

He appears at the end of the hallway, already dressed, his hair sticking up in every direction. There's a picture frame in his hand. "It's ten! Why are you still not dressed? We're so late for work!" he cries, waving his hands. "And I can't find my phone to call my boss." He turns and stomps out of view. "I didn't jot his number down."

"But my watch says it's only three," I say. I am so tired. I wouldn't be this tired if I had not slept in that late. That's when I notice the rest of the picture frames. They are all face down on the floor instead of leaning against the wall. What happened last night while we slept?

A couch cushion hits the wall by the television. "It's ten, Claire. Both our watches slowed, and your phone's alarm didn't go off." Another cushion flies. "There it is." He runs over, almost colliding with me. "I found my phone. Here's yours. I had grabbed it to call mine." He runs to the kitchen. "Crap! I don't have time for this."

I remain frozen in place, now with my cellphone in hand. The time flashes up at me. 10:10. How did we sleep so late? Did the weather do this to our watches? Some weird electrical storm? But how does it slow or drain a watch battery? What made the pictures fall down?

This had to have been Buzz's doing. He's still here, baiting us, taking his time, torturing me and Steven until we croak from stress.

I rush to the kitchen where Steven is leaning over the counter on his phone, talking to someone with the charging cord stuck into the bottom.

"Yeah, I'm on my way," he says into his phone. "Thank you." Then he hangs up. "My supervisor is letting this slide since I work my ass off every day."

I offer my phone. "Take this to work to use since it's charged. Go. I'll use your phone while it's charging and ask if I can still go in."

He nabs it and runs, yelling, "Thanks, honey. I'll text you later."

I rub my eyes and run into the other bedroom, where I have all our important phone numbers written. Searching through the scribbles, I find the office administration number and bound back to the kitchen.

After a rushed explanation, the not-so-patient secretary says I can still show up and get half a day's pay. I message Danielle, explaining that I'm using Steven's phone and I will be there soon. Then I yank on yesterday's pants, a fresh shirt and the first sweater my hand touches in the closet. A pair of socks and my loafers are next. To the wall of the bedroom I say, "Buzz, that was a jerk move. I don't know who sent you, but you have crossed a line. I'm no longer scared. I'm mad. I'm coming for you now." There's no time for applying makeup or proper hair care, so I grab a claw clip to hold my unruly curls back, snatch my briefcase and Steven's phone with the charger attached, and sprint to my car.

23

I arrive on campus at ten thirty. It takes another few minutes to find a parking spot in the full faculty lot and sprint to the science building with my small umbrella, which is of little help against the torrential downpour being blown every which way.

"I'm so sorry," I declare, bursting into Danielle's office, dripping onto the carpet.

Danielle holds up a hand without looking up from what she is writing. "I messaged you not to bother coming in. We don't do half days."

"But the office cleared me to work a half-day. I already used the time clock. Please hear me out," I say, and approach her desk. I inhale and hold my breath for a moment, trying to slow my thumping pulse. "My watch slowed, and my phone alarm didn't go off. Steven's phone died, so he took mine. I didn't get that text." I clutch the edge of the desk and gulp down air, still recovering from the strain of the elements that fought my every step outside.

Danielle heaves a sigh. Her mauve lips thin, and her charcoal-lined gray eyes narrow. "Claire, I am trying to cover for you the best I can, but the office is receiving complaints from my students. Your absences are affecting my ability to do my job and reflecting poorly on me. I'm not calling you a liar, but both those problems sound like something a student would come up with for missing a test. If the dean gets wind of this, another semester's position won't be available to you. I've heard of it happening before."

"I understand." *I understand those complaints are about you, not me.* But regardless of what I know to be true, it's far outweighed by what I don't know. That very thought brings tears to my eyes. I'm losing control of my life, and for the first time, I'm not sure how to get back up. I decide to plead with Danielle, to speak to her better—friendlier—side. "But you believe me, don't you? You saw the state the yard is in. We still haven't discovered what is causing these anomalies. I won't have the blueprints of the house for another week. You understand bureaucratic red tape and slowness, right?"

Her eyebrow rises; her frown deepens. "Perhaps you and Steven should stay at the campus hotel during bad weather. You'd be closer to work."

"I'm not sure that would help," I mumble. Why can't she just believe me? I'm not crazy.

"Why not? It makes perfect sense," Danielle says. Her eyebrow lowers, the frown set in stone.

I lick my lips and count to three before speaking. "Two reasons. One, we can't afford it. And two, well… Do you believe in ghosts?"

Danielle scoffs. "This again? Don't be absurd, Claire. You're a scientist. You need to keep your rational brain on."

"You're right. I know." I pace in front of her desk, sifting, sorting through the ludicrous and rational thoughts. "It sounded absurd just saying it, but there is a reason I can't dismiss that theory yet. Please, I need a distraction. Just let me work the rest of the day? You can call the office. They cleared me. They allow half-days, I swear. At least today they did." Ew, now I'm outright begging. This is not who I am. After work, I'm going to find our hidden basement. A ghost can't cause an entire house to buzz and make birds fall from the sky and drain batteries and slow time. Unless Buzz *is* from the lab. A lab-grown ghost primed for our military to use. And I'm the human guinea pig. Too bad I don't have any remaining friends at Rosebud to ask around for me.

"Fine. Alright. If they cleared you. I don't understand why they are giving you such preferential treatment, though," Danielle announces. I shake myself out of the insane spiral my thoughts are taking. Danielle gestures to me with a pen. "I canceled my scheduled tutoring today since I have a staff meeting at the head office, but you can still tutor without me, right?"

My nostrils expand and contract in my effort not to snarl. I give a curt nod and reach for Steven's phone. I've tutored two students at once, so if I borrow the student contact-sheets found in Danielle's file cabinet and send out a mass text for all students in advanced physics wanting tutoring, they can meet me in the library later. I can prove my worth to them. Danielle won't ever have to know.

*

Steven messages me, saying that the phone battery is dying, so I may not get another message. Then he asks if I got to work. I reply with a simple yes.

Danielle gives me the silent treatment for the rest

of the day. Her dark glare says it all when students beam at me when they pop into her office for tutoring. A few inquire about my health and how happy they are that I am here. I want to explain to them that it's rude to act like that when the professor is sitting not six feet away, clearly listening in by the way she averts her gaze when I glance her way.

When four o'clock rolls around, I rest in my car for a minute before driving away. The tension emanating from Danielle was suffocating. Tutoring struggling students had felt like torture instead of a relaxing exercise. I swear Danielle was staring at me when I wasn't looking. She had replanted herself at her desk after classes, announcing the staff meeting rescheduled. I had rushed an apology email to all the advanced students, explaining Danielle was available for tutoring after all and I could not escape to the library, only for Danielle to turn away every student that came in asking for help. Both she and the dismissed students throw dirty looks my way. It's true I should have asked Danielle if she was answering questions upon returning, but the blatant hostility is immature. If this continues through the final, I may have to find the courage to request a transfer to work for another professor. That would mean assisting a professor in a different subject. I would miss physics. Perhaps an advanced math professor would be an enjoyable challenge. I exhale, filling my cheeks before blowing out like a cartoon cloud. It all comes back to our house. Fix that, and the rest will follow.

There's a note on our front door written in pencil on a torn piece of paper. I rip it off right before I shut the door. Television programs highlighting kidnappings have taught me never to have my back turned to the world while distracted by something on my car or house door. Once inside, I stand my umbrella up in the corner to dry and flip on the floor lamp to read the note.

In shaky handwriting, it states that Steven called Gary from work and Steven would be late home since work was allowing him to make up the lost hours. At the bottom of the note, Gary apologizes once more for his actions. He hopes we can still be friends.

Not me. Steven can if he wants. But not me. I reread the note about Steven. It sounds like my phone died, and he had to borrow the office phone or another cell phone. It makes me wonder how Steven got Gary's number. Maybe it's listed.

I glance around. The pictures are still face down on the floor. It's quiet, and I'll be alone for a few hours. That's good. First, I'll stack all the picture frames in the spare bedroom, and then test out our latest theory: I'm going to use Steven's hammer and tap along the walls and floors in search of a trapdoor. I might even find the courage to peek into the attic. What if the Galloways put the entrance up there with a ladder between the walls to get down into the cellar? If Steven could stomp around up there for minutes on end, I can at least peek inside. With a quick internet search, I'll know what to look for to uncover a hidden door in plain sight.

*

"Claire? Claire? Honey, where are you?" Steven calls.

His boots thud along the back deck, so I crawl toward the sound. "I'm down here," I call out, then sneeze.

He runs down the steps, and his boots and legs appear in front of me through the opening in the wood paneling that's supposed to keep critters out from under the house. I may have "helped" the opening a bit by prying a couple more panels off so I could fit easier, figuring that with so much of the wood rotted away, stained green from years of moss and algae growth, we will have to rebuild this part of the deck at some point, anyway.

"What are you doing under there? It's dangerous. You could get tetanus from a rusty nail.

The opening to get under here is at the front of the house. Why didn't you use that entrance? Can you get out?" Steven crouches down until his face appears.

I've been under the house with a flashlight and a hammer for a while now. There was no unusual hollow sound that might hint at a secret door inside, including the attic, so in my frustration, I crawled to search for a door at ground level. But my search has been in vain.

I crawl toward him until I reach his outstretched hands. The ground has stayed dry considering all the rain, but my hands and knees have found a few wet puddles. I've been breathing through my mouth and trying not to think about what I am crawling through and breathing in. I hand over the filthy flashlight and hammer. He sets them aside and reaches back under to help me the rest of the way out.

When I stand up, he examines me. I glance down, too. Mud cakes my hands and knees. Grime smears my pants and orange running shoes. My shirt has spatters of mud and cobwebs. I haven't been this dirty since boot camp.

He rolls his lips. "I'm afraid to ask what you were doing under there, so I'm not, since you look to be in one piece. Let's get you cleaned up. Next time, wear a dust mask and gloves. God knows what's under there."

I grin sheepishly and trudge up the deck stairs. "Nothing much. Remember how we will get the blueprint in two to four weeks?" I pause by the back door to pull my sneakers off. "I got impatient."

Steven scratches his forehead. "And you found nothing."

"Of course not. This house is a conundrum," I say, scrunching my nose as I get a whiff of something sour on my sleeve. Buzz can live another day.

24

I stand on the deck in my socks, still warm from my exertion under the house, even while the temperature dips. Heavy mist presses into my face and hair as I stare out, trying to take in details I may have missed before. The length and breadth of our backyard is like a foreboding swamp in an evil forest. Sodden bare tree limbs hang low from young, scraggy saplings in the middle of the yard and from larger oaks and firs around the perimeter after years of neglect. Clumps of crabgrass not swallowed by large mud puddles stick up like the spiked haircuts popular in the early 2000s. Creeping vines stretch out from the back property fence, reaching for a new foothold to anchor themselves, a new victim to strangle. Our simple four-sided shed, made of wooden boards weathered to a dark gray and green with algae like the deck, sags to the right under the weight of overgrown foliage.

"Come inside, honey," Steven calls from the kitchen.

I turn to go inside, but freeze halfway, whipping my head back toward the fence. Something just moved back there. A shadow, a form, *something* that wasn't a vine or branch. There's no wind.

"The shed!" I shout and shove my feet back into my sneakers, hopping around to maintain balance. How could we all have overlooked it? "Steven! The electrician! He didn't check back there!"

Steven steps outside just as I snatch the flashlight lying on the deck chair and catapult myself toward the shed. I'm already covered in mud, so what's a little more? And there's still just enough light from the setting sun somewhere behind the cloud cover to ward off my fear of what lurks back there in the dark.

I slow down halfway across the yard. These puddles are like quicksand, clinging to my sneakers until I yank each step forward. Water seeps through my socks, cold and unforgiving. The door to the shed is ajar. That must have been the movement I saw. But didn't Danielle say it's locked up? Didn't I see a lock? Where did the padlock go?

"Be careful not to touch the poison ivy," Steven shouts. I glance behind me to see him on the deck steps, and I motion for him to follow me. He shakes his head. "Why don't we pick the search up tomorrow? I'm exhausted."

I wave him away and thunder back, "Then go back inside. There's a frozen lasagna we can make for dinner. I have to see for myself. Danielle is upset with me for losing work. I have to figure this out now."

"You claimed Danielle understood," he yelled back, crossing his arms. "You insisted on missing work, Claire. Not me."

"I know. I'm not saying you did. Please, I need to figure this out. I can't—*We* can't stay here if this ghost keeps haunting me," I argue. My hand clenches the flashlight harder. The rain is picking up, with rivulets running down my forehead.

"Ghost? I thought we agreed it's just your anxiety causing hallucinations?"

My teeth grind together as I pull my foot from the soft mud the shoe is sinking into and move to a clump of grass. With my free hand, I wipe water out of my eyes. This soaked, dirty t-shirt I'm wearing is as thin as my nerves, and my anger boils over. "How can you say that? You've experienced the same things I have. You even gave the entity a name. Buzz, remember? What if the previous owners hadn't fled? What if they died in their bunker and are haunting us? What if they booby-trapped this house? We might need to move out."

Steven holds up a hand. "Claire. Stop, please. No, we can't afford that. I will make this work. There will be a logical explanation. We will figure it out. But not tonight. Come back. You'll catch a cold. We have all weekend to work on this."

I shake my head. "I'm not coming in yet."

"Fine. Do whatever you want. I'm taking a shower," Steven yells, throwing up his hands. He then turns and goes back inside.

Great, now on top of everything, I've started a fight. But he doesn't understand how this is affecting me. Sure, Steven says he understands, but how can he when he hasn't seen Buzz and the similarities between the entity of Buzz and what I saw that night in the bowels of the physics building? What if what I saw in Montana was an experiment on the supernatural? What if my brain can't comprehend what's there, so all I get is a fuzzy shape? What if Buzz is one of the dead owners and they need help to be laid to rest?

With my resolve strengthened, I lower my head and slog the rest of the way to the shed.

I yank back the door, not caring if it breaks off the ancient hinges, and point the white beam of my flashlight straight ahead to illuminate the small space. Shadows elongate from rusted garden tools and dense clusters of gray cobwebs in the corners and dangling from the ceiling. I sweep the light across the floor to illuminate a large dirt-encrusted carpet square; the same brown shade as in the house, which lies at an angle across the floor, as if someone had just thrown it down and never thought to straighten it.

I sweep the light back towards me. Bingo. A cutout square flush with the wooden floorboards, complete with a frayed piece of rope threaded through holes on one side for a handle. I step toward it, steeling my nerves. God only knows what awaits.

A low buzz tickles my ears. "Not this time, ghost," I growl and grab the rope.

Suddenly, my vision swims, and the room vibrates. A rake falls forward onto me. I shove it off and stare at the trapdoor while holding my hands out to steady myself. I can't tell whether the room or I am swaying. In my peripherals, I spy two shadows rise from the corner.

"No," I shout. "What do you want? Let me help you."

The buzzing increases. Just like last time, and the time before that, one hundred bees becomes one thousand in my ears. I drop the flashlight—the reassuring beam cuts off from the impact—and hold my head.

Keep it together, Claire.

This is for my sanity. For my job. For my marriage.

I fall to my knees. The impact makes my teeth clack together, and I yank the trapdoor open. A concrete foundation greets me. I scream. Foiled again! I slam my hands down on it, over and over, trying to break through. My hands are slick with a dark substance that smears the gray surface where my fists land. The shadows inch closer, reaching.

"Where are you?" I scream, scrunching my eyes shut against the abusive buzzing and hungry shadows. "What do you want from me?"

Hands seize me under my armpits and haul me onto my feet and backwards out of the shed.

"Let me go!" I shout. "Let me go!"

The hands jostle me. I gasp and open my eyes. At once, the buzzing stops. My hands sting. My vision doubles, then clears. I focus on the figure standing nearby. Gary hovers near a tree. I point at him and screech, "You! Don't move, Gary. What did you do to them? Did you cement them in?"

He grasps the tree trunk and shakes his head.

That's when I notice my hand and draw it to my face in horror. It's covered in blood, mud and grime from under the house. I hold up my other hand. It has suffered the same fate. I watch them tremble.

Iron fingers clamp down on my elbow, squeezing muscles and tendons together. I jerk my head up. Steven looms over me with furrowed brows and a deep frown. A fury darkens his gaze. "Stop. Gary swung by to check on us. We heard your scream and came running."

Steven releases me, and I slump into his chest as a strangled sob escapes me. I cry out, "They're going to get me, Steven. There were two enormous shadows in there reaching for me. They're here trying to get me."

Steven maneuvers his arms around my shoulders, steadying me since my legs have turned to jelly. "Let's get you inside."

I point back at the shed. "The shed. They're in the shed. There's a trapdoor, but it's filled in. Did you see them? Did you see their ghosts?"

"You were the only one in there," Steven says, tugging me back toward the house. Our shoes make sickening sucking sounds as they pull free of the mire with each step. I rub my face against his work shirt. He smells of sweat and dirt. Comforting, real.

"You didn't see the shadows with their reaching hands?" I press. They were so close. The temperature dropped the moment I stepped foot into that shed. The buzzing had begun as if on cue.

"Is she okay? Should I call an ambulance?" Gary's voice wobbles from nearby.

"No," Steven says before I can open my mouth to shriek at the old man again. "Thanks for checking on us, Gary. I'll pop by tomorrow to chat if I have time." There's a finality in his tone that's not lost on Gary, and he scurries away around the side of the house.

25

Steven pushes me down into a dining chair. He sets his phone next to mine, and I grab for one, but he places a hand over mine and presses it to the table. I wince at the pressure on my open wounds. He lets go. "You just sit. Do you want me to call Dr. Sternan?"

"No. Oh, Steven, I'm so tired," I cry, and lay my head down on the cool wood of the table. Exhaustion creeps down my limbs like a phantom wave, pulling them down, down. "I just want this all to stop."

"I know, honey." He rubs my arm.

I lift my head and see a trail of blood and mud from my hands smearing the tabletop. My stomach somersaults. "You really didn't see them?" Tears build behind my eyelids. My palms ache from pounding on the concrete. Blood has dried on my knuckles, stiffening the skin.

"No, I didn't." The *'don't upset her any more than she already is'* look is back; his voice tight. "I think weird wiring or something similar is still to blame. Your anxiety is blowing it out of proportion. But I have some good news. I stopped by the military surplus store on my lunch break. He's going to search through his records to see if he wrote anything down about what he sold to the Galloways. I'm trying to help, Claire. I really am."

Tears leak down my cheeks. How do I make him understand I'm not some broken doll? I was so sure I had figured it out. So close. "I know. But what if they are ghosts, and since I walked into the lab—what if that was their experiment? Trying to contact the dead? What if there was some sort of radiation that has opened my mind up to being able to see ghosts now?" I wipe my eyes with my forearm. If Steven hasn't learned that I never give up by now, he's about to. "We need to call a paranormal team out here right away. In fact, I snapped a picture of a number off the campus community board on my way out of the building today." I reach for my phone.

Steven stays my hand at the wrist. He turns it

over, inspecting my scrapes. "You know what? Why don't you enjoy a hot shower first or a nice bubble bath? I gather you came away from this dirtier than I am from working all day. I'll help you bandage your hands if you need it afterward."

I chuckle like a madwoman and peer down at my lap. Mud and cobwebs have painted a grotesque picture on my pants. I nod, conceding. A crypt would smell better than these clothes right now.

He rubs my arm. "I'll get dinner going, and then wash up in the sink here. You shouldn't be pushing yourself this hard. We will do whatever you want, but tomorrow, okay? Please, Claire?"

I nod, my throat tightening. The way he says please always breaks my heart, drawn out, whispered. In a whisper, I force out, "I'm sorry I'm such a wreck. I can't explain how, but I have a target on my back, Steven. I'm trying to heal, but every time I get better, I get slammed back. It's like God is flipping an on-and-off switch for bad things to happen to me since the lab incident. Why can't Rosebud Facility just admit they were running some sketchy experiments? I wouldn't go to the press. I just want this all to stop. I need a break. I'm tired of being traumatized."

Every movement hurts, making me grit my teeth as the raw skin on my fingers comes into contact with the shower knob and bending down to pull up the spout toggle that diverts the water up to the shower head. Hot water pelts down at an angle, pounding the tiled wall. I watch it drain, showing no signs of a backup from a bug influx. Next, I glance at the shower caddy on the wall. Hair products? Check. Soaps and scrubbers? Check. Shaving products, if I choose to bother? I need a new razor. Razor burn with an uneven trim is not what I need on top of everything else.

The extra razors are in our hallway closet. I pull the door open. Steven's voice floats toward me. Tiptoeing into the living room, I eavesdrop.

"No, nothing like that. Nothing to see… Yes, definitely obsessive… Will it be strong enough? … Just one? … Okay. Yes. I will. Thank you. Goodnight."

I tiptoe back to the closet. He's consulting with someone. But about what and with whom? What does he mean, obsessive? Is he talking about me? I'll confront him after I'm clean. I want to know what someone is suggesting will be strong enough. Maybe it was my mom giving advice on how many bundles of sage to burn. Or someone from work advising how to break through the concrete in the shed.

I hurry to shampoo my hair twice, praying that the ghosts don't sneak up when I have to close my eyes for a few seconds. The constant hissing through my teeth as soap and water sting my cuts makes me sound like a pissed-off snake. It's like the pain is a scolding reminder of how I became unhinged, thwarted again by something or someone from the past. But whose past? And why?

I shake my head, continuing the internal monologue while I dress. Anger replaces anxiety. Who knew that becoming a homeowner would be such a messy and terrifying business?

When I emerge from the bathroom, it's dark in the house save for a few lamps on. The curtainless front window is a black, gaping maw, threatening to swallow me into the cold, wet night beyond. I shiver, squinting, searching. What lurks where I can't see? Who—man or creature—is looking back at me?

"We need to cover this window."

"I know," he says, right behind me.

I flinch, then turn to him with a sheepish grin. He hands me a glass of red wine. I blow him a kiss and step around him, heading to the kitchen. I haven't forgotten his secret phone call. Should I bring it up or give him a chance to? There's a good chance that he's got a reasonable explanation. But the suspicion in my gut says otherwise. Momma says I should always listen to my woman's intuition. It's our superpower, and God doesn't want us to waste it.

I tap my nail on the side of the wineglass and glance around the kitchen and dining room. There's an open beer sitting next to a frozen lasagna on the counter. My stomach growls.

"You haven't started cooking the lasagna yet?" I seethe, side-eyeing him.

"No," Steven says with an air of nonchalance. "The oven is still warming."

The oven takes twenty minutes to heat. My shower lasted at least half an hour. Plus the time to dry off, dress, and apply first aid. Everything took longer with two hurt hands. One or two phone calls before turning the oven on would explain it. I huff and step toward the dining table, where both our phones are. "Then don't bother. I'd rather just skip it and make a sandwich." I pick up a phone without looking, purposely grabbing his phone, and scroll into his recent call log.

"Claire, that's my cellphone." His tone is no longer casual, volume no longer hushed. It's not lost on me that he called me by my name instead of "Honey", and I also didn't miss the almost panicked edge, the speed at which he spoke. He holds out one hand to me and points to my phone on the table with the other.

I shrug, hand the phone back to him once I click back onto the home screen, and fake giggle into my wineglass, taking a large swig. "Oh, whoops. That's why nothing was familiar. Guess I'm deeper into this wine than I thought."

A smile wavers on his lips, then he drops it and looks down, focusing on his scrolling. I lean against the counter and take another long sip.

"I was trying to make sure I had saved Danielle's cell number in my contacts. What's the unsaved phone number in your call log?"

Steven's eyebrows furrow. "Dunno. I use my phone for work sometimes," he mumbles.

I lick my upper teeth. "The area code was from Montana." Then I bolt upright and set my wineglass down on the counter. "Steven, I know that number." Even though my stomach is growling and my eyelids are heavy, I will wait all night for him to admit who he called. I have stamina. I was a soldier. I know that number. I call or receive a call from it once a week.

Steven sighs and pockets his phone. He sits and glances at me. "I won't lie. I called Dr. Sternan."

"Why? Concerning what?" I cross my arms. How could a psychiatrist help with a ghost haunting?

Steven waves a hand toward the backyard. "Concerning what you saw out there."

"Oh, Steven, tell me you didn't say the word ghost to her?" I groan. Steven stares at me. The confirmation is in his eyes. Yet, there is no regret. He doesn't know what he's done! I place my face in my bandaged hands. "Oh my God. She's going to have me locked up in an insane asylum!" I howl. "What were you thinking?"

I yawn, my jaw extending to its limit. I could sleep for days. "Whoa, either I'm having a panic attack or the ghosts are trying something else." I reach my hands out, my eyelids fluttering; it takes every ounce of concentration just to stay upright. Steven's form looms over me, his hands grip my shoulders. I grasp his shirt. "Call her back right now." Another yawn. "I can't deal with this. Call her and make this right." Yawn. My eyelids flutter shut. "We are so close to the truth." Yawn. "I can't…"

Steven scoops me up in his arms, kisses my forehead, and says, "Let's get you into bed."

I sense my body being laid down and snuggle into my pillow; it dips to the enormous weight of my head. He pulls the sheets, still cool from the icy night air, over me, and the world falls away.

26

I wake in a puddle of drool on my pillow, disorientation causing my heart rate to speed up. I claw the sheets off me, forcing my gritty eyes open. Gray light swathes the bedroom. A door bangs shut in the distance. I swing my right arm over and grasp my phone to figure out if it's day or night.

The bedroom door creaks open. Steven pokes his head in. "Ah, it did wake you. Sorry about the noise. The cupboard door got away from me. How are you?"

I use my forearms to prop myself up. "Like I drank too much."

He walks over and nudges mushed, frizzy curls out of my face. His chocolate eyes peer into mine.

"Maybe you just overslept a tad. It'll wear off. Do you want breakfast or lunch? It's noon."

"Ugh. Coffee. No food," I groan. Then my stomach growls in protest. Steven tilts his head and stares at my torso. His eyebrows rise. I heave myself up. "Maybe coffee and a bowl of cereal."

Steven smirks. "Okay, sleeping beauty," he says, and pushes me playfully back onto the bed, then leaves the room. I grumble and shuffle after him to the kitchen, switching on the coffee machine while he gets a bowl from the cupboard.

"How much did I drink last night?" I grab the Captain Crunch and slump down into a dining chair.

He shrugs and sets down a bowl and spoon before me. "A bit. You had a bad day. I'll get the milk."

I pour cereal and stare at the dry, sugary shapes. Why did I have a bad day yesterday? I glance up at Steven as he sets a cup of coffee and the milk jug in front of me. He smiles. It couldn't have been that bad if he's smiling. *Come on, brain. Just once, help me out.* I glance behind me, out the window beyond the deck, and spot the shed, its door gaping, a dark interior daring those brave enough to enter. Everything comes flooding back like a slap in the face. I whip my head around. "Did you call Dr. Sternan? What did she say? Where's my phone?"

I'm up and running to the bedroom. Steven is on my heels.

"Claire, wait," he pleads behind me.

I grab my phone off the nightstand and open my contacts. Dr. Sternan has to hear my side of things before she calls the men in white coats. I just hope it's not too late.

"Please, honey, sit down. Maybe coffee isn't the best for you right now. You had a fright. Let's go slow today."

I spin around and glare at him. "Slow? No, if anything, we should work faster. Neither of us can afford to lose any more work because of this haunting. We have to solve this before anything else happens." My finger hovers over the call button under Dr. Sternan's name. I'm not crazy, just haunted. That's all. That would explain everything. I thought it was a being from the lab, but confused what I thought I saw with an actual haunting here in my home by the previous owners.

Steven clasps his hands. "Claire. Your alarm not going off was a fluke. It's not a ghost. We've both had to start new jobs in a new city. We're tired. These things happen. I hadn't even plugged in my phone the night before, remember? If the events were an effect of the same thing, they would have happened every morning."

I want to step back from him, distance myself,

but I'm stuck. The bed and wall are behind me, Steven in front. He's not trying to comprehend what I can. "Are you serious? All of this is happening because the energy, or entity, is escalating, strengthening." His eyes remain blank. But the concern deepens on his forehead. I try again. "How can you be so blind? It's the only explanation." I shoulder past him and stomp out of the room. He doesn't resist, but follows, like a hound trying to figure out a scent. My anger boils. "If you will not help me, and do shit behind my back like call my therapist, then I'll figure this out on my own," I snap.

"Claire," he pleads. "Please calm down."

"I'm not speaking to you right now," I say and stomp back to the bedroom to get dressed. Dr. Sternan can wait. I need to get the paranormal team out here.

There's a gentle tap at the bedroom door. Though it's open, Steven doesn't enter; he leans in the doorway. "Please eat your bowl of cereal, or a banana. Something. I'm concerned about you, honey. You need to eat something. Dr. Sternan was very understanding and offered that all you needed was a good night's rest. I promised I would help you search for answers today. I'm in the middle of something in the garage, but when I'm finished, I will inspect the shed. Okay?"

I regard him. My stomach growls as if in agreement. Had I overreacted? Was this the hangover talking and not the rational scientist in my mind? I've been wrong before. "Okay, I'll eat. But I'm not going out there again. Maybe take the rosemary candle to burn in the shed to protect yourself. I'm going to call that paranormal group, regardless."

Steven nods, his lips in a thin line, and takes a step back. He mumbles about re-grouting in the bathroom and walks back down the hall. I stare out the window, past the soggy, overgrown front lawn and to the tumultuous skies above. Thunder growls, but no lightning flashes; the eye of the storm isn't overhead yet. A large white van rolls by. I just make out the Deadwood Animal Control sticker along the side.

"Hey!" I shout. "There's the animal control van. Maybe they can tell us something." I dash out of the house barefoot, still in my orange woolen pajama pant set. Steven calls after me, but I ignore him.

"Hey!" I holler, waving both arms above my head at the van. "Hey, stop!"

The van's brake lights flash on, then the driver hits the gas and speeds off.

"Hey! What the heck?" I stand in the middle of the road with wind rustling my wild, frizzy mane, tugging at my clothes. The van turns right, barely slowing down. There's no license plate on the back of the van. Isn't that illegal? I'll get the vehicle number most commercial vans have and report it to their supervisor. They must have routes or something for the boss to go by. This is a small town with no place to hide.

Steven shouts for me to come inside as he walks toward me. I glance around the street once more. Mr. Devon is peering through his screen door.

"Hey, Mr. Devon! Do you know—"

He steps back and shuts his house door.

"Claire, for God's sake, come inside," Steven says, throwing an arm around my shoulder and steering me towards the house. "Your poor feet. I'm buying you rain boots for Christmas."

"But why did they drive off like that?" I point down the street, crestfallen, shivering, numb.

"They didn't see you." He hugs me closer. "Do you want me to carry you?"

I hang my head and lean against him. "Then why did Mr. Devon shut his door to me?"

"No offense, honey, but how would you react to a woman running after a car without a coat or shoes on? Come inside before you get sick."

"I just want answers." I register sharp gravel digging into the soles of my feet, but I don't care. My dignity hurts worse. Nobody had ever run from me before. Could they see the monster living inside me? The panic? The anxiety? The sanity leaving my eyes? A dark shadow or two looming behind me?

"I know, honey. Come on."

Once inside, after cleaning my feet, Steven sets me on the couch under our heavy orange blanket with sunflowers knitted by Steven's grandmother and places the television remote in my hand. He then busies himself bringing me a fresh bowl of cereal, a cup of Earl Gray tea instead of coffee, and my laptop. I toss the remote to the other side of the couch, uninterested in hearing people spout doom and gloom about the world. I'm suffering here. I could run a news station out of this place with all that happens every day.

Half an hour later, I stare at the search engine results; my finger hovers over the mouse pad. My ghost investigation options are between a group from this college or one in Salem. I haven't decided if I want students who would recognize me in my house yet. Our conversations with Charlie and Gary about the house flit through my mind. This house has sat empty for about five years. Why didn't anyone in town nab it if the price was so good? What do they know that they aren't telling me? What horrors have we subjected ourselves to? Is it worse for me than for Steven because of my exposure to that experiment in the lab?

The cereal is heavy in my stomach; I ate to shut

the growling up and to have the crease in Steven's forehead relax. I cast the blanket off my legs and traipse to the garage. Inside, I find Steven putting on his leather tool belt. It's the same one he was wearing when he helped me pick up my books the day we met. He had been on a campus construction job while I was working on my master's degree. His award-winning smile won me over that day. Ever the gentleman, he had waited a few more days to ask me out, but never forgot to wave when I passed by the construction site. I still have not told him that I used to wander his way every day, though I had a class on that part of campus just once a week. The memory makes me ache with nostalgia for simpler times. Ah, when I was young, naïve, and free of haunts.

"Did the realtor ever say why the house was empty for so long? If not, can I get the realtor's phone number from your phone?" I twirl a curl around my finger, my thoughts half in the present, half in the past. "Like you said, the probability of ghosts is a little far-fetched." But not so far-fetched that I won't pursue the research.

He straightens. "So you are letting go of the dead bodies in the cellar theory?"

"Not yet. You remember the gross smell coming from Gary's cellar. What if it's not just butchered geese down there? You seem to like him, but I don't trust him. People in grief do crazy things."

"He's just a sad old man," Steven sighs. "He couldn't overpower two people, let alone one. It's not fair to pass judgment when we don't know the full story. Maybe that's why the previous owners moved. Maybe their basement or cellar flooded, ruining whatever they stored down there, and gave up on their prepping goals. Maybe they covered the cellar entrance with concrete to hide it if they constructed it without a building permit."

"Without a building permit?" I hadn't thought of that. My nose scrunches. "So it wouldn't show up on any blueprints?"

He shakes his head.

I slap my thigh. "Well, then, that was a waste of money ordering a house blueprint."

"Sorry, honey. Why don't you just relax this weekend? I'll get some older outlets changed out and recheck the wiring where I can."

My hands fall limp to my sides. "I have to get caught up on grading worksheets." I let my chin drop to my chest and shuffle back into the house.

I'm not crazy. I'm not crazy. I'm not crazy.

27

I gnaw what's left of my thumbnail. Is this a mistake? The students will be here soon. I can't afford the Salem paranormal investigators with their hundred dollars hourly rate. This group requests a donation and refreshments. I pulled a twenty-dollar bill from our grocery budget envelope to give them. I'll go without lunch for a week if I have to. Steven shouldn't have to go without just because I'm crazy—no, *not* crazy. Confused, or haunted, or cursed.

Steven's not interested in participating. He says he'll read with his headphones on in the bedroom. I'm jealous that he's not as worried about the cause of events here as I am. He hasn't seen Buzz yet. He hasn't experienced what I have, the way I have. Words are nothing compared to the brain registering something that shouldn't be there.

But maybe that will change tonight. I'll try to coax the specter to show itself, to reveal who it is and who sent it. And then I will tell it to leave me the hell alone.

*

There are five paranormal team members, but in this small house, everyone ends up climbing over each other. These students, with their cases of electronics and wires and windbreakers with a cartoon ghost on the back, are trying to be professional, asking permission for every setup they do and where they do it. Steven is still watching them like a hawk, regardless.

After one of them asks if they may use an outlet to charge a device, Steven whispers in my ear, "You promise this won't leave the house? My coworkers will tease me without end if this gets out."

I glare at him, then turn my attention back to watching one of the ghost hunters set up a device called a REM-pod on the kitchen table.

"I already told you, yes," I hiss back. "Do you picture Danielle having any respect for me if she finds out? I'm a scientist. But I'm also at my wit's end."

When Steven doesn't reply, I glance at him again. His eyes meet mine, lips thin out, an argument forming in the shadows of his gaze, and then he huffs and looks away.

Good. Because I'm serious. I need answers.

Within minutes, the group of students invite us to tag along to get base readings around the house before they go into what they call "night mode," where they flip off all the lights and wait to hear anything. I kick Steven's foot when his shoulders vibrate with silent laughter. This is a serious matter. Who cares if it's a group of college kids? I point toward the bedroom, but he shakes his head and sucks in his lips.

At eleven, all lights are off, and we stand in a circle near the couch. It's so dark that the students across from me are rough outlines. I can smell Steven's powdery aftershave to my right and a student's bubblegum-sweet body spray to my left. There's nothing audible except the refrigerator's hum. It's cold since Steven turned down the thermostat so that the heater wouldn't kick on and disrupt any sounds being recorded. One student turns on the voice box app on his cellphone, and an awful white noise akin to two pieces of high-grit sandpaper rubbing against each other breaks the silence.

"Did anyone die here?" someone asks the room.

The white noise doesn't speak.

"Are there more than one of you?"

No disembodied voices shout from the box like I've seen on television shows.

I lick my lips. "Were you sent here?" I ask, steeling my nerves.

No reply. Steven shifts beside me. Weight on one foot, then the other. He is impatient or bored. Or both.

The students whisper among themselves about what their next move should be. We didn't tell them what I have been experiencing since they wanted to investigate with an open mind.

Not about to give up, I shout, "Are you stuck in the shed?"

After a few tense moments of listening to blaring white noise, the volume gets turned down.

"There's no equipment set up out there, ma'am. The yard is too wet for our safety and equipment."

"I know. But they can come to the house if they desire. Trust me." I ball my hands into fists. *I won't look a fool, Buzz! Do something!* I shout in my mind.

A flashlight flickers on, and a student walks around us, holding out another device. "This reads the temperature and electromagnetic frequencies. Still nothing out of the ordinary. Maybe we will have better luck during the witching hour."

"Whoa, look at it now!" Another group member

shouts, pointing.

I stare at the device. The green light flashes. Then the yellow flickers on. Then the orange bulb lights up. They stay lit.

Everyone's heads swivel around. The energy in the room is strained. My chest tightens.

"Maybe Buzz heard you," Steven mumbles. I elbow him in the ribs.

The students standing across from us, closest to the kitchen, crane their heads to the right.

"Does anyone hear that?" one of them whispers.

"Oh, no," Steven groans. "Not this again."

I can't speak because I hear it, too.

It's starting as a hum, as it always has done. I count the seconds passing by, staring at the floor lamp that transformed into Buzz my first night here.

The pitch climbs to a buzz, a swarm of bees.

Crack! The voice box explodes with sound. Someone shouts. I grab Steven's hand.

"Deck. Sing. Cart," the voice box screeches.

The buzzing pitch increases.

"Oh my God, it's coming from everywhere," someone shouts.

I cover my ears. Is Buzz or whoever the entity is trying to communicate, or is the box being messed with by the vibration? What did it say? Deck, sing and—

"The deck!" I shout and point. Then I drag Steven with me to the back door. "Follow me, everyone, to the back deck. I've seen shadows out there."

Bodies shuffle around, and a couple of students whisper and whine as I push past them. Someone turns the voice box volume down. We all crowd onto the wooden deck. The buzzing is fainter outside, but only just. It makes me wonder if the house walls act as amplification devices. But if it's out here also, from what direction is it originating? Everyone turns this way and that, raising the EMF meter and voice box into the air and over the railing.

Caw! Caw!

I shrink backwards into Steven's chest, knowing what happens next.

Caw!

"Those crows are flying in a circle around the house!" a student shouts, pointing.

A flash from someone's phone camera illuminates them in the sky. I squint, trying to count the flapping shapes. Three? Five?

The buzzing intensifies.

"Ouch," the students shout, breaking from their reverence of the crows and covering their ears.

The birds break their formation and scatter.

Steven steps back and opens the door. "Everyone back inside."

The students shuffle as one. Steven shuts the door after I press in last. My eyes wobble in their sockets. These students are supposed to help us figure out the source, but they are acting as perplexed and scared as I am.

"Ah!" someone shouts.

I try to edge forward, but get jostled backward as everyone rushes toward whoever shouted.

"Bugs! Gross!" another person shrieks.

Stevens steadies me and flips on the overhead kitchen light. He shouts, "Everyone get back! Anyone with a strong stomach, grab my duct tape from that toolbox on the floor."

I watch through rapid blinks with bright spots of light blinding my vision as a student with a chin beard passes the EMF meter to a teammate and helps Steven shove paper towels down the sink drain and tape the holes shut.

A red-headed girl declares, "I think I'm going to be sick," and runs from the room.

I want to run to the living room, but I'm stuck to the wall, the sound pinning me in place. I want to escape or shrink down. To anywhere but here. *Stop, Buzz! Stop it! You're hurting us! You're scaring us!*

"AHHH!"

The scream comes from deeper in the house. My shoulders tense. Tears prick my eyes. Terror locks down my spine.

"Cassy!" the chin-bearded student bellows and runs out of the room.

"The bathroom!" Steven declares. "We have to block up the bathroom, too!"

Oh, God. My stomach lurches.

Everyone crowds into the living room.

"Come on, Mrs. Simmons. We're stronger as a group." A young man with a long ponytail pulls me with him into the next room. "I reckon this is the poltergeist trying to communicate or show off its strength."

I shake my head; my lower lip quivers. I don't want to play ghost hunter anymore. I want out.

As we wait for Steven and his assistant to finish plugging the holes in the bathroom, the students and I hold our hands over our ears and glance this way and that. There's fear in some eyes and excitement in others. This may be the most activity any of them has ever experienced. I should assure them that it's okay. The buzzing will stop; the bugs will retreat down the drains. After all, I'm the oldest one here and the homeowner. But I can't. In fact, I'm confident that I'm more frightened than any of them.

"It's a poltergeist?" I shout, trying to maintain composure. I can't tell if the buzzing is in my head or outside. Like someone pointed out, it's coming from everywhere.

The student running around the house with the EMF reader in one hand and a hand over one ear makes his way towards me. "A powerful one! The EMF reader is at full strength throughout the entire house! It's not going down!" He waves the machine in my face. Sure enough, every light is lit, and there are no fluctuations. Great. A ghost so damn powerful, it's off the charts.

Tears stream down my cheeks. What am I going to do now?

"Honey? Where are you?" Steven shouts. He shoulders dazed students out of his way. "Are you okay?"

I shake my head no.

POP! POP! POP! Lightbulbs in the kitchen explode. Students scream. Darkness swallows us once more.

"Everyone calm down!" Steven bellows.

Someone whimpers. It could have been me. I don't know. I'm frozen again.

Cold air wraps around and through my clothes as the thousands of bees buzzing in my ears drill their way into my brain, shattering my nerves, my rationale.

"Oh my God," someone gasps next to me.

"What is that?" someone else squeaks.

My eyes dart left and right, trying to catch sight of the *thing* without wanting to envision what's coming for us.

Then I see him. Or them, more like.

Dark shadows, blacker than the night, start creeping into the room from the hallway.

Soul-sucking creatures are descending, groping for their prey.

"Everyone out the front door. Go now!" Steven declares.

The students don't hesitate. They bolt. Someone pulls the storm door open so hard that it slams into the living room wall.

At least they're getting to safety. I'm stuck. Maybe it's fate. Let them take me.

Spare Steven, I plead in my mind. *He's innocent, like them. Just take me and*—

"Honey, come on!" Steven yanks my hand.

He thrusts me out first and then slams the door shut behind him.

I stumble, falling forward, but hands grasp my shoulders and direct me to the driveway and then to the street where the students huddle by their van.

"I'm not staying here, Steven. I'm not," I blubber. My body convulses as he envelops me in his arms. Icy rain pings off my face and soaks through my sweater.

"Come into the van, Mrs. Simmons," the redhead offers. The group parts and ushers me up into a seat. When everyone sits down and Steven has his arm around me, rubbing my biceps as I continue to shiver, someone rolls the van's side door shut.

"I'm not crazy. I'm not crazy," my mental chant babbles out of my mouth.

Steven murmurs into my ear, but it's still ringing, so I don't hear his words. I shut my eyes.

"Hey, I can't hear the buzzing anymore," someone announces.

The other students agree. I gulp down another sob and open my eyes.

They're right. The buzzing has stopped. Or we are far enough away from the house. Maybe I'll buy a camping tent and just live in the driveway. Or do they have a ghost ward up in this van? Were they smart and burned sage, or had they placed a talisman in the glove box beforehand?

I sag into Steven's chest. I've survived another encounter, another night. But it's not over yet, whatever *it* is.

"What *was* that?" someone exclaims, awe in their voice.

The man with a chin beard turns around where he sits in the driver's seat. His gaze falls on me. "I think it's a poltergeist. Mrs. Simmons, you say you theorize it's targeting you? Well, based on research, when the activity is this strong, it's the actual person being haunted that is causing the poltergeist activity."

My mouth falls open. Me? I'm the haunter? I'm haunting myself?

"What? No, there's no way. Don't be ridiculous," Steven scoffs.

His annoyance helps me break through my stupor. "Yeah," I pipe in with a tiny voice unfamiliar to me. "I've been calm, and it still happens."

"Maybe it's your energy escaping from holding it in all day. Like a release valve," the student with a ponytail offers.

I wish I could remember their names; they rattled them off once upon arrival, but my mind was already in overdrive and wasn't paying attention. Something in what he is saying strikes a chord. "Like radiation?" Like being exposed to an experiment where they were testing the conjuring of ghosts or whatever else could have been happening in the lab that night? My throat tightens. I grasp Steven's hand and focus on my breathing. In one, two, three, four. Hold one, two, three, four.

Mr. Ponytail doesn't seem to notice I'm having a panic attack. He shrugs and glances around the van. "Don't know. Maybe check with a Reiki practitioner. They read and fix people's auras. My cousin knows one in Portland."

Steven shifts in his seat. "No. That's enough. If

you can't tell us what is causing the sound, then we are done. Your hair-brained theories are stressing my wife out. The phenomenon has stopped, so we can go back inside." He reaches for the van's side door.

I gasp and grab at him. "I'm not going back in there."

"Neither am I," two others say in unison.

"Please, not tonight, Steven," I beg.

He peers into my eyes, and I spot the worrying crease on his forehead deepening.

"Fine. I'll go pack an overnight bag for us and get the money for these guys. But I'm not gathering up all your equipment."

"We don't want the money," Mr. Chin-beard says. "This experience was payment enough. Since it's too much work to gather everything myself, perhaps I can bring these guys back tomorrow in the daytime to pick the gear up? I wish I had invested in a good camera to video tonight. Maybe some other time."

"Yeah, that'll be fine. I'll text you when we are getting home tomorrow. Mind if my wife stays in the van while I go in? My car keys are still inside."

They don't mind, and I am grateful. One of them blasts the heater in my direction while the others change the subject to things like college football and the upcoming holiday season.

I am not crazy.

28

"Dr. Sternan? I know it's not our scheduled time for a session, but something major has happened."

It's nine in the morning. I'm alone in the hotel room while Steven gets us breakfast down the street. We found a vacancy at the hotel next to campus. I slept well; I want to steal this downy mattress. If I dreamed, I don't remember. Why should the figures visit me in my dreams when they know they can visit in the real world now? Steven thinks I have adrenal fatigue and told me to stay in bed until he returns. I won't tell him, but I figure the ghosts want me alone, so there is no witness to their evil deeds. That's why I'm on the phone now. I want a witness. Not today, ghosts.

Not today.

"That's all right. I've been eager to hear from you, Claire," Dr. Sternan admits. "Steven called me a couple of nights ago saying that you thought you saw ghosts in the shed and that you assume there are bodies buried in the backyard. Why didn't you tell him about—what did he call the figure? Oh, that's right, Buzz, from your first night in the house?"

I slap my forehead and slump into the overstuffed chair. "Why don't we have sessions over speakerphone so you and Steven can compare notes?"

"Now, Claire, I took an oath and haven't forgotten it. I didn't tell him anything. He did all the talking. All I offered was that you had a terrible panic attack and needed to be put to bed. He asked whether a sedative would help. I told him to give you one of your anxiety pills. That was all." Her voice is stern, grounding.

My teeth grind. That doesn't justify Steven sedating me without my consent. He must have opened a capsule into my glass of wine. I knew I felt groggier than usual the next morning. They hit me harder than when I take an antihistamine. We will have a big talk later. The bitter sting of betrayal, even if for my own good, grows a little more, like that of a paralyzing bite from an

Amazonian spider. Pretty soon, I'll commit myself to a hospital, if only for a reprieve from the people out to get me.

"Okay, okay. We will talk about that on Monday after I hash it out with Steven. I want to talk to you about last night. We had a team of paranormal investigators come from the college to see if they could pick up anything. It was more to find out if their machines would go off. We were hoping to find the source of the buzzing. It's affecting us and the fauna around the house. I suspect the neighbors can hear it, too, and aren't saying anything. My theory is they are trying to protect their property values." Or this is just a strange town with ley lines that are wreaking havoc. I need to call Momma and get some advice for cleaning up dangerous energies.

"Something happened," Dr. Sternan postulates.

I slap my knee. "You bet. All their machines and gizmos weren't reacting at all for an hour. Then, at eleven, boom, the buzzing began. That set off their gadgets. Scared everybody. We had the lights off, and we had asked the spirits why they were here." I then look heavenward, trying to remember the exact timeline. Everything happened so fast. "Do you know what a voice box and EMF reader are?"

"I've seen a ghost hunter show, so yes, I'm following. Go on."

No admonishments or groans about believing in the paranormal? That's a first. I continue. "Well, I remember the voice box saying the word deck, so I had everyone go to the back deck where we could see the shed and maybe glimpse the shadows I've seen back there. You remember me asking you about raccoons?"

Papers shuffle in the background. "Yes. You wondered if raccoons grow to be big in Oregon. Can you talk a little slower, Claire? I'm making some notes." Her voice is still even and nonjudgmental.

I focus on the room's door, listening, but no footsteps approach. There must be long lines at the cafe. We are on campus. The science building is just two short blocks over.

"Okay. So outside, crows are circling overhead, cawing. Not scary, but it was strange. Meanwhile, the buzzing increases, hurting my eyes now. The students were complaining about the anomalies affecting them as well. Steven then ushered us back into the kitchen." I pause so she can scribble this down. "And that's when the bugs started coming out of the drain again."

"Bugs?" Dr. Sternan gasps. "Again?"

Didn't I tell her about the bugs? Whoops. "Yeah, real, live bugs, Dr. Sternan," I enunciate. "I know you mentioned that the other occurrences were a possible shared delusion of some sort. But is it one when birds and bugs are acting strange at the same time?"

"No," Dr. Sternan draws out. "I'd say not. This sounds awful, Claire. I can't imagine what was going through your head. Can you tell me?"

I swallow bile as it rises along with the memory. "I felt helpless and frozen. It was all happening in perfect sequence. Every incident I, alone or with Steven, have experienced since I arrived was happening all at once, as it did in chronological order, but in minutes instead of days. I—I cried."

"Goodness. I would have too. Where was Steven when this was happening?"

I stand up and glance out the hotel room window that overlooks the parking lot. He said he'd walk to the nearest cafe, about half a block away, and come right back. How long have I been talking with Dr. Sternan?

"Claire? Did you hear me? Is everything all right?"

"Uh, yeah," I say, walking the three steps back to the bed. It is the weekend, and we are near student housing. There's bound to be a long line. "Yeah, Steven was there next to me last night. Then, he and one student handled the bugs as we did last time. He taped over the sink drains and faucets. When they ran to the bathroom, that was the one time he wasn't next to me. Why do you ask?"

The sound of pages turning and a pen scribbling fills the silence before Dr. Sternan speaks again. "How is he reacting to all of this?"

He hadn't been a wuss like me. "He was, well, annoyed, I guess. I don't think Steven believes in ghosts. I don't even know if I believe in ghosts. Though we both agree that something is going on at the house. But we are at odds about how to find the source. He gets upset when I come up with a new theory. Understandable because they are more hair-brained than what others suggest."

Dr. Sternan hums, and her pen scratches across paper. "Anything else from last night that affected him?"

I tap my knee. "I remember that every time the buzzing worsened, or if something new happened, he made us move as a group to another room. The last straw for him was after the bugs, when the lightbulbs in the kitchen exploded. He shouted for everyone to get out of the house. We ran to the investigating team's van to get out of the rain. He told the group leader to shut up after the guy claimed it was *me* that was causing all the poltergeist activity." I chew my lower lip, fearing what her response will be.

"I'm glad he did," Dr. Sternan states.

I inhale and release my sore lip. "Really? So, you

don't think I'm cursed or hexed or—but exposed to some kind of radiation in the lab that they haven't tested me for? What if they didn't know there was an experiment going on down there? Dr. Sternan, should I see a doctor?"

"Whoa, whoa, Claire. Breathe."

I clutch my chest and start counting. Dr. Sternan urges me to do a second round.

"Okay, Doc," I announce when my pulse slows. "I think I'm—"

A card key unlocks the room door. I crane my head around. Steven enters with a brown paper sack and two coffee cups in a four-cup cardboard holder.

"Steven just got back. I should go."

Steven's eyes narrow at me. "Why? Who's that?"

"Dr. Sternan. I was just filling her in on what happened last night. I'm hungry and want to eat breakfast with you," I half admit. My other half of truth is that I want to keep questioning Dr. Sternan on why she's so interested in Steven's whereabouts last night. I also want to know why he was gone so long and why he sedated me after the shed incident without my consent. I've never questioned his motives and whereabouts before, but if an unbiased third party is, shouldn't I?

Dr. Sternan pipes up. "Claire? I'll let you go. But do one thing for me between now and our session tomorrow. Draft everything you have experienced since your arrival on Sunday. And don't even think about going down that rabbit hole of ghosts and poltergeists. Do you understand?" Steady and stern. Just what I need.

I almost said, "Yes, ma'am," like she's a schoolmarm. Instead, I say, "You got it, Dr. Sternan. I'll have Steven help me recall his side of events, too. I'll call you on Monday."

By the time I hang up and toss my phone on the bed, Steven has set out the marionberry muffins I requested and takes the plastic lids off two cups of coffee. He glances up. "The first place's debit card machine stopped working, and I don't have cash. A kid in line announced he was going to the next closest bakery, so I followed him."

I give his biceps an affectionate knead and plop down at the little table for two by the window. "I'm sure it's great. You got your steps in, and I had a productive talk with Dr. Sternan. She wants me to record everything that's happened since I arrived. Can you help me recount what you experienced, too?"

"Sure," he says in the process of stuffing a quarter of one muffin into his mouth. "Mmm. Grrd."

"I've seen marionberry ice cream in the grocery store. I'll get some when it warms up." I chomp down and relish the sweet, whole fruit pieces in the dough, then sip my lukewarm coffee. It's no better than what I brew at home, but don't mention it.

Steven shoves the rest of his breakfast into his mouth and brushes the table crumbs into his hand. He gets up and dumps them into the little trash can by the window. "Huh," he says. I look over at him. He points down to the parking lot. "There's that animal control van again. I wonder if they're working in this place today?"

I rush over. Sure enough, there's the white van parked two spaces from our car, with Deadwood Animal Control on the side and a license plate on the front ripe for picture taking. No running this time! I spin and launch myself toward the door, grabbing my phone and room key on the way out.

"Claire? Where are you going?"

There's no time to explain. These animal control people are going to get a reckoning from me for driving off. Then, I'll make them explain why they were on our street. What are the creatures they are searching for? Have they caught something already?

The elevator dings open on the ground floor, and I sprint outside. The van is still there. I skid to a halt by our car. I don't want someone to call the police on me for taking pictures of a random car, so I pretend to accept a phone call and lean against my

Subaru. I hit record on my camera app and have the lens facing the van. I chat about work as if I'm talking to Danielle, assuring her that I've finished Friday's work. Then I pretend to be preoccupied with the ground, saying a lot of yeses, and wander back and forth by the van's hood. When I'm satisfied I have enough video footage, I say goodbye aloud and head inside.

The man behind the reception desk eyes me with a tentative smile and then glances outside.

I wave my hand and titter. "Sorry about that. Urgent calls from work. They thought I had a missing file. But they found it."

The receptionist's shoulders relax. "Oh, yes, that would be stressful."

"While I have you here," I say, and lean against the counter. "I noticed the animal control van parked outside. I need to get rid of the family of raccoons in my attic, but I don't see a phone number on their van. Are they staying here at this hotel?"

"I'm sorry," the receptionist replies, shaking his head. "We can't give out that information. Perhaps you can leave a note on their van windshield for them to call you?"

I plaster on a fake smile. "What a great idea! I'll just go up and collect my bags and husband to check out first."

After getting over his initial panic about why I ran out, Steven says he understands my dilemma with photographing a car that's not mine, and writes a note to put on the van while I pack.

We check out and hurry to the parking lot.

The van is gone.

29

There are still no websites or contacts to be found for Deadwood Animal Control. I print out the screenshot of the license plate. Even if my phone dies or the data disappears, I'll have this hard evidence in our lockbox. Lesson learned from last time.

After the students leave with all their equipment later on, and as I type up a rough draft of events for Dr. Sternan, Steven calls information for the closest animal control company. They patch him through to one in Eugene. After hanging up, he explains to me that they had never heard of a Deadwood Animal Control being set up and had warned Steven to stay vigilant. It could be a cover for burglars casing places out.

My jaw drops. We weren't home last night, and the van had parked near us at the same hotel. "Steven…"

"I'm way ahead of you, honey," he assures me. "Keep working in here. I'm going to call the police station to report it. Send me the video you took of their van. Then I'll snap photos of all our stuff too and back them up in the cloud for insurance."

He leaves the room, and I lean back in my office chair. Steven has agreed not to replace the broken door until we figure out what's going on, or else I wouldn't ever step foot in here again. New theories and connections emerge in my mind. The van sitting outside nearby, the buzzing, us running from the house multiple times in fear, and neighbors acting cold. What if they are experiencing something similar, but are too embarrassed to admit it since it implies what I have thought—that ghosts are haunting their house or they are going insane? What if these shady people in the van have a homemade sound machine from parts bought at the military surplus, and it's meant to drive people from their homes long enough for them to burgle?

My fists and jaw clench. What if our neighborhood is their testing ground and they are happy that I'm freaking out? How would they know I have anxiety from experiencing something similar in a lab far away?

I type with renewed fervor, adding comments in the margins for Dr. Sternan—connections, theories. It is all based on reality. All based on hard evidence. I snort out loud. How could I have been so irrational that I thought I was causing this activity? Then I sober up. Anxiety. Stress. Lack of sleep. Past trauma. My brain is fragile. But that doesn't mean I'm weak. This evidence is solid.

I am not crazy.

Dr. Sternan will be proud of me.

Heck, I have half a mind to pat myself on the back.

But not yet. First, we have to catch these crooks.

I lick my lips, letting my imagination grab hold. Perhaps if I can solve this, Dr. Sternan will submit a report to the Rosebud Research Facility about my extraordinary progress, and the review board will consider rehiring me to pick up where I left off.

*

I wake Monday morning to my alarm, none the more rested. After speaking with local police over the phone, Steven had gone out and bought extra locks for the windows and new locks for the front and back doors. The police claim there's not much they can do for us, but promised to send a patrol car around the neighborhood and run the license plate number of the van. We had gone to bed with a hammer on the floor by Steven for protection and a glass of wine in our bellies to pacify our nerves.

After we triple-check the locks, we share a deep kiss by our cars before leaving. Finally, we agree on something. We are on the same side, with the same bad guys to look out for.

I am going to research pricing of security and trail cameras for the front and back yards on lunch, and Steven says he will spread the word about the suspicious van. If we have time tonight, we'll make posters using a snapshot of the van and hand them out to our neighbors.

We all need to be on the same team right now.

*

When I arrive at Danielle's office, the dean, Kelly Vargus, whom I recognize from the photo on the college website sporting the same shoulder length jet black hair, dark blue business suit, and intense gaze, is speaking with Danielle by the bookcase. I clear my throat. Danielle bids me good morning, and Dean Kelly nods her greeting. I'm not sure what to do next since they are blocking the place my briefcase and thermos go.

Dean Kelly glances at Danielle, who nods once. Dean Kelly motions me to a chair in front of Danielle's desk, and then walks around the desk and sits in Danielle's chair. Danielle follows behind and stands next to her, smoothing her tweed calf-length skirt down the sides. Her gaze doesn't meet mine. There is something interesting on the ground in front of her. My stomach tightens.

"Please have a seat, Dr. Simmons. I would like to speak with you for a moment," Dean Kelly says, motioning towards the chair again.

I roll my lips and perch on the edge of said chair, placing my briefcase by my feet.

"I have heard many good things about you, and I know Dr. Bayer is grateful to have you as a teacher's aide." Dean Kelly brings her hands up and folds them atop the desk. "However, your recent sporadic absences and late arrivals are painting a different picture."

I straighten my spine. Excuses flit through my mind. I open my mouth. Dean Kelly holds up her first finger. I snap my jaw shut, teeth clicking from impact.

"This is your official first and last warning. The students come first. If you miss one more day of work, we will have to let you go."

I turn my attention to Danielle. Her gray eyes flit up to mine, and then back to the floor. I shift my gaze back to the dean. "But I've caught up on the work Professor Bayer has assigned me. It's in my briefcase. I'll even work on the weekends to tutor the students. The circumstances of my absence were beyond my control. I can prove it."

"I'm sorry, Dr. Simmons. We cannot give preferential treatment, no matter who your mother is or what is going on in your life. All new employees go through the same probationary period, and the same rules apply."

Who my mother is? Momma helped me find this job. As in, 'found the position available'. I still had to submit my resume, interview, and wait for an answer like any other applicant would. I grit my teeth and count to five. "Dean Kelly, with all due respect, it does not matter who my mother is. All she did was tell me about the position availability, and I resent the fact that you assume she helped me become employed here. My credentials are superior to those of a teacher's aide qualifications, and I interviewed well, if I say so myself."

Dean Kelly glances at Danielle. My neck heats. My jacket is too hot. This is the last straw. There will be no more friendship, no more first-name basis between Danielle and me. Professor Bayer is acting as if she is powerless in this situation with her eyes downcast, acting like a scolded puppy. This is just like the research laboratory bureaucratic nonsense all over again. A lot of avoidance and silence.

Professor Bayer shrugs. The dean frowns at her and turns back to me. "Alright. I retract that remark. Apparently, I'm mistaken. But I still have to give you that warning about missing any more days."

I shoot a glare in the professor's direction. The human resources department here hired me, not the dean, so I can't hold that comment against Dean Kelly. But someone has been snooping into my private life. How else would they know my momma has school board connections? And whether it was Professor Bayer or one of her friends in the administration office, I won't stand for it. I won't lose this job. I relax my face and meet Dean Kelly's gaze. "I do not understand. I haven't used all the sick days available as outlined in my employment packet."

"That's for employees who have passed the probationary period. Before that, you have three fewer days until you pass probation," Dean Kelly explains. I frown at her. No one had explained that to me. She stands up. "I believe that is all I have to say. You are now informed. Please try not to lose any more work, Dr. Simmons. We need your help here, and the students do like you." Her gaze softens then, bordering on kind and apologetic.

This is a woman with a demanding job, being made to do the dirty work.

"Yes, ma'am," I say, sitting up straighter.

Dean Kelly doesn't bid Professor Danielle Bayer good day, doesn't even glance her way, when she leaves the room.

I squint my eyes at Professor Bayer. *I'm onto you.* She raises her eyebrows.

"You could have warned me about the fewer sick days while on probation," I flick her way.

Danielle crosses her arms. "Don't take your frustrations out on me. I didn't know myself. I've never missed a day." Then she lets her arms fall to her side. "Let's have that be the end, please. I'd hate our relationship to be damaged over such a small thing. She just waltzed in here a few minutes ago. I had no warning."

It's my turn to cross my arms. Slight thing, indeed! This is my livelihood we're talking about. I open my mouth to tell her just that, but the local church bells peal in the distance, signaling the hour. If we don't move, we'll be late for class. I nod, opting to be civil since I am at work. "Okay. I guess it doesn't matter, anyway. We've narrowed down the suspects. It's only a matter of time before the police arrest someone."

Professor Bayer snatches her briefcase and runs to me. Her gray eyes are bright. I lean back. She grabs my arm. "Tell me everything while we hurry to class. I've been wondering what progress you've made."

I follow her out, pulling my arm out of her grasp. After that little charade, I'm still suspicious of what she or someone she knows said to Dean Kelly. I fight the desire to roll my eyes and to tell her she doesn't deserve to hear about it.

But she is my boss until I find something else, so the least I can do is to be amicable. After today, I will be job hunting. I haven't felt at home in Deadwood. It's too rural, and the locals stare while you grocery shop, and this rain…

I shrug as if our breakthrough isn't a big deal. "A suspicious van parks in the neighborhood almost every day. They drive off when I go outside. We called the police, who suspect burglars. We agree they have some sort of device meant to drive us out of our homes long enough to steal our belongings. Which reminds me," I add, snapping my fingers. "I might call the police back and tell them to get records from the military surplus store. The owner said something to me that makes me suspect him."

"Really?" she huffs, reaching for the classroom door handle, and pauses. "I honestly don't know what to say. What you had described over the last couple of weeks had sounded fantastical, I admit. This sounds much more logical and scarier. I sure hope the police take it seriously."

*

"I thought I was losing my mind," I admit to Danielle after the last student leaves. I am calmer and have decided that I was premature in declaring to myself that Danielle and I are no longer friends. Nothing she has said or done throughout today has triggered my suspicions further. We had an amicable day; students were alert in class, no one stared at me, and Danielle lent me a scientific journal on the newest developments in quantum computing that a colleague from her past had sent her. So, for now, I'll tamp down my hurt and try to forgive and forget. And not miss any more days of work.

"It was happening to me whether I was home alone or if Steven was there. My theories range from someone pranking me from Rosebud Research Facility to the ghosts of the past homeowners requesting help to pass over to the other side. I couldn't speculate any other reason since we had an electrician check out the wiring. Steven thinks we should make a sign about the suspicious van and hand it out in the neighborhood. We could all be sitting ducks for these sadistic crooks." I'm sitting in the chair facing

Danielle's desk, tracing my finger along the armrest. I shouldn't stress about admitting to believing in ghosts. I have anxiety, and Danielle would be the only one besides Dr. Sternan who would understand how the mind spirals under stress. "Steven has had to slip me anxiety medication when I couldn't calm down."

Danielle nods and lays down her paperwork. I meet her gaze, noting the crease between her eyebrows like Steven gets when he's concerned about me.

I sigh. "What? You can say it. They need to lock me up in an asylum."

She shakes her head. "No, no. I wouldn't say that at all. Goodness knows you've been through a lot." She pauses, her lower lip disappearing between her teeth for a moment, her gaze distant. "I just had a thought. What if the van theory doesn't pan out? It couldn't be Steven, could it?"

"Huh?" My brain has hit a wall. Nothing she just said makes sense. Steven as the perpetrator? My Steven? How could she even surmise that? My thoughts flit to Dr. Sternan's questions concerning Steven's whereabouts and his reactions. I had stopped worrying about him once the police were called about the van.

"What I mean is, is your marriage doing alright?" Danielle asks.

I can't come up with anything to say. I want to say yes. We are usually on the same side, but the last couple of weeks have been trying for us. As it would be for any couple. I lean my head to one side, regarding her. I hate when people grill me about my personal relationships. It's too intimate; vulnerabilities exposed to those who don't know the entire story.

"We're great. He's my rock."

"I don't mean to pry, but I worry about you. I suppose I watch too much Dateline… But they say there are more ways to abuse a partner than physically. If your relationship is rocky, I'd check him. He works in construction, right? Knows about electrical things?"

"Stop." I mean it. I'm done. "No. Steven would never. He—no, he has experienced this too. Why would he do it to himself? No."

Danielle shrugs. "On one show, the partner poisoned themselves along with their victim to throw suspicion off them."

My phone rings. Thank God, a distraction. The caller ID flashes. "It's Steven." My heart thumps against my sternum. Did he somehow know that we were talking about him? Shouldn't he be at work? "Oh no, what if they've burgled our house already? But we have so many locks now."

"Answer it," Danielle commands, pointing at my

phone.

"Steven?"

"Hi, honey. Can you come home? Like right now?"

I glance at Danielle and then at my watch. It's three thirty. Do I risk asking to go home early? "I don't think so. The dean warned me not to miss any more work or she'll fire me."

"What? When? You haven't used all your sick days."

I sigh. "Yeah, that's what I thought. But Dean Kelly says new employees on probation have fewer days to use than full-fledged employees. And before you say anything, yes, I explained my absences were justified, and no, it didn't make a difference." I inhale. "So, what is going on? I have half an hour left."

"I got a call from Gary about seeing someone from his upstairs window snooping around our backyard. My boss let me go home to investigate. Well, by the time I got here, the place was swarming–" his voice drops to a whisper — "with police dogs, FBI, and the military. They want to speak with us together."

The blood leaves my face, my brain, to pool in my feet. "W—Why? Did they catch the burglars? Did they burgle our house?"

"I don't know, sweetie. They're not saying

anything. I begged them not to go to your work, which they agreed to if you come home. They won't let me into the house."

I clench and open my free hand. Again and again. "Oh, God. Okay. Um. I—let me ask."

Danielle leans forward and says, "Your face is ashen, Claire. What's wrong?"

Tears prick my eyes. Where are my words? My mouth is a desert. "Um, there's people at the house who want to speak to me. Um, police officers are waiting."

Danielle rises from her chair. "Are you sure that's wise? You look and sound scared."

"Claire? Don't tell Danielle anything, please. Don't bring anyone with you. I'll be here. I'm not going anywhere."

I stare into Danielle's wide gray eyes and swallow. "Okay. Um, Danielle? Can I go? I'll work an extra half hour tomorrow, I promise. He says the police will come here if I don't show up. I don't want to cause any trouble."

Her eyes narrow. Then they relax, and she nods. "Okay, if you must. Yes, please don't bring the police here. Dean Kelly won't appreciate that. Go. Quickly. Don't use the time clock. I will write an excuse slip for you and turn it in."

I stand and hesitate.

"Go," Danielle waves me on.

"I'm on my way, Steven."

"Law enforcement is blocking both entrances to the street now. Maybe your theory about bodies on the property is true, after all."

Progress. Finally.

I am not crazy.

30

Two unmarked black SUVs parked sideways block the entrance to my street. A soldier holding a rifle in one hand is waving and shouting at a local station news van inching forward in front of me. I slow to a stop and watch the news van turn around while a camera person leans out the passenger window, trying to record everything happening past the blockade. Why would army reservists need to be called in? Is the disappearance of the Galloways a federal investigation? Did they not pay their taxes and need to be confirmed dead to dissolve their debts?

"Or are the Galloways part of the theft ring, trying to get their house back?" I whisper to myself, my eyes widening.

A rap on my driver's side window rips me from imagining escalating scenarios of how the Galloways met their demise or joined a crime ring. The reservist who waved the news van away motions for me to roll down my window.

"Street's closed until further notice," he barks. "Do you live nearby?"

I nod. I meant to point, but my hands have fused to the steering wheel. The coffee I drank right before Steven's phone call whirlpools in my stomach.

"May I see your driver's license to verify that?" The soldier leans down so his head is level with mine. His green eyes search my face and the car's interior.

"Uh, y—yeah," I stammer. My right hand peels off the steering wheel. I push my jacket away and pull my briefcase from underneath it onto my lap. The soldier steps back; both hands gripping his rifle. I freeze. "My wallet is in my briefcase," I explain, motioning with my head.

"Okay. Slowly, though. No surprises."

I gaze at him. For a soldier, he seems young; his face is youthful. Maybe, like me, this is the most action he has seen. I wonder what he's seen or been told today? My hands work the latches, and I open the case as if I'm in a slow-motion action shot.

"What's going on?" I ask.

He remains silent, watching me until the lid on my briefcase is open all the way. My wallet, thermos, phone, and a lone file folder filled with student papers to grade lay inside.

"Okay, get your license out. All I can say is that we are waiting for a person of interest to surface."

"Surface?" I hand over my license and my Veteran ID card, hoping it will loosen his tongue once he sees he's in the presence of a former Air Force enlistee.

He glances at both cards and then back at me. "Where were you stationed?"

"Montana was the last place I lived as a reservist." I give him a wavering smile. *It is so hard to smile when I'm nervous.*

The young soldier stares back for a moment, and then motions to the nearest van. The car backs into a driveway. The reservist points down the street. "Keep your speed low with your hands where we all can see them. Park in front of your house and get out slowly. Don't make any sudden moves. They didn't tell me much; only to allow anyone who lives on this street to go home. They want to interview all the owners. The FBI brought us in, just so you know. And when the feds bring us in, some real shit is going down. Stay safe," he says. Then he slaps the roof and backs up.

I exhale and release my foot from the brake, allowing my car to roll forward. My foot hovers over the accelerator, too scared to go any faster in case one of the many soldiers or FBI agents milling about with rifles and attack dogs becomes trigger-happy.

Most officers turn as I roll by and gaze at me. Some speak into their walkie-talkies. I keep scanning for Steven. Three more houses until ours. Steven promised he wouldn't go anywhere. He promised. Then I spot him at the edge of our yard that connects to the Davis property. Steven has his arms crossed and is watching our house. A few feet from him, I spy Charlie Davis speaking with a police officer in his front yard. Charlie points at me. The police officer he's speaking to reaches for his walkie-talkie, not taking his eyes off me. I refocus on the road and pull over right by Steven.

More police and military personnel pivot toward me and watch. My stomach sinks further. That confirms it. They were waiting for me.

Steven walks towards me. I get out of the car, keeping the door open with my hands at my sides, and meet him a few steps away.

He hugs me tight, rubs my back. There are no words he can say to make this moment any easier, and he knows that. It just matters that he's here with me.

I glance up while still in his embrace, towards our house.

"I've already retained a lawyer, honey. Just in case," Steven whispers into my ear.

I pull away from him. A string of people wearing blue and black jackets with the large FBI logo on the front are exiting the house holding file boxes and filled clear bags with one word printed on the outside.

EVIDENCE.

"What the hell are you doing?" I thunder at them. They are taking our stuff again. I'm sure my new laptop is in one of those boxes, along with some of Steven's tools. Just like last time. Not again. "Put those back," I screech at the unwavering line marching to an unmarked white van parked in our driveway. "Nothing we have will help you with this investigation!"

Steven puts his arms around my chest, holding me back from running at them. "They have a search warrant, honey. There's nothing we can do."

"Claire? Claire Simmons?"

Steven and I jerk our heads to the right to see a decorated military officer walking towards us, shadowed by a police officer with handcuffs in one hand and the other resting on his gun in its holster. I shrink back into Steven's chest. My vision sways. This is worse than last time, when only a few military police rifled through my office. Local law enforcement, FBI, and the military have all converged at my home right now. This is a whole new and unimagined nightmare.

"Claire Simmons," the military officer states again and stops a foot from us. I want to demand the warrant for searching our house, but dots dance across my vision. The officer motions the police officer forward. "Claire Simmons, you are under arrest for breaking the Nuremberg Code."

International ethical standards for human experimentation. When did I break that?

Do they assume I made all this buzzing racket and gave myself anxiety and panic attacks?

"Are you all insane?" I screech, shoving Steven away. "I'm the victim here! We both are!"

"Please place your hands behind your back," the police officer deadpans.

"Steven," I plead wide-eyed to him. "What do I do?"

He steps around me, placing an arm in front of me, blocking me from the officer. "Hey, I told you she would come quietly. You don't need to handcuff her in view of the neighbors. I'm coming with her, too." Steven turns to me. "Claire, say nothing. I have our lawyer on speed dial. We will see what they want. I'm sure it's a big misunderstanding."

He already told them I would go without question? He spoke for me? He knows better than to speak for me. He's not my keeper. Who got to him? I snarl, "Why did you tell them that? I'm innocent. And you damn well know that."

"Sir, please step aside. This is protocol," the military officer says. "You can meet us at the station, Mr. Simmons, but your wife is a flight risk."

My body shakes. I've never run away from a situation in my life. Who claimed I am at risk of doing anything? I continue to stare into Steven's eyes while hands pull my arms back and cold metal snakes around my wrists. Was it him? Steven's arms hover in the air, half reaching for me. He stares back, with a mix of concern and helplessness written in the crease of his brow and the slackness of his mouth. Someone states my Miranda rights. Steven drops his arms to his sides and mouths, "I'm sorry."

"I didn't do anything!"

I am not crazy.

31

I'm pressed down into the back of a nearby police cruiser and wait until they close the door to peer out. Steven is talking on his cell phone and walking towards my car. I hope he has half a mind to get my briefcase, jacket, and keys before following in his truck, if he follows. Or is this the last time I will ever see him? Tears prick my eyes at the mere thought he could be behind this, as Danielle insinuated. What tipped her and Dr. Sternan off about him? Steven plops into the driver's seat of my Subaru, closes the door, and starts the engine, headlights coming on. Then he just sits there.

Tears roll down my cheeks, and I preoccupy my mind with box-breathing. A police officer sits in the driver's seat and starts the car. An armed reservist climbs into the passenger seat, and we pull away from the curb. I glance upwards and see that our trees are full of birds of many colors and sizes. Black, blue, brown. Am I stuck on the set of an Alfred Hitchcock movie, or stuck in a fever dream? None of this can be real.

I lean my head back and stare at the roof of the car. How am I breaking the law? If anything, I am a victim of an awful prank or theft ring. I have no lab equipment to work with. So, who called the Feds? I gnaw my lower lip until I taste blood.

I'm not crazy. I'm not imagining things. Someone is doing this to me. It's someone else. Not me.

Maybe the people in the animal control van had something to do with it. Did they make the call and frame me? Are the Galloways still alive and watching from a distance? Or if it is someone from the lab behind my arrest, does their experimenting fall under the Nuremberg Code? Am I an easy scapegoat since my mental health has been called into question and I have a therapist? Can I still trust Steven?

I grit my teeth and close my eyes. Of course, I can trust Steven. We said our own vows at our wedding, written together. He promised to always have my back, as I would his. But Danielle's words swirl around my brain. Even Dr. Sternan wondered how our relationship had been going. Had he reached the end of his tether with me and was searching for a way out? But why buy a house and relocate? It's been so much work. We had used my military loan and payout to make the down payment. The house is in both our names. He doesn't have any debt. His grandmother is still in Montana, which he admitted upset him to leave her behind; his parents and siblings have been on the East Coast for years. It makes little sense for him to be so antagonistic. There would've been more obvious signs. But if not him, who? And why attack me at home? Why not at work or in my car? Was it because they knew that what they were doing to me falls under the Nuremberg Code, and thus didn't want to harm the public? But why torture me? I *am* a member of the public.

We arrive at the police station, and there is no sign of Steven. I am marched into a white-walled interrogation room where I'm directed to sit in a metal chair facing an unpainted metal table in the middle. They switch my hands to be handcuffed in front of my body and lock the handcuffs to a raised iron pipe with each end welded to the tabletop. The chair I'm now seated in faces an enormous mirror on the opposite wall. My butt turns to ice within moments, and goosebumps pop up along my arms. Shivers convulse my torso. I curse the nervous hot flashes I get when stressed, that being the reason I had peeled my coat off before driving home.

An MP stands guard by the door facing me when the police officer leaves. I'm not the Hulk, so why the security? I open my mouth to ask, but remember Steven's words of warning about speaking. I'll wait and hope I don't become hypothermic. Steven will get help. I wonder where he is. On the other side of the door? Pacing in the lobby? Shouting at people and demanding to see me? Had he lost his temper and is now locked in handcuffs too? He keeps a cool head, but is a muscular guy and protective of me. At least I still hope he is.

A man in an FBI jacket with a matching blue nondescript baseball cap on, cleft chin and a straight nose enters with a file folder in one hand and stands on the other side of the table, regarding me.

"I'm not talking until my lawyer and husband are in here," I declare through clenched teeth, so they don't chatter.

He nods once and walks out.

I count the minutes as they drag by. Then I give up and count the hair on my red and numb knuckles.

Sometime later, Steven, a mystery man in a gray suit about his height, and a police officer shorter and much rounder about the waist, enter the room. I raise my head from where it lay on my arm. I'm exhausted from being cold and kept in the figurative dark.

Steven's brow creases, but keeps his distance from me. They must have given him a list of rules to follow so that he could be in here with me. "Handcuffs, really?" He gestures to me. "She wouldn't hurt a fly. And she's freezing, shaking. Crank the thermostat and bring her jacket, or I'll add to the list of things I'm suing you for."

My shoulders droop. Oh, Steven. My rock. My big teddy bear with his warm eyes and tousled brown hair. How could I have ever doubted your love and loyalty to me? I blink back tears.

The officer doesn't budge. "Just following protocol, Mr. Simmons. The jacket of hers you brought in has to stay in evidence to be tested for chemical residue."

"Can I give her my jacket, then?" Steven implores. "Your people already searched the pockets and lining."

The police officer glances at the wall behind him. Ah, yes, it's a one-way mirror. Then he turns to Steven and nods once. Someone watching must have given the okay in his earpiece.

The man in gray hasn't spoken. He peers at me, and then at anyone who is speaking, sizing them up. I size him up. Friend or foe? A well-tailored suit, shined shoes, speckled gray hair. His facial expression remains passive.

Steven peels his Dickies work jacket off with its warm red flannel inner lining and wraps it around my shoulders. My neck and shoulder muscles melt as delicious heat seeps into me. "Thank you," I whisper.

His hand gives my shoulder a squeeze, and then he steps back to his place next to the officer, gesturing to the man in gray. "Honey, this is Mr. Terry Sinclair, the attorney I have retained. I have filled him in on what's been going on. Let him do the talking unless he says it's okay to speak, alright?" I manage a weak nod. Steven then rubs his hands together. "Okay, I'll be in the waiting room if you need me." He reaches one hand toward mine.

"No touching," barks the officer.

Steven sends a glare at him, gives me a sympathetic frown, and draws his hand back.

"Go. I'll be alright," I lie to him, wondering for how much longer I can survive handcuffed to a metal table, freezing to death, and alone except for the guard and whoever is staring at me from behind the one-way mirror.

Steven pivots to our attorney. "She gets panic attacks. Dr. Sternan is her therapist if you need information. It's on the list of phone numbers I gave you." He gazes at me until I motion to the door with my head, then leaves.

The police officer crosses his arms over his protruding belly, and we both watch Mr. Sinclair grab a metal chair and place it next to me, then sit down.

The same cleft-chinned FBI agent from before enters with an evidence bag.

"Hey, I didn't say bring anything in here," the officer growls. "Who are you? Get out of here."

"My name is Agent Jeffers, with the Federal Bureau of Investigation. We appreciate your cooperation, but this is where we part ways," the newcomer says with a flat expression. "The Pentagon put Big Haus in the lead on this case. You can leave."

My mouth flops open. Someone from the Pentagon is involved. Who is Big Haus? Was it the decorated officer who announced I was being arrested? They sound like a mob boss. My heart thumps against my sternum, and I toss a scared glance at Mr. Sinclair, who puts his finger to his lips. I strain in the handcuffs to press a finger to my neck artery and start counting down from one hundred.

"Hands on the table," shouts the police officer.

I sneer at him. "I'm checking my heart rate."

"Hands on the table," he enunciates.

Mr. Sinclair murmurs to me to follow

instructions. I lower my hand, but keep counting down. Five people in this tiny room are five too many. The least they could do is have the military police officer step out since there are three grown men here and me, chained to this freezing table.

Agent Jeffers steps to the table, gestures for the police officer to take a step back, and pulls an object from the evidence bag. It's a large black box with a few red dials on top. He places it in front of me. "Do you know what this is?"

"Don't answer that," Mr. Sinclair instructs.

I glance at him, then at the agent, and shake my head. I really don't know. If I were to venture a guess, I'd say it was some sort of electrical control device. Did they find that in the fake animal control van? The agent and my attorney stare at each other for a moment. I continue my backward counting.

"What have I been arrested for again?" I need more time to think. To process. To analyze and defend myself.

Agent Jeffers repeats what was told to me back at the house: I have been conducting illegal human experimentation using military-grade weapons.

"That's preposterous, and you know it," I say and grasp the chain locking my handcuffs to the table. Mr. Sinclair shushes me.

I scowl at him and clutch the cold links of metal tethering me to this place tighter. The icy, unforgiving material sharpens my concentration. "No. I have been trying to figure out what the hell has been happening in our home since moving here." I jab a thumb toward my chest. "I'm the victim, not the one doing it. I've had to deal with whatever has been happening in my home from the very first night. Whatever has been happening in that house was there, set up, before I arrived." I slam my hand down on the table. "I can prove it if you haven't incinerated all the evidence you took."

"Watch your tone," the police officer snarls.

Agent Jeffers turns to the officer and points to the door. "Leave. Now."

The officer stomps out of the room. One down, three to go.

Mr. Sinclair warns me not to speak anymore. I wave him away and say, "This goes beyond your comprehension, too. I can prove my innocence with airline tickets, my cab fare, grocery receipts, you name it. I've kept it all. I've hired electricians, an exterminator, and paranormal investigators to help us figure out what's going on. I've even gone around to our neighbors to see if they've experienced anything."

Jeffers takes out a notebook from his jacket and sits in the third chair across from me. "An alibi. Sure. Let's see how tight it is."

I point to the mirrored wall opposite and address

anyone who may be watching. "You had better be recording this, because I don't enjoy repeating myself." Then I straighten my spine and tell the agent, "I flew here from Louisiana, got a cab in Eugene, and arrived home alone. Steven had gotten the inspection done and all the papers signed with the bank days before and would not be home until the next day, Monday." Am I implicating Steven? He's a victim of this, same as me. But facts are facts. He can provide his own alibi with receipts if he needs to. I continue. "So, I was putting books in my bookcase and then called my therapist, Dr. Sternan, since I forgot our earlier appointment time. During our conversation, something in the house buzzed. Dr. Sternan couldn't hear it, so I raised the phone so she could listen and turned around. That's when I saw a figure standing in the corner. I ran from the house after telling Dr. Sternan that there was someone there with me. Once I stopped running, I realized I was on the side of our house. Dr. Sternan helped me calm down since she was still on the line, and I got the courage up to—"

"Hold on. Can you describe the figure?" Agent Jeffers asks.

"Black and fuzzy."

The agent raises an eyebrow. "Have you ever seen the same figure before?"

I suck in a breath. I smell a trap. "I can't say that

I have."

Beside me, Mr. Sinclair is scribbling on a yellow legal pad, muttering to himself.

Agent Jeffers ignores him, keeping his focus on me. "Can you describe this figure in greater detail? Right now, it sounds like you are describing a teddy bear."

I roll my lips. *Slow down. Get the facts right.* "A black and fuzzy, two-dimensional humanoid-shaped thing, I guess you could say. About my height or taller. I was terrified. So there is no way I would want to do an experiment that brings *them* around or the buzzing sound. But here we are. They are here haunting me."

The other eyebrow arches. "Fuzzy, two-dimensional shapes are haunting you."

I'd cross my arms if I could, but the handcuffs are restricting my range. Instead, I frown at him. He huffs. My annoyance overrides my anxiety. I hate when people dismiss what I say. "That's what I said. These things, and the buzzing, and the bug infestation, and the excessive bird activity around the house, and, and once our house shook like an earthquake, but none of the neighbors felt it. Or they conned us. I have witnesses to it all. Except the figures. Apparently, only I can see them," I ramble.

The agent holds one finger up and peers at the wall behind me.

"Steven didn't tell me any of this except the buzzing," Mr. Sinclair mutters.

I roll my eyes. "See? I told you. It's beyond comprehension. It's easier to chalk it up to coincidence or old-house issues. But I understand the pattern. I have a doctorate in physics."

"Sshh," Mr. Sinclair urges.

I roll my eyes once more. "Oh, please. Like they don't know everything about me already. I was in the military, Mr. Sinclair. And if the Pentagon is involved, they know you top to bottom already as well."

Agent Jeffers clears his throat. "Okay, going back, you got the courage to reenter the house that first night. Go slow and don't skip any details."

I angle my head to one side. "You mean you lot hadn't already riddled my house with listening devices? Because it was fantastic timing when things happened *after* I got home."

"You think *we* are doing this to you?"

I shrug. "Well, someone is."

Mr. Sinclair whispers to me to cease talking.

"No," I snipe at him. "Leave if this case is too much for you. I'm done trying to figure this out on my own." I lean so I can stare at the one-way mirror, sensing someone important, like whoever Big Haus is, is watching and listening. "I understand I shouldn't have been nosy about what

I was hearing in the lab building that night and gone to investigate on my own. It was my ego and nosiness that made me want to know what was happening in a lab down on the fifth level. I shouldn't have opened the door, even though there was no sign that an experiment was underway. I don't care if I ever find out what was being tested. I need to move on." I inhale. There. I admit what I have been fighting in my heart since the incident. I scrub my face. I have also broken the non-disclosure agreement. Great. With a sigh, I sit straight in my chair, look at the agent, and say, "That first night here, I plucked up enough courage to sneak back indoors. Then I saw something by the fence—"

"What was it?" Agent Jeffers leans forward, pen at the ready. His thumb presses the pen top down with purpose. *Click.*

Suddenly, I'm back on my porch in the darkness, cold mud soaking through my shoes, my heart thumping, a large shape moving in the shadows. "I—I don't know. It was dark, and there was this figure hunched over like an enormous dog or raccoon moving by the back fence."

"So you aren't sure?" Both Mr. Sinclair and Agent Jeffers ask in earnest.

"No, I'm not. And I told my therapist so. Speaking of which, I have court-ordered phone appointments with her on Mondays. She'll report me for not calling tonight."

"This is Dr. Sternan you are speaking of?" Both the agent and my lawyer ask in unison again.

They share a sharp glance. Their attention on the same things isn't lost on me. I lean forward and grip the edge of the table, its glacial, unforgiving nature acting as an anchor under numb fingers. "I can name everyone else who has been a witness. Even my neighbors can hear the buzzing, I think. At first, I thought the old guy, Gary, was doing it, or had something to do with it. Wait, where is my briefcase? Does Steven have it? He can get the numbers for you if Mr. Sinclair doesn't already have them."

Agent Jeffers holds up a finger. "Okay, hold on. I need the proper release form. I'll see about getting your phone or having your husband provide the numbers he gave your attorney." He leaves. The military police officer by the door remains a statue, staring at the opposite wall.

Mr. Sinclair turns to me. "Claire, please listen to me. You cannot assume these people will vouch for you in the way you assume they will. State that you want me to be present during each witness statement. People will lie through their teeth to protect themselves. And the Pentagon will cover its own people at any cost. Any of the witnesses could be the culprit trying to get you in trouble. I am here to protect you from that happening. Please trust me."

I stare at the one-way mirror. "Oh, I know all about how far they will go to cover their asses."

Agent Jeffers returns half an hour later with a clipboard and my phone in an evidence bag. "I got what numbers I could from your husband. We have him sitting in a room two doors down if you, Mr. Sinclair, desire to speak to him. Mrs. Simmons, Mr. Simmons confirmed, you act scared every time there is an incident. So much so that he felt compelled to call Dr. Sternan in one instance. My colleague got a hold of her, and she will be on a call in a while." He sits down and points to the clipboard, his demeanor becoming rigid. "Right now, we need you to tell us what you know about that apparatus," he points with his other hand to the black box still sitting on its evidence bag, "and how it came to be found on your property."

"Where on my property?"

"Claire, please. Let me ask the questions," Mr. Sinclair urges. I nod and purse my lips. He turns to Agent Jeffers. "Where exactly within the Simmons' property line was this located?"

"Under the back porch stairs."

"Well, then someone dropped it there after last Friday because I was under the house Friday night, and there was nothing there," I announce triumphantly.

Mr. Sinclair groans.

I splay my hands. "Look, I know how it sounds, but I was searching for a cellar door. The previous owners were eccentric, so I figured they stored some weird stuff in a hidden cellar, and that was what was causing all the anomalies," I explain. "But when I found the cellar door in the shed Friday night and opened it, there was a slab of cement covering the opening. Then the buzzing started again, and Steven pulled me from the shed."

Agent Jeffers' back straightens. "So you are telling me that you hadn't gone under the house or into the shed until last Friday night?"

I nod. "Correct. The electrician inspected underneath, but not the shed. And the exterminator peered under the house, but didn't crawl beneath or go to the shed. The backyard is a swampy, overgrown mess, and no one ventured to guess the phenomenon was originating from there. Steven can tell you about the house inspection. No one reported anything out of the ordinary about the wiring or construction of our home."

"But you've been living at your house for weeks. You didn't store any tools or gardening equipment in the shed when you moved in?" Agent Jeffers presses.

"No. We don't own any gardening equipment. We left all that at our condo in Montana when we sold it. Steven keeps all of his tools in the garage or my office unplugged. Whatever was in the shed or cellar came with the house. Steven and the bank can verify that."

Agent Jeffers crosses his arms. "I still find it hard to believe you didn't at least open the door to peek in to see what the bank might have left behind for you to use. We've seen your yard; there's a lot of work to do."

I glare at him. "It's winter. There's no point. The weather has been gross, and we have been busy with our new jobs. Besides, a friend told me to be careful because of all the poison ivy growth around there. There was also a padlock on the door. I think. Steven can verify. I don't know who took the lock off."

"Advised by whom to be careful?" Mr. Sinclair and Agent Jeffers ask. Another shared glance.

This is what I feared. They'll question everyone. Pretty soon, they'll insist on calling my parents. Upsetting them is the last thing I desire. "I don't need to bring anyone else into this. My job is on the line as it is. I can't afford to lose my meager salary. I wouldn't even know where to buy something like that," I motion to the box, "much less the funds to buy one. I'm sure you'll examine my bank account, if you haven't already."

The room door opens. A wall of a man dressed in a military officer's uniform enters. Towering over six feet tall, not including his cap, and with double-wide shoulders, it's a miracle there's room in here for him. But the cramped space is not what has anxiety and annoyance playing tug-of-war in my consciousness. He dismisses the military police officer.

"Oh, hell, not you," I say.

A smirk curls up at one corner of the newcomer's lips. "Stand down, Mrs. Simmons. I'm on your side."

I harrumph, then roll my eyes. "Like you were last time?"

The officer faces my attorney. "I'm Air Force General Hall. You have been told my codename, Big Haus."

I watch with mild interest as Agent Jeffers' whole countenance relaxes while Mr. Sinclair's shoulders bunch up to his ears, and he writes more on his pad, flips over another page, and writes more.

The general continues. "I'm taking over from here, Agent Jeffers. You can stay, but I'm sitting in that chair. Been standing all day, and this bad knee of mine is aching."

Agent Jeffers gets up and makes his way to the

door. "I'll be behind the glass. I want to understand why you are on her side when you were the one to call us to investigate her."

My eyebrows rise. "I'm not saying shit." I glance at my attorney, who stares with a bewildered expression back at me. I would be too, since I had just been spouting everything I knew. But this is different. I'm not scared of Agent Jeffers or any police officer. But this guy? He was the deciding vote on the panel at Rosebud Research Facility that suggested I fabricated my statement and had suffered from a psychotic episode, which got me dismissed from the Air Force and Rosebud facility.

My wounded pride from our previous encounter starts a fire in my belly. I concentrate on that sensation and snipe at him. "You thought you could make everything disappear with that non-disclosure agreement, huh? But your secret experiment has gone too far this time. I will whistleblow so hard, it will slap your department before the Supreme Court." I lean forward, staring into his face. This sudden confidence reminds me of one night at three in the morning, soon after I finished boot camp. I and some other Air Force cadets had to repel down a cliff in the pitch dark. They made us stare over the edge first to fill us with fear, calling us chickens. No one else offered to go first, and always wanting to be the best, I volunteered. They strapped me up, and I hopped over the edge, flipping the bird at the lieutenants hazing us. I threw up at the bottom, since my stomach was in my throat throughout the entire descent. They hadn't warned me how many boulders and bushes would be in my way to navigate. But I earned the higher-ups' respect that night, and I never got hazed again.

General Hall leans forward as well. "I am on your side, but so help me, I can get these charges to stick on you if I desire."

Mr. Sinclair lays a hand on my forearm and says, "Claire, please heed my advice."

I lean back and make the motion of zipping my lips shut. Then, I gesture for the general to continue.

"That's better. What I was going to say is that yes, I agree you wouldn't know where to buy such an apparatus or have the funds to buy one. In fact, that and the other stolen military property are traceable back to Europe."

I sit up, lightbulbs going off in my head. "Don't tell me, it's the same type of equipment that you find in the labs on level five?"

"Yes."

"I knew it! Hallelujah!" I shout, jangling my chains. "So why am I still chained up like a criminal?"

General Hall raises a hand. "Not so fast. We still need to figure out how so much equipment found its way onto your property and who is behind it. You yourself are still under investigation."

Hope simmers in my chest regardless of the insinuation. One of my legs bounces under the table, my brain still thinking, processing, still sluggish because of the time of day and being in this cold coffin for so long. "Wait. It just sank in. So you found more than just that thing in the bag? Where?"

"In your bunker."

"But there isn't one. The door to the cellar just opens onto cement," I argue. "And it's not my bunker."

General Hall shakes his head. "Don't play games. It's on your property, so it's your bunker. We know that is a false door. We found the actual door."

I lean back, mouth gaping. "Actual door?" I screech. "How? Where? That was the only door in the shed. I searched around the house with a flashlight for hours. Were there bodies too?"

"No, it's under the shed."

"Under the floorboards? But there weren't any foul smells."

"Claire," Mr. Sinclair warns under his breath.

General Hall tilts his head to one side. "You really don't know, do you?"

"No." I shake my head and glance at my lawyer, licking my lips. I need to evaluate what I'm going to say next, so I don't piss the general off again. "I'll say the same thing I told Agent Jeffers. If you have been investigating me for a while now, then you will know, and will see on my bank statements and phone records, that we have been hiring professionals to figure out what's been going on at our house. The ghosts are getting stronger from the increased electrical discharges."

General Hall's lips thin.

Another light bulb turns on in my head. "Oh my God, it was you in the fake animal control van, huh? There were never any burglars. Your little FBI buddies have been spying on me. And it still hasn't occurred to you that I might be innocent?!" I try to raise my hands, but am stopped by the chained handcuffs. Their cold metal edges dig into the soft tissue around my wrists. I wince and lower my hands back down.

Mr. Sinclair lays down his pen, a shiny ballpoint with writing on the side. Probably his name or firm. "General Hall, are you charging her or not? Because if not, un-cuff my client. She has cooperated with you. Way more that I would have allowed had I had the power to shut her up."

General turns from him to me, then chuckles. My cheeks flame. The general asks the mirrored wall for Agent Jeffers to come back with keys.

Agent Jeffers pops in and takes the cuffs off. I massage my red wrists and numb fingertips, and then thrust my arms through the sleeves of Steven's jacket.

"I'm not saying we are not charging you for now. But we appreciate your cooperation, Mrs. Simmons," General Hall states, watching me. "And no one is going anywhere until we find the person responsible."

"So long as you have a scapegoat to cover your ass," I grumble. Same tune, same record, same voice.

"That's strike two," General Hall says.

I roll my eyes. They're getting a workout today.

"There is no law that says my client can not speak her mind, General," Mr. Sinclair poses. "These strikes will not hold up in court. I will press charges against you for harassment if you don't stop."

I swallow a snicker, smiling instead, and thank him. That just earned Mr. Sinclair an extra star on Yelp.

General Hall cracks his neck. "Who is it, then, is the question."

Agent Jeffers, who has been hanging out in the corner since unlocking my cuffs, straightens. "I could get the form to fill out for a list of everyone she knows."

"Everyone I know is still alive, though," I contradict. Do they think the ghosts are someone I know?

General Hall's eyes widen and his mouth falls open, as if I had just spoken in tongues. "What are you talking about? I want to find who put the scientific equipment in your bunker. We don't need to interview everyone. That would take too long. I need to know with whom you've kept in contact from your past employment."

"No one, General. Honestly. All my friends disowned me. Check my phone and computer. I'm sure you already are. I talk to a few people here as well as my therapist, and my parents."

Agent Jeffers pulls out his little notebook and flips through it. "You claim a friend warned you not to go near the shed. Who was it?"

Mr. Sinclair raises a hand. "Before my client says anything, I need a written statement that she has been cooperative and you can assure that no retaliation befalls her for giving names. That includes her current employment and the bank that owns her home or any other assets the Simmons have."

I nod. "Oh, that's good, Mr. Sinclair. I also need my record cleared from the Air Force."

"It was when you signed the non-disclosure agreement," General Halls drawls.

"No. What I mean is, I need a full pardon and full retirement benefits as punitive damages. I was going to stay in the Air Force until retirement age or longer. You took that career away from me. I'm still paying my parents back for lawyer fees. I don't care what shady shit you all are playing at. I just need to move on from my past mistakes and stop being haunted."

We stare at each other. I fight the urge to blink.

General Hall inhales sharply and breaks our stare. He makes a notation on the clipboard in front of him. "I can't guarantee your request, Mrs. Simmons, but I can try. If you help us uncover the true culprit."

I look at my lawyer, who nods. "Okay, you have a deal."

Because I am not crazy.

32

I squirm in my cold metal seat to stretch the dull ache from my lower back above the complete numbness of my rear. "Can Steven sit in with me as I compile names in case I forget one?" I stretch my arms over my head under the scrutiny of all present. What are they going to do, re-handcuff me? Not likely with Mr. Sinclair at my side.

"No," General Hall says, pointing behind me. "We have Mr. Simmons writing a list of his own. Then we will compare the two lists for any discrepancies." He readjusts his cap. I notice the gray around his temples has spread since we last met.

Mr. Sinclair glances around at all of us, then

insists on seeing and speaking to Steven to confirm he is okay with this arrangement. Agent Jeffers volunteers to escort him, and they leave.

I crack my neck, rub my arms, needing more blood to flow to my head and extremities. Do they keep these rooms so cold to dull the senses of suspects? If so, it's working. These white walls and metal furniture are making me forget what the outside world looks like. Will I ever be warm again? "Wouldn't it be more time-efficient for Steven and me to pen one list together?" Whatever gets us home faster. My stomach growls. A glance at my watch confirms that it's past dinnertime. I still have lasagna in the freezer from Friday. Mmm, or a hot cup of soup. We always keep a few varieties in the cupboard.

"What if it's him that's doing it?" General Hall poses.

I jerk my head up and stare at him. This again? Why does everyone suspect Steven? "Like I've told everyone else, I won't even consider it. He's a good man, and he doesn't have any knowledge of physics. We are happily married, a foreign concept in this day-in-age."

General Hall arches his eyebrows. "How can you be so sure? We found plenty of textbooks and reference material for physics experiments in your house."

I lick my teeth and purse my lips. He's grasping at straws, and I hate nothing more than a weak argument. My mind brings up past concerns friends in college posed to me when I started dating Steven. Won't our education level differences cause conflict? What about our cultural and racial differences? I crack my knuckles under the table. So help me, if the general makes his argument about race. I shake my head to dispel those memories from view. "Those are mine. That stuff makes him fall asleep. He's more interested in architecture and building houses with his hands, not in understanding how the universe works."

"Someone built everything in that bunker. Regardless, everyone, including you, is a suspect until we can whittle the names down. You should act that way too," the general warns. I slump back into the chair. He has a point. I hate not knowing who I can trust or having Steven's reassuring hands holding mine. I wonder if I should give his jacket back. Maybe in a few minutes. His lingering aftershave is good for my nerves.

"But the bodies were there before I arrived, right? That's easy enough to prove," I press.

"I have no idea what you are talking about."

I squint at him. "The earthbound bodies belonging to the ghosts. The ghosts that are haunting me."

He shakes his head.

Mr. Sinclair and Agent Jeffers return.

"Claire, please don't speak to anyone without me present. I can't protect you if I don't hear what you say," Mr. Sinclair says as he settles back into the chair next to me.

I shrug and lie. "I just asked him to repeat what he's already stated. Are you representing Steven too?"

Mr. Sinclair turns to General Hall. "Is there any cause to?"

General Hall shrugs and gazes at me. "Everyone is a suspect until proven otherwise."

"I'll inquire." Mr. Sinclair stands. "We may need to call in my associate to cover him. I can't protect you both when separated."

I reach out a hand to stop him. "Ask him if he wants his jacket back for a while. I'm warmer now."

Agent Jeffers accompanies my attorney out of the room again.

I drop my head into my hands, scratching my scalp. My stomach growls again, and a headache beats against my temples. "Can I have a cup of coffee? Or something to eat? Steven too?"

General Hall pokes his head out the door and barks at someone, "Go get us some stuff to eat and drink."

Mr. Sinclair and Agent Jeffers slip back in.

"Steven doesn't need his jacket, nor does he feel the need to be represented. He says to focus on you and he will be cooperative," Mr. Sinclair says after a heavy sigh. He reads over his copious notes.

I smile at this minor victory. Steven's actions have always spoken louder than his words. A man who stands by his convictions. He's innocent. He loves me. Then the warmth in my gut freezes. Someone is after me, though. After us. We are a team, after all, joined by marriage. But I can't fathom who. Everyone likes Steven. Maybe there are people who don't like me, but is their dislike enough for them to spend time and energy disrupting my life? Whoever it is must be psychotic.

The door swings open. A military police officer enters with a document for me to sign. They explain it's for the proposed deal between me and the Air Force, and another to fill out with names. Mr. Sinclair snatches both papers from me and reads them over once, twice. Time ticks by.

He alters clauses and wording on the pages and gives them back to the agent without allowing me to sign or fill them out. "Get these edits approved by the judge, or my client isn't signing."

The officer leaves. Mr. Sinclair returns to reading over his notes, as if that intervention on my behalf had never happened. I regard him and then glance at the general. General Hall looks impressed, too. His frown has an amused slant. I'll have to ask Steven what kind of fee Mr. Sinclair is charging and whether we should always have a man like him on retainer. With the frequency I talk to superiors regarding my employment status and law enforcement, it would be a logical action.

I am not crazy.

33

The tip of the ballpoint pen I've borrowed from my attorney hovers like the beak of a bird ready to snatch a worm.

"I need Mr. Sinclair present during each interrogation, General Hall."

"Agreed. Now, sign the legal agreement and then write the names on the other page in two categories. On the left go the names of people you have talked to about your house or life, and who may have been to the house. In the right column go the names of people that know about your residence and its location, but may not have visited or that you have not been present when they did," he instructs.

Mr. Sinclair gives me a thumbs-up and watches me scrawl out names. I try to remember them in order of the dates they visited. Steven, Danielle, Gary, the electrician, the exterminator, and the paranormal group go in the left column. Our bank name, real estate agent, house inspector, parents, military surplus owner, and the other two neighbors I spoke to go into the right column. Then, I tap the page and stare off into the distance. It's been two long weeks, and I've been around many people. I don't want to forget anyone. Do I include the cashier at the grocery store? Or the nice old man who owns the hardware store? What about the gas meter person or the mail carrier? The garbage collector? With a sigh, I add Dr. Sternan to the right column and cab driver to the left before sliding the paper towards the general.

He scans it; the downward tilt of the brim of his cap hides any expression he wears. Then he glances up at me. "Did the cab driver act suspiciously?"

"No, but he drove me home from the airport. I don't know how far-reaching you'd like me to go. I could add the mail carrier, meter reader, the entire street of neighbors—"

"No, no. This is fine to start with. We have our own list of names garnered from surveillance." He stands up as Agent Jeffers enters the room with a paper of his own in hand.

They converse in hushed tones in the corner before both leave without saying a word to me.

Mr. Sinclair yawns next to me, and I hide my yawn behind my hand.

"How much longer do you gauge they will be based on past cases of yours?"

He rubs his arms and shakes his head. "I couldn't say. I've never taken on such a complicated case. Your non-disclosure agreement doesn't help. That general has a huge upper hand over me." He then pats my shoulder and leans back in his chair. "But don't fret; I'm a competent lawyer and don't let things like big names and titles scare me. I don't like bullies, and that's how your husband described what happened to you, and I can see it happening again."

I thank him, and he gives me a solemn nod.

Agent Jeffers' head pops into the room. "Who is this Dr. Bayer? Your physician?"

"No, the professor I assist at the college."

His head disappears for a moment and then pops back around the door. "How is your husband acquainted with her?"

Mr. Sinclair sits up and readies his pen. I don't answer until he nods at me. "She offered to come over the first week I arrived to inspect our yard, since she used to work for her dad's landscaping business. We had her over for dinner that same night as a thank you, and they talked. She's the one who gave the advice I told you about avoiding the poison ivy."

"And you accompanied your husband to the military surplus shop?"

"Yes. The first time. We were hunting for bug traps after they crawled up our drains in the house the night before. It was gross."

"And you've never met your real estate agent in person?" I confirm I haven't. He nods and leaves the room.

Mr. Sinclair finishes writing my statement, then asks me to describe the military surplus owner. Was the owner curious about our house? Curious about how long we had been there?

I shrug. "No, not to my recollection. But he did mention I wasn't the only ex-Air Force soldier in town, and that I was nicer than that person. His daughter thought the soldier wore a disguise."

Mr. Sinclair's eyes widen. "Why didn't you tell the general?"

"I heard that," a voice echoes through the room.

Mr. Sinclair points at the one-way mirror. "They have a hidden speaker installed on the side. Now, I need you to remember more details of what the owner said about this person and say it aloud for them to hear behind the glass, too."

"His daughter helped this person, and she

thought they were wearing a cheap disguise. But when I pressed him for more information, thinking it peculiar myself, he said his security cameras are fake—they don't record," I say, facing the mirror.

Mr. Sinclair mutters that that's a shame.

A police officer enters loaded down with a few wrapped sandwiches, a shopping bag full of chips, and another bag full of various sodas. I grab the first two sandwiches within reach, snatch a bag of Fritos, and a Coke. Then I inquire about Steven. The officer says he'll be heading to Steven's room next.

Another officer enters after the other leaves and hands a pillow and gray wool blanket to me and my lawyer. "It's going to be a long night. Try not to spill on them." He pauses, then says, "We've brought in a couple of people from your list for questioning. Try to get some rest."

"Who?" Mr. Sinclair and I ask in unison.

The officer motions to the wall with his head. "Big Haus doesn't fancy me saying."

The next few minutes are silent except for our chewing and slurping sounds. I wrap myself in the blanket like a burrito and roost on the pillow, hoping that it will ease the ache growing in my lower back.

Mr. Sinclair burps, then stands to brush crumbs from his lap. "That was the best fare I've eaten in a police station, even if it was from the vending machine. My compliments," he says and salutes the blank wall.

I crack open a second soda. "Can we have a bathroom break soon?"

Agent Jeffers walks in and says he will escort both of us to the bathroom.

"Can you walk us to the one farthest away so I can stretch my legs?"

He shakes his head. "No, there's only one in this building. But you can exercise in this room if you don't mind an audience." Then he turns to my attorney. "We are setting up our video call with Dr. Sternan. I'll escort you there once we drop Mrs. Simmons back into the room."

*

I end up opting for some gentle yoga stretches while Mr. Sinclair is a witness to Dr. Sternan's interview. Or is it an interrogation? Is she a suspect? But she's been so supportive of my healing journey.

As I transition into the downward-dog pose, I run through everyone on the list I provided. No one seems capable of such a terrible thing. Even grumpy Mr. Davis with his big dog. It must be someone I don't know or remember from my past. But who? And why? Or is this all one big, chaotic coincidence? Did the ghosts come with the house, or did they manifest with help of the electrical devices?

No, I tell myself, there is a connection to me. There has to be. The figure's resemblance and the stolen lab equipment are too much of a coincidence. I remember being so perplexed when I arrived with the security officers. The laboratory was missing evidence of people and equipment. The lights being off was another giveaway. I remember being blinded when I walked in the first time. Then my eyes adjusted, and those figures were standing in front of me.

I am still restless. Maybe the two cans of caffeine soda weren't the best idea. I step to another section of the room away from the table and begin doing high-kicks to burn off some energy and get my blood flowing. It's still cold, both in temperature and surroundings. My watch says half an hour has passed since Mr. Sinclair left, but it could have been an eternity. The white walls, gunpowder-gray metal table, and neon lights overhead are pressing in on me, making me doubt my innocence, my sanity.

My attorney enters with Agent Jeffers, interrupting my jumping jacks. Mr. Sinclair lays his briefcase down on the table and then his legal pad.

I finish my set and rest my hands on my hips.

"Well?" I ask, pushing back curls from my face.

My attorney smiles and gives me a thumbs-up. "She vouched for you and had taken screenshots of timestamps of your meetings to back up what she said," he explained, then did some arm stretches. "Dr. Sternan is a great material witness. This is an interesting case. I am as perplexed as everyone who the culprit is."

I cross my arms. "I'm glad you're having so much fun. Meanwhile, I'm going to lose my job, and my neighbors think I'm a criminal. I'll become as reclusive as the Galloways."

"The Galloways? Who are they?" Mr. Sinclair asks. Agent Jeffers also perks up, putting a bag of chips down.

I purse my lips. What if it is the Galloways getting revenge for us moving into their house? What if they never went far and are spies from a different country using their bunker for nefarious deeds? I rotate toward the federal agent. "It may be worth looking into them. Tim and Laura were the owners before us. Reclusive and weird, based on what our neighbors say. They abandoned the house or died there. They may have disturbed some indigenous graves as well. Gary Tubman from next door used to do yard work for them. He's weird, too. There are some gross smells coming from his basement—the entrance is in his hallway."

Agent Jeffers nods while listening to me, then nods again at the end, in between shoving chips into his mouth. "We did, we are, and we will. That old man hadn't cleaned up the two geese he admitted to slaughtering. It made me throw up. Big Haus got him to spill everything he knew about the Galloways and sent him to a retirement home for the weekend on the government dime before you arrived this afternoon. We are homing in on the Galloways' whereabouts as we speak. They are very much alive. An agent in Utah has found their farm." He touches his earpiece, glances at the one-way mirror, and nods. "Alright. You two are welcome to watch as we interview your real estate agent."

"So they aren't dead, nor have they been spying on us here? Then the ghosts are from long ago?" My head jerks back. "Wait. Our real estate agent? Why? She's a spy?"

"Spy?" Agent Jeffers and my attorney ask.

"Oh, well, the narrative in my mind has an international spy involved in the research of conjuring ghosts, and I'm the unfortunate citizen to get caught in their path," I mumble, wringing my hands with cheeks aflame.

When I glance up from my intense interest in the floor tiles, I catch the men exchanging a glance that says, *'She watches too much television.'*

"We don't dabble in the paranormal. Nor is that why we are here," Agent Jeffers says. "We are going off a hunch Big Haus has. He thinks you might be onto something when you proclaimed that the person or persons behind this phenomenon had set up their equipment before you arrived. So we are bringing in everyone that had access to your house before the Sunday your plane touched down in Eugene."

My stomach drops. It takes two tries before I find my voice. "Is—is that why Steven is being held in a room and not able to sit with me?"

Mr. Sinclair lays a hand on my shoulder. "Steven told me not to tell you. He says he is innocent and will do anything to help with this investigation."

I hug myself and pull away from my attorney. "I know he didn't do it. He's Steven Simmons. And that means something." I swivel to Agent Jeffers, tears stinging my eyes. "No matter what others infer about him, it's all lies. He works hard and would do anything for me."

"Big Haus is the lead on this investigation. It's a good sign your husband is so compliant, okay?"

"Stop calling him Big Haus!" I shout. "His name is General Hall, and I don't trust him." I stamp my foot. "His is the signature on my discharge papers, and he petitioned for my permanent leave from

Rosebud Research Facility." I point to the mirror, hoping he is watching. "He got the judge to approve a year of court-ordered therapy. That's the reason Dr. Sternan is in my life. At least she vouches for me. This is all a sham!" I heave, hand on my chest. My throat tightens. "I am not crazy!"

"Jesus!" Agent Jeffers exclaims.

Mr. Sinclair reaches toward me. "Should we call Dr. Sternan?"

I shake my head, leaning away from him. "No," I say, my voice hoarse. "I'll just do my breathing exercises for a minute."

The men wait until I calm my wheezing. I smooth out my trousers and zip up Steven's jacket. "Okay. I'm better now. So, why are you letting me watch an interrogation?" I remind myself that all these police and agents are working for the general. If I don't trust him, I shouldn't trust them either. Mr. Sinclair may be my only hope of staying out of handcuffs. "What's the game?"

Agent Jeffers scratches his cheek. "General Hall wants to see your reactions to what she says. He says the realtor burst into tears after they sat her down. When they grilled her about why she was so upset, she cried out that she knew it was a bad idea to sell you and your husband the house." He smirks when I gape. "Still interested?"

34

Agent Jeffers leads us down the barren hallway and opens an unmarked door, gesturing for me to enter first. If I hadn't known better, I would have thought he was shoving me into a broom closet, since the interior is dim. General Hall is leaning over a clipboard proffered by a police officer. I'm glad it's not the same mean one that handcuffed me to the table. That guy can eat rocks. The general glances at me, dismisses the officer, and gestures for me to approach.

My feet anchor to the floor. I don't want to be within fifty feet of this man, much less the three feet allowed within this narrow room. Mr. Sinclair slides past me and nods at the general. Then he stares through the glass of the one-way mirror and beckons me. I shuffle forward, keeping my eyes focused on anything but the general. General Hall can eat rocks too, for thinking Steven could have anything to do with this.

Mr. Sinclair points and whispers, "Are you sure you've never met her? No video calls or pictures from around town on advertisements? Is she familiar at all?"

It's like I'm at some sadistic alien zoo, pointing at caged species that don't seem to care that we are there. But the lady sitting at a table in a room identical to the one I was in moments ago cares very much about her surroundings.

This woman, lacking the plump face of youth but without the deep lines and pull of gravity that come with living on this planet for many years, makes me place her age around forty-five or fifty. Her pink puffer jacket is half zipped up, mousy hair in a claw clip with lumps all over her scalp. There is no makeup gracing her ashen face, or, like me, after a long day of work, any makeup had worn off. Her puffy, red eyes dart here and there. The ceiling, the door, the wall through which we are staring at her. They had the courtesy of not handcuffing her. That was the most humiliating I've ever felt, besides my last day carrying my box of personal effects from the research facility where I worked for over a year.

At least Steven had warned me about the police presence at our house. How did her partner, or kids if she has any, react when the police knocked on her door tonight? Did the kids break down? Did she have to tell her partner not to wait up? That this will take a few minutes? Or perhaps she's a single mother and had one of the older children watch the others since the cops wouldn't allow her the time to call a sitter. I wish I could tell her what the police won't: it's not just a couple of questions and get back to your life. The room doesn't get warmer, and neither does the company about to join her. The questions are sneaky and intrusive. I want to hold her hand and sympathize with her. This woman is about to dissolve into a puddle of anxiety, like I was.

But I can't stop watching.

When her eyes halt their erratic search of her surroundings, her hands fidget. Clasping together, touching her face, her hair. Now back to her blouse sticking out from where the jacket's zipper ends. Now, pinching the charm on her necklace between her fingertips. Does she know the secrets of our abandoned house? *Anyone could be the culprit*, I remind myself.

I lean forward and squint at her necklace. Ah, yes, a gold cross. I'm disgusted with myself watching this woman's anguish. Did I look that pathetic when handcuffed to the table? Do they have video of me stored on a hard drive? I swallow hard and glance at my attorney.

"I've never seen that woman in my life, Mr. Sinclair," I state in a low tone. How high is too high of volume to speak here? Is this room soundproof? Steven never even described our real estate agent to me. Why would he? It would seem weird if he had. Same as if he had described the bank loan manager handling our mortgage. Who cares what someone's outward appearance is, as long as they do their job right, right? "And I don't think she did it," I add. "Her countenance doesn't scream psychotic. But she is nervous about something."

"We are of the same mind, Mrs. Simmons," General Hall agrees, using his normal speaking volume. "You two don't need to whisper. She can't hear us. I wanted you here in case anything she says jogs your memory of something or someone. As long as you keep your composure. Do you think you can do that?"

I sneer at him. Out of the corner of my eye, Mr. Sinclair shakes his head at me. I swallow what I want to say: can he handle being a decent human being for once and not treat everyone as an enemy of the state? Especially when he says he is on their side or doesn't suspect them. I manage one nod, eyes still narrowed to show him I'm not happy. He smirks.

Just then, Agent Jeffers enters the interrogation room. The federal agent introduces himself to the real estate agent, calling her Mrs. Carter. Then he sits and opens a file in front of her. "Have you ever seen this woman before?"

I crane my head; my nose an inch from the window.

As if reading my thoughts, General Hall states in a bored tone, "It's a picture of you. What he shows her isn't as important as what her face reveals when her words don't."

Good Lord, what did my face reveal? But it must not have been that bad since I'm on this side of the glass. Then again, what if he is a double agent and still building a case against me? I shuffle to stand on my attorney's other side.

Mrs. Carter straightens from peering at the picture. "No, sir," she says, her voice wobbling. "Who is she?"

"The victim."

The woman's hands fly to her chest. "The victim?" she chokes. "The house I sold to Mr. Simmons and his wife is a murder scene? But I sold the house only about a month ago. Why am I implicated?"

"This is Mrs. Simmons."

Mrs. Carter's features crumble. "Oh, no," she

groans. "But Mr. Simmons was so nice. Please tell me he didn't do it."

Agent Jeffers leans forward. "Mrs. Carter, I can not divulge who we theorize did it. But if you can answer a few questions for us, that would help us with the investigation. The sooner we get through them, the sooner we can get you home."

The woman nods, licks her lips, and clasps her hands atop the table. "Ask me anything. Anything. That poor girl. Oh, I'll never sell another abandoned property again. I swear. I didn't want to in the beginning, anyway," she blabbers on. "I had heard the haunting rumors, but never imagined that evil spirits could cause someone to murder their loved ones!"

Agent Jeffers holds up a hand. "Hold on, hold on. First, you said you thought it was a bad idea to sell them this property. Then you said you didn't want to sell it. Why the hesitation when it was such an easy sell and you didn't believe in the rumors?"

Mrs. Carter wrings her hands on the table. Tears leak down her cheeks, and I can imagine the cold sweat running down her back. Her fingers press into her cheeks, and she makes an anguished sound.

"I'm sorry, I didn't catch that," Agent Jeffers says.

All of us in the secret closet lean forward toward the glass, straining our ears.

"I took the listing on as a favor," Mrs. Carter repeats, sniffling. "Sales have been slow even with the economic boom this town is having, and I have bills to pay. I had to call in favors to help the Simmons get into that house. The bank was very hesitant to approve a VA loan for the abandoned property. They didn't fancy selling a reputedly haunted house to a veteran."

I ogle at the general. He smirks and touches the side of his nose. Something *was* going on at that house before I arrived. He knows way more that he's admitting to me. The jerk.

"A favor to whom?" Agent Jeffers implores.

The real estate agent's head pops up. I watch her eyes dart around the room.

"Is she here? Is she on the other side of the wall watching?" She stares at the mirror we are observing her through, then points toward us. "Is she implicating me? Or saying I made up the ghost stories and didn't get her the house first on purpose? Because I didn't do anything, Mr. Jeffers. I'm a vegetarian and animal rights activist. I couldn't harm an animal, much less a person. I volunteer at my kid's school. I'm a good person. It was the bank that wouldn't give her a loan, not me. There was nothing more I could do for her. It was a miracle that the Simmons got the house. The bank should have bulldozed the property and started over."

"No one is watching us, Mrs. Carter. This isn't an HBO crime series," Agent Jeffers replies, feigning exasperation. I would bet he's chuckling to himself right now, knowing how many of us are watching. It makes my stomach churn.

But I will see this through. I am not crazy and am becoming enraged at the culprit the longer I am in this building. Look at how many lives they have disrupted! How am I supposed to go to work tomorrow as if nothing had happened? I'll need an entire day to explain everything to Danielle.

Agent Jeffers has asked another question, but I am so deep in thought that I missed it. Something happened at that house. Either before the Galloways left, or soon thereafter. And why isn't anyone asking what the haunting rumors entailed? Mrs. Carter seems to know.

I lean towards my attorney to ask when Mrs. Carter says, "My friend, Danielle Carrol, wanted to buy the house first. But she didn't get approved. The bank told me there was too much suspicious activity in her account. I haven't spoken to her since."

I jerk my head back. "Danielle?"

General Hall turns to me. "Could it be the same Danielle Bayer you work for?"

Wait, no, she said a different last name. I blink

several times. "No, must be a coincidence."

"Are you sure?"

I regard him through narrowed eyes. "There are a lot of Danielle's in the world. I'm more interested in what the haunting rumors are. I want vindication."

General Hall waves a hand at me and leans towards a panel of buttons, holds down one, and speaks into a small microphone protruding from the wall. "Jeffers, ask her to describe her friend."

Agent Jeffers leans forward. "Can you please describe Mrs. Carrol for the record?"

I gag at how sweet Agent Jeffers made his voice sound. I'm glad he didn't try that on me. I would've punched him. My hands clench. This poor woman doesn't know how dangerous these men are. They'll rob her of everything if they want to; everything save for her name, and they might take that, too, if it pleases them. I'm a prime example. The name Claire Simmons means nothing to the scientific community. Who knows what falsehoods future employees might dig up about me, released from Rosebud Research Facility. If I come out of this alive, I'll make sure that Mr. Sinclair checks they wiped my military record clean and puts an end to any salacious rumors spread by former colleagues.

"Where is her attorney? Where is her

protection?" I ask Mr. Sinclair.

His lips thin. I spin around to the general.

"But she doesn't understand—"

"It's better this way," General Hall barks at me. "We'll be here hours more for no reason. If she is an accessory, she will face the consequences. Otherwise, she will go home."

I suck my lips in and bite down. That poor, poor woman.

"Well, um," Mrs. Carter begins, staring at her hands while her fingers roll around one another. "I think it's just Miss. My friend, or maybe it's ex-friend now, is not married. We've known each other since grade school. I was stunned when she popped up here in Deadwood and called me looking for housing. She didn't say what kind of work she does. We've grown apart, and she has always been a private person."

General Hall goes back to the microphone. "Her appearance, Jeffers. We don't have time for a life story."

Were these friends' remains found along with the electronic equipment on the property? "Why did you arrest me with all that fanfare and police and soldiers if there was a body on the property? That was stupid. You probably tipped the murderer off," I snipe at the general.

He goes back to the microphone. "Get Mrs.

Carter something to drink. Stall before she answers. I need a minute." Then the general turns to me and shakes his head. "Stop assuming things and wasting my time. There were no remains, just equipment. No fingerprints or DNA either. Else, we wouldn't be here. We assume the person or group behind these events has a gigantic ego. They are trying to prove how intelligent they are. There is a link between you, the stolen equipment, and the incident that got you sacked, and I need to know why. I don't want to hear about ghost nonsense."

I scoff. "Someone could have told me to set my mind at ease. I know what I saw in the lab and at home. It wasn't normal. Someone fudging up an experiment too big for the facility to handle invited something into the world."

"The equipment was back in its proper storage space within the week, and scientists with clearance apprehended. But they won't tell us who was heading the experiment or who was monetarily backing their project. They're too scared of the consequences," General Hall says with an air of superiority, his chin rising, peering down his nose at me. "The culprits here bought the stolen equipment we found on your property on the black market at a considerable price, or were the ones who stole it." He widens his stance. "Why someone would shell out that amount of money just to torture one household makes little sense. It would draw too much attention—as it already has." He smirks when my eyebrows rise. "I surmise it is someone from the facility, and this is their side project using the equipment, and you landed right in their lap by moving here. I fired and banned everyone apprehended from working in a government job again. There is no such thing as a perfect crime. I will find out who they are and what they are working on."

"Wait, is this you admitting you *didn't* know what was going on that night at the facility?" I glance back at my attorney. "Make a note of this, Mr. Sinclair."

"Way ahead of you, Mrs. Simmons," he says, bent over, using his upheld knee to write on his legal pad.

I shift back to the general. It's my turn to smirk. He shakes his head. "Good Lord, you are annoying," he mutters. "No, I'm saying nothing. We need to move on." Then he says into the microphone, "Okay, Jeffers, get her to talk."

I roll my eyes and edge closer to the mirror. *At least being annoying is better than being a jerk.*

Agent Jeffers requests that Mrs. Carter describe Danielle Carrol's appearance in the same nice-cop way. She takes two more sips of her tea before setting it down. From the tick in her cheek upon swallowing, I suspect it tastes like tepid, dirty dishwater. She's got to be using the action to stall for time or out of politeness.

"Dark blond hair, blue eyes, light skin, tallish."

"And you took on this house to sell to her as a favor?" Agent Jeffers presses.

Mrs. Carter swipes loose strands of frizzy brown hair back from her face. "Danielle found me through an ad in the local paper. My agency featured me because it is my tenth anniversary of working there. We went out for lunch a few times to catch up. It turns out she has alumni connections to the college my oldest son wants to attend. Danielle asked about cheap houses she could flip since she took a temporary job, but then the bank denied her loan two weeks before Mr. Simmons called me for a viewing. You see, I hadn't been aware my office had re-listed the home in the real estate papers. Before Danielle had applied for the loan, she'd promised to type a letter of recommendation for my son, which she followed through with. I am grateful. Nothing shady. I have my reputation to maintain as a real estate agent here." She sits taller.

Agent Jeffers flips through pages in his folder. "What car does Miss Carrol drive?"

"When I showed her the house, she was driving

a silver Nissan."

I breathe a sigh of relief. The Danielle I know is very different. Both in appearance and style.

"And when was the last time you saw her?"

Mrs. Carter leans her head back for a moment, then forward. "Well, I thought I saw her the other day, but when the lady turned after I called Danielle's name, she kept walking like she didn't know me. So maybe it wasn't her. The lady I called out to was wearing glasses, overalls with a black long-sleeved shirt, and her hair was a lighter shade of blond. I remember wondering why Danielle chose that shade of color for her hair. I could have been mistaken. I haven't spoken to Danielle since breaking the bad news that the bank didn't approve her loan. And I haven't seen her in person since showing her the abandoned house."

Professor Bayer wears glasses, has blond hair, grey eyes, and dresses nicely. Her name is Danielle. She drives a BMW. I can't imagine her in overalls unless she were doing yardwork for someone.

But the guy from the military surplus place said the service person had driven an old Nissan. Was it silver? Could Mrs. Carter's friend be the doomsayer?

I'm being watched.

General Hall is studying me.

I blink and roll my shoulders back.

"Are you covering for someone?" he asks me.

"No. It's just who she thinks she saw and my boss have a couple of similarities. It is a small town. But the Danielle I know has gray eyes, not blue. Her hair color is light blonde, not dark, and she drives a nice car. The surplus owner said an ex-Air Force person, who drove an old Nissan, had bought the weird stuff. Professor Bayer never mentioned being in the military, even when she found out I was. All she mentioned was that her father was military. And I've seen a lot of Nissans around town. You should bring her friend in, not mine."

He points to the glass. "People change their looks. Contacts, hair dye. Focus. Your expression changed when she described glasses and overalls. What about that gave you pause if the two women are not the same person?"

I glance at Mr. Sinclair. He nods, pen at the ready. I consider all I have perceived of Danielle. "I can't imagine my boss, Professor Bayer, in overalls unless she was helping someone with their landscaping. It's a hobby of hers. At work as a professor, she wears high-end brands. Like the other day, she wore a Gucci skirt. She drives a BMW. On my first day, she stated she liked to uphold the image of her title as a doctoral recipient since she had worked so hard for it. I don't blame her. I would do the same if I had the money."

"Anything else?" General Hall prompts.

"She never mentioned knowing about my house. She followed me home and didn't act like she'd ever been there."

The general scratches the beard stubble sprouting along his jawline. "And what is she a professor of?"

"Physics. *Theoretical* physics, where they sit and *think* about physics and don't care about experimentation. *Experimental* physicists figure out how to test their theories."

"Right," he declares. "I know that, but I wanted to hear you say it. You have a problem with denial, Mrs. Simmons. Life will get easier for you once you get over that." Then into the microphone, he says, "Jeffers, come out and escort these two back to their room. Tell Mrs. Carter you'll be back soon."

"Wait. Why do you keep trying to connect to the Danielle I know?"

"She's a suspect."

"In what universe? First, the coursework in all her classes is too much for her to keep up with. That's why I'm her assistant. And we are so exhausted at the end of every day. Second, are your ears clogged? She is a *theoretical* physicist, not an experimental one. Same as me. I do coding for the computers that experimental physicists use. We don't test hypotheses. Third, she's too smart to be involved in this kind of shadiness. The reason she is here is that her grant money dried up."

General Hall ushers us out of the room and locks the door behind him. Agent Jeffers meets us in the hallway and leads the way, with the general bringing up the rear behind me.

I walk backwards and say to the general, "Danielle Bayer is not this Danielle Carrol. You are going to cause me to lose another job. I'll sue you if that happens."

"We've been following leads as long as we've been tracking your movements, Mrs. Simmons. If you know better, then explain to us why Danielle Carrol, and not Danielle Bayer, has been an employee at two renowned laboratories in the world with a father that was in the Air Force from 1980 to 1991?"

35

For the professor's sake, I hope it's all a terrible coincidence. Or it's a case of stolen identity. Or that she lied about having a doctorate or working in research facilities. I could forgive that. People protect their insecurities in the strangest ways. I chew on my thumbnail and lean back in the cold metal chair. That would at least explain why I am better at helping the students with their physics problems.

"Do you think my boss faked her resume and isn't a physicist?" I ask Mr. Sinclair.

He cracks open a Sprite; the last soda left in the bag of drinks from our feast earlier. "Either that or she is the evil mastermind behind this whole thing.

Dots of evidence eventually make a line."

"I don't like how easy that would be. Just like when they picked me as a scapegoat. Why would an evil mastermind help me debunk this thing? I've told her almost everything that has happened. She's been sympathetic. Oh, and she has the same physics equation tattoo. That's how we connected. It is our love of physics that strengthens our friendship."

He shrugs. "This whole thing sounds like someone has a vendetta against you. Or it's all an incredible coincidence. Either way, I'm with you until the end."

I pull the rough, gray, woolen blanket tighter around me and lean forward against the table, elbow on the top, my chin in my hand. "But what about all the other people on our lists? It's a bit on the nose, isn't it? My boss is the mastermind behind a secret organization using black market stolen equipment on *my* property. Don't you suppose she would have picked a different profession and identity to hide behind?" My leg bounces. "No, I can't believe it. It sounds so ridiculous as I say it aloud. It's got to be someone else. The barista who makes my coffee at work sometimes and gets it wrong half the time, or the dog walker that can see when I come and go from the house."

Mr. Sinclair sets down his now empty can of soda

and covers a belch with his hand. "I don't know, Claire. I've seen and heard stranger things in my career. If there's one thing I've learned, it's that humans are unpredictable. There would be no need for psychoanalysts or therapists if they were predictable. We'd be able to stop crime waves before they happened and elect the right people to political offices." He stands and stretches. "I know you don't like the general for past reasons, but he's earned his position. Guys like that deal with colossal problems in the world. If he's involved, this is not just a petty scheme to get back at you. These are dangerous people who aren't worried about what happens to you or anyone in their way. I advise we stay amicable and communicate anything that you can remember of importance. That tattoo of yours, for one. I'll add it to my notes as well."

"Yeah, yeah, okay," I say, then yawn. My eyelids are heavy. This must be the end of the line for the caffeine in my system. "I wonder how Steven is doing. I wish he were here with us. They'll let him go now, right?"

"I don't know about them releasing him," Mr. Sinclair says and walks over to the door, knocking twice. "But that's not a bad idea. I'll check."

A military policeman pokes his head in.

"I'd like to check on Mr. Simmons' welfare two

doors down. I represent him and his wife."

I gape, then shutter my expression. He represents me, so he is lying. I wonder how often a lawyer fibs—how far they know they can go without being arrested? Is Mr. Sinclair trying to prove to me how far he will go to be my attorney? *I kind of don't have a choice, man. Steven hired you, not me.*

The officer nods and allows Mr. Sinclair to leave the room. Poor Steven, all alone. At least I have our attorney for company. But I'd rather have Steven present. We could compare notes. He could reassure me that everything would be all right.

My fingernails and the tiny hairs on my knuckles have been inspected by the time Mr. Sinclair returns. He falls into the chair beside me and heaves a sigh.

I give him a moment to scribble more notes before turning to him. He aged five years in the time away; the lines around his eyes grew deeper, longer. His hair is shaggy, long strands falling forward over his face.

"Mr. Sinclair?" My voice is small.

He leans on his hand and glances over at me. "First, Steven wants me to extend his love to you for thinking of him. But Claire, I'll be frank. I just spoke with Agent Jeffers in the hall. People are talkers in this town. Agent Jeffers has been snooping around everyone Steven knows and interviewing them. People at his construction work say he's been muttering to himself a lot. Words like ghosts, and wind, and illness. Neighbors who can see your front yard say he doesn't appear happy when he arrives home. They are claiming Steven always stands outside his truck, staring at the house for a full minute before entering." Mr. Sinclair runs the other hand over his face. "The military surplus store owner thought Steven was acting controlling and possessive of you. He's seen your husband on more than one occasion at the shop. Are you sure there aren't any personal details you are leaving out about your relationship with Steven? Something you could be in denial about?"

I've frozen, still processing the first half of what Mr. Sinclair stated. Why was Steven muttering about ghosts? Has he seen Buzz or the other one and not told me? I gulp. Then I remember and snap my fingers. "He went a second time to ask about the records of the Galloways. Ask him. The general gave him a chance to explain himself, right? This has been an attack on both of us, remember? Steven has been trying to help me since I have anxiety." I bury my face in my hands. How selfish I have been! "I know all of this has been hard on him over the last few weeks, but he only kind of expressed it once. He works so hard, and I've been doing all the complaining. I'm the worst."

A hand rests on my shoulder, and Mr. Sinclair says, "You both have been through a lot. He loves you and isn't going anywhere. I advise taking a vacation together after this is all over. I'm no marriage counselor, but I've seen this happen a lot. It sounds like your marriage has become strained, Claire."

"I believe you are right. Two other people have inquired about how we were doing—how Steven has been treating me." I scoff and sit back up. "As if he were the one doing these awful things to me and himself." Then I meet Mr. Sinclair's gaze, a fire kindling in my stomach at the insinuation. "He has done so much for me." My eyes well up. "He's my best friend. My only friend," I sob, and I shove a fist into my mouth to cover the ugly sound; there's no controlling my emotions tonight.

"Okay, that's enough. Now my client is upset. This is pushing my ethics," Mr. Sinclair yells at the one-way mirror.

I wipe my eyes and glance at the mirror, then at my attorney. "What? What's going on?"

Mr. Sinclair won't meet my gaze. Shifting eyes, thinned lips, tense shoulders. I know the signs of a guilty conscience.

"What did you do?" I growl.

The door opens, and General Hall steps in. "Before you attack him, Mrs. Simmons, it was my idea. I pressured him, but the cameras weren't recording. We just had to be sure about what you felt for your husband. He is still not above suspicion."

I jump up, the metal chair crashing to the floor behind me. "Be sure?" I thunder. "That I'm capable of emotion? That I love my husband and I know for a fact that he loves me?"

The general nods once. "Well, yes, actually. Just tying up loose ends."

"I should sue you for emotional distress," I hiss. Then I turn to my attorney. "And you are so fired."

Mr. Sinclair stands and buttons his jacket. "I agree. But this case isn't over yet, Mrs. Simmons. We can talk about my ethics after you are free. I have a job to do. General Hall, that was over the line. I can't believe you talked me into that."

I shoot a scathing glance at him. Steven and I will deal with him later. I imagine a discounted rate is in order for that misconduct.

General Hall shrugs. "I know her better than you do. She's tough, but still human." He meets my hard gaze. "And that's a good thing, Mrs. Simmons. So, if you'd like to join me, we are about to interview Professor Danielle Bayer. Or whatever she is calling herself these days."

Of all the backhanded compliments. I blink. My hands clench again and again. I stomp out of the room; General Hall navigates ahead of me to lead the way. Mr. Sinclair follows in silence.

I say over my shoulder, "Since this thing keeps dragging on into infinity, I'm guessing I won't make it to work tomorrow. You are going to make sure I keep my job and my husband keeps his, Mr. Sinclair."

"Yes, ma'am," he replies.

*

Another tiny closet with a window. Steven won't be joining us. "Again, tell me why you called into question my loyalty to Steven, and his to me?" I grill the general.

He heaves a sigh, pulls off his cap, scratches his buzzed scalp, and replaces the cap. "In our subsequent interview with Mrs. Carter, she elaborated, saying that when she thought she saw her friend, a man was conversing with the woman. Mrs. Carter waited for them to finish talking before calling out her friend's name. When we showed her some pictures of men, she pointed to Steven's picture, adamant it was him she saw."

The blood leaves my face. "When?" I whisper.

"The morning he went to get breakfast while you stayed at the hotel. We were observing you observing us, if you remember," he says. "I also had an agent shadow Steven. They can corroborate."

I freeze, remembering who I was talking to. "Stop. You are trying to trip me up. He was just being cordial, saying hello. Mrs. Carter would have blabbed if anything more scandalous were happening. Professor Bayer lives in an apartment near campus. She was probably getting breakfast as well. Steven and I had had quite a night. The worst yet. Then, when he returned, I had been talking with Dr. Sternan and had told him about your pest control van. It slipped his mind." I raise my chin. "Nice try." But I store it away for later, to ask Steven his side of things.

The general shrugs, then his head turns. "We'll see. Ah, here we go."

Someone opens the interrogation room door. Professor Danielle Bayer walks in first. She's as immaculate as the day I met her. I would have concluded it was morning, and she was on her way to work. Maybe she was. I glance at my watch. Nope, it's almost midnight. Had they let her get dressed? Every strand of blond hair is in place, her mauve pout lined, mascara black as night. She even has her briefcase.

"Is she representing herself?" I wonder aloud.

"She could play an attorney," Mr. Sinclair says, with a hint of awe in his voice. I don't blame him.

She could take down a corporation dressed like that—an impressive image of confidence to behold.

"That's how she dresses every day."

General Hall scoffs. "And you're sure your husband just forgot to tell you he ran into her?"

I sneer at him, I'm sure not for the last time tonight. "She's not his type."

Steven admitted to being attracted to women of color when my friends questioned his white-boy intentions in our first month of dating. *'A little messy, a little feisty, a curvy body, and mind of her own is what I'm into,'* was what Steven shot back at my then college best friend who had grilled him. Then Steven had wrapped an arm around me and said, *'And I've found all that, and more, in Claire.'*

Back in the interrogation room, Agent Jeffers settles into a metal chair opposite Danielle, just as he had with Mrs. Carter. Danielle's face remains neutral, her posture straight.

"Can you please state your legal name for the record?"

"Dr. Danielle Bayer," she states without hesitation.

Agent Jeffers flips open a folder and slides a paper in front of her. "That is not what your birth certificate says. Your last name here is Carrol. Your mother's maiden name is Bayer."

"Congratulations, agent. You know how to look

stuff up. I legally changed it a long time ago."

So she is Mrs. Carter's friend from school? But why would she pretend she hadn't seen Mrs. Carter? Was she embarrassed because she was wearing overalls instead of her usual more upscale attire? And that would mean she knew about our house. A heavy knot forms in my stomach.

Agent Jeffers takes the birth certificate back from Danielle. "You kind of fell off the face of the earth for a time, Miss Carrol. It's curious that it coincides with when you changed your name."

"It's Dr. Bayer to you," Danielle snipes. Then her features cool, and one of her shoulders rises and falls. "It was a bad time for my family. Nothing that's your business."

"Everything is our business if national security is on the line, Dr. Bayer," Agent Jeffers spars back.

Danielle's chin rises. "I don't know what you're talking about."

"I know you are an intelligent woman, Dr. Bayer, so I will cut to the chase," Agent Jeffers says. "You are a physicist who has had clearance in research facilities that use the most advanced lab equipment in the world. Then you quit, and your entire life goes dark. Your bank statements reveal frequent but large cash deposits for several years until this recent professorship. Who was bankrolling you?"

"Family. It was a family matter that I was helping

with. There was an illness. My father was dying."

General Hall chuckles next to me. I glare at him. He glances my way. "Not the worst lie that I've heard someone make up. It's more like she's drawing from an offshore account to cast suspicion from herself."

I huff and say, "So quick to judge. Her father suffered from post-traumatic stress disorder. Not that you would know what that is."

He rolls his eyes and turns away. Back in the room, Danielle's composure hasn't changed. She could be a mannequin, sitting in a window display, fresh for viewing.

"Okay, so you took a teaching job here in Deadwood and reconnected with your friend, Mrs. Carter," Agent Jeffers states. "Can you confirm that she and you viewed the house currently occupied by the Simmons?"

Danielle's lips purse, then relax, and then purse again. "We viewed a few homes from the sidewalk. I never went in. The front of that dilapidated property was enough for me to pass. She offended me; had the audacity even to show me such a house. That's when I broke contact with her."

But she had applied for a loan, according to Mrs. Carter. I frown. Is Danielle's ego so fragile that she will lie so blatantly to a federal agent?

"Why didn't you mention you had been to that

property before when Mrs. Simmons invited you over?" Agent Jeffers pressed. That lie must be of little consequence since Jeffers is ignoring it.

"What good would it have done?" Danielle snaps back. "They bought the property, not me. She asked for advice on how to handle the yardwork, and I gave it. The end."

The federal agent leans back in his chair, crossing his arms. "And you've never been back since?"

Danielle shakes her head once.

Next to me, General Hall rubs his hands together. What a monster. Did he do that when I was in the hot seat? And when Jeffers questioned Steven? What a sadist.

Agent Jeffers pulls out additional sheets of paper from the folder and slides them across the table. "Can you confirm this was you driving a silver Nissan and also driving a black BMW?"

Danielle leans over the pictures, then sits back, shrugs. "The picture is too blurry. I can not confirm nor deny."

"No, it isn't. Face recognition software could discern whether it is you. Do you know this picture of your parked Nissan can place you within a hundred yards of the Simmons' property, Dr. Bayer?" Agent Jeffers says, tapping the picture on the right. "Do you remember being on the same street as the Simmons' property last Friday night?"

I gasp, reach forward and dig my nails into the ledge of the window. What was she doing there driving that car? Was it even her? *Why isn't she asking for a lawyer?*

General Hall turns to me. "Did you experience anything Friday night?"

"You know I did." *Not you, Danielle. It has to be someone else. It must be.*

"What time was that again?" Mr. Sinclair implores.

I nibble my lip, watching Danielle's impassive reaction, her cool gaze. Nothing is fazing her. I'd be sweating bullets if I were in her position. "Steven had just gotten home from working late. I was in the backyard, and sunset was ending. So, whatever time that was. I had a flashlight. Steven went back inside, and I went into the shed. That's when the buzzing sound started. I opened the false cellar door, thinking I had solved the puzzle. But there was only concrete. The noise worsened then." I shut my eyes, reliving how angry I was and Steven dragging me back out. My fingertips of one hand glide over the scabs of the other palm as if I'm reading Braille. "Steven pulled me out, and Gary Tubman was there as a witness. Gary had come over to check on us." I peek over at my attorney to gauge his reaction.

But he's focused on General Hall, who is nodding

like a bobblehead. Then, the general turns to the microphone.

"Ask her what she was doing on the street," he says, speaking to Agent Jeffers.

"What were you doing on that street at eight o'clock on Friday night in the silver Nissan, Miss Bayer?" Agent Jeffers cross-examines.

Danielle's jaw twitches. "It's Doctor Bayer. I worked hard for that title. Since when was driving in a rental—since my car is in the shop—to a friend's house a crime now?"

"What friend?"

"How is that relevant?"

"What's the address?"

The ringing in my ears overshadows Danielle's reply. Doctor Danielle Bayer. Formerly known as Danielle Carrol. Placed near my house around the time I experienced buzzing. *"Dots of evidence eventually become a line."*

"But how?" I inquire aloud. "If it is her, how is she getting into my shed? And she said the Nissan is a rental, but Mrs. Carter says that's what she drove months ago. Does her mechanic only have one car for loan?"

General Hall raises a hand. "Again, people lie. She could own both cars. You are obsessing over the wrong thing, Mrs. Simmons. The 'how' she is getting into your backyard is simple. Simpler and more pertinent than why she sometimes drives an older car. Agent Jeffers proved his theory of how while we were waiting for you to arrive from work today." Then he leans back over the microphone. "Jeffers, work your magic. It's confession time."

"Magic?" I ask, glancing at my attorney. He just shrugs.

General Hall chuckles. "You two are about to see why I picked Agent Jeffers to work with me on this case."

Mr. Sinclair and I lean toward the glass. Part of me hopes we are on the right track, because I desire to go home to my bed and mend anything that needs it with Steven. The other half of me is heartbroken and hopes it is not Danielle. Over the last two weeks, I have worked so hard to build our relationship, to defend her when Steven claimed she would use me.

Is she General Hall's newest scapegoat since I put up a fight?

Or have I been so blind and naïve as not to see what everyone else can?

Whatever it takes to prove that I am not crazy.

36

My eyes are dry, head heavy. "Can I get a glass of water? This place is sucking the life out of me."

General Hall sighs and turns to the microphone while pressing a different button on the panel. "Front desk, send someone with a bottle of water to interrogation closet three, please." He turns to me. "For an ex-soldier, you don't have very good stamina."

I wrinkle my nose at him. But then turn my attention back to the one-way mirror. Agent Jeffers is shuffling through papers in the folder on the table. If I didn't know better, I'd say he's flustered, unsure of what question to ask next.

I can tell Danielle thinks so, too. She's watching

him wearing a smirk that I have seen twice over the last couple of weeks. Once directed at me; once directed at a student. Both times resulted from asking Danielle to clarify something she had said. Is this the ego that the general inferred? Is there a dark side to Danielle that Steven alluded to?

I shudder; my attention glued to Danielle's face. I wonder when the agent's magic will kick in. A hand passes me a bottle of water. I don't blink while my hands work to unscrew the lid and bring the bottle to my lips. Cool liquid passes down my throat and into my stomach. I recap the bottle, gripping it hard enough for the plastic to crinkle in my hand; a harsh sound in the otherwise silent room.

Finally, the federal agent closes the folder and rubs a hand over his face.

"Having trouble, Mr. Jeffers?" Danielle croons. "Because that happens when someone is innocent." She draws circles on the tabletop with one manicured fingernail, her lips parting and stretching back, flashing pearly white teeth.

I tilt my head. Is she *flirting* with Agent Jeffers? I run my tongue over my own teeth. It's been a while since I've been to the dentist.

"I'm innocent, Mr. Jeffers," Danielle says softly. She bats her eyes. "I have a class to teach in the morning. You know where I work. The next generation isn't going to teach itself. Why don't you let me go, and we can discuss questions you have over coffee?"

Gag me; this is a new side of Danielle I've never seen. She had better not have tried these moves on Steven. I'll punch three shades of purple into that pretty face if she has. I relax my grimace and blink. What if this Danielle has nothing to do with the experiment and everything to do with just trying to be a homeowner? The white picket fence American dream, and all that? What if she's just a spoiled brat and searching for that one sucker to give her anything she wants—to be at her beck and call? My fingernails dig deeper into my palms.

Oh, you hussy. I bet you don't even have a teaching certificate. I bet you're just a failed actor fudging your way through life with your pretty hair and nice clothes.

Agent Jeffers leans towards Danielle; his hands travel halfway across the table, palms down. I'm dumbfounded. Is he smiling? A scowl of disgust? Or is this like playing poker, and no matter what he says, he keeps a straight face?

"You should have a mirror on the other side so we can see Agent Jeffers' face," I grumble.

Back inside the interrogation room, Jeffers whispers, almost too low for us to hear through the speakers, "You know, professor, I believe you. This is all just a formality. Between you and me, we are trying to build a case against your assistant, Mrs. Claire Simmons."

My eyebrows shoot up. So do Danielle's. General Hall reminds me Jeffers is playing with her, working his magic. Regardless, my heart hammers against my ribcage. *Good Lord, they could have warned me he was going to say that!*

"How do you evaluate her as a person, Dr. Bayer?" The federal agent is using his low and sweet tone again.

Danielle sits back in her chair, her expression softening into a grin. "Honestly? Crazy. Living in a fantasy. The woman can't get to work on time and has an arrogance that would stun the devil. She thinks she can do my job better than I do!"

My blood goes from cold to boiling, nails continuing to dig into my palm. "Oh, this bitch," I growl. "Steven was right about her. What's next? That she's going to say that she adulterated the ink on my Halloween invitations?"

General Hall grunts and relays my question to Jeffers.

Danielle throws her head back and laughs after Agent Jeffers asks her. Actually cackles like a Disney witch. When she pulls herself together, she glances in the mirror's direction, then back at Jeffers. "That was my genius at work. I injected a bit of disappearing ink that wouldn't mix with the other ink into the cartridge so that what she printed out would fade while everything I printed afterward appeared normal." She shrugs. "A harmless prank. A little new-person-on-the-job hazing. I was trying to gauge what her threshold was for stress and to take her ego down a peg. Teaching is a hard job, and as I just stated, she acted like she could do my job from day one."

I fling my hands into the air. "Holy hell! Who does that to a new hire and calls it a harmless prank? My neighbors hate me thanks to her."

"Yes, yes, it was mean of her. But that's nothing compared to what we are going to pin her with," General Hall says through his teeth. He gestures for me to pay attention to the proceedings in the interrogation room.

"Did you know she got fired from her last job at the Rosebud Research Facility in Montana?" Agent Jeffers inquires, leaning forward as if he and her were just two friends gossiping over coffee.

Danielle snickers. My nostrils flare. Is she playing the game back, or is this her sadistic way of trying to impress the federal agent? Whatever her intention, I want to vomit. On her.

Agent Jeffers splays his hands. "What's so funny about someone being fired from their job? I presumed that would shock you, since she is your assistant."

She flutters one hand in the air. "Oh, please don't try that psychological crap on me. She told me everything about that night a week ago. It serves her right, ruining those poor scientist's careers. I saw all the red flags cropping up over the last couple of weeks and have been trying to get her fired. Unfortunately, the dean doesn't consider my concerns to be valid."

"I didn't tell you anything!" I shout, as if I'm in the room with her. "How dare you? I didn't ruin anyone's career but my own."

General Hall shushes me.

"But," I say, pointing at her.

He points to his ear and then back at Danielle.

I cross my arms and glare through the glass. Agent Jeffers reclines back. How can he stay so cool when it's as if a volcano is bursting its top within me? He should slam his hand down onto the table, shout in her face, arrest her for slander.

"No, she didn't," Agent Jeffers says finally.

"Damn right, I didn't," I mumble.

Danielle crosses her arms, her mauve lips frowning. "Excuse me? How would you know?"

I glance at the general. He is staring at the two seated, eyes narrowed. Is the agent's subdued demeanor a sign that he is getting what he wants? Is a confession of some sort near? Why did Danielle lie about my ruining careers? She knows nothing.

"I'll state again how intelligent a lady you are, Dr. Bayer. Some peers say brilliant," Agent Jeffers croons. "Surely you didn't conclude the Simmons' house is the only residence we've bugged over the last week? Someone using a burner phone fed that information to you."

My eyes widen. Those rats! Dirty, stinking rats. Next to me, Mr. Sinclair is scribbling again, muttering to himself. Good. Incredible. Danielle is ogling the agent as well. But she hasn't squirmed, spoken, or even blinked.

Agent Jeffers scoots forward in his chair. "So, Dr. Bayer, would you like to tell me who told you that Claire's actions got multiple people fired at the facility? Or about how she interrupted an experiment? An experiment that the department hadn't approved? An experiment with three unauthorized individuals present who had snuck onto the grounds? One of whom matches your description from video surveillance that was recovered, even though your cohorts tried to corrupt the film?"

Danielle's slim throat contracts for a split second. Her lips thin, then relax. "You're telling me that little brat obeyed her non-disclosure agreement and told no one what and who she saw?"

From my point of view, Agent Jeffers doesn't fidget. Maybe he is smiling now. Or has an eyebrow raised. I, for one, am melting from the inside out, starting with my stomach.

"We will tell the judge you were cooperative if you tell us who you work for," Agent Jeffers says. His glacial tone makes me shiver. It reminds me of the metal chair back in my interrogation room. Such a juxtaposition from his silky warm tone a moment ago.

Danielle smiles. It's the same stretch of lips as when she was flirting. But this time I flinch. This is a dangerous woman. A woman I called a friend until a few minutes ago. Everything, from my admiration to any friendship I held for her, curdles to stone in my gut. She's been whispering deceit in my ear that fed my fears this whole time. We fed her food and information. I interlock my fingers on top of my head.

"Oh, you are a simp, aren't you? I'd be dead within a day of talking. You are not the only person who keeps tabs on me. I'll face a jury with this weak case that you assume you have against me," Danielle says. She waves a hand over the folder and papers littering the tabletop. "For whatever it is you think I've done. Because I haven't admitted to doing anything."

Agent Jeffers stands and picks up his file folder. "An officer will be in to tell you your rights and escort you to a jail cell, Dr. Bayer."

General Hall leaps to the microphone. "Ask her why she targeted Mrs. Simmons instead of working on the experiments."

"But before I leave, I'm curious to know, Dr. Bayer. Why did you waste so much time and energy on torturing Mrs. Simmons? Why didn't you bring in an experimental physicist to run the equipment? It would have taken so much time to learn how to. Or why not just transport your employer's equipment to a more secure location and continue your research?" Agent Jeffers places his hand on the doorknob and relaxes his stance, as if saying he doesn't care what she says. "You would have been another step ahead of us. Your hands would've been clean."

She plays with the bangles on her right hand for a moment, then peeks up at the glass. My breath hitches. Can she see me somehow? Does she sense I'm watching?

"Because of her nosiness, she has set back scientific progress in physics for years. No one will push the boundaries of what we know about the universe, and what we call reality, like my employer. I was ready to pack up and move, but then Claire had the nerve to say she developed anxiety from her little experience." Danielle scoffs. "She doesn't know what anxiety and paranoia are. My father, a *real* soldier, developed *real* stress disorders that eventually killed him. His disintegrating mental health destroyed my family. But the Veterans Association offered none of us therapy." Her eyes scan the ceiling. "I couldn't believe it when the front office mentioned her name, saying she is my new assistant here in backwoods Deadwood. Then, there she was, feet from me, day in and out, a little princess, complaining about her non-existent problems while living in the house my employer told me to buy with my money after securing the equipment. Claire iced the cake with trying to be chummy, and had the audacity to suggest we collaborate on grant writing as if she were at my level of intelligence." Her frown deepens, eyebrows furrowing; she rests her glare upon Agent Jeffers. "I wanted to give her a real problem. I need her to feel destroyed, hopeless, like an insignificant nothing." Danielle smirks. "My employer understood, since she bungled their schedule up too for what the investors were demanding. My employer gave me three weeks to destroy her life. I almost did it in two."

Something trickles down my face. I swipe my palm across my cheek, and it comes back wet.

"We've heard enough, General," Mr. Sinclair says. He puts a hand on my shoulder. "Can I get you anything, Claire?"

I wipe my eyes again and shake my head. My heart has sunk to the floor. Danielle is still sitting in the chair with perfect posture, acting as if the room isn't thirty degrees, the metal chair uncomfortable, that it's the middle of the night, or that she just confessed to actively trying to destroy my life. How much further was she planning to go? How many more nights was she going to play in that underground bunker, directing those waves of energy and sound at me before I ran away, leaving Steven and everything behind? She had everyone fooled. Me, most of all.

General Hall follows us out of the room.

"I need to get out of here," I whisper, my voice hoarse.

This time, the general doesn't have a scathing remark.

This time, he stays silent.

37

Agent Jeffers and Mr. Sinclair escort me and Steven to my car after filling out release papers. They talk about what just happened as if it were a football game, something they watched from the sidelines and cheered for the same team. Steven shakes their hands twice and thanks them—no hard feelings, and all that.

I can't speak, and won't shake their hands. My anger still simmers beneath my shock. I want to yell at everyone for their part in my misery. I want to scream in the faces of the federal agents and General Hall for stalking me from their van and trying to pin everything on me, knowing it wasn't. And finally, I'd berate myself for not getting the security guards first all those months ago at Rosebud Research Facility. All this *is* my fault because all of this—minus Danielle's involvement in the illegal experiment—was more or less avoidable. My right hand is in Steven's firm grasp, with the other clenched deep in Steven's jacket pocket that I'm still wearing. Tears of shame and exhaustion sting my eyes.

Steven then assists me into the passenger seat. I scrunch up into a ball after he clicks on my seatbelt and kisses my temple. My eyes remain wired open. The world is different now. Shadows loom from fences and trees. I watch them, worried they will transform, that they will slither toward me. Danielle or something more sinister will materialize behind them, directing their actions.

Large, dark shadows moved in the backyard. That was Danielle, going in and out of the shed.

The buzzing and vibrations, and nightmares. All caused by Danielle yards away underground. No wonder it was always after work. She couldn't be in two places at once. And it sounds like there was more equipment than just the box they showed me. So that would explain why it happened when I was at home. Danielle couldn't pack all the machinery up and follow me around town.

Something at the back of my mind nags at me. I'm forgetting something, something important.

There's a police officer keeping vigil over our street to make sure none of Danielle's associates try to seek revenge and attack us. The front desk officer said there would be a police cruiser driving around at all hours for a week, per General Hall's orders. Steven is relieved, squeezes my knee; he just wants to get some sleep before work. I remain silent. The looming task of job hunting is ahead of me. There's no reason the college will keep me on after this.

Steven keeps an arm around me as we enter our house for the first time in almost twenty-four hours. The dark street behind us doesn't betray anyone peeking through their blinds.

As I step into the dark living room, I remember what I forgot and freeze. Steven bumps into me.

"What is it?" he asks through a yawn.

I point at the floor lamp once he flips the switch. He glances from it to me, confusion written on his face along with dark bags of stress and lack of sleep under his eyes.

"There's nothing there."

"No, not now. I just remembered the figures I saw. Buzz. Was that all in my head since you never saw them? Is my brain broken? Can I see dead people now?"

Steven rubs his face. "Honey, you'll be fine. It was her machines causing the hallucination. Can we please go to bed? I have to be up in four hours."

His voice is heavy, pleading.

I hug myself and peer into the dark corners. "You go on. I need to shower the smell of the police station off me."

*

When I arrive at Danielle's office the next morning, taking constant sips of coffee from my thermos, hoping the caffeine will hit me at some point, I am met with a locked door and a note that reads, "No classes today. Contact front office with questions."

Half an hour later, I'm still waiting outside the dean's office. Dean Kelly finally emerges to send me home for the day, maybe longer, and doesn't provide a hint about whether I still have a job, or what will happen to the students after I inquire how to help them.

"Go home, and enjoy the day off, Mrs. Simmons," Dean Kelly says, sounding as exhausted as I feel. "Don't fret about the classes. You look like you could use a nap, regardless. I'll contact you with any updates, alright?"

I nod and trudge back to my car, texting Steven on the way.

Back home, I can't keep my eyes open. I lie down

on the couch, and fall into a deep sleep.

Sharp rapping on the front door yanks me out of a dream. Once I hop up, the fleeting essence of a dream vanishes. Were there figures? Was I alone? I smooth my hair back and peer through the window. It's General Hall in his uniform; cap tucked under his arm. I groan. After yesterday, I hoped I'd never have to see him again.

"General Hall," I say with a grim smile once I unlock and open the door. "Do I need to call my attorney?"

That solicits an impish grin. "No, Mrs. Simmons. This is purely a social call. Do you have a minute to talk? It's about the case, if you're interested," he baits me.

"Um, yeah, sure." I open the screen door for him with one hand and attempt to smooth out the wrinkles in my blouse with the other.

He enters and pauses in the middle of the living room, peering around.

"Will you give me a moment to freshen up, sir? You caught me napping after they sent me home from work since there's no teacher," I explain, knowing full well that he already knows. He knows even more regarding my job security and prospects.

General Hall nods.

"You can use this time to collect all of your

listening bugs. I'll shell out whatever it costs to get a detector. One beep and I'll haul you to court."

A deep chuckle escapes him. "And here I was, worried that this case had softened you. No, you shouldn't find any leftovers. As I told you before, I was and am on your side. We took them out when we were searching your house. And *that* was to make sure that professor of yours didn't plant any unsavory devices."

I gape, then slam my mouth shut, and scout the corners and outlets in the room for the telltale tiny round lens they use on television.

"We found and discarded a small video camera attached to the shed that pointed at the house," he says. "Go freshen up. We'll talk more over coffee."

When I return, I find General Hall has placed his cap on the kitchen counter and is standing at the back door, gazing out the window. The police have wrapped caution tape around the shed. It wasn't hard to deduce where Danielle was sneaking in. Someone had chopped back vines to reveal a gaping hole cut into the back fence. Agent Jeffers had left a note on our dining room table that explained not to go out there; the department would decide whether they would fill in the bunker with cement or leave it for us to use. We need to pretend we don't have a shed for now. A year could pass before anything gets decided. The speed of bureaucracies, and all that.

"She was living a double life," General Hall says, turning around.

Another nod for him, and then I fill the coffee machine with fresh water and grounds. "What's going to happen to her?"

"Well, that's the main reason I wanted to speak with you." His hand goes into his pocket. "She has friends in high places."

I cross my arms. "Did she lawyer up? Isn't she a threat to national security?"

He shakes his head. "You need to understand that there are people even more powerful than me. Someone got the local judge to post a ridiculous bail instead of no bail, as I had requested. An undisclosed party paid using an offshore account, all before anyone thought to inform me this morning."

"So, go arrest her again," I say, gesturing towards the front door.

The coffee gurgles into the pot behind me. A silence stretches between us.

He slumps into a dining chair. The opposite of what I want him to do. "If we can find her. The CIA is considering the case. But I don't expect they will take it on."

"Wait. Find her? She did a runner?"

"Not a runner, a disappearing act. And if her

friends are as high up as we are thinking, we'll never see her again. But at least we recovered our stolen lab equipment from Europe." His dejected tone says it all. Danielle has bested one of the best.

"Do you suppose they'll punish her for getting caught? Is the mafia involved?" If I were her, I would've demanded a new identity from Agent Jeffers in exchange for information.

"Haha, no. The mafia couldn't afford her. She's in some foreign politicians' pockets. So don't go searching for her," he warns, focusing on me.

No fire sparks in my chest for justice. Maybe it's my lack of sleep, my exhausted mind and body. I am numb. But at least I'm home. I am not crazy. That's what matters to me. "Even if I had the means to, I wouldn't. I'm quite content where I'm at, as long as all this buzzing has stopped."

"I'm glad to hear it. Yes, that bunker is empty now. Anything else, get checked out by a doctor." He gestures behind me. "Cream and sugar, if you have it."

I spin around and pour coffee into two mugs, then bring them and the condiments on a tray.

"Want anything to eat?" *Please say no.* I don't care that he was on my side this time. He got my career derailed, made me upend my life, Steven's life. I still haven't received an apology for that. The small protection detail with police cruising the area at night is the least he can do to make up for all the crap I've gone through.

My shoulders relax when he shakes his head. I lean back in my chair and sip the hot brew. My mind wanders. How strange these past few weeks have been. Buzzing sounds, birds, slowed clocks, bugs, and figures. I jerk my head up.

"General, what are the figures?"

His eyebrow drifts up, and his cup goes to the table. "Figures?"

"You heard me. What are the figures I see when the buzzing happens? At the laboratory as well. Their appearance made me get the security guards at the facility. You heard about that part, right? Well, one came here and haunted me," I ramble. "I know you said you weren't investigating a ghost, but there was something there. And here. Please. It's the last time I'll bring it up."

His other eyebrow arches. He leans forward. "So you weren't making that part up in the interrogation room? You actually saw them at the facility? And here too? Fascinating."

"Are you making fun of me?"

The general shakes his head. "No. I am not. One scientist we interrogated reported that as well. The figure's appearance was unexpected," he explains. "In fact, a few neuroscientists are interested in trying to copy the experiment to see if the—were they fuzzy in appearance, too? Just as you described to Agent Jeffers?"

I stare at him. My mouth is dry from being open. I blink, registering that he had asked me a question. I nod, still agog.

General Hall smiles wide enough for top and bottom teeth to show. Straight and white. Whiter than what I would have expected from a coffee guzzler. It sends a shiver down my spine; a smile made of mischief, like that seen on the wolf in *Little Red Riding Hood*. The general scoots forward in his chair. "Did they move or stand still?"

"Uh, um. I guess… Well, the one I saw here stood still. But the last couple of times…" The last time two were at the window, the door had locked me in, and Steven had to break it down to rescue me. "There were two outside of the house one night. Steven never saw Buzz or the other one."

"Buzz?"

I shrug, letting loose an unsteady giggle. "We named it Buzz because the top of its head had a flat top, like a buzz cut. I want to know if it's a ghost." I gulp, ears heating as I realize what I am saying. "Not that I believe in ghosts. I just want to understand what I experienced."

He leans back with a stoic expression. "Interesting. I wouldn't blame you if you did. There is a lot we don't know. That's why science exists." Then he studies his mug, which he's rotating in his hands. "Would you be willing to participate in the study if we secure the funds?" A quick glance at me. "I can make sure it's worth your while. You can tell us if we are on the right track."

I snort. "No. And don't bribe me. I never desire to see another fuzzy humanoid thing ever again." Then I meet his gaze and emphasize, "Ever. Again."

His lips thin, but he doesn't speak. Then he points from his mug to the coffeemaker. "Mind if I?"

I wave at him to help himself. Whatever will keep him talking. Questions have been collecting in my brain these last few minutes. There is so much that I don't know; I need to understand what happened to me.

"May I inquire what the original experiment was for? Did you ever find out from the scientists employed at Rosebud?" I lick my lips. My knee bounces under the table.

General Hall sits back down and concentrates on stirring in his sugar and creamer. Then he taps the spoon on the lip of the mug, lays it down, and peers at me. "Can you keep a secret?"

"Either you trust me or you don't," I say, crossing my arms.

A smirk crosses his lips. "Alright. I don't suppose

anyone will believe you anyway, so here it goes. Have you heard of St. Elmo's fire or the Philadelphia Experiment?"

I angle my head to one side. "But I didn't see any blue flames like St. Elmo's fire."

"But you heard buzzing."

My eyebrows scrunch together. "Okay. I mean, that's why we thought it was an electrical problem. But the Philadelphia Experiment involved an entire ship that disappeared using physics that doesn't exist. Some drunk naval guy from the forties made it all up, right? I don't see the connection."

"Well, physics has come a long way since the forties," General Hall says, scratching his head. Then he takes a sip of his coffee. "The Pentagon recently discovered that the experiment's classified documents are missing. These are some good beans. Local brand?"

"Oregon local roaster, yeah. You can take the rest of the bag with you. I have another," I say, waving a hand, not wanting him to deviate from the story. "So, it was a real experiment? What is the connection? Nothing disappeared from this house."

Another long sip. "Ah, that beats hotel coffee by a mile. Okay, Miss Impatient, the connection is that there are two forms of physics that affect electromagnetic fields. The scientists were creating a strong current right next to an area of space being stripped of its field. Vibrations and buzzing are side effects of both experiments. They were playing with the very laws of physics that hold our universe together. In very close corridors. Dr. Bayer must have remembered your reaction from the lab and recreated similar effects on a smaller scale, concentrated at your house to freak you out."

I lean back and whisper, "Field equations."

"Which ones?" the colonel asks, leaning forward. "A physicist assisting us with the investigation hypothesized something similar."

I tilt my head in thought. Her tattoo placement should have tipped me off. The inside of her wrist? Not only would that have hurt like hell to get done on such a sensitive area, but seen by her daily, reminding her what she does. Only a genius, one with more comprehension and vision than Einstein himself, could combine and calculate so many constantly changing variables. "There should have been copious notes. Book's worth. There was nothing like that in the bunker or her apartment?"

He shakes his head once. "There was nothing written. Not even a damn laptop. She must have forwarded everything days ago. And her team would have been sending encrypted notes on how to set up and operate the machines. Hell, she could have gained a secret engineering degree while off the grid to help her independent work. We have people scouring the postal offices in surrounding counties in case there is a physical paper trail, and have internet code breakers looking for clues. Books, as in plural, amount of information, you say?"

"I—I don't know. But maybe she combined multiple field equations into one super-equation and committed it to memory. It's so complicated. So complex. It's not my area of expertise. My brain hurts just thinking about the possibilities and probabilities of error." I shake my head. "No way. It's so volatile. I'm surprised Danielle didn't blow up the bunker, or herself. I swear my eyeballs were going to pop out a few times."

"Would serve her right," the general mumbles into his mug.

"Regardless, it doesn't explain the figures. Coronal discharges of blue light, I would understand. But not grainy humanoid figures."

"No, it does not. That's why we are now interested in the experiment. We also want to know who in the world is financially backing it. Danielle and her team may have stumbled on a way to bend or rip apart reality."

"Are you talking about alternate universes? As in, like, on some level, she was successful, and those figures aren't from our reality?" My mouth flops open again.

He doesn't snicker. Not so much as a twitch of his lips. The general stares back at me with blank eyes. A poker face. "Do you really want to know? I can get you working at Rosebud within the month."

I blink. Do I want my old pay back? Yes. Do I want high-level clearance? I think so, if it helps my career. Do I want to conjure more figures *on purpose?* I shudder and close my eyes. No, I won't. I can't. I already told him I don't want to be involved anymore. That is the truth. I love physics. Hard physics. Physics that govern *our* universe. "No, I don't want to know," I say, waving both hands in front of me, pushing the temptations from my mind. "Just keep her away from me. I need to stay in this reality. I need to ground myself in mundane tasks and find a stable job for a while. Steven and I have this place that needs work, and it isn't so bad when the place isn't crawling with bugs and birds." I remember what the taxi driver said. "I hear it's nice here in summer. You can't judge a place in winter."

That elicits a nonchalant shrug from the general. He reaches into his jacket and retrieves an envelope, then passes it to me. "Fine. This might help."

I tear it open and read the letter. Then reread it. It's a welcome letter from Deadwood College

Board, similar to the one I received when they hired me for the teacher's assistant position. Except instead of the assistant, it states that I have accepted the teaching position for all the physics classes Danielle taught. Along with the proposed professorship salary. Slightly more than I was earning from Rosebud Facility. I frown and scrutinize the general's face. This is too good to be true.

"Well? Do you want it or not?" he asks.

"How? Does Dean Kelly even know about this, or did you make this on your computer?" I accuse him. This is a sick joke, if so. It's like dangling a carrot in front of a starving rabbit. How high will he make me jump for it? "What's the catch?"

"No catch. And it's on the up and up with the dean. She likes you. Cross my heart," he promises, crossing his chest. "She's the one who got a hold of me with Mr. Sinclair's help after he had made good on the promise of you not losing your job. The students want you, even signed a petition and turned it in yesterday." The general then raised his mug in salute. "You start tomorrow. Meet with Dean Kelly at her office at seven, and then classes resume on Thursday."

My mouth guppies. My heart swells. The students do like me. Danielle, brilliant as she may be, didn't want to nurture their brains or see their potential like I do. I contemplate whether I want to do this. It may not be so boring if I imagine it to be like heading a team of scientists at Rosebud Research Facility. Lending a guiding hand and overseeing their success. And I can still apply for grants, or practice writing proposals, at least.

"I wholeheartedly accept."

General Halls nods once, then stands, grabbing his cap. "I knew you would. You have the spirit of a leader. I'm sorry we can't accept you back into the Air Force, but you can still make a difference with these kids. Well, I suppose that's everything. Oh, and you'll get your files and laptop dropped off by the end of the week. I'll see myself out."

I grab the bag of coffee for him and lead the way to the door. He steps past me and turns around.

"Congratulations on your promotion. This is my thank you for helping me uncover a kingpin scientist from that unsanctioned experiment." He pulls out a slim black box with an orange bow tied around it, like that for jewelry, from his inside breast pocket and hands it to me.

I hold the box at arm's length, ready to hand it back. "Does this mean that I can live my life now? No more surveillance or accusations against me? Will you leave me alone now?"

With a wink, he states, "I might check on you from time to time. Just to make sure you're staying out of trouble." Then he turns and walks to an SUV parked in our driveway, and drives away without glancing back.

I retreat into the house and secure the door. With two fingers, I pull on the bow's end until it unravels and slips to the floor. Still holding the box away from my body, I lift the lid and gasp.

On a black velvet base, a gold nameplate sits under a thick orange card that says, "Anticipating the recruitment of your graduates to our research facilities.-General Hall."

I pick the card up to examine the carved nameplate.

DR. CLAIRE SIMMONS, PhD.
Department of Physics

My eyesight blurs as tears flow. A smile stretches across my face.

The slow lane in life has never looked so good.

Epilogue

Tim and Laura Galloway's arrest makes local headline news. They had confessed to running from the bank for not paying their mortgage. Their purchased survival bunker and its expensive installation had drained their retirement savings, and they then had to choose between paying their bills or eating. It surprised us to read that the military surplus owner was *not* their dealer. The article didn't divulge who the Galloways had bought the bunker from, but mentioned it was a contact arrested in Utah living on the same plot of land as the Galloways.

"It wouldn't surprise me if Danielle's financial backer somehow found out about the bunker and its absent owners from their black-market contacts," Steven muses.

It makes perfect sense to me. If General Hall ever pops in for a visit, I'll ask him. "So long as those contacts stay away," I say, spreading more cheese on a cracker from the cheese and jam basket sent over from Mrs. Carter. She had also included a letter that said she was beyond embarrassed to have forgotten to send over a congratulatory basket when we first moved in. Then she states she was happy to hear that I am alive and well and Steven wasn't a murderer. Included was a business card with new contact information since she, too, wanted to distance herself from her dealings with Danielle. I chuckle to myself, knowing that if Danielle wants to contact any of us, she will have no trouble doing so. But I hope she never gets an inkling. "Another?" I offer Steven.

He leans forward, securing the laptop on his lap, and opens his mouth so I can pop another of our snacks in. The multiple tabs open on screen are for several airlines, so that we can find the best price on our upcoming summer vacation to visit my parents in Louisiana and his family scattered about on the East Coast. My new position and subsequent raise were a welcome bump in income, only for Steven to get a promotion at his job and a significant raise. Now, we can afford landscapers to do the colossal amount of yardwork for us and repay my debts if we stay where we are and don't take on any more costly projects.

"How was your session with Dr. Sternan yesterday?" Steven asks after swallowing and wiping crumbs from his face.

I set down the cracker smeared with jalapeño jam I was about to stuff in my mouth. "Great, as usual. The meditation tapes she recommended I listen to before bed are helping my lucid dreaming. Last night, for the first time, I felt myself thinking of the dark figures, stopped, began thinking of a garden, and my brain plopped me into Momma's garden when I was a kid. I remember pretending her green bean poles and colorful pepper plants were the walls of my fortress." I turn to him. "What do you think about building some raised garden beds? Or a greenhouse? I can check out some gardening books for this climate from the college library and talk to Momma."

Steven beams. "Claire? Are you there? Is this the same girl I married that scoffed at the idea of caring for an indoor plant in our first apartment because, and I quote, 'I deal with hard, cold facts, not messy green-for-a-week things that I will inevitably kill.'?"

I snatch up the nearest decorative pillow and smack him in the face. He falls back, laughing hard.

I scowl at him, trying to suppress the laugh bubbling inside. "I'm surprised you're not more surprised that I want to stay here longer, you turd."

Steven pushes the laptop off his lap and pulls me to him, kissing my head. "I'm not surprised because I know you and love you. Beneath that scientist exterior, you are a big old hippie, just like me. This little town has some quirky folks, but none so kindhearted and evolved as my honey. You fit in wherever you are because of that. Your eyes are always open and see things most miss."

Snuggled against Steven's chest, I gaze over at the floor lamp where Buzz first materialized. 'Evolved' and 'see things most miss.' That is an understatement of the century. I bite my lip and wonder when a good time will be to tell Steven that Buzz still materializes in the house every other day. Will I ever know if Buzz is just an image burned into my brain, or an actual entity studying me since I am one of the few humans to see them?

Then I smile.

Who's crazy now?

Acknowledgements

There is so much we don't know about our universe and reality. And that's what fascinates me. In this beautiful, chaotic world we live in, there is still so much mystery.

Luckily, I don't have to rely on non-human entities to share ideas! Some of my human friends and family I would like to thank is my cousin Jessica for your brilliant PhD-level knowledge of physics and enjoyment of fiction to help me give more believability to my far-out stories. Thank you to my other beta reader, Ryan, for understanding the assignment and offering writer advice where you can give it. Also, a big thank you to my husband—my biggest supporter—who loves listening to paranormal stories with me, which led to the birth of this story.

And thank you, my readers. I wouldn't keep writing if not for your encouragement and eagerness to find out what I am writing next. I have a whole notebook of story ideas, so there will always be something to look forward to.

Also By Author

The Ausurnians Series (by Alisha Trent)
    Book 1 Into Ausurnia
    Book 2 The Rise of Athelia
    Book 3 (upcoming prequel)

Follow A.A. Trent on Facebook, Instagram, Threads, and soon to be on YouTube for audiobook versions.